Jake Arnott

Born in 1961, Jake Arnott lives in London. His first novel, *The Long Firm*, was a major critical and popular success. It was subsequently made into a BBC TV series, which was nominated for two BAFTA awards. His second novel, *He Kills Coppers*, was also made into a series by Channel 4. He has since published the novels *truecrime*, *Johnny Come Home*, *The Devil's Paintbrush* and *The House of Rumour*.

JAKE ARNOTT

THE
FATAL
TREE

SCEPTRE

First published in Great Britain in 2017 by Sceptre
An Imprint of Hodder & Stoughton
An Hachette UK company

First published in paperback in 2017

1

Copyright © Jake Arnott 2017

A CIP catalogue record for this title is available from the British Library

ISBN 978 1 473 63776 4

Typeset in Adobe Caslon by Palimpsest Book Production Limited,
Falkirk, Stirlingshire

Printed and bound in Great Britain by Clays Ltd, St Ives plc

Hodder & Stoughton policy is to use papers that are natural,
renewable and recyclable products and made from wood grown in sustainable
forests. The logging and manufacturing processes are expected to conform
to the environmental regulations of the country of origin.

Hodder & Stoughton Ltd
Carmelite House
50 Victoria Embankment
London EC4Y 0DZ

www.sceptrebooks.co.uk

Since Laws were made for ev'ry Degree,
To curb Vice in others, as well as me,
I wonder we han't better Company,
Upon Tyburn Tree!
But Gold from Law can take out the Sting;
And if rich Men, like us were to swing.
'Twou'd thin the Land, such Numbers to string
Upon Tyburn Tree!

John Gay, *The Beggar's Opera*

CONTENTS

ONE

—

The

TREE

of

LIFE

Dear Applebee,

'All of you that in the condemned hold do lie, prepare you, for tomorrow you will die.' This is the cheerful song they recite to those who await the journey from the doleful prison of Newgate to the fatal tree of Tyburn. At midnight comes the peal of St Sepulchre-without-Newgate, the execution bell, whose sound is carried through an underground passage to the very cell of the doomed wretch. Twelve double tolls are rung and each woeful chime makes its demand. It is the bell of Old Bailey that calls *When will you pay me?* But we all know the account will be settled soon enough.

I write to you in the hope that you might provide some credit in the meantime. For as you are aware if the condemned confess to the chaplain here, that holy man will likely sell the contents of an unburdened soul on Grub Street. He might earn twenty pounds if the story is a good one. All those sins remembered in *The Last Dying Speech of* _____ or *The Ordinary Account of the Behaviour, Confession & Dying Words of the Condemned Criminals Executed at Tyburn.* A pretty pamphlet sold for sixpence at the criminal's own hanging.

Prisoners have learned that it is far wiser to deal directly with a publisher and earn a little money to pay the fees, the *garnish*, the gaolers charge for any comfort in this purgatory. That is why they send for you, John Applebee, known to all in this particular branch of the trade as its finest exponent, and that is why I trust you are found by this letter. For I can offer you a work that I am certain will interest you as the man who made his fortune with *The History of the Remarkable Life of*

John Sheppard as well as *The True & Genuine Account of the Life & Actions of the Late Jonathan Wild.* This new account might capitalise on the success of these previous narratives, for we will meet both of these infamous gentlemen within: the housebreaker Sheppard; the thief-taker Wild. And what follows will eventually form a history that links them both: the tale of the woman who tempted the young Sheppard away from his apprenticeship to a wicked life and betrayed him to the corrupt Wild. I present to you the story of Elizabeth Lyon, never fully told before, that lewd soul known as Edgworth Bess, now awaiting judgment here in Newgate, who has agreed to confide to me the details of her adventures and misfortunes. As justice draws near it is surely time for her to give her own testimony.

In the biography you printed of Sheppard he said of his lover Bess: 'A more wicked, deceitful and lascivious wretch there is not living in England.' So now hear her evidence attentively that you might be certain of your own and the reader's verdict. Accordingly, I enclose with this letter the first chapter of her story. If it meets with your satisfaction and we can agree terms, I will send you the rest in instalments.

It is, of course, hoped that the moral of this confession might keep the public sensible and cautioned of temptation, even where its sensational details might incline them to be otherwise. All should be warned of the salacious nature of some of the elements described in the recounting of this wretched life. But sincere penitence insists that every sin should be depicted in all its wickedness and true justice requires a full report of its own shadow.

And to that shadow-land are we now headed, with its queer

4

customs and foreign tongue. I have retained Elizabeth Lyon's use of the thieves' vernacular so the readers might acquaint themselves with the strange dialect of this wicked world, whose *canting-crew* contains *filchers, bung-nippers, spruce-prigs, punks* and *mollies*: the *St Giles' Greek* better known as *flash*. For example, in *flash* talk the evil trade of Edgworth Bess is spoken of as *buttock-and-file*, that is, whore and pickpocket. If possible a full glossary of terms should be provided in the end pages. A guide for the reader, like the link-boy who leads with a lantern through the alleys at night.

For you will know to beware of that other whore and pickpocket: the writer. That hackney-scribbler always ready to filch someone's life and fence it cheap. Dissipated talents who trade in feigned sentiment and dulled wit, those poor wretches who reside in Grub Street. It is said that this thoroughfare was once called Grape Street and before that Gropecunt Lane where, as the name suggests, the very lowest forms of harlotry could be found. You may think, as many do, that its present inhabitants merely follow this tradition. I have some reputation in this dubious profession but can be trusted to write a faithful account and to deliver it in a timely fashion. For the moment, however, and for reasons I will explain in due course, I wish to remain anonymous. So I would beg your indulgence and request you direct your reply to my subject here at Newgate.

You might consider this just another petty story to be sold and one of doubtful value but I am certain that in the publishing of this account a handsome profit could be realised. As you know, now is the fashion for criminal narratives, ever more extreme and each loudly boasting its authenticity. Most are badly told lies. But if the public really craves the truth, to hear the lamentable voice calling out of the condemned hold, I can assure them that each word that follows comes from the very mouth of that hell.

So here begins the tale of Edgworth Bess, related by me in her own words and a darker narrative for those that would look a little closer. A hidden history that must be told in secret: of lives too scandalous even for the *Newgate Calendar*. And of love lost, which is the saddest story of them all.

I am, sir, your most obedient servant,

the author of the below

THE TRUE & GENUINE ACCOUNT
OF THE LIFE & ACTIONS OF
ELIZABETH LYON

I

I was born in the small town of Edgworth, some ten miles north of London, the year Queen Anne came to the throne. If any seek significance as to why the place of my birth was later to provide my notorious alias, they might note that the old Roman road from there makes one straight line to London, without a single turn or bend in it, and ends directly at where Tyburn now stands. So this was my swift journey from innocence and, in truth, I was headed for the gallows of that wicked city too soon and far too young.

For I was not always so harsh in my manners or so coarse in language. I grew up in a noble household and as a child I learned some etiquette, some reading even. I used the proper words for things then, not the canting tongue I would later be schooled in. When I tell the flash citizens of Romeville that I grew up in a gentry-ken, they laugh, but it is true. A fine country house in a small park with an ornamental garden, a fish pond, and a summer-house – that was my world when I was a child. Our master, Sir Wickham Steevens, had it built in the classical style with the great fortune he had made in the Americas.

I lived downstairs, of course, in a small room I shared with my mother. She was servant to Lady Steevens and, though the rules of the house were strict, I was allowed some liberty when young and was raised partly with the family. I was always expected to fetch and run errands, but there were times when I took the opportunity to gain some education in the little while I spent with our master's children. Learning by imitation and enquiry rather than direct instruction, I acquired a fickle wit but a keen and curious spirit.

The staff were ruled by Fenton, master of the household, a stern cove who had served as a sergeant in the Foot Guards. He ordered all the servants, the footmen, the cook, the kitchen maids and the gardener. He chided me sometimes for being too familiar and warned me that I would soon have to learn more of duty.

My happiest memories were of playing, and my dearest play-mate was Richard, the eldest child and only son, who was but a year older than myself. I was as fond of the boys' games as those the girls played but I had a warmer affection for Richard than for his sisters, who in their turn could be quite offhand with me. As I grew to be their servant they soon forgot that we had once all been mere children together. Because of the closeness of our ages, Richard had a gentler recollection of when we were almost like brother and sister.

My mother died when I was thirteen and I took her position. Within the next two years I grew tall and strong and my figure ripened at hips and bosom. The master's son now looked at me differently. He would still act towards me in a playful manner but there was a new game to be learned.

It happened one day that he came running up the stairs calling up to his sisters. I came from where I was alone in a room and met him in the doorway. I said to him, 'Sir, the ladies are not here. They are walking in the garden.'

His breath was quick, his manner bright and full of haste. He clasped both my arms. 'Bess,' he hissed. 'That is all the better. Are you here alone?'

I nodded and his eyes sparked with mischief as he pushed me back into the room.

'What is it?' I asked, as he turned from me to close the door on us both.

He took hold of me once more, pulling me to him tightly and kissing me on the mouth. Even as I pushed him away I felt my blood fire up. He reached out to trace my cheek gently with his fingertips. 'Bess,' he whispered.

His face came close to mine, eyes hooded, the mouth a trembling pout. His lips brushed mine and he seized me once more. I was possessed by a strange fear as I yielded to him. Not of him, though. He was but a stripling and I might have wrestled him off. No, my fright was at something inside myself.

Presently he stopped and we stood just looking at each other, both scant of breath and in wonder at a strange new joy discovered. I remember noting at that instant how Richard looked all the prettier in a disordered state, his curls falling loose over a dampened brow, his cheeks flushed in a rosy glow.

'Bess, I am in love with you,' he told me.

And that spell worked its glamour on me. A foolish girl tranced, never doubting the truth of what he said. I believed these words as if I had uttered them myself and there lay the folly: Bess was in earnest but Richard was not.

He went to the window and looked out. 'My sisters are coming back,' he said, and turned to leave the room. As he passed me he took my hand and kissed it, holding my gaze all the time. 'Will you be mine, Bess?' He let the question hang in the air as he rushed out, calling to the daughters of the house as he thundered down the stairs.

The next few days passed with hardly a word shared between us but we rarely missed the chance to trade a glance, smile or gesture. Those silent expressions made me as heady as his spoken words. More so, perhaps, as they told of some great secret that could not by reason be deciphered, only by the senses.

Then the day came when all his family were out on a visit and the house was empty but for the maids below stairs. He found me in his sister's chamber, rudely caught me up in his arms and carried me to her bed. Once more he spoke of his love for me as he unlaced my stays. He set to work on loosening every part of my rigging, then unpinned the handkerchief at my bosom. I gasped as his eager hands sought out my naked flesh. I did not quite know all his intent, as I was innocent then, so I offered little resistance to his attention. Indeed, I was too pleased with this new game to think of where it might lead. Then Richard thought he heard somebody coming up the stairs so he got up and urged me to reorder my dress.

It was then that he took my hand and put a guinea into it. Well, I was as charmed by the money as I had been by his words. I imagined that the coin was a token of love, not a bargain for it. He asked again, 'Will you be mine, Bess?'

And I nodded, thinking that this was a promise of the heart. I kept the gold piece he gave me on the table by my bedside.

By arrangement he came to my room in the middle of the night. I lit a candle and he crept into my bed. I stayed his hand as he pulled at my shift but he entreated me with such persuasion, saying all would be reckoned well when he came into his estate. Once more I did not doubt the honour of his words, being of such childish inexperience that I thought of love as but a simple story ending in marriage. And so I soon lay exposed before him.

With a sigh he ran his hands across my form, examining it by the yellow flicker of the candle and remarking at its beauty in a way that appealed to a vanity I'd never known. My excitation quickly matched his. And the very urgency and danger of my predicament spurred me on, especially as the debt of my virtue seemed secured by some destined guarantee. All these things blew the coals of my desire and I readily gave myself to him.

A fierce pain soon gave way to tantalising pleasure. Richard seemed possessed by some demon as he bucked away at me. I felt the yearning of joy, just out of reach, lost somewhere in the frenzy of sensation. Then he shuddered violently, his whole body clenched in some furious ecstasy. For a moment I thought that this spasm might be a fit of the falling sickness. Then he groaned and with an addled-headed grin rolled over and fell into slumber.

Sleep did not come so readily for me, though. I snuffed the flame and lay in the gloom, brooding on my circumstance, wondering idly on imagined prospects, bewildered but utterly ignorant of how forsaken I really was. And it was this vain attempt at comprehension that contributed to my ruin, for I slept late and woke to find Richard still in my bed. I tried to rouse him but it was too late. One of the other maids had seen him and told the mistress of the house what she had witnessed.

So we were discovered and the shame of it laid bare to the whole household.

Richard's mother was in a fury. 'You have let this whore snare you, is that it?' she demanded of him.

And he meekly agreed to this hateful lie. 'Yes, Mother,' he muttered, becoming her little boy once more. 'She took a guinea for it.'

'Is this true?' she asked me.

'He entreated me,' I tried to explain. 'He asked me, "Will you be mine?"'

'And so you were his?'

'Yes, madam.'

It was then that Lady Steevens spied the coin on the table by the bed. She picked it up and held it in front of my face. 'For a guinea?' she sneered. 'You took this from my son?'

'No!' I protested. 'He gave it to me.'

'Forgive me, Mother,' Richard told her, 'but she led me astray.'

It is said that with repentance of sin comes a hatred of its object, and that the greater the affection felt in the act so the detestation will be more in proportion afterwards. If that is the case then Richard might well have been telling the truth when he told me that he loved me before as he treated me so cruelly afterward.

And so, in those flash terms I was soon to learn, love is a sharper that works the queerest of drops. I had my innocence filched from me and, thus peached, I was dismissed from the household.

'Take your guinea,' Lady Steevens told me curtly, 'as the wages of your sin.'

But for that accursed coin, all I had was a meagre bundle of my possessions. Fenton escorted me to the gate with a sorrowful look on his face. 'I warned you not to be so familiar, Bess.' He shook his head and sighed. 'But this is cruel. Far too cruel.'

'What am I to do, Fenton?'

'Make for London, child. You'll find work in one of the grand houses there. But be careful, my dear.'

He bade me goodbye. I was fearful at being turned out of doors into the wide world but I knew that all I could do was follow his advice, to journey to the great city and find some employment there.

So I left meekly but vowed that one day I would come back and take vengeance. I would make them pay somehow for my ruin. With the gold coin I bought a place on the next stage-coach for town and was soon on that straight road to Tyburn.

இ

Arriving in London I felt a fierce assault on all my senses: the bewildering parade of people and carriages in the streets, the mad bustle of business, the shriek and clatter of its traffic. And the stench! Scattered heaps of filth, dead fish and offal, dung everywhere. Ragged beggars clamoured at every corner. I held my little bundle close and made to walk in a manner that might show I knew my way. But I was hopelessly lost.

The world there was so close and stifling. Even the grand houses Fenton had spoken of were often crowded in terraces. They stood proud above the squalor below but elsewhere lay darker streets and alleys cluttered with wretched dwellings and menacing inhabitants. All was discord and tumult to a forsaken country girl.

I was as shocked by the harshness in manner of London's citizens as I was bewildered by the sharpness of their tongue. I would, of course, soon learn a new way of speaking. Indeed, the reader will be tutored in it also as they follow my tale.

But for the moment all I sought was a friendly face and counted myself lucky when a kind-looking lady of middle age approached me. She wore silks and a bonnet and had a large beauty spot on one cheek. 'You look new to town, my dear,' she told me.

I nodded.

One hand held a fan, the other stroked my face. 'Then you must be careful,' she went on. 'London is a wicked place. Full of danger for a young maid like you.'

'What am I to do?' I beseeched her.

'Come with me, my dear. There's a position for a serving girl in a good house, if you'll take it.'

'Who are you?'

'Call me Mother Needham.'

But as she went to link her arm with mine a younger woman came between us and pushed her away. 'Leave her be, you old trull,' said the interloper.

'Touted her first!' answered the elder.

'Touted her last, too.'

And so an argument arose that proved a lesson in the peculiar discourse of the streets. *Tout* meant to see or to look: I could follow that at least.

'She's no game pullet for you,' the new arrival went on, grabbing me at the elbow. 'Offer you work, did she? Say Romeville was a wicked place and she could look after you? Well, this abbess will want you for her nunnery, sure enough. She's a buttock-broker.'

'Blow the widd, would you?' Mother Needham called out, her voice now coarse and shrill. 'Then blow all of it and tell her you want her for your own academy!'

'Least I won't sell her to the colonel. Like you did me.'

Mother Needham stopped still and squinted at the young

woman. 'Punk Alice,' she declared. 'You've grown. I'd hardly recognise you.'

'I was but a child then. Like this dell.' Punk Alice turned to me. 'Come, let's wet the neck. Will you take a cup of prattle-broth with me?'

By this I learned that we were to take tea together as she led me to a nearby tea-house. There Punk Alice explained that Mother Needham was the most notorious procuress in the whole of London and would approach girls who had arrived fresh from the country and offer them work as servants. She would first sell them to the colonel, an evil rake with a taste for young virgins known as the 'Rapemaster General of All England', then set them up at her brothel in St James's. There she would work them day and night for little pay, making them hire the very clothes on their backs and throwing out any that fell sick or into disfavour. I was truly shocked by this, but with the relief in avoiding this fate came fear and, indeed, confusion at what plans this Alice might have for me.

She related everything to me with many of the strange words and phrases I had heard her use with Mother Needham. This was the first time I had come across the thieves' cant known as flash and I learned slowly how to patter it, as they say. A canting-crew can hide the meaning of what they communicate to outsiders but it seems to have another purpose all of its own. I swear that as I became versed in its strange terms it changed how I saw the world, how I heard it and how I comprehended its meaning. And once you master this way of speaking you become its slave. You become a flash one yourself and can never truly be anything else.

We walked to Covent Garden and reached the piazza by sunset. That great Square of Venus was ending its daily trade and preparing for its nightly commerce. Alice pointed out the beaus and the bloods, the gentlemen of fashion, the toasts of the town, all dressed up fine. She insisted that, it being my first day in London, we go 'for a dish at Moll's', meaning Moll King's coffee-house, not much more than a shed in front of the church that I came to know as a most popular meeting place where parties might consult on their nocturnal intrigues. There, they might make assignations (though to effect consummation they might need to find other premises). At Moll's all society, high and low, went to see and be seen.

Quite a throng had gathered outside on the steps and portico of the church. There was a buzz of conversation and some lively comments made in our direction. Punk Alice hustled me within and we found a bench in an inner saloon she told me was called the Long Room. I noticed above the fireplace a framed print of a fellow in mask and motley crouching behind a woman on all fours baring her ample buttocks as he kissed them. It was entitled *The Curious Doctor*.

We were waited on by a black serving-girl, whom Alice hailed as Tawny Betty. The coffee at Moll's is laced with strong spirit: brandy, rum or arrack. I had not tried coffee before, let alone hard liquor. The effect of them together both quickens and dulls the senses at once. In a calm reverie I watched a mizzy-eyed man try to rouse a sleeping strumpet, who lolled asleep, her ragged handkerchief fallen and her bosom exposed. A soldier broke into a bawdy ballad and some of the company joined in. I smiled, quite unperturbed by my disordered surroundings. Half of me knew that I had fallen into a low and debauched place while the other half reasoned that if this was Hell it was a merry place indeed.

All at once the hubbub hushed as a thick-set man entered. He wore a fine brocade coat and a long powdered wig beneath a tricorn hat but as he turned his head I noted a brutal countenance contrary to his noble bearing. His appearance was undeniably striking: a once handsome face etched with livid scars and coldly vigilant eyes of the palest hue. He walked with a loping gait, one leg dragging a little, pounding out a mournful rhythm as a silver-hilted sword swung at his side. All the assembly marked his entrance, though none dared look directly at him. Except me, of course. I sat staring with all the foolish curiosity of innocence. He caught my gaze and held it fast: in an instant I was trapped by his pallid stare. Then he reached into his coat and, seeing the butt of a pistol poking out, I gasped, thinking he was about to draw it. He grinned at me as he pulled out a pamphlet and held it up for all those in the Long Room to see.

'*An Answer to a Late Insolent Libel*,' he declared. 'Sixpence a copy, and here's a free issue for Moll King's reading room. Where is she?'

He dropped the bound tract onto a table as Tawny Betty led him through to find the proprietor.

'Who is he?' I whispered to Alice.

'Jonathan Wild,' she replied. 'The new thief-taker.'

I thought I knew something of that breed of men. We country folk imagined them as bold fellows who recovered stolen goods and apprehended villains in the wicked city.

A rake had picked up the pamphlet and begun to read aloud from its detailed frontispiece. There was some general discussion and the gist I caught was that there was a dispute between Wild and another, in a similar station, called Charles Hitchen. The rake holding the paper was ragged and wild-eyed but his deportment bore some trace of the stage, as did his voice when he intoned: *'Wherein is prov'd in many particular instances who is originally the Grand Thief-taker; that a certain author is guilty of more flagrant crimes, than any thief-taker mention'd in his nonsensical treatise; and he has highly reflected on the magistracy of the City, in the said scandalous pamphlet . . .'*

'This is his reply to Hitchen's accusations,' Alice explained.

'What accusations?'

'Of villainy. Each blames the other, then boasts of his own reputation as a whore might protest her virtue.'

I thought to question this as they surely both sought to uphold the law but Alice had turned to hear more.

'*. . . set forth in several entertaining stories, comical intrigues, merry adventures. With a diverting scene of a sodomitish academy!*'

At this the room broke into an uproar.

'Wild has really blown the widd now!' cried Alice.

'Why, all Romeville knows that Hitchen's a molly!' called another.

I had yet no notion of what they spoke.

Wild came back into the room, baring a blackened tooth as he grinned. He snatched back the pamphlet and held it up in a gesture of triumph. 'Gentlemen,' he said, with a slight bow of the head. 'Ladies. You see before you the new thief-taker general. Never mind Hitchen. He's nothing more than a madge-cull.'

He tossed the paper down and made his way over to where we were sitting.

'Thief-taker general,' said my companion, with a hint of mockery in her voice. 'I remember you when you were just Mary Milliner's twang.'

'Punk Alice.' Wild sat at our table, addressing her while staring at me. 'You've fresh prospects, I see.'

I looked to Alice. She shrugged.

'Anything for me?' he went on.

'Nix my doll.'

The thief-taker sighed and shook his head. 'You'll come to the gallows with no credit at this rate, Alice. Now, cant this.' He leaned forward so as not to be overheard. 'Let all the prigs know that as the trade goes at present they stand but a queer chance if they deal with Hitchen. And if they have made anything and carry it to the fencing-culls or vamp it to any flash pawnbrokers they are likely to be babbled. So, when they have been upon any lay or planning to speak to any purpose, let me know the particulars. Otherwise they'll run the hazard of being scragged.'

Punk Alice nodded. Jonathan Wild turned once more to me. 'And who's this dimber mort?' he asked.

'Bess. She's just come to town from Edgworth,' Alice answered.

'A flat one, eh? Take care, Edgworth Bess. This one will want to play a game of flats with you.'

He stood up and scanned me once more with his steely glare and I felt some quality of his power. His pale blue eyes bestowed a share of the attention he held in the room, and as all looked upon me I was charmed. I knew at once that this was a man who knew how to rule others.

'Welcome to Romeville,' he said, with a smile. 'We'll meet again soon.'

Then he turned and walked out. Moll King's resumed its revels with his departure. I felt fairly lightheaded with all the excitement of the day so I was quite relieved when Punk Alice stood up and announced it was time for her to show me my new lodgings. I hoped for some rest and sanctuary, little knowing what misadventure lay ahead.

It was dark as we left the coffee-house and the lamps of the link-boys glowed here and there, marking out a constellation across the cobbled piazza. One of the theatres had just emptied its crowd, and now a boisterous audience set forth to make its own drama. We passed the column with its sundials and gilded sphere. On its steps women sat selling hot milk and barley broth. I was led up a side-street to a quiet and respectable-looking terrace.

'Welcome to our house of civil reception,' said Punk Alice, as she ushered me up some steps to the front door. As we entered, a surly footman roused himself from a chair in the hallway. 'Fetch Mother,' Alice snapped at him, and he skulked off to some back parlour.

While we waited I felt great trepidation. I was fearful of what might happen to me in that strange house but full of determination also. I spied a Bible lying open on the hall table but I took it for yet another ruse. Circumstance decreed that I could not hope for God's blessing but I might yet find mortal favour. My further ruin seemed already certain. What mattered now was my survival of it.

Presently a silver-haired woman appeared wearing a velvet mantel. Alice introduced her as Mother Breedlove.

'Ah!' she declared, upon seeing me. 'What a fine kitling we have here. What is your name, child?'

I was about to answer, 'Elizabeth Lyon,' but something stopped me. It was as if I was no longer that person, no more the callow girl from the country. I felt I had already changed to fit this wicked new world and find my way in it. I was wilfully consenting to the destruction of my virtuous self, perhaps, but that person was no use to me now. Some guile, or merely the pretence of it, was necessary if I was not to be seen as helpless. 'I am known as Edgworth Bess,' I told Mother Breedlove, repeating how the man Wild had called this new creature into being.

Both women laughed heartily at this and I knew I had earned some credit of notoriety. From that moment on I reasoned that in a bad world there is little point in being good.

'Best tip the dell some prog,' said Mother Breedlove.

We followed her through to the back parlour and she bade me sit at a table on which supper had been laid out. Though hungry I scarcely managed to eat more than part of a cold capon's leg, so full was I with a nervous tremor. I had less trouble with the drink poured for me. I had never tasted red wine before but I loved it at once for the richness of its flavour and the instant warmth with which it endowed me. And soon it worked its power on me as I felt a marvellous transportation from disquiet. Mother Breedlove and Punk Alice talked more in the strange cant that I was only just beginning to understand but I no longer struggled to follow it, just allowed the haze of conversation to diffuse around me. I returned their smiles and Alice poured me another glass.

I not only felt my senses wrapped comfortably around me but something else, something unknowable, something like prophecy. This was the effect of the drink on me: like a premonition that everything would be well, a vague but certain promise of happiness. And it was this feeling that would hold me in its thrall. The elation one might feel in having done a virtuous deed, without the arduousness of undertaking such a task. Pure pleasure in idleness, a celebration of nothing and for no reason.

I started as I felt a hand at my elbow, rousing me from my

reverie. 'It's time for Alice to show you to your room,' said Mother Breedlove.

'I'll take her up to Sukey's old cribb,' added Alice, as she stood.

I felt giddy as she helped me to my feet – the entire house appeared to reel about me. Alice put an arm around me and we climbed the stairs together. I was shown a fine room with a dressing-table and a gilt-framed looking-glass. Escorted to a large canopy bed with its curtains tied at each post I sat down and caught my breath.

Punk Alice began to unlace my stays and loosen my dress. I thought nothing of it at the time since I had spent most of my life helping the girls and ladies of my household in this manner. Then, stripped down to my shift, she held my shoulders and kissed me full on the mouth with a great eagerness. For a moment I had the notion that this was merely the London way of bidding one goodnight but as her embrace of me became tighter and more urgent I knew that she was fixed on some keener purpose.

I was shocked at first but soon gave in to the will of my assailant. Fatigued by all the events of the day, as well as the effects of the wine, I was easily steered by the firm command of one with as much knowledge of my body as of her own. For her hands moved over every part of it, caressing and squeezing me with the same intent young Richard had had but with far more expertise. As she withdrew to undress herself I lay back gasping on the bed beneath her.

Alice had a strong, sturdy frame. She was but five-and-twenty and had seen the worst of the streets, yet she held herself with a pride that gave me a strange kind of hope. She pulled off my shift.

'You're a long-meg, aren't you?' she said.

I took this to be a comment on my frame since even at that young age I was tall and big-boned. I laughed. 'What is this?' I beseeched, looking up at her.

'This?'

'This game.'

Now it was her turn to laugh. 'Yes, it is a game I'm going to teach you. The first of many,' she replied.

'The man Wild mentioned a "game of flats".'

'Yes.' She laughed once more.

'Like a game of cards?'

'Yes. But we'll not be studying the history of the four kings.'

'No?'

'No. We'll play the queens not the knaves. Here.'

She climbed onto the bed, her strong legs straddling me. Leaning forward she kissed me first on the mouth, then on my chin and down along my neck. I gave a little cry of delight, my mouth wide and head thrown back. As my body arched upwards I felt her face between my breasts, her tongue following each curve. Then she raised her head and looked down at me once more.

'Here's a pair to open with,' she murmured.

With finger and thumb she teased the bud of each nipple and bestowed kisses on them until they were quite hard and pointed.

'The deuce of diamonds,' she declared, rolling off me to lie at my side.

'What is a sodomitish academy?' I asked her, as she stroked my face.

'Never mind Sodom,' she told me, tracing a line along my body. 'Tonight you'll learn Gomorrah.'

And so I let myself be led through this wicked city of the

senses, curious to know what I might find of myself there. She bade me look down at my own flesh as she smoothed her palm against my belly, reaching down to the cleft between my thighs.

'Here,' she said, touching the rounded patch of jet-black hair. 'Here's the ace of spades. That's the trump.'

I giggled as her fingers played amid those curls. Then I sighed, feeling utterly pliant in her hands, stretched out before her as she took possession of me. There came the fervent and yearning sensation I'd felt when Richard had taken me. But Punk Alice found in me what that boy, in his clumsy haste, had been oblivious of, and with a quickening caress I was transported to a delirious ecstasy.

She continued to explore this part of me, skilled in all the modes and devices of exquisite pleasure. She was curious to know me intimately, and as she felt me within, I was moved to confess to her that I was not as flat as she might have imagined. Thus I told her of how I had lost my maidenhead.

When I recounted my disappointment in the act, as well as my betrayal in affection, she told me, 'Never trust a man for love or pleasure. Money and cunny are the best commodities. We trade one for the other. But among our own selves we'll be free.'

'Our own selves?'

She curled herself around me, softly humming a haunting air. 'But among our own selves we'll be free,' she sang the words this time, in a cooing tone with a plaintive and wistful cadence.

For some minutes her manner and gaze were distant. Then she turned and spoke to me intently: 'Remember, Bess, this is your property.' She touched me below once more. 'Your own freehold. You can rent it out but let no one own it except yourself. Now, here's a trick. I'll lay my queen of spades on your queen of hearts.'

She embraced me again and so we shared the night together.

I awoke with a start at dawn, for a moment not knowing where I was. Then, spying Punk Alice sleeping beside me, I pondered my state. What had I lost? My virtue? No, I decided. I'd never had any. Now I was to consider what to gain. I would learn new tricks, subtle crafts and trades. And in the years to come I would take as gospel her advice not to trust men for love or pleasure. Until, that is, I met Jack Sheppard.

Dear Applebee,

Thank you for the ten guineas received on account and your
comments upon the text.

You rightly protest that many will complain of the possible
corrupting influence of this story, that Bess rather flaunts her
bodily crimes and pleads little for the mercy of her soul. But
you know as well as any that this might be her final whoring
and could well be a draw to the public. From a shadow-world
a shadow-gospel is rendered: the flesh made word where only
the intoxication of sin can be offered as mitigation. And
though I'm sure that the idle reader may appreciate this, it is
to be hoped that when her case comes up before the next
sessions she can deliver a better defence than that. But, then,
you know the old jest about a jade who plied her trade by the
Temple: that if she had as much law in her head as she had in
her tail, she would be one of the ablest counsels in England.

Now, it may be argued that decency demands a moral to the
tale, and one that stretches beyond the scaffold that awaits
such sinners, for otherwise this is wicked learning, bad wisdom
that is itself a vice. What was the Tree of Knowledge but
Creation's first gallows? Yes, this is man- and womankind's
fatal tree. Some blame the serpent, some Eve for the Fall, but
who planted the evil sapling that grew with the heavy fruit of
its branches hanging so low and tempting? The same cruel
God who decreed His one and only Son should be strung up
on a wooden gibbet. It was He who cursed us with conscious
thought.

In our intelligence we share some guilt in preparing this

work for the press and, though I agree to the terms of its publication as set out in your letter, I crave a little space to reflect upon my own predicament. There is another story to be told but we will come to that later.

For there is scant time, I know, until the final date and much work to be done. I once heard a chaplain promise a condemned man, 'I'll tip you as handsome a coffin as a man might desire to set his arse in but I need half a dozen more pages of confession.'

This is a grave undertaking, after all. You yourself have said that for this account of her life to be a success poor Bess must hang for it. Then she'll have a fine audience at Tyburn and an eager readership for this pleasant Newgate pastoral.

So there's the moral for you. The blight of knowledge endowed in these very words. Each letter a crawling creature of sin. I sometimes rue the day I learned to read and write. I might have found a more honest trade.

I remain sir, your humble servant,

the author

II

I was soon set to work in what Punk Alice called (in one of the many flash terms she used for our establishment) 'Mother Breedlove's Vaulting-School'. And I learned from her that our trade there was, in the most part, giving a performance. We began with costume, and I was rigged out in a fine mantua gown in pale blue silk with brocade front and hooped skirt. Alice pulled hard on the cords of the bodice, squeezing my form with its whalebone stays, narrowing the midriff and raising the breasts provocatively. When I protested at how this constraint restricted my respiration she insisted that the shape would make the man equally scant of breath.

'The tighter the dress, the looser the morals,' she jested.

Then, with some time spent before the glass practising this impertinent posture, and a quick lesson in the application of paint and powder to the phiz, we left the dressing-room and proceeded with rehearsal. Punk Alice considered that the best way for me to learn was to watch one of the other jades as they presented their repertoire.

One of the cribbs had a dark closet attached that could be

accessed by a separate door. A grille had been inserted in the panelling that masked it, and through this the occupants of the main chamber could be touted unawares. Alice pattered that this booth was often hired by male visitors to Mother Breedlove's. And it was from this little opera box that we were audience to Polly, one of the most popular girls in our academy, as she entertained a cull (as the men who hired us were known).

The pantomime had already started as we took our seats. Polly knelt before the cull, who had unrigged to his shirt and took his machine (as Alice called it) in her paws. Looking up at him all the time, wide-eyed and imploring, Polly offered breathless phrases of desire and encouragement. The importance of feigning one's own response of pleasure was pointed out here as it was noted that, strangely, most men prize this reaction as greatly as they do their own gratification.

We looked on as she reached out and took a curious device from her dressing-table. Alice told me that it was a cundum, a sheath made of sheep gut that could prevent both the Covent Garden gout and the siring of any unwanted squeakers. Polly slipped it over the shaft of his machine and fastened it with a pink ribbon. She then stood and, still holding him by that most vulnerable part, led him to a couch that had been positioned on the opposite wall to the secret closet so as to give the best view of the spectacle. Punk Alice nudged me, as if to indicate that the dumb show had ended and the main act had begun.

Having first confirmed that this was the posture he desired, Polly climbed onto the upholstery and raised her rump towards him. Looking back over her shoulder she gave that same plaintive gaze and moaned in mock ecstasy as he inserted himself. She provided the main part of the dialogue here, entreating him with 'Oh! Yes! My captain! It is too much!' while he merely rejoined with grunts and the occasional curse until all at once he improvised his little death scene and the play was at an end. At this he was soon dressed and dismissed downstairs, and so I learned that the great drama by which men set such store could be swiftly dispatched as but a comic interlude.

❦

I quickly went from understudy to the taking of roles in the academy, ever conscious of the element of pretence in our work. Though there was always danger in the act. Sometimes a cull wouldn't want to use a cundum or there wasn't one to hand. And, frankly, a jade would get lazy and rather think of the quick tempo of the play than its safe traffic. So then there were the other ways: a sponge dipped in vinegar hidden in the commodity or a quick syringe after with some purgative to clear out what was left behind. The worst of it was that we mostly feared life rather than death: of being with child rather than the pox. It was to the best if a thing could be dealt with before one felt the quickening of it. After that there were places where they could rid you of it but all faced that with dread. Some swore by a herb called pennyroyal, but Punk Alice told me to take no heed of that as it was poison. There were dark tales of jades who had lain-in secretly and had left the child to the world's mercy or even stifled the squeaker themselves.

All of us agreed in our trade to make the culls our prey and not otherwise. If the act could be finished by the paw or between the shanks that was to the good. The trick was to put much excitement into the prologue so that they might discharge their part in an opening scene.

Then there were the bleeding-culls, those who might part with their loure without much more than a feel of the goods, and the watching-culls who paid to tout others perform. Strangest of all were the flogging-culls, though it seems that this particular vice has long been popular in England. Indeed, in my first years of this life, the pleasure in castigation was quite the fashion in Romeville, with even a learned treatise on its application circulated widely in the city. Many a time I had the breeches down of some lusty cull to birch his bare backside. I once wore out a full penny-worth of rods on one ancient rake and Punk Alice, who touted me fustigate him from the dark closet, declared that I could easily take employment on Hart Street with Mother Burgess, who ran an academy entirely dedicated to this practice.

Many of us dreamed of finding a keeping-cull who might set one up in luxury, and there was always some prattle of a jade who'd become the mistress to a gentry-cove. Punk Alice confessed that, as a dell, she had been kept by an old Dutch merchant who had treated her well but plagued her with an insistence that she declare her true love for him. He would implore her thus in his broken English until she could bear it no longer and jabbered at him, 'Damn you and your queer tongue! How can I love rotten teeth and stinking fifty?'

And that was the end of that.

Mother Breedlove could be strict and was determined to keep her academy in good order, but she had a charitable spirit that could be appealed to. She was hopelessly devout (the Bible in the hallway was sincerely meant) and she regularly attended the gospel-shop of St Paul's by the piazza. Edifying works of Christian teaching could be found scattered around, and framed verses from scripture or religious pictures hung alongside obscene prints on the walls of each cribb so that (as she put it) 'each jade or cull might repent even while they sinned'. Punk Alice had long used this yearning for goodness for her own ends, playing upon Mother's better instincts and demanding what she called the 'liberty of the gate'.

It was this spirit of freedom that I foolishly followed. For I might have escaped this sinful world for good and found honest work in a respectable household, as old Fenton had advised me. But I learned too swiftly the temptations of luxury and idleness. What I knew of a servant's life was mostly drudgery, and though a whore's employment might be distasteful, there was always a chance for easy money or being kept.

So I sought, like Punk Alice, mere respite from the vaulting-school and, like her, became determined that I would not be too confined by it. But once outside I was led astray further and learned yet more wicked practices. I came to know the parish they call the Hundreds of Drury, all the back-streets and side-alleys off that crooked road, which runs down from St Giles to the Strand. Here I was Edgworth Bess and none of the canting-crew had any notion of the fresh girl from Daisyville I had once been. Indeed, I was soon insensible of her myself.

So, when business was slow we might pad it to Moll King's to look for prospects or go to the Black Lion, a boozing-ken nearby, to take lush with our own tribe. And what an industry of vice we found in the Hundreds, where the poor apprentice might find meagre lodgings. Here were ken-millers, bung-nippers and low-pads – that is, housebreakers, pickpockets and those who rob upon the street. So many were plying an evil trade, there were as many villainous professions as there were respectable ones. If half the city was making then the other half was taking, and all of Romeville was a prig's paradise for those of us in the flash world.

Even the landlord of the Black Lion, Joseph Hind, who professed the honest craft of button-moulding, was said to have turned queer bit-maker as he had all the tools to forge coin. Here I gained knowledge of many tricks and developed a fondness for gin. The lightning, as we called it, would rouse my spirits free at first, then hold them fast for its longing. The love of this joyous and melancholic lush would bring much misfortune, as would my calling, the vocation of buttock-and-file, for which I became famous. And this was first practised in the episode that follows.

On the day of a hanging the streets were so full around the procession from Newgate to Tyburn that it was best to pad outdoors for trade than to wait around at Mother Breedlove's. There was scarce a tavern, ale-house or brandy-shop along the route that did not fill with an idle audience eager for the gape-seed. The cart would stop at the Bowl Inn at St Giles and here the condemned would take a drink and toast the mob. A murderer might be jeered but most were simple thieves, flash like us. A cheer would go up as one of the damned drained his clanker and tipped the old jest that he'd settle the bill on the way back. Some might boast of being a neighbour or a near acquaintance to any of those about to be scragged, and those on the cart would smile for a moment on their last day of fame, hoping that some balladeer might make a song of their plight.

One Monday we got to Tyburn early and found ourselves in the push close by the scaffold. The gallows formed by three cross-bars on three posts is sometimes called the Triple Tree or the Three-legged Mare as it can scrag a trinity of felons at one go. Nearby is the wooden grandstand, known as Mother Proctor's

Pews, where for a penny you can get a good tout of the poor coves being turned off. I could not quite cant then what the coves and morts took from this gape-seed as they watched Jack Ketch string a fellow to the tree. To tout that moment when the horses pulled away and the cart moved off, to see the condemned dangle and caper in the air. Was it to snatch some spark of the soul as it flew up to Heaven or dropped down to Hell? Or was it to see how the wretch faced death, begging for mercy or standing proud?

The one thing certain was that the moment the poor wretch swung was the best time to pick a pocket. That instant was a fine stall for the bung-nippers, for all glaziers were on the one dancing the Tyburn jig and insensible to those diving for their watches and snuff-boxes.

So Punk Alice and me stuck close with the push of ground-lings, touting out for a lay. Soon a dandyprat-cull in a full-bottomed wig approached and Alice nodded to me to show that she thought we might nab from that one. I smiled at him.

'Would Sir care to join us and perhaps go for a pint of wine later?' I asked him.

His ruddy phiz beamed and we stood either side of him. A pamphleteer passed by and the dandyprat bought a *Last Dying Speech* of one of the condemned for sixpence.

I sidled closer to him and implored the man to patter some of these final widds as I had little reading and Alice none.

'It seems that the fellow is to hang for outwitting the Bank of England,' our cull explained. 'He says, *I come hither to hang like a pendulum to a watch, for endeavouring to be rich too soon.* Oh, that's good, that's very good!'

'Isn't it?' Alice rejoined, then said to me: 'Speaking of a watch, let's speak with his. Stall the cull and I'll dive for the clickman toad.'

'What?' said our cull, not canting what we jabbered.

'Read us some more,' I entreated him, then followed my sister's instructions. Leaning across to tout the pamphlet, I pressed my bosom against him. Punk Alice set to work, gently unfastening the gold watch from his waistcoat pocket.

'If the poor man had wanted to make easy money out of banking,' said the cull, distracted by my movements, 'he should have invested in the South Sea Company.'

That was the first time I'd heard of this queer business, later called the Bubble, but in the next few years there was prattle of it everywhere. I once imagined this bubble to be some actual creature or edifice to be touted in those southern waters where the rich got their money. I stroked the man's stupid phiz and pointed further down the tract asking, 'What does he say there?'

'Er,' he cleared his throat. '*I was never a murderer, unless killing fleas and such little harmless creatures fall under the statute, neither can I charge myself with being a whore-master, since the female gentry of the Hundreds of Drury had always the ascendant over me, not I over them.*'

Alice and me laughed heartily at this, feeling a fond pity for the condemned cove, though none at all for the cull we filched from. By then I had my shank between his and was rubbing against his breeches. Keeping him merry and conscious of the growing weight in that place, rather than the loss of it elsewhere, I looked to my partner and she winked to let me know the deed was done.

We bided a moment as the push we were part of moved forward and took the opportunity to slip deftly back through it, thus shabbing off from our prey. Alice had a fob of lead that she'd left in his waistcoat pocket so that, in luck, it would be some time before he twigged the watch was missing.

And so I began my career as a buttock-and-file, learning all of the tricks of the pickpocket trade. It always amazed me when some flat citizen might declare hanging a deterrent to that felony, when we might make so much at one.

On the way home we called by the Black Lion, hoping to find a fence for what we had spoken with that afternoon. And it was that very darkmans I first met two natty-lads who were to play their own part in my story and its sad conclusion.

Joseph Blake was a sullen rogue known as Blueskin because of his dark countenance. He was part-blackamoor and a dimber cove. With some workhouse schooling and an abiding respect for learning, he was a sharp one but his early inclination to villainy had damned him to a crooked path. His only diligence in self-advancement now was to be studious in infamy.

James Sykes was a powerful-looking man known as Hell-and-Fury, not for any particular ferocity of his demeanour but for his ability to pike faster than the devil. He had been a running footman to the Duke of Wharton and a champion athlete. He still ran two-mile races for high wagers on occasion and was canted as the best skittle player in all of London, but his principal occupation was now as a low-pad. It was prattled that he tutored a crew of spruce-prigs, those who dress and dance like the gentry-coves and make society balls and the opera their lay.

But those proud rogues turned meek when Punk Alice handed them the watch we had dived for.

'Best take it to the prig-napper,' murmured Joe Blueskin, and I canted he meant the stern cove I had touted that night in Moll King's.

'Bitched by Wild, are you?' Alice demanded, with a fierce look in her glaziers.

I was still largely ignorant of the practices of this self-appointed thief-taker general but I had heard his name pattered with fear throughout the Hundreds of Drury. I twigged that he had built a reputation on his ability to recover stolen goods and for his bold courage in the apprehension of those prigs who thieved without his sanction. The power he had to peach or acquit made him the terror of the flash world as well as something of a hero to flat society.

'He might be the devil, Alice,' said Blueskin, 'but who else might the likes of us deal with except Merry Old Roger?'

'Then damn him,' she jabbered back, snatching the clickman back from his paw. 'I'll find my own fencing cove or else vamp it to a pawnbroker.'

I sat mum-chance on this discourse, intrigued by what could inspire such fear in Joe Blueskin and disdain in Punk Alice. But in the days that followed I became ever more sensible to all the prattle of the canting-crew that buzzed about Wild. And, though I touted peery of the prig-napper by lightmans, by darkmans came queer fancies of that pale-eyed demon. He haunted my dreams, perhaps with the very power that held sway in all of Romeville. I knew somehow that it would not be long before I would learn of his dealings first-hand.

Padding it home from the Black Lion one night, with no thoughts of business or its solicitation, I came across a foppish fellow very pot-valiant. He invited me to stroll with him awhile, perhaps drawn in my path because I was not calling out or rudely importuning, as the common jades of the Hundreds of Drury do. I took him for an amiable but easy cull so after a few pleasantries I directed him to procure a carriage for us both so that I might take him back to our academy.

Once we were on our way, the fop began to make quite free with me. I, too, let my paws explore his person but only in order to twig what was carried on it. He was quite insensible of my true intentions and driven by two devils: the lush and the lust. The first swiftly overwhelmed the second and he fell into a slumber. I quickly dived him properly this time and found a gold watch and chain, a green leather pocketbook fringed with silver and a fine snuff-box. We were in Little Russell Street where the road narrows, and as the coach idled a moment, I took the opportunity to brush upon the sneak. Gently fastening the door behind me I shabbed off quickly and quietly.

But as I touted my haul back in the presumed safety of my cribb I was overcome by a terrible fear of what I had done. I took some gin but it did little to calm my mood. When Mother Breedlove came up to see me she quickly twigged the strangeness in my manner.

'What's the matter, girl?' she asked of me.

'Nothing,' I insisted. 'I'm just tired from walking.'

'And while you were walking?'

I blushed that she might see inside my soul so easily.

'Come now, Bess,' she entreated, and poured another glass of lightning. 'Tell your old mother everything.'

I took a gulp of the spirit, then babbled all, showing her the loot now in my possession. She shook her head slowly and clucked her tongue.

'You know I don't allow my girls to steal from visitors to the academy,' she pattered.

'But this was on the outside.'

'Yes, but you bring it back here.' She sighed and gave a heavy shrug. 'Look, I know what to do. Stow those things under your bed for now. And get yourself ready. There's a gentleman waiting below.'

I thought no more of it that darkmans. Later I considered telling Punk Alice about the affair but felt a sort of shame at how lully I had been in screening it. I pondered on going to patter with Blueskin or Hell-and-Fury but twigged that this might complicate matters. In the end I decided to wait and see what Mother Breedlove could arrange. A week later she showed me an advertisement in the *London Journal*:

Lost, the 1st of June, a gold watch, a snuff-box and a shagreen pocketbook, trimmed with silver with some notes of hand. The said items were lost in a coach on Drury Lane at about 10 o'clock at night. If any person will bring the aforesaid items to Mr Jonathan Wild, in the Old Bailey, they shall have a guinea reward.

'What does this mean?' I asked her. 'Is this from the owner?'

'Of course not. I went to Wild so he knows how these things were stolen and that the owner will want to be discreet about their recovery.' She pointed to a line in the text. 'See, "some notes of hand". That's a nice touch. Shows that the gentleman could be identified whereas he might prefer to be anonymous.'

'What shall I do now? Must I go and see Wild?'

'Wait for him to call for you. That's the best way.'

And so I tarried, in reasonable fear but also with some crank excitation for the summons of the prig-napper.

It was at the end of lightmans a few days later that I was called to his rooms by the Old Bailey. There was a grand sign on the jigger: 'Office for the Recovery of Lost and Stolen Property'. I knocked and a servant came to the door. When I had pattered my business he nodded, then turned to call in a disdainful tone: 'A lady to see you, sir.'

'Show her in, Quilt,' came a voice from within.

I was led through the ken to where Jonathan Wild sat at a desk piled with papers and books. He squinted at a small note-book in his paw, his phiz a full frown of lines and scars. He looked fiercely nettled, his grinders clenched in thought as he marked something off with a quill. I grew fearful in waiting for him to look up, my shanks trembling as I stood before him. But as he raised his head and touted me, his face opened out into a smile, his bright glaziers scanning me eagerly.

'Edgworth Bess,' he pattered softly, and I smiled back, foolishly proud that he had remembered me.

'Mother Breedlove . . .' I began awkwardly, but he raised a hand to stop me.

'Mother Breedlove has told me everything.' He sighed and scraped back his chair to stand up. 'Oh, Bess, a few months up from Daisyville and already fallen into bad ways.'

'I wish only to make amends, sir.'

'Indeed.' He nodded, padding around the desk to come next to me. I flinched a little as he took my paw in his, but his palm was surprisingly soft and warm. 'Are you still in possession of the loot Mother Breedlove told me of?'

'Yes.' I caught my breath. 'I'm sorry. I haven't . . . I haven't brought it with me.'

He let go of my hand and wheezed with laughter. 'I should think not,' he said. 'I wouldn't want stolen property on my prem-ises. Anyone might take me for a fence.'

'But you'll want to return these items to their owner, won't you?'

'All in good time. You're still quite the flat one, aren't you, Edgworth Bess? Well, you'll learn plenty today if you care to.'

The glare of his bleach-blue eyes promised mischief. Once more I could not forbear smiling at him. 'What am I to do?' I asked.

'Wait and see. You're in luck. The owner of what you filched has contacted me and has an appointment presently. Bide a while in the other cribb where you might hear our discourse. Then you may see how things are done.'

He took me by the arm and led me to an adjoining chamber. I stood close by the jigger and listened as the gentry-cove I had dived all those nights before dupped in. I could tout a little through the crack: the cull looked as sober now in his rigging as he did in his senses. A crown was handed over as the prig-napper's initial fee and Quilt brought prattle-broth for both men. Wild asked all sorts of questions about the circumstances of the theft and I could hear the scratching of a pen as he made copious notes. This was more for the appearance of knowledge than the acquisition of it, as he told me later. I looked on as he played his part as the great master of detection. He knew all the facts already, but the way he seemed to be twigging a meaning for each new sample of the truth made him seem a prodigy of intelligence. In time he asked for a full description of me. The fop was able to offer little that could be incriminating but that I was quite tall and long-limbed. Wild prompted him with details of his own. I felt quite a thrill of terror, so quickly did they paint a clear picture of me.

'Yes, I think I know who that is.' He called to his servant: 'Quilt! Where was Edgworth Bess the Tuesday before last?'

'On Drury Lane, sir,' came the reply.

Wild touted over to where he knew me to be screened and tipped me an artful wink. 'Yes, she's a sly jade, that bitch,' he said. 'I'll have her safe before morning.'

I quaked, thinking of how, if peached, I could go to the gallows for this crime.

'Oh, sir,' the gentleman protested. 'Don't take her up. I won't prosecute if I can help it. I'd rather lose these things than see a poor wretch hang for them. Can we not come to some arrangement?'

'Come, sir,' the prig-napper goaded him sternly. 'If we bargain that might compound a felony. Justice must be seen to be done.'

And for a moment I thought that all was lost, that this was a trap and I was queerly snabbled.

'But . . .' the gentry-cove implored, as if canting my own distress.

'But,' Wild grinned, 'you'd rather not have your virtuous wife and her innocent children know how you came to lose your snuff-box, watch and pocketbook.'

'Yes. Yes, that's it exactly, sir.'

I gasped with such relief that I thought I might be heard.

'I could make her come and ask your pardon,' Wild went on, looking over to me once more with a smile still on his gob. I twigged then he had been playing me.

'I'd rather forgive her *in absentia* as it were,' said the cull.

'Very well, sir. I foresee that it will cost some twenty guineas for the recovery of these articles, with all the expenses, the fees if they have been in pawn.'

'In pawn?'

'Let us hope so, sir. If this low jade has kept these things all the while they might be damaged, especially the watch. No, eighteen, nineteen, I'll do my very best to keep it below twenty guineas, sir. You have my word on it.'

'And your own costs?'

'Not a farthing more than the crown I charge for my services, sir. Come to me next Thursday and we should have the matter settled.'

And so the prig-napper led the dance like a cunning caper-merchant and the gentry-cove departed, satisfied that his mystery had been solved and convinced of the thief-taker general's prestige as a stoic agent of the law. Wild then bade his man Quilt to open the jigger and beckoned me through.

'That's how to make proper loure from buttock-and-file work,' he pattered, 'whatever Punk Alice might tell you otherwise. I know how to work the drop on these culls. They never like it known how their goods were filched so I play on that. What say you?'

'You're a sharp one, sir. For a while I thought . . .' I stopped, thinking better of admitting my terror. But Wild touted that fear.

'You were scared, weren't you, Bess?' He came closer.

As I nodded, he reached out and gently stroked my bare throat. 'That's good,' he whispered. 'Never forget how easy it is for me to scrag such a pretty neck.'

I gasped yet it was such a soft touch. He hummed and closed his eyes as if sensing me quiver with his fingertips. Then he opened his glaziers and withdrew his paw. 'So, time for your reward, Bess.'

He counted out some coin from his bung and pressed it into my palm. 'Three guineas. Will that suffice?'

I agreed, even though I knew he stood to make twenty from the deal.

'Good. And you'll sup with me?' he asked.

The calm authority in the delivery of this invitation banished any thoughts of declining it, so I let Wild take my arm as we padded out onto Newgate Street with his loyal Quilt following behind. We dupped into a tavern nearby, and as we made our way through to a snug corner at the back of the ken, I noted the fearsome regard with which the coves and morts touted my companion. As I caught the odd stare I, too, was looked upon peerily, as if I had earned some respect simply by being with the prig-napper. I must confess that I revelled in this small snack of tyranny, unused as I was to the courtesy it provoked. Indeed, when the bluffer came to our table and addressed me as 'madam', I looked around, wondering who he might be pattering with.

We had a fine dinner of roast partridge and much French wine. There were many interruptions as our table was approached by those begging a brief audience with the thief-taker general. And here I learned how he ruled the lower world of Romeville just as I had touted earlier the way he put the bite on the gentry-coves. All of the canting-crew seemed drawn to the sphere of his orbit, ready to babble their tribute. Wild knew all the secrets of the wicked city, his power measured by such broad intelligence.

Then a scrub ballad-singer wandered in singing a mournful air and pleading for some coin. The bluffer came forward to throw him out but Wild called the ragged troubadour over. The ken hushed as the poor wretch started again in a sad and lilting tone. *'Oh don't you see yon lonesome dove, in yonder willow tree,'* he sang, with a bene voice that was hard to credit to his mean and haggard phiz. *'She's weeping for her own true love, as I will weep for thee.'* And I touted that the prig-napper's eyes were glib with tears. He reached for my paw and turned to me, his muddled glaziers, which could have been grey or blue, now mizzy as a pair of shucked oysters. When the song was done he reached into his bung for a silk wiper and dabbed away some heartsick remembrance.

The man offered another ballad but Wild shook his head and tossed him a shilling. 'Now pike it,' he ordered briskly, and nodded to some rogue who was waiting behind.

This cove had a jewelled brooch to trade for its reward and though he asked a little too much for it he quickly secured the bargain.

'Damn,' Wild muttered, as the man departed. 'He caught me in a fond moment. Mark that bastard down, Quilt. See if we can't find someone to go evidence against him for next sessions. Well, here's a gift for you, Bess.'

As he picked up the bauble and pinned it to my gown I touted that something melancholic yet dwelt on his phiz. Later, in the cribb upstairs, it was soft affection he craved as much as the vigour of lovemaking. I was to learn that, like many ruthless men, Jonathan Wild was driven by wistful sentiment. His ruthless brutality had been tutored by private pain where every past loss called out for future gain. I spied the sadness in him as clear as the marks upon his flesh. His battered countenance, like some ancient bust, bore a kind of maimed beauty. I saw the silver plate on his cropped and wigless crown that fixed a fracture of the skull. There were wounds upon his soul as well. He pattered bitterly of the four years he had spent in the trib and how he had taught himself the trade of thief-taking by working for the quod-culls there. Now his pale blue glaziers were ever watchful. I spent many nights with him yet never caught him in slumber. It was prattled that he slept with his eyes open.

45

He would call upon me at Mother Breedlove's with rum jewellery and fine rigging of silk and satin, and he would tip me much prog and lush. But his best gift was the knowledge I canted through him of how things worked. That great mystery of Romeville where every petty felony was solved by regulating its crime. Only such a dishonest man could know the whole truth of our fallen world. I was proud to know the cleverest man in London.

We went to the playhouse on Drury Lane and touted a dreary tragedy of some Romish gentry-coves, then a lively pantomime of a necromancer. Wild cheered at bold Caesar presented as a villain and clapped at how a harlequin pawned his soul to Merry Old Roger. He could be bene company for the darkmans, curious and contrary like me, clever without any schooling. And I got used to being looked upon with that respect when I was out on the pad with him. I had this rum feeling of being safe, for a while at least, even though I knew that he traded in people and kept a huge ledger book of every prig in London.

'I'll never lose you, Bess,' he pattered to me one lightmans, with a queer kind of affection to his voice. 'Once someone is part of me I never let them go.'

I did not cant the meaning of this and took it instead for a kind of bargain that I might earn something from. I had by then become too familiar in a circumstance that I should have twigged to be temporary. And I argued with Punk Alice when she told me to be peery of putting any trust in the prig-napper.

'Don't look to him as any keeping-cull, Bess,' she warned me. 'He already has six wives.'

I had heard this prattle of Jonathan's cruelty to our sex from other jades. I took it for mere smokiness on their part and indeed proof that I was special as he had treated me well. Then I touted him out on the pad one lightmans with a new dell from Mother Needham's.

So I returned to the cloistered sinfulness of the abbey. I had foolishly imagined an easy way out and now it was back to work at the vaulting-school. When I walked abroad I noted that I was now touted as before: a simple jade to be gawped at with none of the privilege I had enjoyed with Wild for an escort. Worst of all, I looked down upon myself now, canting myself as a worthless trull. I grew timid of the world and hardly dared to pad it out for long, which made me miserable.

Punk Alice cared enough for me to refrain from pattering that she had been right all along. Instead she noticed how I brooded in confinement and seemed determined to take me from that state. 'Come, Bess,' she implored. 'Let's take a stroll.'

'Where to?'

'To Moll King's. Or to the Black Lion.'

'Why? So that we might furnish a room for the greedy or curious?'

'Bess?' Alice frowned at me. 'What is it?'

'I wish I were invisible,' I told her.

'Invisible?'

'Yes. Or else be able to wander without being touted upon with either lust or contempt. We never know which is which since they both wear the same look of malice.'

'Oh,' Punk Alice nodded slowly, as if comprehending something I scarce had hold of myself. 'Is that what Edgworth Bess wants? Then it will be arranged.'

'Now you play with me.'

'This is no jest,' she said, with a gleam of mischief in her eyes. 'Sunday night it'll be. Tell Mother we're going to evensong.'

47

And that night she came to my jigger with a bundle of men's clothes. At first I thought she had unrigged a couple of culls and was planning to dive them.

'Careful, Alice,' I said, hustling her into my cribb and out of sight. 'If Mother Breedlove touts you filching, she—'

'Bess,' she interrupted. 'These are ours.'

'Ours?'

'Yes. Come.' She heaved the clothes onto my bed and began to strip. 'Let us get rigged for this evening's walk.'

She had procured for both of us fine jackets and pale breeches, lace-cuffed shirts and embroidered waistcoats. Alice showed me how to bind the breasts with cloth so that the swell did not show so much beneath. Once rigged, we adjusted our men's wigs so that the line of jaw and cheekbone might seem strong and forceful, then secured our hats on top. Finally Alice helped me pull on a pair of polished leather boots and we stood together before the glass.

'What a fine pair of bullies we make,' she declared.

And indeed we looked handsome in our new apparel. I was tall enough to pass for a pretty youth. Alice was short but broad in the shoulder and with great confidence in manly deportment. She showed me how to pad it like one of them, and as I copied her I had to stifle my laughter. Soon I had grasped enough of this peculiar gait to proceed and continue the learning of it by falling into a rhythm beside my tutor. And so it was that we set out together as two young bloods on the town.

We avoided the boozing-kens and coffee-houses that we normally frequented and headed for those places of resort where we were not well known. As my confidence in a gentlemanly demeanour steadied I felt a wondrous sense of liberty. And strong lush certainly helped in becoming a man since there does seem to be some sort of insensibility to it. I stuck to small drams of lightning or brandy, though, rather than quantities of ale or wine. In the manner of my drinking I could stand as well as any cove, but in pissing it away I might not pass so well.

Punk Alice told me that she had padded it out at darkmans in this manner before to go thieving since it offered a complete disguise, though she confided that it also gave her pleasure at times to dress as a cove. 'Part of my soul belongs like this,' she said, with a smile.

We could not resist strolling up Drury Lane and taking the calls from the poor jades who plied their trade on the streets there. Alice was bold with them, answering their cries with lewd pronouncements of her own. But at length I became weary of our private masquerade. 'I can't keep this up much longer,' I said.

'It is still early yet,' she replied, although it was past ten o'clock.

'In truth,' I admitted, 'I grow tired of being a man.'

Punk Alice laughed out loud and declared, 'Then we'll go to Mother Clap's!'

She led the way up towards St Giles and we turned along Holborn. I twigged in horror that she was now planning to conclude our night out as young men with a visit to a brothel, since most of our vaulting-schools are known by their mother's name. I knew of Mother Griffith's in King Street, Mother Needham's over in St James's, even of the academy of Mother Burgess where the flogging-culls are catered for, but I had not yet heard of Mother Clap's.

'Alice,' I protested, 'you go too far. You cannot expect us to pass as culls ourselves.'

'Don't worry. We're for another kind of academy. One that you were curious of yourself.'

'What?'

'Oh, yes. You asked of it on our first night together.'

I still had no notion of what she spoke. We passed the Bunch o' Grapes tavern on Field Lane and ducked into an alleyway by the arch opposite. Here we found the jigger to what seemed a coffee-house. There came the muffled noise of music and merry-making within. Punk Alice knocked and pattered something I could not fathom to the bully who answered, and we were shown through to the main room of the ken.

Here there were some forty or fifty coves making riot. In the corner someone scraped at a fiddle and in the middle of the floor there was dancing. There were a few jades, perhaps six or seven, who paraded or made postures to applause and catcalls. A more lively school I had never known, or a stranger one, since none of the coves took much notice of the morts present. Indeed, I looked again and saw the men kissing and caressing each other. Punk Alice caught my astonished eye and said: 'Well, you did ask me that time what a sodomitish academy was.'

I had heard madges and mollies talked of as foppish and effeminate. But here were all types of the species, many as manly as any cove. They pattered their own kind of flash, an arch slang that seemed not so much to hide their difference as to express it, to bring it into being. This was the molly dialect and they called each other by their 'maiden names' such as Miss Fanny Knight or Primrose Mary. There was a bewildering assortment of rank: Madame or Miss, Aunt, Lady, Countess or Princess. Some titles seemed simply to reflect the trade of the person such as Dip-candle Polly (a tallow chandler) or Small Coal Kitty (a collier's merchant).

We began to draw attention and curiosity as we made our way through the push. In a low voice Punk Alice pointed out a back parlour known as the chapel where couples might go for 'marrying'.

It seemed that the mother of this academy made her loure more by letting out rooms than the actual hiring out of people, though it seemed that could be arranged too. I asked Alice about the morts present.

'The morts?' She frowned at me.

'Yes.'

'Oh, Bess,' she smiled. 'There are no morts bar us. It's just a festival night.'

'What?'

'Come.' She took my hand and led me to where the ladies were lined up. 'Come and meet Princess Seraphina.'

The princess looked impressive in a fine mantua gown and powdered face and she made a mock-curtsy as we approached. Close up I could see that she was a cove. With a sweeping gesture my companion took off her hat and wig and revealed herself in a low bow.

'Your Highness,' she said.

'Punk Alice!' Princess Seraphina declared, in a hoarse shriek. 'You're a bold one. Look!' he pointed out to the assembly. 'It's Punk Alice!'

There was an uproar in the room at this, and as the princess and the punk stood together, the room broke into applause. Someone called for a song, the fiddle started up, and they stepped forward to render the ditty I had heard that first night at Mother Breedlove's:

Let the fops of the town upbraid
Us for our unnatural trade,
We value not man nor maid,
But among our own selves we'll be free,
But among our own selves we'll be free.

So that darkmans I saw a world turned upside-down. And I first met the one who sets down my story: Billy Archer, known at Mother Clap's molly-house as 'Princess Print', since that was the trade he was first apprenticed in. He was then, like me, one whose youth had been lost to the flash world, though he ever pursued the vocation of poet and hackney-scribbler along with other less respectable trades.

And now years later he has found me amid the condemned of Newgate and convinced me to unburden the sinful details of my life to him rather than the chaplain. He has his own confession to make but you will hear of that soon enough.

Dear Applebee,

So the curtain is pulled back and the author revealed. Edgworth Bess impeaches me for my own transgressions (though you'll note that I indict myself by allowing my own pen to record her accusation). The tongue loosens as judgment approaches.

I have withheld my name up until now as it risks being tainted by gossip and scandal. I did warn you to beware the writer. You know my work, Applebee, as I have laboured for you in the past, setting down the memorandums of the condemned and preparing criminal narratives for the press. I was one of your many 'garreteers'. Now you might know something of my life.

For I concealed my true identity to temper the shock of what I intend to add to the narrative of myself and to soften the prejudice the general reader might feel towards me with a more prolonged introduction. Bess has unmasked me a little sooner than I had bargained for but I did intend eventually to add my own wicked story to hers. In time I will offer a tale of unnameable offences, not to be uttered among Christians. And however the audience might then condemn me, they can be certain all my sins will soon be paid for. Now you all know me for what I am, I offer a true testament of my own and one that deserves a hearing.

At least you'll agree that I am ideally suited to lend a convincing voice to Elizabeth Lyon. Who better than a molly? There is always the need to dress up the prose, to add some powder and paint, as any jade might. This is no travesty in the telling but rather a performance, as they say in the French theatre, *en travesti*. A little pretence always helps to bring out the truth. Then I might play her sympathetically, for the public at least, if not for the court.

As I am well versed in the flash world, my knowledge and experience might illumine the darker corners of this history. You knew me as one of your best sources and I can be called upon to provide a certain background to Bess's tale with my own testimony.

In reply to your enquiries as to her upcoming trial she was found in possession of six silver spoons belonging to a hog-butcher in Clerkenwell a week ago and now stands indicted of robbery and housebreaking, that is felony and burglary in legal terms, both capital offences. The next sessions are due to be held in three weeks' time on the 2nd March so we will have the sentence then. Poor Bess. I too have some dread of that final date.

So the work proceeds apace with the added expectancy that the date of each letter I send brings us closer to the final judgment. All we will need then is her last dying words before the gallows, so there will be time, as she puts it, for me to make my own confession. But before that here is the third part of the story of Edgworth Bess.

Your humble author, in times past known to you as

William Archer Esq.

III

Within a couple of years I had fully learned my trade and grown accustomed to my life among the Hundreds of Drury. There was ever a risk to it but also a chance for easy profit, though what was spoken with was often as quickly melted. We citizens of Romeville thought ourselves the sharp ones, that the flat world feared us, and a cheap pride made us consider that we were wiser than the culls we made from. But we were mere lully-prigs compared to those who filched from whole nations and called it honest.

For the biggest lay in those times was this South Sea Bubble and the stock-jobbers who worked the drop down in Exchange Alley. They were keener sharpers than any in the flash world. Selling paper that promised to make men rich! It seemed a carnival trick, but for a while it worked its magic. Many a time we would tout one of the sudden wealthy in a coffee-house, some former tradesman looking awkward in his fine new rigging and silver-topped cane. An easy cull for buttock-and-file work.

Even Mother Breedlove invested one hundred pounds and was sure that she could soon give up her wicked livelihood. All the

jabber was of speculation, of projects, projections and new enterprises. The prattle was all of shares and bonds.

'We have but one commodity to sell,' Punk Alice lamented to
me, 'and the interest on that tends to decrease as the years pass.'

It was pattered that the South Sea Company was set to make
a fortune in trading in the newly discovered parts of some distant
continent. Not yet, mind, but in a future you could bet on. A
queer game: somehow so much could be made by something that
had not even happened. If any prig could have comprehended
such a lay or a sharper cogged their dice so well, they might have
been elected to Parliament rather than sent to Newgate.

Then the Bubble burst and it seemed the whole lay had been
a dream. The great squeaker of society had idly blown through
a pipe in soap and water and conjured a colourful sphere that
floated in the air for a passing moment. Then: *pop!* Many who
had chanced to gain so much lost all and faced ruin. Those done
up led a general outcry against the prigs of Exchange Alley who
had put the bite on the whole country, while those who had made
good loure when the market was up sat mum-chance. Of course,
the culls that had been bilked by their own greed were liable to
jabber loudest about morality and corruption but it was prattled
that the King's own ministers, those great prig-nappers of state,
had screened some of the sharpers. Many said the bankers and
the stock-jobbers were as bad as high-pads and should be scragged
as such. But to us their sin was simple. If any were found guilty
it was only that they had committed the worst of all felonies:
that of getting caught.

So, all of Romeville woke up one morning like a fuddled rake
who had spent too long at the gaming table the previous darkmans. Someone had to pay and it was no surprise that the debt

fell to us below. For even before the crash the rapid change in fortunes had made those at the top peery. As the low rose and then the high fell, a great fear took hold of the gentry-coves. Now with so much lost, what remained was all the more smokily guarded. Laws were passed to increase the severity of punishment for theft as this seemed the only way to secure the protection of property. Ever more minor offences against capital now became capital offences and fifty new reasons to be scragged were given to the justices.

And though none of us in the flash world felt we were working any harder there were constant reports on the increase of our industry. Alarming accounts of crime appeared everywhere, in newspapers, pamphlets, in printed narratives. The public loved nothing better than something to tremble at. That and the stories of the brave thief-taker, his gallant exploits in the capture of villains and speedy recovery of stolen goods. Yes, Jonathan Wild reaped the benefit of the new scare that haunted the city: he fed upon the terror. The gentry-coves in Parliament passed something called the 'Black Act', which gave more power to the prig-napper as well as increased the reward for the peaching of offenders on his recommendation. Romeville touted to Wild to keep the peace, and looked the other way as he stole yet more for his own corporation.

I still saw him. He would call on me at Mother Breedlove's and take me out on occasion. As one of his many mistresses, I learned that he was as dab at ruling morts as he was at bitching coves. He inspired a queer sort of loyalty among the jades, despite all the prattle of his cruelty. It is pattered that power can blow the coals as readily as a pretty face, and even I nursed a crank affection for Wild. In truth I never did fully cant the queer feelings yet stowed in my heart, though my head twigged that it was best to keep on his right side. His protection, or at least the promise of it, was a bene thing to have.

He had begun to style himself 'Thief-taker General of Great Britain and Ireland' and set about milling any crew that challenged his authority in London and beyond. Appointing Quilt as 'Clerk of the Western Road', he sought to control the routes leading into and out of the city, bitching the high-pads that worked the rattling-lay outside Romeville as well as the low-pads that filched within.

Meanwhile there were calls for moral reform, saying that lustful vices were the cause of so much lawlessness. With all her loure gone in the Bubble, Mother Breedlove endeavoured to recoup her losses by employing more jades and running her academy with less discretion, but this brought the poor mort greater ruin. Informers from the Society for the Reformation of Manners (a dismal crew set up to make the whole world flat) must have touted the increase in this trade and babbled it to the justices for a crew of constables was sent with warrants to close our vault-ing-school. Mother Breedlove and Punk Alice were arrested and taken away. The rest of us were thrown out onto the pad.

Our mother was peached for keeping a bawdy-house, fined ten shillings and sentenced to be whipped at the cart's arse along the Strand. The poor cow never fully recovered from the ordeal.

Punk Alice was sent to the Wood Street Compter for two months. All of us jades gathered enough loure to pay the garnish that would keep her out of the Hole, that vile dungeon of any trib where those with no gelt are cast. Yet on the third week of her confinement she caught the gaol fever, the dread pestilence spread by lice in those filthy places. Her skin was hot and covered with a rash when I got in to see her. I dabbed at her brow with a wet cloth. Her cheeks were flushed, her glaziers bleary.

'Who is it?' She frowned at me, her mind part lost in delirium.

'It's Bess, Alice.'

'Bess.' She gave me a thin smile. 'My own Bess.'

'The same.'

'Careful, sweetness. Don't catch this fever.'

I held up a nosegay and pressed it to my phiz. 'I'll get you out of here,' I promised her.

So I went to see Wild at his offices. He had been imprisoned himself in the Wood Street Compter all those years ago and from working the system there had taken his first steps in the thief-taking business. He sat at his desk scanning the pages of his huge ledger of prigs.

'Bill Spiggot,' he jabbered, scarcely looking up as I dupped in. 'Know any babble on his crew?'

I shook my head.

'What about the Hawkins brothers? Or Valentine Carrick? I hear Joe Blueskin's been seen with his men.'

'I'm sorry, Jonathan. I've come about something else.'

He sighed and I padded around to where he sat.

'It's damned hard work keeping order in this wretched town, Bess. Most of the canting-crew see sense but there's always some wild rogue thinks he knows better than me.'

I leaned over and stroked his phiz. 'Then take a little holiday,' I pattered softly in his lugg. 'Call it St Monday and leave Quilt in charge. Then we can have a bene time together.'

He closed his glaziers and gave in to the caress for a moment. Then he quickly twigged what I was up to and sat up with a start. 'What do you want?' he demanded.

'Punk Alice is in the Wood Street Compter.'

'I know. Who do you think kept you out of there?'

'You?'

'Yes, so you've already run up some credit. Why should I lift a finger for Alice?'

'Because she's a friend.'

'Your friend. You recall that night we first met in Moll King's?'

'Yes,' I said, remembering it as the very night I had become Edgworth Bess.

'I asked Punk Alice if she had anything for me. And what did she say?'

'Nix my doll,' I said, and the words sat flat on my tongue.

'Yes.' He grinned. 'Nix my doll. Well, why shouldn't I return such a compliment?'

I put an arm around his neck and slipped onto his lap. 'I'll make it worth the trouble,' I whispered.

༄

Later Wild pattered the deal. 'I run a business, Bess, so I have to keep my accounts balanced.' He tapped the great book of villainy that lay next to the bed. He had brought it with him even as we climbed the dancers to the cribb above his office. 'For every one I acquit, another must be peached somewhere down the line. I'm like the recording angel.' He let out a dry laugh. 'For Judgment Day.'

I got up and began to rig myself. I felt Wild tout me as I picked up my gown. I shrugged. 'I don't have anyone to give you,' I told him.

'I don't mean now. I mean when the time comes. That'll be

the agreement. I'll need to take a lot of bodies off the pad to clean up Romeville for the gentry-coves. I'm going to break all those crews who won't be bitched, you just watch, Bess. So, you promise to give me a person, anyone I might ask for, mind, or it really is nix my doll. Only then you can have your pal out of the trib. Agreed?'

I thought for a moment, not truly canting how diabolical this bargain was. It would mean selling a soul on tick, as it were, but I could not conceive of anyone in the whole of the canting-crew that I would not gladly damn to save Punk Alice. I padded back to where the thief-taker lay. 'Agreed,' I said, spitting on my paw and offering a handshake.

Wild found a beak to grant bail and offered to stand the surety of it himself. I piked it over to Wood Street with the warrant and ordered a carriage to convey poor Alice to a cribb in the Hundreds. But her fever was much worse and I canted with horror that my dearest friend was slipping away from this world. As I settled her in bed she touted up at me and sighed. 'You didn't make a deal with the prig-napper, did you?'

'I'd make a deal with Merry Old Roger to save you, Alice.'

As I pattered those widds I knew how much I truly loved her.

'Thanks for getting me out of the trib,' she said, with a smile.

I brushed the hair from her phiz.

'Well, I'm free now,' she went on. 'Soon I'll be free for good.'

'Please . . .'

'Hush. I need a long rest, nabs. You take care of yourself.'

'I'll fetch a physician.'

'A nim-gimmer can't help me now.' She reached out and took hold of my arm. 'I wish you hadn't put yourself in Wild's bung on my account. But I'm glad not to die in prison. Thanks, Bess.'

'Don't patter so crank.'

'Watch out for yourself, Bess. Brush upon the sneak.'

She rose up from the mattress and I bussed her on the forehead.

'Step lightly,' she whispered. 'Stay free.' With a groan she lowered herself down on the bed and fell into slumber. These were her last words. In two days she was dead.

∽

So I was on my own in Romeville once more. I began to pad it with Poll Maggot, a sly jade as well versed in the buttock-and-file as I was. We found lodgings in Vinegar Yard off Drury Lane for a shilling and sixpence a week and began to work two-handed from there. It was a decline in circumstance but I bore it the best I could, reasoning that since the end of the Bubble all trade was at a lower rate. Dice can run uphill or downhill; only by cogging can we know how they'll fall.

I had to stow my feelings. Thinking too long on the passing of Punk Alice would have sent me to Bedlam. She might have led me down the wicked path but she was a true guide through all the twisted alleys I had padded. With more love for me than I could ever return, she had never grudged the debt of her affections. I grieved that I had never pattered how much I cared for her, but there was no time for tears. The only way to pay her back was to keep moving, to honour her memory by surviving.

I owed Jonathan Wild now, so I was peery of approaching him for help. And after what had passed with Alice his favours seemed to have the air of ill luck to them anyway. Besides, the thief-taker was busy fixing his rule on Romeville.

With his henchmen he cornered Bill Spiggott's crew at the

Blue Boar in Westminster. They were peached by the Reverend Joe Lindsey, a soul-driver who had turned to gaming and when done up by that had become a rum prig. One of the gang kicked away but they tracked him down through the Hundreds. I was in the push that saw him make a last stand on the pad, drawing a sword as the prig-napper calmly padded forward with his own blade at the ready. They stood guard on each other for a moment, then one of Wild's posse came behind the prig and clubbed at his back with a cudgel. I touted the cold spark in Wild's blue eyes as he ran the man through.

Then it was prattled that the Hawkins brothers' gang had been taken. They had nettled Wild by snaffling from the Earl of Burlington on Quilt's Western Road and not giving the corporation a fair snack of the loot.

That left Valentine Carrick's crew yet to be snabbled. A battalion of low-pads that clicked on the streets of Romeville, they holed up in a dram-shop in London Wall from time to time. I heard it spoke that Joe Blueskin was padding it with them on the sly.

Poll Maggot and me now dupped into the Black Lion most days. It served as a place to meet culls and as a flash-ken where we could sell on what we had spoken with. It was well used by Blueskin and Hell-and-Fury, who still worked for Wild. So we fenced through them, letting the prig-napper take his snack so that all was bene with him. We would pal up with those natty-lads when a lay might suit a cove and mort couple or even a brace of them. At other times it was good to have a pair of strong and well-dressed young bloods on hand. Poll and Hell-and-Fury took a liking to each other and soon she was trading buttock as well as file with him. He was a virile cove, she assured me.

In turn I found myself more in the company of Joe Blueskin, though we were not so well matched. I found him proud and haughty, a little too aloof for my liking. And though he was very dimber, he seemed all too familiar with his own beauty. I even thought of babbling on him for padding it with Carrick's crew, that he could be the body I owed Wild for springing Punk Alice. It seemed a cruel trick to play but that was the rule of Romeville: peach or be peached.

One darkmans we were in the Black Lion together when Billy Archer himself came in. He had a book to fence and he showed it to Blueskin. 'It's a volume of Pope's translation of Homer,' Billy said, nodding over at me. 'Sorry to hear of Punk Alice, Bess. God rest her soul.'

I smarted at this and took a gulp of lightning. 'The wicked jade's more likely palled up with Merry Old Roger,' I jested, as if to hold my grief at bay.

Blueskin was turning the pages.

'See?' Billy pointed. 'The wrath of Achilles.'

'Where did you speak with this?' asked Blueskin.

'Why, it's not stolen, Joe,' Billy protested, in mock outrage. 'It was a gift from a dear friend.'

'If you say so.'

Billy was at ebb-water at this time. He had struggled to make loure as a hackney-scribbler and he'd lost what he'd set by in the Bubble. 'Times are hard,' he declared, patting his pockets. 'I've scarce a face except my own. Half a guinea?'

'Half a shilling more like,' Blueskin countered.

'Five.'

Blueskin shook his head but he was already absorbed in the volume. It was said he loved reading so much that when he had once milled the ken of a scholar he sent some loure to him after to pay for the books he had spoken with.

'You'll take four?' he offered at last, and the deal was done.

Billy left us, and Blueskin idly leafed through the copy in his hands. The crank words I'd said of Alice nettled my head and I brooded on how lonely I was without her. I started to patter with Blueskin and found myself seeking confidences in him that I would never have if we had been in a push. I expected him to jest with me but he let his guard fall for once and told me something of about his own life.

His mother was a white woman who ran a brandy-shop in Wapping but, as with myself, he knew little of his father. He had been told he was a black slave who worked as a servant in Mayfair but had never known any more than that.

'I am what the Spaniards call a *mulatto*,' he told me. 'And the citizens of Romeville, a St Giles' Blackbird!'

The laugh he gave at this was loud but dry and flat.

'That's just foolish prattle,' I said.

'Oh, I care nothing of what people call me,' he declared, 'but I'm a stranger everywhere I go.'

I touted then that his arrogance was but a mask of sadness. His phiz might fit many places yet truly belonged nowhere but for the tribs, the bridewells, the houses of correction, he had been in and out of since he was thirteen.

We took more gin and I shared some of my past with him. The lightning always helps me jabber and all at once we were conversing in an intimate and condoling manner. This was a change from the usual discourse in the Black Lion, where the crew's patter is but boasts of what was made and the great lays yet to come. All at once we were just two lost souls amid the

65

Hundreds of Drury. And we had but one thing in common in our flash life: Jonathan Wild.

'I was apprenticed by him when he was still Hitchen's assistant,' Blueskin pattered. 'He takes young lully-prigs off the pad and trains them up for the gallows.'

'And he docks all the buttock-and-file jades,' I replied in turn, 'then pays them with the reward from what they filch.'

'You've got to hand it to the prig-napper. He's a clever bastard!'

So we drank his health, since we could hardly begrudge him his methods. In our idleness we had let ourselves become his creatures, fattened up for the devil and bred to prig or peach for him.

'It's prattled that you're padding it with Valentine Carrick,' I said.

Blueskin shrugged.

'Be peery,' I told him. 'Wild means to mill that crew.'

'I tip the prig-napper his due.' He sighed. 'I just want something on the side, that's all.'

I now felt bad in thinking of clearing my account with Wild by squeaking on this dimber youth. I was feeling fondly pot-valiant and the streets were a blindman's holiday. Blueskin offered to pad with me back to Vinegar Yard.

'Bene darkmans,' he said, as he stood at the jigger.

I gave him a buss and felt his lips full and soft against mine. I invited him up, but as we climbed the dancers, he said, 'I'm no cull, Bess.'

'A stallion then, are you?' I laughed.

He reached out and took me by the hand. 'I just don't like it bought or sold, that's all.'

'Then among our own selves we'll be free,' I said, and led him up to my cribb.

66

I sparked the candle and we unrigged in the flickering light. His skin was not blue, of course, but rather a deep umber that glowed in the glim like polished wood. He had a fine frame and as he came to embrace me I pushed him back onto my bed and climbed up to get a better tout at him.

His body was firm and glib, with whorls of fine black hair that traced a line all the way down his belly to where his machine stood dark and proud. He groaned as I took hold of him there. 'Douse the glim,' he whispered, pointing to the glimstick.

But I shook my head, happy for once to gape and not be gape-seed, to take rather than be taken. Soon dragon rode upon St George, as they say, and I had my joy with dimber Blueskin. Then he turned me over and had his. All was fair since none had been gulled of their snack of the delight.

So I had known enough trust in a cove to find pleasure with him, in spite of what Punk Alice had said. Though not enough for love, perhaps. I liked him well enough and he blew my coals, but I touted for the morning sneak when he might come and thieve my heart and he never did. Perhaps he felt a little too bitched by me and I too proud for him. He fancied himself the wild rogue, to be ruled by no one, and I the haughty jade who needed no man. In truth we both belonged to the prig-napper. We all did in the end.

Valentine Carrick's crew was hunted down and Blueskin was once more forced to play the double game. A Chelsea pensioner had been chivved to death in Piccadilly and it was babbled that it was the work of Valentine's low-pads. There was outcry among the flats and the gentry-coves, and a rum amount of loure was offered as reward for their snabbling. So as the crew went to ground and a hue-and-cry was called, the beaks and constables led their posses down all the alleys of the Hundreds of Drury. Blueskin was taken by Quilt and Wild in Southwark, though he had been left out of the information. In his anger he lashed out and took a sabre-cut to the head. The thief-taker told him he was lucky to plead evidence and he was sent to Wood Street Compter for a spell while the rest of Carrick's crew were scragged. Wild kept Blueskin in his corporation, though, tipping him three shillings and sixpence a week for garnish, and even sent him books to read in the trib. It was clear that teacher was playing mouser and mouse with his pupil.

Then Mother Breedlove died and there was a big funeral in St Paul's by the piazza. Every punk, dell, jade and buttock filled the aisles; all the whores from the great Square of Venus were gathered together in the gospel-shop by Moll King's coffee-house. Even the autem-divers, those who rob in church, observed a special sabbath from their trade so none of the congregation's bungs were nipped or pockets filed that day. When the soul-driver called Mother Breedlove 'a devout pilgrim' we all had to stifle a snigger but then came the hymn 'O God Our Help in Ages Past' and my glaziers pricked with tears that never came. As we sang I grieved for Mother Breedlove, for Punk Alice, for my own damned and lonely soul. Then, when the dirge was finished, I locked away that grief in the condemned hold of my heart. And I thought none might dub the jigger to it. For I knew then that I had no hope for years to come, no shelter from the stormy blast and no eternal home.

⁓

There are so many stories, fanciful narratives and downright lies as to how I became acquainted with the notorious Jack Sheppard that I am myself confused of the circumstances and the correct order of events. Since I became his relict, this is the tale all want to hear. I have told it many times, perhaps with additions or subtractions in each telling, for the account book of memory shows a meagre debt to oblivion and none can truly tout the final tally. So, I expect no credit from this particular rendering, only for you to judge in your own sessions. If I yet stand condemned as the one who corrupted the innocent Jack to a life of vice and felony, the wicked, deceitful and lascivious Edgworth Bess, then so be it.

I first saw him in the Black Lion as one of the many apprentices that dupped into our boozing-ken at the end of lightmans. Finding freedom from their labours, those young culls would imagine themselves wild rogues or natty-lads rather than near slaves of some sullen master. Melting what loure they had on ale and gin, and with their heads lush-lightened, they would try to patter flash as if by doing so they might share the liberty of a canting-crew. We laughed heartily at these flat boys as they sought to sharpen their tongues in such a manner.

Though short and slight and cursed with a stammer, it was Jack who often held the floor among them. He had a lively charm about him. A pale phiz like a cherub's and dark glaziers that sparked with a strange glim, his wide gob would stretch out in a broad smile or purse in a curious pout. He was a dimber little thing. Lithe and agile, he would twist and gesture like a harlequin. And rather than hold back his stutter he would chant its rhythm as bold as a balladeer. Then the mob would hang on each word and an old jest would patter fresh as it staccatoed from his pretty lips.

One night I passed in earshot by his crew, just as he was improvising the end of some wicked tale.

'Th-then,' he said, with one hand raised, 'the c-cull d-docked the d-dell in the d-d-darkmans!'

There came a laugh from the apprentices that was cut short as I passed through their company. Jack looked up and, as I caught his eye, his whole being froze into a posture of shocked contrition. I grinned at him and said, 'Stow your widd, nabs. I can cant what you prattle.'

His bleach face tinted red, and as the boys howled at him, I could not forbear to ruffle the locks shorn so close to his small and dapper head.

I began to fence a crank fondness for Jack and he was framed in my mind as a fiery little angel. I soon learned that were he to be of that host he would most certainly be one of the fallen ones that defied the Almighty, for a glim spirit of rebellion was bound up in his indentured soul.

Poll Maggot saw something of this by his expression and demeanour. One night in the Black Lion she turned to me and nodded over to where Jack held forth among his pals. 'Something about that one,' she said.

'Jack?' I squinted over to where he was sitting.

'Yeah. Something in his looks.'

'He's a dimber cove,' I said.

'Perhaps.' Poll laughed. 'But, no, it's not that.'

'What, then?'

She turned to me with a frown and pattered all solemn: 'He looks born to hang.'

And maybe one could tout that fate on his phiz even before he started filching. Something lost in those big black glaziers that could shine with a defiant wit at one moment, then darken with a fathom's depth the next. Yet I saw something pure in Jack back then. He might have made good in the flat world, had he not been just too clever for it.

In those days he affected a polite and courteous manner towards me, as if I was some gentry-mort. I twigged that he was peery of me. Being such a long-meg I towered over him when close. When looking up from my shadow and stuttering: 'B-B-B . . .' I would bite my gob with my grinders to stifle a snigger. He seemed flattened in my presence and, given my flash reputation in that quarter of Romeville, he had good reason to be wary. And though there came a certain ease of familiarity, he looked at me intently with those dark glaziers.

He was in service to a carpenter, on the last year of his appren-ticeship, a dangerous time when the impatience to finish its term provokes all the temptations of liberty. Time's a rum prig, and I believe Jack felt the few months left of his indenture stretch away into eternity. His youth robbed, he would soon look to the world to vamp the debt of seven years' slavery.

'I'm a good w-w-worker, Bess,' he complained to me, over a clanker one evening, 'but my b-boss won't teach me no more. I still hardly know how to b-b-build anything from scratch, he just has me job from k-ken to ken, fixing what others have made.'

Jonathan Wild dupped into the Black Lion as we pattered and the apprentice boys crowded him, knowing of his fame and keen to hear the rum tales of how he had bravely taken some high-pad or wild rogue for the fatal tree. I noted Jack's gaze stray over in curiosity. Then the prig-napper touted me and came across. 'Bene darkmans, Bess,' he said. 'Have you been screening yourself from me?'

'Of course not,' I lied. 'I've been busy, that's all.'

71

In truth I had steered clear of him since the business with Punk Alice.

'Yet you found time to melt with Blueskin. Oh, I scan it all, Bess,' he chided, noting the glim in my glaziers. 'You really shouldn't let these natty-lads burn the ken.' He grinned, baring the blackened grinder in his gob.

I shrugged, hoping that Jack would not cant what the prig-napper pattered.

'How is Joe?' I asked.

'I tip him enough loure for the garnish.' He frowned. 'Even got a nim-gimmer to dress his wound. I look after my coves, see? My morts also.'

As he reached out a paw to me, Jack looked on with those deep eyes of his. Wild followed my gaze and noted the sullen youth with such fine features. He tipped him a frown that brought out all the scars on his phiz.

'Sir.' Jack nodded with a cold politeness.

'Who's this?' Wild demanded gruffly.

'Jack,' I pattered, contriving a rough introduction. 'He's an apprentice.'

'A diligent one, I trust,' mused the prig-napper.

'I h-h-hope so, sir.' Jack's bright face glimmed with a slight blush.

'What's your trade, son?'

'C-c-carpentry.'

'Indeed? I've always got work for those skills. Might be able to put some your way.'

'Jonathan,' I protested. It was my turn to chide as I twigged what wicked labour he pattered of.

But Wild widened his pale eyes, lolling them at me in a

mockery of innocence. 'I merely mean,' he insisted, 'to fix the jiggers and glazes of those coves who have been filched from. Now, if you'll excuse us. Come, Bess, sup with me. Let's kick away from this wretched flash-ken and to the Lyon's Head for some turtle soup.'

And so Wild took my arm and led me away. I glanced back and caught a sad look in Jack's blank phiz, and the smoky way he touted after me. I wondered what he really thought of me and my life.

After that, I did not see him in the Black Lion for some while. I twigged now that he had some yearning after me but reasoned that my behaviour with the prig-napper had warned him off and canted that this was for the best.

But one darkmans, when the moon glimmed full and sharp over Drury, I spied him padding it home to his lodgings on Wych Street. It was gone midnight and his master had locked him out, having warned him earlier of such a curfew.

'Which is your cribb?' I asked him.

He pointed to a glaze high up on the third storey of the ken. 'Then you'll have to sleep upon the pad,' I jabbered.

He grinned at me, his gob wide, his eyes starry, then shabbed off a few paces. All at once he turned and piked it towards his master's house. Leaping like a mouser, he found a ledge to balance on, then climbed up swiftly, finding gaps in the brickwork that he could use as easily as dancers. All the time he brushed upon the sneak, moving as silently as a ghost. In a handful of moments he was by the window he had fingered to me.

'B-b-bene darkmans, Bess,' he called out, then dubbed the sash and rolled himself in.

I was astonished by this display, perhaps acted for my benefit to prove he was not merely a dull apprentice. This 'power of his early magick', which the later accounts of his life patter of, had an artfulness to it but something purely natural too. A gift that seemed to spring from some boundless energy within. He was like an imp from a world beyond, a free and glim spirit that could never be held fast. Enchanted as I was by this performance, I soon learned that I was not the only audience for his pantomime of liberty.

Prattle of his talents soon spread through the Hundreds of Drury. That he entered in and out of his lodgings at his pleasure and made a jest of locks or bolts became a common tale for the apprentice boys. They would jabber that he could twist and climb like a cat, let none keep him out or hold him in, but that he also struggled against the very bonds of his indenture. Mr Wood, his master, was a mild and sober man whose family observed the sabbath. Jack had strayed from that righteous path and now spent the evenings and the Lord's Day as he chose. He was becoming well known for his quick temper and for the first of all sins: disobedience.

Biding his free hours in the Black Lion he was drawn to idleness, away from the flat world of industry. This boozing-ken was an open trap to one like him and he soon picked up flash habits, drawing the attention of the canting-crew.

I caught him at the end of lightmans pattering to Wild over a clanker of ale as a small push looked on. I called for a dram of lightning and slyly padded it over. I could twig by the way they jabbered that the prig-napper meant to snare the youth, to use him as a prig, and I wanted to stall him from that, I don't know why. I conceived a chance to draw Jack away from this wicked company but he had his back to me. Wild had the corner chair, always preferring to sit where he could scan the whole ken, and so he noted my approach.

'Bess!' he called loudly, somehow twigging that I was brushing upon the sneak.

Jack turned and I was not the only one who touted how those doleful glaziers peeped up at me.

Wild gave a cruel laugh. 'Why you've an admirer here, Bess,' he pattered. 'I'll hazard he'd like to woo you. But he's a touch tongue-tied.'

The push around the two men gathered closer, keen to see how the prig-napper would play the young apprentice. Wild always looked for the weakness in men, that he might use it to bitch them.

'Jonathan, please,' I implored him.

'I would tell him that he need not use those words he so clearly has trouble pattering, just enough loure, which he could get when he works for me. I might even let him have you for free.'

Poor Jack's milky face flushed crimson and his gob quivered in wrathful humiliation. 'B-B-Bess—' he began, but Wild jumped in quickly

'Y-y-yes!' the thief-taker retorted loudly. 'B-B-Bess!'

And the entire company roared with laughter.

Jack stood up from his chair, his sinewy body shaping up in fury. For a second it looked as if he might strike Wild. The whole ken hushed and the prig-napper leaned back and took hold of the hilt of his sword, baring his grinders in a lethal snarl. 'J-j-just a j-j-jest,' Wild jabbered softly, pulling the blade out a little.

The youth glared down at the older man, his paws clenched and his glaziers glim with hate. Then he turned and stormed out of the Black Lion. I bided awhile, just until the commotion was quelled and replaced with another. Then I shabbed off and piked after Jack down Drury Lane.

'If I h-h-had a s-s-sword,' he muttered, as I came alongside him.

'If you had a sword you'd be a dead man.'

We padded it together and I waited for his rage to douse. I knew that Wild's mock-stammer cut deep. Like many, Jack loudly joked at his own impediment so that none else could be heard to do likewise.

'It was a stale jest,' I told him.

'He s-spoke ill of you, too.'

I smiled. 'It's gallant of you to think so, Jack. But I'm used to such patter.'

Jack stopped on his heels and turned to me. 'W-w-what is he to you?' he demanded.

I shrugged. 'The same as to all of the canting-crew. He rules us.'

'I d-don't understand.'

'That's for the best. The flat world stays safe in its innocence.'

'And w-what are you to him?'

'You know me for what I am, Jack.'

He sighed and shook his head, then carried on walking. 'Next time.' He swore softly, still a little red in the face.

So I grabbed hold of his arm to cut him dead. 'Listen,' I said, ready to jabber as clearly as I could. 'Wild is not a man to be played with. Do you want to know what the prig-napper is really about?'

He frowned and nodded. We were now at Long Acre with just a glim left of lightmans.

'Then let's go to Moll King's,' I told him. 'And I'll blow the whole widd for you.'

It was early enough to find a table in the Long Room at the coffee-house. We sat and had a dish together with a dash of arrack. Coffee and strong spirit is the best lush for prattle and Moll's buzzed with it. A crew of fops in the corner jabbered over the news in some journal as I pattered the true narrative of the thief-taker general. Jack sat open-gobbed, his glaziers wide with amazement.

We went out onto the piazza and I hoped I might have set him on a steadier course. 'You might be vexed by your present master,' I told him, 'but the prig-napper's a worse one.'

'A c-c-curse on all masters!' he cried, all fierce and proud.

It was as if the spirit of Punk Alice had come back to haunt me.

The Square of Venus was filling up with that motley push, the gentry-coves and the canting-crew. What I had pattered was meant to warn him, and had he but heeded the words, he might have been safe. But the tune was a siren-song, luring him onto the rocks. For now the labour of day was over and the riot of night had begun. Jack was determined to make a darkmans of it.

We went to the Rose and the Shakespeare's Head where Jack called out a toast: 'For all those b-b-born under a th-threepenny planet!' I steered him away from going back to the Black Lion lest we meet with Wild again. We finished in the Cock Tavern on Bow Street by which time he was quite pot-valiant. He would be locked out again and he railed against the bonds of his indenture. 'You'll be free soon enough,' I told him.

For most lush slurs the speech, but booze tempered Jack's stammer. He turned, his phiz a gape-seed of sadness, and pattered softly, 'Will I, Bess? Will I?'

He padded it with me as I headed back to Vinegar Yard. As

we passed his lodgings I expected him to leap up at the ken as before but he said he would walk all the way to my cribb.

'Well,' I said, as we reached my jigger, 'are you going to come up?'

'I haven't . . .'

'What? You've no loure? You can owe me.'

'No, B-Bess. I n-never . . .'

Then I twigged that this was a confession he had yet to enter the academy. So I took him by the paw and led him up the dancers with a promise that I would go easy with him.

The surprise for me was the vigour and energy bound up in that little body of his. I have never known, before or since, a man with so much passion. And I was shocked by my own feelings, caught off guard by a fierce desire. When Jack caught his breath and swore that he loved me, I smiled and tried to make his words a jest but I felt the truth of them in my senses.

He woke me early with some prattle that he might show me something. My cribb was the sky-parlour of the ken, and sliding up the sash of the glaze, he found a way of climbing up onto the roof. He pulled me up there to sit beside him on the tiles. It was peep of day and we could tout across the rooftops and chimney-stacks to see the church spires rising from the gloom of the city, pointing at something better. The morning star that is Venus or Lucifer glimmed low over Romeville and from the end of the world came the pale blush of lightmans. I asked him what it was he wanted me to see.

'This, Bess,' he pattered, with a sweep of his paw. 'This. It's ours. All ours.'

And I canted this as a moment to savour, something precious filched from the drudge of day to darkmans. I did not dare to

78

imagine at the time that it would mean any more than that. I canted that I would have to wake from this foolishness and stifle any tender feelings.

For a jade stands but a queer chance if she pals up with a cove who is neither twang nor stallion. I might have given up the game for some keeping-cull but I could not afford to let myself go for some poor apprentice. I had my own trade to attend to.

So when I next saw Jack in the Black Lion and he bade me patter with him in a quiet corner of the tavern I did not spare his feelings.

'I'll b-be a journeyman in less than a year,' he said.

'If you keep to the terms of your service.'

'Y-y-yes. B-b-but th-th-then we could be married.'

I was nettled at this, ever peery of those culls who think they can save you and with some fine widds fetch your soul out of pawn.

'And until then you want me for yourself?' I asked him.

'B-B-B—'

'What am I to do in the meantime? Starve?'

At this the poor boy was an ugly sight, his whole person a quivering stammer. I ventured then to put an end to his misery.

In those days Romeville was full of soldiers. The previous spring had seen three whole regiments camped out on Hyde Park in peeriness of another Jacobite rising. That night a crew of fusiliers dupped into our boozing-ken. I left with a lusty corporal, making sure that Jack was a witness to it. I touted him staring deep into his clanker, his pale phiz a full page of sorrow.

But Fate takes you where it pleases. The next lightmans I found myself padding it through the Hundreds with the corporal tracking after me. He had melted all his loure and was jabbering

79

that I had stolen from him. I feared he might call for a constable so I looked around for somewhere to hide. It was then that I twigged I was right outside Mr Wood's yard by Wych Street and there was Jack fixing the panels of a jigger.

He looked up and smiled as I sneaked into the premises, perhaps thinking I had come to visit him at his honest labour and had thought again on his offer of betrothal. As I raised a finger to my gob to tell him to stow it he stuttered out my name loudly and so I was blown.

The soldier appeared with his hue-and-cry and all at once Jack's glaziers glimmed with fury. He shouted at us both and threw a piece of wood that missed the corporal but caught me on the shoulder. In anger as with passion, little Jack was driven by some infernal engine. Such was his rage that the bold fusilier hastily beat his retreat. I tried to patter my thanks to him but he turned away from me and went back to his work.

I heard later that a quarrel with Mr Wood over work done on a boozing-ken in Islington had come to blows. It seemed certain that he would break measures and quit service before the end of its term. I kept out of his way, knowing that a hot-headed youth is trouble to everyone, flat or flash.

But one night he sought me out at the Black Lion. There was a calm look in his phiz that I could not fathom. 'I'm sorry, Bess,' he pattered.

'What for?'

'Th-that time in Mr Wood's yard.'

'I forgive you,' I said, half jesting.

'I've g-g-got you something.'

I frowned as I touted the smile on his gob. It was if some great change had come about in his life. And indeed it had. For outside he tipped me half a dozen silver spoons that he had taken from an alehouse he had been jobbing on in the Strand. He asked me to fence or vamp them for him and came back to my cribb in Vinegar Yard.

And so he began his new trade, his first taste from the fatal Tree of Knowledge. The soul-drivers always peach the mort for being the tempter of the cove. As if all mankind were a bleeding-cull to have the bite put on them by a sly jade. It is for this first felony they say we women have such a queer chance of it in the world. But it was Jack who came to me, tracking his own crooked path from flat to flash.

So he wooed me in that wicked manner, with the promise that one day we might settle down in flat society. He had his own ideas as to how we might ply a trade by palling up and proposed that we form our own corporation. He would finish his apprenticeship in carpentry (that would in the meantime give him many an opportunity to filch on the sly) just as I might follow my own craft by lightmans. By darkmans we would work together. Jack had much to learn from me but he had all the skills necessary to be a rum prig. And if we held onto our loure rather than melt it all we might have enough to set ourselves up by the time Jack was free of service and his own master. Then we could be a respectable couple and all the rum lays of our past would stand as the mere follies of youth. It was a fine scheme and we swore that we would sit mum-chance so that none might blow the widd of it.

But I soon learned the danger there was in thieving without the sanction of the prig-napper. I filched a gold ring from some cull and no sooner had I vamped it than two constables of the watch came for me at Vinegar Yard. I was taken and locked up at St Giles' Roundhouse for the darkmans. That might have been the end of our little enterprise but for Jack. When he heard what had happened he was driven into that glim fury of his. He stormed in, demanding to see the beadle of the trib, dinging the cove down when he appeared and taking the keys from him.

'What are you doing here?' I demanded, when he unlocked the jigger of my hold.

'I've c-c-come to set you free, Bess,' he declared, in affectionate fury.

To set you free. Those widds burned in my heart like a crank blessing. And it was the moment I truly fell in love with him.

This was foolish patter, of course, but it was his defiance of the harsh reason of Romeville that gave Jack his power. All of us in the canting-crew knew that if you were snabbled you had to make a deal, sit mum-chance or peach someone. Not Jack Sheppard: he had his own creed and he jabbered it like a soul-driver.

'They'll n-n-not take us, Bess. And if they t-t-take us they'll not h-hold us.'

This passion overcame me and I canted then that we were meant for each other. Though in truth I was peery of those feelings inside me, I learned to fear for him too. For his impulse seemed always to be this defiance of the bonds of authority rather than what could be made or spoken with. Yes, love is a crank spirit, free but awful dangerous.

We were lucky that nothing came of the incident at St Giles' Roundhouse, though I made sure we steered clear of that trib. And I tried to tutor Jack in his new trade. For though he had all the skills and agility in dubbing the jigger or starring the glaze, when it came to the actual business of crime he could be as queer as a lully-prig.

From a piece-broker's shop in White Horse Yard where he had been fixing the shutters, he stole a large roll of fustian of some four and twenty yards. God knows how he thought to fence it and I touted him trying to sell it to the natty-lads in the neighbourhood at a shilling a yard. I was nettled at this crank lay and did not let him stow the cloth in my cribb when he could find no buyers for it. So he took it to his master's and hid it in his trunk there.

I knew from experience that small items of great worth are the best for filing. Dive for whatever is easiest to hide, fence or vamp. I pattered all of this to Jack but, as with his other apprenticeship, he would be ruled by no one, not even me. He had to prove himself a master so he went back to the piece-broker's premises the following midnight and, after taking out the bars from the cellar glaze, dupped into the ken and stole some silver plate and seven pounds in coin from the till. He then replaced the bars most expertly so that none might see the ken had been milled from the outside; a mort lodging there was suspected of the felony.

But Jack took his booty to Poll Maggot's cribb. He claimed it was because I was still nettled at him but I was smoky of that. Poll took her snack of that lay and I learned to tout peery of the sly jade.

And there was still the fustian to get rid of. With Jack away from his lodgings so often, it was no surprise that his own master, Wood, found the filched cloth and went to the piece-broker. Jack threatened the cove he had stolen from and claimed that he had been given the fustian by his own mother. She agreed to screen him and they spent a whole lightmans walking around Spitalfields with the piece-broker, pretending to search for a weaver who had never existed.

After this Jack could bide no longer with Wood so he quit his apprenticeship early. I was nettled at this but in the end canted that it would be for the best to get out of Romeville for a while. So we shabbed off to Fulham, finding lodgings by Parsons Green. He set himself up as a journeyman to a master carpenter there, lying to the man that he had served out his time in Smithfield. We lived as man and wife then, so far from the Hundreds of Drury that none might doubt we were a respectable couple. I would keep house and he was out earning honest loure. Though for our wedding gifts he lifted from a gentry-cove's house in Mayfair, where he was jobbing, seven pounds ten shillings, a rum amount of silverware, seven gold rings, some fine rigging and linen besides. This kept us in high style for some months.

Away from the stench and filth of the city, we breathed a cleaner air and spoke in gentler tones. We lived among the middling sort, of respectable trade or business, and pattered their soft language rather than the harshness of the flash tongue. We could even think like them awhile.

It was a quiet life if a dull one. One day I found myself falling into something like weariness, though I was hardly tired. I wondered if I might be sickening, then twigged that this queer humour was boredom, a feeling I had not known for some years. I realised then what made the gentry-coves so fretful and fond of novelty.

But there was little time to indulge in any idle fancies for we woke one morning to find that old trull justice back in our lives. Who knows what we might have become if she had only left us be? A warrant was out for Jack and he was taken before the chamberlain at the Guildhall for having broken his apprenticeship. Mr Wood's brother lived by Parsons Green and had touted him.

The matter was settled out of court so that he was clear of his master. But now he could no longer work as a journeyman until he had completed a new set of terms. This was the end of the flat world for Jack, and we returned to our vagabond life.

Back in Romeville, amid the Hundreds of Drury, we had a thieves wedding with all the old canting-crew. A sword was put on the floor and we hopped over it in a ceremony older than that of the soul-driver in the gospel-shop. And the wicked congregation sang together:

Leap rogue and jump whore
And then you are married for evermore

Our own corporation was back in business and Jack swore we'd be bitched by no one. He made a toast to me with a glass of lightning and he was drunk enough to jabber without stuttering: 'No one will stop us now, Bess. We'll rob anyone who gets in our way.'

Dear Applebee,

And so Bess falls in love and now faces her greatest peril.
For any bond that holds us fast can surely hang us too. I
should know. I was born with a very noose around my neck.
Entangled in the cord of life that joined me to my dear
mother, I was nearly choked as I came into the world. Only
the diligence of the parish nurse saved me from being stran-
gled at birth. Yet I spent my life seeking that treachery of
attachment, and Bess, too, joins with Jack knowing full well
each step with him is but one nearer the fatal tree.

Desire has ever meant danger to me, as it does to all those
cursed with my nature. Now might I relate of that other
underworld with affections and passions that justice forbids
even the naming of. For I am of that kind condemned in sin
for the very instinct known to us as love.

So the theme of my story entwines with that of Elizabeth
Lyon as well as many of the events detailed. I, too, became a
creature of the thief-taker general, a spruce-prig in his corporation, even as I laboured for you as a hackney-scribbler,
setting down the memorandums of the condemned.

So I become part of the tale as well as the telling of it. And
what follows might serve as my own criminal testimony.
Though for all the offences I committed I feel the guilt of but
one: that I betrayed my own kind. And the cause of it saw the
rise of Jonathan Wild.

It all began some months before Edgworth Bess came to London when I first attended Mother Clap's molly-house. It was a festival night with fiddlers, dancing and entertainments. I was a printer's apprentice, barely seventeen, and was shocked to see men kissing and cavorting with each other so openly. And I gazed in frank amazement at those mollies who danced and sported as women. Yet for all its strangeness I at once felt something familiar amid this curious assembly. A parish orphan born and raised in the workhouse, I ever lacked a sense of true belonging. Here I found the kinship of my own race of men.

I was in the company of Johnny Hookman, a sailor who lodged with me at my master's house. We shared a bed and there he introduced me to Sodom and all the exquisite customs of that forbidden city. He had just arrived in London from a long voyage, taking some rest before finding another ship or looking out for another trade since he had spent so little time upon the shore of his own country. His long, black-ened hair was braided behind in a tarred pigtail; he had bright green eyes in a face tanned with the sun and weathered by the four winds. He moved with a fluid ease, a lilting gait still adjusting to dry land. His firm and clefted jaw framed a fine mouth with a ready smile.

He had seduced me with a fierce ardour and I was fearful at first. Then came an awakening passion and I was woken from that long dream of life to a new world, a new sense of being. This realisation came to me like memory, as if I had always known that I was a molly. And I was curious of all aspects of this state, if wary of its hazards.

I confided to Johnny that I was intrigued by those men who

dressed in feminine attire, so he took me to meet the most striking of that crew. Princess Seraphina wore a white gown with a scarlet cloak and fluttered a fan most expertly. She held me by the hands and pulled me to her, looking me up and down. 'You're a pretty one,' she said. 'Have you tried masquerade?'

I shook my head.

'Well, you've the phiz for it. Oh, but your hands!' She held up my fingers stained with ink. 'You'd have to do something about them, dear.'

'I'm a printer's devil,' I told her, explaining that this was the name for apprentices in my trade.

'A devil indeed! An angel more like,' she replied. 'A princess like me. Yes! Princess Print! That's what we'll call you.'

So I was duly baptised with this maiden name (as such epithets are called in the molly dialect) and learned that Johnny Hookman was known in this way as Saltwater Sally. He was called upon to dance for the assembly as at this he was very skilled, having spent much of his youth in the taverns about Wapping. He showed us a fine hornpipe, then demonstrated some of the curious movements he had learned from the savage women of the South Seas. At last I took him by the hand that I might dance a measure with him myself and kiss him openly and before others without shame.

Just as I did this there was some commotion at the door as somebody entered. A tall and portly man in a tricorn hat with gold fringe. It was Charles Hitchen, under marshal of the City. I had known Hitchen from when he had been the main thief-taker and Wild was but his assistant. They would patrol their jurisdiction together from the Temple Bar to the Minories and the under marshal would often stop by Clerkenwell workhouse where I resided to collect the spoils from a crew of boy thieves of that area known as the Mathematicians. I became something of a favourite with Hitchen – he would always tip me sixpence if I took a message for him. Jonathan Wild, on the other hand, seemed to view me with some sort of contempt. All of the canting-crew whispered of a rivalry between the two thief-takers.

Now the crowd parted a little for him as he strode in and the fiddlers held their bows a moment as the room held its breath.

'Evening, Your Ladyship,' someone called at last.

Hitchen turned and made a pout. 'Why, Dip-candle Polly,' he declared. 'You're a saucy one!'

The throng let out a roar of laughter, the band struck up once more and then I knew that Hitchen himself was a molly. I had heard talk of how in the evenings he liked to stroll across Moorfields to watch the wrestling matches or cudgel-playing and that the path dividing that wasteland was known as 'Sodomites Walk'. But I was innocent then and yet to know what that truly meant.

Mother Clap herself came out to greet the under marshal and, no doubt, to make him a present of some of the takings. I noted then that Hitchen had company: behind him lurked William Field, his chief lieutenant among the Mathematicians. Field had a cast in one eye, which made it seem that part of his attention was drawn elsewhere. He spied me and with a grin nudged the under marshal.

'Young Billy,' Hitchen said, when he came over to where I

stood. 'I thought I'd see you here soon enough. But I've not spied you among the Mathematicians lately.'

I had run with that crew when I was still at the workhouse, though not as a thief: I was more of an accomplice. A staller, they called me, one who might serve as a decoy or to give false directions if the hue-and-cry was raised. My fresh face and innocent demeanour were perfect for a lookout. But though I loved to observe the lurid drama of Romeville, I had other ambitions. 'I'm apprenticed now, sir,' I assured him. 'In a respectable trade.'

With a wry smile, Hitchen scanned the room. 'Indeed, yet you still find time for naughtiness. Well,' he sighed, 'I wish I still had you out there touting for me. Keeping an eye on a certain party.'

'Wild?' I guessed, knowing all the recent gossip of the enmity between the two men.

'I should never have taken on that baboon!' He reached down and grabbed my collar, stooping to whisper at me. There was gin on his breath. 'He wants my job, you see. But I'll have my revenge on him. He'll soon feel my curse. And publicly, too!'

He then confided some of the dangers of the shadow-world I had entered, telling me that he protected the molly-houses and certain parties that frequented them. 'We have to stand together,' he said. 'Otherwise we might hang separately. Now, if you ever have any trouble from the Society for the Reformation of Manners, make certain that you are brought before me. You understand?'

'Yes.'

'Good.' He ruffled my hair. Then he strode away.

Field dallied for a moment, one eye glaring, the other with its faraway squint fixed on some distant prospect. I thought I detected the hint of a sneer on his lips as he nodded at me. I frowned. He turned and followed his master.

It was getting late and I noticed how men might pair off and retire to a back room. Johnny explained that this chamber was known in molly dialect as the chapel and told me that what they did there was called marrying.

'Are we married, then?' I asked Johnny, as we walked back to our lodgings that night. He laughed and slapped me on the arse. I thought I heard someone following us. I looked around but there seemed nothing but shadows. As I turned back I noted my companion had grown sombre.

'In truth I am already married, Billy,' he told me.

'What?' I said, with some surprise. 'You have a wife?'

'Only the sea.' He let out a bitter laugh. 'She's my mistress and a cruel one at that. Oh, yes, when you're being tossed to Hell by waves as tall as churches all you can think of is dry land. But once you're back it's not long before all you can think about is the sea, of getting another ship and going out again.'

He spoke of all the terrors and torments he had faced, of all the mates he had lost and how every new voyage raised the odds against him. 'When there's a storm I'll think, If I ever make it back this time I'll stay there. But the sea keeps hold of you. You settle awhile, maybe find a job, get yourself a sweet-heart, but you're just biding your time. The sea's still there in your dreams, waiting for you.'

He had worked the land, toiling as a gardener and hoping that by turning the earth he might somehow plant himself back into it. He had even laboured for a sexton, digging graves in a cemetery.

'And there I was one day, Billy, shovelling the dirt out of a hole, and a voice came into my head saying, "Take a good long look at this dry grave, John Hookman, for your tomb will surely be a watery one."'

'Don't say that,' I told him, and held onto his arm.

The following day I was hard at work at that other kind of chapel, as we call the print shop in our trade. And I was indeed a printer's devil for it is surely a diabolical apprentice-ship. My principal duties were cleaning: the floor of the chapel, the privy of the necessary house, and the ink from the type and from the large leather pads known as balls that were used to daub it, all with a special liquid used for this purpose, known as chamber-lye, viz. human piss. A black art I studied, stained in ink and reeking of urine, like the spawn of some damned underworld. At any spare moment I was set to work on the perplexing task of sorting the hellbox where the used type was thrown to be distributed back into the job cases.

Yet despite these hellish conditions I had a great enthusiasm to learn this profession. Watching the production of a fresh page of text when the fly pulled it from the bed of the press and hung it up never ceased to fill me with wonder. No matter how well acquainted I became with the mechanics of the chapel, this moment yet seemed miraculous and made me feel proud, despite my humble and blackened state, just to be part of the mystery of this trade.

I noted that few of my companions shared this sense of awe: there seemed little interest at the press in what was actually being printed as most in the trade could not read at all, but for the compositor known to all as father of the chapel. He wore a cross-hatched frown all day as he scanned a hand-written page propped on his random, and plucked at the type from the job cases, playing his frame like a delicate harpsichord.

A proof page was always run off from the galley on the correcting stone before it was locked into a forme and put to bed by the pressmen, and I might help the father with it as he had trouble with his eyes. So, I had the opportunity to observe closely how a text might be prepared for the press. Sometimes writers themselves would call in at the chapel with particular ideas of how they wanted their work to appear. I was always keen to get a good look at this breed of men, perhaps expecting some bold hero. I must confess that even then they seemed to me quite a haggard species.

On Tuesday we had to labour into the night for it was then we printed the *London Apollo*, a weekly journal with news and gossip of the town, essays, short poems or ballads and a question-and-answer page (where enquiries were answered on dress, manners or etiquette, as well as on foolish miscellany, such as whether the wine turned from water by Christ was white or red, or why a monkey fed on meat is inclined to eat its own tail). There were also advertisements and letters to the editor.

I remember the week the *London Apollo* began running flash-ballads in its pages because there was a new fashion for these modish songs in the canting tongue. We were done by three in the morning and I could catch a few hours' sleep. I crept into that small cribb in my master's house, above the chapel, that I shared with Johnny, careful not to rouse him.

As I climbed into bed beside him I watched him dream, rocking in slumber as if still feeling the motion of a ship at sea.

Then I was up again at seven to deliver the journal to all the main coffee-houses in the City. I had got to know something of this world of the 'penny university', where so many of the newspapers now being printed in London were read and discussed, and after doing the rounds for my master I might slap my coin on the counter like any man of quality and proudly read the pages of the *Gazette* or *Mist's Weekly Journal*.

That Wednesday evening I ventured into the Smyrna on Pall Mall where the finest wits were said to gather. I spied a trio of them gathered by the left side of the fire as I meekly ordered a dish of coffee and the latest edition of the *Guardian*. Affecting a casual air as I perused my paper, I glanced across at this trinity of thinkers.

One stood above the others, his sharp profile hovering like some bird of prey. The second perched on a high-backed chair, a tiny figure twisted like a question mark, his chin cradled in a hand as he sternly elbowed the armrest. The third was stretched out on a divan, his form as well upholstered as the couch he reclined on. While his companions sported full-bottomed wigs, this one wore a scarlet satin cap of Turkish style that framed a fleshy and effeminate face.

I slyly edged along the counter better to overhear their discourse and found to my astonishment that the subject was myself.

'Might we not measure the liberty of thought in our nation from this?' remarked the man standing. 'That the humblest bootblack can order his newspaper and form his opinion as easily as any educated gentleman.'

They, too, had noticed my hands, stained sable with ink.

'And that the paucity of it is,' replied the one hunched in the chair, 'that he might prove a better critic than any of them.'

'It's a shame he wastes his penny on Addison's new rag,' said the first. 'A shallow draught to intoxicate the brain.'

'Perhaps he intends to use it in his trade,' said the portly man on the settee. 'I can think of no better purpose for it than to wipe the shit off someone's shoes!'

All three broke into laughter at this. I felt a fire in my cheeks as I turned to face them. 'Begging your gentlemen's pardon,' I protested, 'but I am not a bootblack.'

This merely inspired yet more merriment.

'Then what, pray, is your noble calling?' mocked the tall, birdlike fellow.

'I might ask you all what trade you labour in,' I retorted. 'Is it any better than mine?'

'Impudent boy!' The seated question mark straightened up in exclamation.

'Ah! Fearless youth that tempts the heights of art,' sang his horizontal colleague.

'You are all writers, are you not?' I asked.

They nodded.

I raised my hands, palms upward. 'Ink, sirs. It is your lifeblood, is it not? Then I am bloodstained in your service. A humble printer's devil.'

'That's rather good,' someone murmured, and I found the courage to continue.

'You know that each word, each letter has its particular place and that the judgment of their position determines all. How you frame your argument and set it down, how you compose each page and press on until the end. This is the muse for you but toil for us.'

The man in the satin cap rose up from the divan and clapped his chubby hands. He reached out and patted the leg of his seated friend. 'See, Pope? The voice of industry!'

The standing man smiled at me. 'Mr Gay has an indolent fondness for labour. I do believe that he loves work so much that he could watch it all day.'

'You forget, Swift, that I was an apprentice once myself,' returned Gay.

'We do not forget,' Pope interjected, 'but perhaps you should.'

'Would that I could.' He sighed. 'Now, give the boy a pinch of snuff. He's earned it.'

Swift leaned over and proffered his opened snuff-box. This gesture was a ritual commemorating any clever comment or pertinent question made by a lesser wit in their presence. I was to learn that Pope, Swift and Gay were already renowned as three of the best minds of their age. They were masters of satire, a form that I was yet fully to understand but by instinct I comprehended something of it in their very persons and how they were named. Pope was imperious and inclined to pontificate; Swift the quickest in wit, swooping and soaring on the wing, like the bird that never finds a satisfactory perch; but it was Gay's label that had the keenest edge of parody. It is true that he looked a merry soul possessed of a natural gift for comedy. He loved to play at being the fat and lazy buffoon turning his keenest mockery upon himself so that none might beat him to the insult. But a deep sadness dwelled in his heavy-lidded eyes. His was the bitter melancholy of disappointment.

It was by John Gay that I was truly befriended. He had indeed been an apprentice in his youth, bound to a silk mercer in New Exchange by the Strand, so he had some fellow feeling in his regard for me. With no private means he had to live on his own wits or on others' patronage so it was from him that I wished to learn. As his recent play had failed after barely one performance at the Drury Lane Theatre he had to rely upon employment as a secretary to a duchess.

He liked to call me 'Bootblack Billy', an affectionately satirical nickname from our first encounter. Though there was some truth in Swift's observation that he was attracted by the image of rough and manly labour, Gay himself affected a very feminine disposition, his smooth and fleshy form either languid or capricious. And his own indenture had been far from arduous, working at the counter as shop assistant. He had been, as he put it, 'lost in a maze of fashion'. He would wistfully catalogue the equipage of female dress: the silks, the rich brocades, the mantua gowns, the hoop skirts and petticoats, the whalebone stays that tightened the waist. He once confided that borrowing a chambermaid's nightgown for the evening had incited the most pleasing of dreams. In his daily manner he wore the smock of the clown with an easy passivity that hid who knew what mysteries.

He certainly shared none of the furious vigour that powered the rest of the literary world. I learned that most writers reserved their sharpest wit for attacks on each other, forming factions and cliques in the war of criticism. While some fights broke out on party lines (that tedious quarrel between Whig and Tory), the most enduring engagements were in the vicious settling of personal scores. A bad review or a public slight could be a declaration of a long battle of letters. The pamphlet had become a weapon used by all in London to wound their enemies. Indeed, I was soon to be caught in such a paper war myself, the coming one between Charles Hitchen and Jonathan Wild.

At any spare moment I studied in the penny university of the coffee-house or haunted the booksellers in Paternoster Row. At leisure I read whatever I could; the poems of Rochester became a special favourite of mine. At work I watched the father of the chapel compose each page at the random with a delicate art. I was but a dreamer, and in all those places I looked for a kind of romance: I had always felt that I was somehow special.

Even as a humble parish orphan I had bestowed upon myself a charmed life, born in the workhouse itself, my mother a 'lewd person and a common night-walker' taken in by the steward after being found lying in the street nearby by a constable of the watch. In a filthy and insensible state the poor wretch delivered me to this world and I swung by my neck on the rope of life. And as the parish nurse saved me so was a two-fold luck bequeathed: it was said of me that I might be spared a death by hanging as I had already been scragged once and lived, just as those born with that membrane known as a caul over their face are rendered immune from drowning, having already survived a measure of that fate; and in cheating a two-legged gallows it would be my fortune to play truant to the three-legged mare of Tyburn. But I gave a poor exchange for this double reprieve for as my mother gave birth to me so I gave death to her.

My mysterious paternity provoked wild imaginings and I grew to think of myself as better than the other parish orphans. My Quaker guardians spoke of a 'light within', while I looked inward and saw darkness. As they talked of friendship, honest dealing and sobriety, so I dreamed of pomp, luxury and enchantment. I felt a stranger in their midst, a changeling child. I was a quiet, pretty boy who quickly learned how to please and be charming but I fear they mistook my shyness for humility: I longed somehow to rise above them all.

In some matters of schooling I had thrived under their care. In words and letters I proved quick of study and my memory yet retains the physical joy in which I first comprehended the alphabet. These characters whispered to me and gave me comfort, as if the dim shape of each letter conjured the shadow of my mother just before she gave up the ghost. Every line and curve became the movement of her mouth as she formed her final blessing to me, the sound of her voice, of her last breath. As I learned to read I mouthed each syllable and, with greedy delight, I suckled at words.

My most precious possession of infancy was a small stitched chapbook called *Tom Thumb's Alphabet*, printed by woodcut on cheap paper. *A was an Archer, who shot at a frog, B was a Butcher, and had a great dog.* That the first letter spelled my surname seemed some great omen, that this might be the index of my very existence. I swear that it was from this bright and battered volume that I first truly learned the power of the heroic couplet.

So, instructed and prepared for labour in the mechanical trades at the workhouse, I was lucky to be apprenticed to a printer from the age of fifteen. If I could learn the compositor's trade it was promised that I might one day become a man of substance. Yet I longed to be the opposite. Intoxicated by words, I already nursed a calling to the most dangerous of vocations: that of a poet.

And I was drawn to the lurid drama of the Hundreds of Drury with its tales of wicked jades and bold highwaymen, as well as to some of the true knowledge of that bright and guilty world. I was exploring the streets of our great and wicked city. Some scholars call London New Troy after some lost myth of antiquity. The flash world names it Romeville, though I doubt from any classical allusion. I think that this is merely a corruption of *rum ville*, meaning that it is a good town for those in the canting-crew, though I confess I grew fond of some of the seemingly grandiose terms of this St Giles' Greek. Profane or high-flown, there is always a richness to its vocabulary.

For language itself was ever a sensual pleasure to me, and as my palate became conversant with a whole glossary of slang words for vice, I began to compose songs in the flash tongue. This began as my own amusement but soon I was entertaining the journeymen as we laboured in the chapel. Being quick-witted on the shop floor could oft-times save me from being picked on, which can ever be the fate of any apprentice. Indeed, I could be quite consumed in showing off, conjuring the rough comedy I had learned from the streets in improvising a canting song or two.

One Tuesday the editor of the *London Apollo* was in the chapel checking the layout with one of the writers he employed. He was lamenting that there was as yet not enough content for this edition when the father smiled and said, 'Well, young Billy here could tip you a ballad.'

The writer gave a disdainful laugh but the editor shrugged and beckoned me forward. 'Come on, then,' he said. 'Let's hear it.'

So I gave them 'The Ballad of Poll Tricksy', a ditty I had been working on at idle moments. It went like this:

> Poll Tricksy would pad it all night
> She'd tip you a clanker of lightning
> On the culls she would put on the bite
> Her twang a queer bluffer and frightening
> But babbled by a pipe of a quail
> She was snabbled straight into the trib, sir,
> So the bitch she must pad it in jail
> The condemned hold is now her cribb, sir

'I say,' the editor clapped and turned to his colleague, 'that's rather good. James, set that down, will you?'

'Oh, no, sir,' I insisted, taking up a quill myself. 'Allow me.'

I wrote it out in my fairest hand and signed it at the bottom, thinking I knew something of copyright. I was paid a shilling for this, the first writing I ever sold. I can still recall the utter joy I felt at seeing my own words in print.

By good fortune I managed to find Mr Gay on his own at the Smyrna and could not forbear showing him the piece. He nodded and smiled gently as he read it. 'Oh, an infant tongue that too soon learned the canting art,' he mused, and at once I felt foolish.

'It's just some jest,' I said, with a shrug.

'Well, it follows a native tradition in verse.'

He said this with a sparkle in his eye and I feared that he was mocking me. But he went on to speak of Thomas D'Urfey, who wrote popular ballads and bawdy country songs. Gay admired any attempt to capture the voice of common experience. He took me to a tavern and we shared a bottle of claret.

'Welcome to Grub Street, Billy,' he said, patting me on the shoulder. 'Remember, the pen is no easy trade. D'Urfey is in his sixties. He's written more odes than Horace, more comedies than Terence, yet he's as poor as a beggar.'

'Then why do it?' I asked.

'Fame.' Gay's eyes flashed as he breathed the word. 'Fame. His throat yet burns with a thirst for it.'

I was drunk with more than wine that night. I had just turned seventeen and felt that I'd already found a foothold on Mount Parnassus. I would learn the compositor's profession by day and write by night. And not just trifling comic ballads but great idylls of some deep and tragic resonance.

I had such confidence then, and I wonder now at how I dared feign such a precocious temperament. But youth marvels at a sense of its own cleverness. I could not imagine anything that might hinder my lofty ambitions.

But in my life with Johnny I had to be cautious. We screened ourselves, living in close passion by night while by day we assumed a most sober and detached manner. He carried himself with a fierce manliness, so few would guess his inclinations, and made it a study to be seen as God-fearing and sabbath-keeping. All the time he followed a secret gospel. When I once questioned him as to the sinfulness of our relations he had his own reading of scripture.

'We might be scragged for what we are, but it is no crime for us to do what we wish with our own bodies. David had his Jonathan,' he declared, showing me the verses in the Book of Samuel, from his pocket Bible, which spoke of the love between the two men. 'God is love,' he would say, quoting from St John.

But at times I would spy an absent look on his face. From our lodgings in Ludgate he would look to the river when it was full and high, seething with swirling eddies. When the tide was on the turn he was drawn by the swift current running past the Pool of London. Then he could be as cold and distant as the sea.

Soon there was fresh drama in Romeville, and I discovered what Hitchen had meant by his revenge one Wednesday when I was making deliveries to the coffee-houses. A new pamphlet was being circulated and given out gratis entitled: *The Regulator: Or, a Discovery of the Thieves, Thief-taker, and Locks . . . in and about the City of London, with the Thief-taker's Proclamation: Also an Account of all the Flash Words now in vogue among the Thieves, & c. By a Prisoner in Newgate.* It was a curious document, purporting to expose the nefarious activities of the 'Regulator', who was clearly Wild (though never named). Badly written and its print poorly composed, with garish headings in black letter or Gothic type, the whole gaudy tract was an attack on Wild and, though it claimed to be authored by a 'prisoner in Newgate', it had clearly come from Charles Hitchen. The flash world now had its own paper war and I somehow knew it would mean trouble for me.

Then one Friday evening three constables broke the door of our lodgings as we lay abed. They claimed to have a warrant accusing us of 'unnameable acts' and had come to arrest us. Johnny knocked one of them down with his fist and ran out of the house but I was taken and bundled into a waiting carriage as my master Henry Pammenter came out onto the street and loudly denounced Johnny and myself as sodomites.

As the carriage pulled away I turned to one of my persecutors. 'Are you from the Society for the Reformation of Manners?' I demanded, with as much courage as I could muster.

There was no reply to this. One of the men sneered at me.

'You must take me to the under marshal,' I went on.

'Must we, indeed?' he retorted.

'Yes,' I was running out of breath. 'Charles Hitchen. You know, the thief-taker.'

'Oh, we're taking you to the thief-taker all right.'

I was driven to the Blue Boar by the Old Bailey and led upstairs to a parlour that served as an office. All my fears had a moment's reprieve as I imagined that I was being brought before the under marshal and soon a way would be found out of my predicament. But as I was shown through I saw another sitting at the desk before me, scratching a quill on the fresh page of a vast ledger book.

It was Jonathan Wild.

'So, Billy Archer's a molly,' he said contemptuously. 'Can't say I'm surprised.'

As he dismissed the constables I spied William Field sitting in the corner.

'Don't think you can run off to Hitchen, now,' said Wild, as if scanning my thoughts. 'It's too late for that. I've got testimony on you, Billy. You were touted at Mother Clap's.'

I turned to Field. He gave me a cock-eyed grin. 'You bastard sneak,' I told him.

'Careful, Billy,' said Wild. 'William works for me now, not Hitchen. So do you, if you want to save your neck, that is. You've seen this?' He tossed a paper across the desk at me.

It was Hitchen's pamphlet. 'Yes.'

'Well, you know something of the Grub Street trade, Billy. What do you think?'

I picked it up and leafed through it once again. 'It's not very well done.'

'No, I didn't think so. But it demands a reply. I've a hackney-scribbler working on it already.'

He explained that he was dictating his reply to the pamphlet's accusations to a journalist who would then polish the text and make it ready for the press. But in addition he intended to solicit a contribution from myself. 'We want you to spice it up a little, Billy,' he said, with a cruel grin. 'A nice chapter placing Charles in that molly-house. William here tells me you're something of a scribbler. You could pen it yourself.'

'You want me to peach Hitchen for sodomy?'

'In a manner of speaking, yes. Unless you want to hang for it yourself.'

So I was ordered to write 'A Diverting Scene of a Sodomitish Academy', the final section of Wild's tract against Hitchen, an account of the under marshal cavorting in Mother Clap's. I was advanced a guinea for it.

Field took me to lodgings in the Hundreds of Drury, along with some writing materials furnished by Wild. 'All of the Mathematicians have gone over to Wild,' he told me. 'And most of the rum prigs will, too. He offers greater rewards for goods spoken with. Better prospects, see?'

'Even if you're more likely to be peached by him?'

'That's the luck of the draw, Billy.'

'Bad luck if you're scragged,' I said.

'Well, you know what they patter.' We had reached the house where I would be staying. 'Better bad luck than no luck at all.'

'So you betrayed Hitchen, just like that?' I demanded, as we climbed the stairs.

He shrugged. 'Don't worry, Wild will let Hitchen keep the molly-houses. You'll be safe enough, Billy. A pretty phiz like yours could earn good coin from the madge-culls.'

'Bastard sneak,' I muttered. We had reached the top.

'Remember,' said Field, handing me ink, pen and paper. 'I only betrayed him with a widd in someone's lugg. You're going to do it in black and white.'

So I set to work on the hated task. Yet I could not forbear from mustering all my talents in the writing of the article. I even found that I had picked up some talent for journalism from all my time at the penny university and in the print shop. I managed to bring some authentic colour to the prose, describing the use of maiden names and some of the sly humour of the molly dialect. I fear I did it all rather too well. I was just writing how one madge might complain to another that *he ought to be whipped for not coming to school more frequently* when a knock came on my door. It was Johnny Hookman.

'You're safe,' I gasped, as he embraced me.

'Yes, Billy, so are you,' he muttered, and I felt his closed palm draw down my cheek, then the knife within against my neck. 'Peach me, did you?'

'No.' The blade was at my throat. 'I swear.'

'Then how did you get away?' he demanded angrily. 'I saw them take you.'

I begged him to let me explain and as I showed him what I had written for the thief-taker he folded the knife back into its clasp. He shrugged. 'Thought you'd babbled on me.'

'No.' I sighed. 'Just on the entire molly species.'

He grabbed me once more, now in a rage of mere lust. We coupled swiftly and in a most savage manner. All the fear and suspicion, the anger and indeed hatred one can feel when cursed with this nature seemed bound up in our fierce love-making. Then he stood and gathered his things.

'What now, Johnny?' I asked, as he buttoned his breeches.

'Got a ship.' He told me he had signed up on a merchantman bound for Virginia.

'And what will I do?'

Johnny looked around the room, at the pile of papers on my makeshift desk. 'Write, Billy. Maybe it's what you're good at. You'll be a famous poet yet.'

Then he kissed me and was gone.

I received another guinea when I delivered my work. Wild's *An Answer to a Late Insolent Libel* quickly circulated throughout the coffee-houses, a much more professional job than Hitchen's ill-judged broadside. And Wild had the intelligence to charge sixpence for his pamphlet rather than to hand it out free, thus setting some notion of value to his opinion. All of the under marshal's accusations were cleverly refuted or dismissed but it was my final chapter describing Mother Clap's that provided the *coup de grâce*. Hitchen was presented as being very merry in this assembly, dallying amid some young sparks and openly displaying his desire for them. And so I anonymously provided the satire that broke his reputation. I had betrayed the secret of the molly-houses and defamed their protector. Now Wild had a clear field to take over Romeville.

He had studied his craft well and learned how to deal with the canting-crew. They knew him as a man to be feared, ruthless and always ready with violence. And though the under marshal was more lenient with his thieves, they knew they could get more money from the new thief-taker. Wild would impeach or break a man without question and any rogue stood more chance of being hanged by him than by Hitchen but, as Field had observed, they also had the opportunity to gain more. Raising the stakes tends to make men more reckless and continue playing when they should rather quit the gaming table.

Hitchen could be pompous and haughty with the gentry and lacked the patience in dealing with stolen goods, too often fencing or pawning them himself without giving time for the owners to be readied to pay the high rewards on demand. Wild had a more subdued manner, and would carefully inveigle the quality with his intrigues.

Above all, Wild had a true instinct for power. He allowed Hitchen to collect from the molly-houses as well as certain other academies and to keep his title of under marshal. Wild had no interest in this mere municipal appointment but instead had the ambition to declare himself 'Thief-taker General'. In this bold act of self-creation he set his own mark on London.

And, having won the paper war, Wild now knew how useful the press might be to further his reputation. His pamphlet had been produced by Thomas Warner whose shop was by the Black Boy in Paternoster Row and who also printed Applebee's *Weekly Journal*. It was from this time I began to place articles about the thief-taker's exploits in that as well as other London newspapers. Wild was keen to promote himself with stories of daring arrests and swift retrieval of ill-gotten loot while the press became all the more keen on this new journalism as it brought with it fees from advertisements for the recovery of stolen property.

But my earnings in Grub Street were as yet haphazard and I could not go back to my master's shop in Ludgate. It was said that I had broken the terms of my apprenticeship and Mr Pammenter would not even see me.

So I had to find new ways in order to survive. I began running errands for Mother Clap's, which earned some coin. I saw Hitchen there on occasion as he still collected money from it under Wild's sanction. He was still in shock after his sudden fall from grace.

'You're the only one I can trust, Billy,' he told me, completely unaware that it had been me who had betrayed him.

On festival nights I might perform with Princess Seraphina and sometimes after a song or a measure the hat would be passed around. Soon enough I was fetched to oblige the company of a cull and paid a crown to go with him to the chapel. So this became another profession I followed.

I apprenticed myself all about town in my new trade. As well as at Mother Clap's, I could be found at the Yorkshire

Grey by Bloomsbury Market or the Three Tobacco Rolls in Drury Lane, strolling outside in the Royal Exchange by day and padding the Sodomites Walk in Moorfields by night. The piazza was quite a marketplace for my commerce as were the bog-houses on the east side of Lincoln's Inn Fields.

In all of these places I would make a bargain, as long as it brought me enough benefit. My looks and youth were a desired commodity, and I learned to thieve and pick the pockets of the madge-culls. It was in those days that I first met the bold jade Punk Alice, who taught me how fierce one had to be to work the streets.

And in filching from some gentleman I might steal a pocket-book containing some personal details. Then I could send a note promising to return it in exchange for payment to prevent me impeaching the poor fellow for sodomy. This was the evil habit of the trap: I did not care to see how I turned on my own kind and instead I reasoned that this was fine vengeance against the whole of creation for making me what I was.

And there was danger in the streets: violence, poverty and sickness stalked every corner, every alleyway. It is said that in London the rate of death is higher than that of birth, so the whole city might slowly wither away were it not for all those strangers: those Jews, Italians, Huguenots and St Giles' Blackbirds that dup into Romeville year upon year. And so it grows, a great emporium, a fat beast of commerce that wallows on the river with the lucky few feeding on its body, the rest scavenging its waste.

My first winter amid the Hundreds of Drury was the hardest. It was so cold that season that the Thames froze over and there was a frost-fair by London Bridge that stretched from the Temple Stairs to Southwark. A great carnival of delights for all the senses except the pleasure I traded in. For the frigid air can rouse many passions in men but rarely lust. And so I faced a decrease in my wages at the very time I needed extra coin for food, fuel and warm clothes.

Coming out of Mother Clap's one freezing morning, I spied a strange figure waddling down Field Lane. A stout gentleman all trussed up in a heavy surtout greatcoat, double-buttoned and wrapped at the front. The collar was up and a silk cravat tightly knotted at the throat. He wore a flapping hat with its uncocked brim let down at the sides, an old bob-wig covering his ears. A fat and ruddy face peeped out of this bundle and hailed me. 'Bootblack Billy!' the rotund apparition called. 'Just the fellow!'

It was John Gay. He took my arm, and as we sauntered down towards Holborn Bridge, he explained that he was writing a poem about walking the streets of London. I could not help laughing as if this was some mad jest, for Gay was the least suited in temperament, inclination why, in his very body for such a physical pursuit. I always saw him as wilfully indolent, fond of inert pleasures. Yet he claimed to be serious.

'Walking is an art, Billy,' he told me. 'It must be practised judiciously. You will note my careful preparations.' He tapped his thick cane at a pair of sturdy square-toed shoes with well-hammered soles and low heels. And I noted that he sported none of his habitual finery. His coat was of plain close-knit kersey with no embroidered flourish or lace trim, his hat unedged, his wig undressed. And in this manner he set out to discover our great city, like some fearless explorer.

'No coach or chair for me, Billy,' he declared, prodding at the filthy cobbles. 'Think what ancient shoreline we follow beneath this pavement. Only by walking can we truly understand this space we inhabit.'

'Just by walking?' I asked.

'Yes, Billy. There is yet a science to it. An art, of course. "The Art of Walking the Streets of London", that will be the rubric of my poem. But its title will be "Trivia".'

'Trivia?'

'Yes. It has a double meaning . . . well, a triple one, I suppose. It does not refer only to that trinity of the lesser arts, no, it also means *tri-via*, you see? The meeting of three roads. Trivia was the Roman goddess of the crossroads, and she will be my muse. In space, Billy, and where the three streets of time converge: morning, day and night.'

We had just reached Holborn Bridge and he was already short of breath. I wondered if this fancy of his was not just some ridiculous farce. It was hard to tell with Gay as he was always joining the mundane with the classical in some vast heroic satire. He panted steam and nodded down at the Fleet Ditch below.

We looked into the black river that winds its filthy way through London and forms its main sewer. Part congealed by the cold, it churned with a lulling murmur. In its lazy current, foetid garbage lolled and bobbed.

'Another goddess,' sighed Gay.

'No,' I protested.

'Yes. Cloacina. In Rome she presided over the Cloaca Maxima, the great drain of the Eternal City. The goddess of the sewer. Here she guides the Fleet.'

We crossed the bridge and followed the banks of the stream.

'This tributary forms the very innards of the city,' he went on. 'The digestive tract, the guts, the fundament.' Gay turned to me and smiled, saying, 'Oh, yes, Cloacina is a dirty goddess. And a lusty one.'

He conjured a story as we walked of how Cloacina, like many a classical deity, falls in love with a mortal boy. Emerging from her underworld in the form of a blackened cinder wench she seduces him in a dark alley. In his tale Gay contrived to make this son of men a humble bootblack, as the goddess of dirt would esteem his grimy looks as a sign of beauty. He was also, of course, directing her desire upon me since he used my ancient nickname.

And he in turn took the part of the goddess in the telling of it. I had long wondered if Gay was like Seraphina, and loved to dress or become like a female. Or if Cloacina was merely a maiden name and he was one of those gentlemen I had sometimes made bargains with who yearned to walk on the wild side of Romeville and consort with rough boys of the street or shirtless youths of industry. But I never did find out whether he was a molly or any other kind of a cull. Some men hide it well, others deny it fiercely, even to themselves. But with Gay the mask was himself; there was no dissembling, merely a happy vigilance and a delight in transformed sentiment. For some men the greatest mystery in life is themselves.

Through that winter I walked with him as he began to compose his mock-epic odyssey. There seemed no plan to how he mapped out his wanderings: he chose to merge with the crowd at times and move with their ebb and flow, or leave it to chance as to which way he might turn. This was the modern experience, he told me, where every individual might enjoy the freedom of the city.

'Though the world takes so little notice of me,' he soon complained, so quickly worn out by our meanderings, 'I need not take much of it.'

Yet in space and time we travelled. Around the Seven Dials where seven streets count the day and from each other count the sun's circling ray. From there to Covent Garden, its cobbled piazza grouted with ice, where apprentice boys, like Furies, played a warlike football game, the colonnade of the temple their goal.

We crossed the hoary Thames where the frost-fair's tents formed a pitched encampment, a wintry army laying siege to the city from its icy plain. Here were booths and stalls, gingerbread sellers, ninepins-playing and great blazing fires where spitted oxen turned.

Then at night I led him through the maze of courts around Drury Lane. We watched the jades that stood and worked the passing trade at that point where Catherine Street descends upon the Strand. I pointed out all the sharpers who might put the bite on culls there. The files, the twangs, the guinea-droppers. When it got late I waited for the moment that he might make a bargain with me.

He paid for my time and made me a gift of the first book of Pope's translation of Homer, but he would leave me at night with merely a brief embrace and a cheerful salutation. He once confided that he had himself made something of a profession out of friendship. He had lately gained the patronage of the Earl of Burlington, who had built that great palace in Piccadilly.

He encouraged me to continue to write and longed to hear my stories. He told me that Swift had written from Dublin, suggesting that Gay might write a 'Newgate pastoral', some epic set among the thieves and whores there, so he was keen to hear of the canting-crew and the new thief-taker.

'I often wonder why the talents of statesmanship seem so scarce in society,' he mused, 'since those who truly possess them are every month cut off in their prime at the Old Bailey!'

As well as my meagre Grub Street work, I penned the occasional flash ballad but I longed to write something more lofty and substantial, a great poem that came from the heart. Yet that part of me had grown hard and unyielding. And in wanting some fine emotion to inspire me it was not lack of feeling I possessed but an excess of it. I had made bargains with so many men, finding some desire but little satisfaction, all intimacy tempered with betrayal and suspicion. I knew somehow that true art must come from true love, but all I could muster was feigned sentiment.

I endeavoured with a song about Johnny, transposing his desire for me into a sailor at sea longing for his fair maid back home. The paltry lyric came in a counterfeit spirit:

When on Afric's dark shore his ship was blow'st,
He recalled the pale hue of her ivory coast.

So I gave up, conceiving that Johnny was but my first love and scarcely the best. It was a last love I dreamed of, one that I could cherish ever after. Then a fine muse might take me and I should prove a great poet as well as a great lover. But that was not much more than an idle fancy as I worked the streets and, in truth, I looked with a cold eye, searching rather for one who might act as my patron while earning coin and finding pleasure where I could.

A Swiss count had begun to stage masquerades at the Haymarket Theatre, which was open to the public after the performances held there. I would sometimes procure a ticket for these 'Midnight Masques' as they were excellent occasions for both wicked work and fine entertainment. Here one could spy gods and goddesses, sailors and shepherdesses, Greek and Roman heroes, fierce Turkish warriors all in vizards or Venetian half-masks.

Masked and dressed as a woman, I could flatter some fop and, as we danced, easily pick his pocket. And if my pretence was by chance unscreened the shock of it might prove a useful distraction. Oft-times it proved a happy discovery for the man and a bargain could be made.

I had learned all the tricks of female performance from festival nights at Mother Clap's with Princess Seraphina. For myself it was merely a game and I indulged in the fleeting pleasure of its transportation. For the princess it was a sublime art and, indeed, part of her very existence. And there were others of this persuasion, even those who journeyed from woman to man in this fashion such as Punk Alice.

I met her there one night dressed as a hussar. We palled up and worked together awhile at these carnivals. In this feast of fools the loose dress and secure disguise robbed the gentry of their restraints of modesty and made them easy prey for Alice and me. With her as the beau, myself the belle, we could work the drop *en travesti*. And, being roughly the same size, we could swap our clothes once more if further confusion was called for.

Punk Alice loved the liberty those balls gave her. Often she complained bitterly to me that there were no molly-houses for the female race. But there she might find a lusty girl for herself. In disguise many lost their self completely, then found out who they truly were. 'Who knows the truth of love, Billy?' she said, when I told her once of my search for such a thing. 'Love is a masquerade. Merely wear its mask and it might yet unmask you.'

'I just never seem to find it.'

'Then let it find you. And take it when you cán. I had an exquisite night last week with this long-meg jade at our academy.'

She spoke of Edgworth Bess and it was through Alice that I first became acquainted with Elizabeth Lyon. I was to know her over the years merely as one of the many women who worked the Hundreds of Drury, never imagining the great notoriety she would gain, or that I would eventually be the one to set down her tale.

Perhaps inspired by all this dissembling at the Haymarket, I now tried my hand at writing for the stage and completed a set of ballads for a harlequinade at St Bartholomew's Fair. The show proved some success amid the jugglers, puppet booths and performing animals of that riotous carnival. I foolishly promised a great epic for this gang of players and the following year they presented my *Siege of Troy*. But these wretched comedians quite forgot most of my lines and proceeded to improvise or work the cheapest jests they could with the audience. So Paris was killed on the spot by Menelaus (though he kept coming back to life only to be dispatched once more), bold Achilles decided he would take

Helen for himself once it was revealed that she was played by a pretty boy, and a great burlesque was made of the Greeks emerging out of the arse of the Trojan Horse.

And, to my shame, in brashly hoping for some minor theatrical triumph, I invited John Gay along to witness this debacle. Nevertheless he enjoyed himself.

'Poor Homer!' he exclaimed, weeping with laughter.

'Poor Billy,' I muttered darkly.

'Yes, yes.' He patted my shoulder. 'Poor Billy, but take courage, you are young. There'll be plenty of time for greater failures yet.'

He confided his own disappointments: a five-act pastoral tragedy that he had laboured over all year had its staging cancelled at the Drury Lane, and though he continued to subsist on the patronage of Burlington he had found no place at Court, or any independent means. He was in a jovial mood, however. A new collection of poems looked set to gain him a substantial advance from subscriptions.

By late spring Gay had received most of his payment, and as he presented me with a copy as a gift, he gave me some advice. He had started to invest the fees he had earned in South Sea stock and encouraged me to do likewise with any monies I might have access to. Shares had already taken a five-fold leap in value, and in a fevered atmosphere of speculation, there appeared no limit to what might be gained by this miraculous enterprise.

I gathered together all I could, pawning possessions and borrowing money from all over town, went down to the stock-jobbers in Exchange Alley and bought one hundred pounds in share certificates. Gay had invested ten times as much, but any amount put into the scheme from whatever rank of person seemed set to solve all the woes of society. Stock rose over two hundred and fifty points in the first two days of June and we revelled in bright fantasies of plenty.

That summer seemed a golden age, a new era in which art and commerce would be reconciled. For Gay there would be no more need for patronage or to chase after Court appointments. And I would no longer have to bargain, or steal, or hack away in Grub Street. I lived on credit, like a gentleman, getting further into debt without a care. For now I was set to be worth two thousand pounds and all the canting-crew in Romeville eyed me jealously. But they were busy also.

A crew of highwaymen began preying on Exchange Alley, knowing that at every hour cash was being taken in and out of that street by those culls trading in the Bubble. It was whispered that Hawkins's gang was doing most of the filching, and good money would be paid for any information.

One day I was called into Wild's office. 'You're looking very elegant these days, Billy,' he declared, eyeing me up and down. 'Mixing with the gentry-coves, is it? Or just pretending to be one.'

'Perhaps,' I said, with a sour smile, 'a little of both.'

'What do you know of the Earl of Burlington?'

'Not much.'

'I hear you know that poet friend of his. I want you to find out when the earl might be coming to town next. I hear he's got some rum loure to invest.'

I knew that Gay had been visiting Burlington's manor house in Chiswick and I learned from him that his patron was coming up to town on a certain Monday evening with six hundred guineas to deposit. I passed this on to Wild and sure enough their carriage was robbed on Richmond Lane that night.

Then Wild bade me place an article in Applebee's *Weekly Journal*, recounting how the Earl of Burlington and two other persons of quality had been set upon by highwaymen, who had made off with six hundred guineas along with a large blue sapphire ring and three gold watches.

This worked as an advertisement for the victims to come to Wild. Only Gay seemed suspicious as to how the thief-taker had known about the robbery and the contents of the haul *before* Burlington or any of the others had actually reported it. He observed all of these dealings with bemusement but never directly spoke of my complicity in them. We would meet at White's coffee-house when he was in town and he might ask after certain details, his gentle curiosity clouded with ironic wit.

In any case, things did not go according to plan for Wild with this scheme. He was offered one hundred pounds for the recovery of the sapphire ring alone, then found out that Hawkins's crew would no longer deal with him. They had sailed for Holland to fence their booty there. Wild was furious and swore he would take his revenge on them at the earliest opportunity.

And I missed out on my commission for the information but at that time I did not care. My stock was still rising and I fancied that soon I would be free of Jonathan Wild's intrigues for ever.

All through that high summer Billy Archer was out on a spree, happy as a skylark and utterly indolent. I had thought that a life of leisure might afford some interlude for me to write something of quality. I had reasoned for so long that it was only the lack of time and circumstance that prevented me composing exquisite odes or solemn tragedies. I took lessons in dancing and swordplay, I even learned to ride, but for the most part I was overcome by an easy lethargy, and in the stupor of merriment, days and nights collapsed on each other in luxurious exhaustion. And I wrote nothing.

Indeed the whole of London seemed to attend lazily upon a great carnival of speculation. The playhouses could hardly compete with the drama, as Exchange Alley now became the great amphitheatre of the city. This was the spectacle of our age and the Bubble became the very muse of Romeville. In the sweltering heat of the season, all were gripped by the fever of stock-jobbing. As well as the South Sea trade every day brought some new fantastical scheme for public investment. An invention to extract butter from beech trees, a policy for insurance on horses, a printing machine, a portable aquarium to bring fresh fish to Billingsgate, a mechanical gun that might fire continuously with round or square bullets depending on whether the target was Christian or Turk. Clouds of ideas, dreams of exquisitely fashioned vapour. Everything was floated upwards to be realised in some far-off time, a great and prosperous future we would all live in.

It was madness but few questioned any of it as long as the stock was still going up. Gay was in a trance, engrossed in the prospect of being worth twenty thousand pounds on paper. Friends had urged him to sell some of his shares, to put aside enough real cash to perhaps secure a hundred a year.

'I asked them what that would mean,' he told me. 'You

know I have no head for figures. Well, they said, "It will make you sure of a clean shirt and a shoulder of mutton every day." Imagine that, Billy! A clean shirt and a shoulder of mutton!'

And we both fell about laughing. I was already living five times that and was able to put it all on a tally. As a South Sea cove with great prospects I could borrow as much as I wanted. Until it all came tumbling down.

In August news of a plague spreading north from Marseille made everyone uneasy, as if a punishment for greed was coming for us all. And so it was. At the end of the month the share price stopped rising. In September it began to collapse. By October all credit had been squashed flat.

I thought the shock of it would kill Gay and, indeed, there was a spate of suicides after the crash. But his defence as ever was irony. A new muse had been called into being with the bright art of speculation, he insisted, and the principal dreamers of our age were no longer poets or dramatists but bankers and stock-jobbers. As we soaked our sorrows in wine, he made this impassioned speech: 'How can we hope to compete with such an imagination? Such flights of fancy and illusion! With metaphysical inspiration they conjured visions of the Land of Cockaigne, of El Dorado with all its golden millions. Each share certificate issued with such lyrical enchantment. And with every element of theatre the third subscription sold: the comic folly, the tragic fall. The meta-morphoses of Ovid were nothing to these astonishing trans-formations in fortune. Bravo!' He held up his glass and howled this Italianate call of approval lately in fashion at the opera. 'Bravo!'

As it turned out, he managed to salvage something from the

Bubble as did many of the gentry who had faced utter ruin. The new prime minister, Walpole, endeavoured to rescue some of the banks by rescheduling debts and transferring liabilities. He also screened some of the higher-ups who had made mountains of cash out of others' misfortune. But I think part of Gay's sanguine disposition during this crisis was that somewhere in his heart he did not want independence. He had spent so much of his time in another bubble, that of patronage, and it had now become a way of life.

There was no such comfort for me to fall back upon, though. I was running from my creditors and it was hard to know which way to turn as I owed money all over town. I had to sell my books and pawn the fine jewels, watches and snuffboxes I'd bought on tick in my days of fortune. I was rudely awoken from the ease of leisure and now faced years in a debtors' prison. I could not bear the thought of rotting away in the Fleet or the Marshalsea, and there was but one man in London who might save me from this fate. I went to his offices at the Old Bailey.

'Not so much of a gentry-cove now, are you, Billy?' Wild declared, in a mocking tone, then leaned forward over the desk. 'But you still look like one. Dress like one. Talk like one. Have you forgotten where you came from?'

'No.'

'Good. Because I haven't and I can put you right back there. But in the meantime other coves might be fooled by you.' He shrugged. 'I'm putting a crew together, Billy. You might want to be part of it.'

It was not an invitation to be declined. And so I became one of Wild's spruce-prigs, a particular race of thief that would assume the personage of a gentleman. With my fine looks, rich clothes and ability to affect the speech and manners of the gentry I had become something of an expert in this species of fraud. Many times I had worked the beau-trap lay, a beau-trap being one who puts the bite on some young blood new to town and eager to spend his money on its delights but utterly ignorant of its wicked ways.

But now the lay of the spruce-prig came when we worked together as a crew. Wild had us tutored most excellently in etiquette and deportment. He even hired a dancing-master so that we might learn all the fashionable dances. This wicked choreographer, a certain Mr Lin, was something of a thief himself and gave us good advice at how to pick a pocket while executing a nimble minuet. Equipped with the best finery and with some playing the part of footmen or valets in livery, we would prey upon balls and masquerades, opera nights and assemblies, and as we capered amid polite society we would nimbly dip and file the aristocracy. And as the thief-taker himself rose up to become part of this world so the spruce-prigs formed his entourage. It was rumoured that he was planning a spectacular raid for the next season.

A reluctant member of Wild's corporation, I became acquainted with the crew that frequented the Black Lion. William Field, whom I had learned to be wary of, and Hell-and-Fury Sykes, who tutored those acting as servants in the spruce-prig lay. There was Joe Blueskin, with whom I shared a love of books, and, of course, Edgworth Bess.

I could appear most sociable and at ease in the various worlds I inhabited, flash or flat. Yet I ever felt a great loneliness and my heart called out for some deep and lasting companionship. Of course, I continued to write and dream of some great romance in art as well as life. But I was a mere hackney-scribbler, placing articles in the press about Wild and gaining some reputation as a good source for those stories of crime that were all the fashion. Sent to record the lives of notorious villains I used the skills I'd learned as a thief as much as a writer. For to steal a soul it is best to step lightly and touch softly. My principal employer became yourself, as your *Weekly Journal* specialised in reports of this kind. You also published pamphlets, broadsheets and even bound collections containing the last words of criminals about to hang. This new and burgeoning market attracted some of the great talents of the age – even that Grub Street colossus Daniel Defoe had started to pen criminal narratives for you. I was but one of that humble crew, known as Applebee's 'garreteers', as for the most part we dwelled in those sky-parlours of Covent Garden.

None of us guessed that a new and shocking story was about to emerge from the Hundreds of Drury: the rise of the thief-taker general and his fall, instigated by the escapades of the infamous prison-breaker. Back then, few would have seen little Jack Sheppard as the nemesis of the great Jonathan Wild. He had had but a short career in crime and there seemed nothing particular about it, just another apprentice getting himself into trouble. And at first no one saw anything special about him, except Elizabeth Lyon. They made a strange couple: Jack a wiry bantamweight, Bess a buxom long-meg. And that might have been the only thing to mark them out, were it not for the events that follow.

Two

—

The

TREE

of

KNOWLEDGE

THE TRUE & GENUINE ACCOUNT
OF THE LIFE & ACTIONS
OF ELIZABETH LYON

IV

CROUCHING on the ledge I peered down at the gaol yard below. Even in the darkmans I could tout that it was a long drop. Our cell was four storeys up on the top floor of the New Prison in Clerkenwell. I looked back at Jack, his bright eyes glimming in the gloom.

'Go on, Bess,' he whispered. 'I've got you.'

He gave a short tug on the rope we had fashioned from a sheet and my petticoats. It ran through the milled bar of the glaze and was hitched around my waist. I feared it might not take my weight or that Jack might lack the strength to lower me safely to the ground. But it was my neck or his: if we did not kick away from this trib another cord would soon fasten him: the hempen knot of Tyburn.

So, I plucked up courage and remembered our first night together at Vinegar Yard when he had pulled me onto the roof at peep of day and we had touted out over Romeville. Shuffling to the edge of the stone sill, I turned and gripped the rope. But as I readied myself to launch out into the night air I had not much care for either Jack or myself. My real terror was for the little stranger inside me.

❧

For some months after our Westminster wedding we had kept a brandy-shop in Lewkenor Lane. It was a bene screen for the flash life and it had brought in rum loure also. By early spring we had some thirty pounds set aside from the takings alone and I canted that we might make a flat trade of it one day. In the meantime Jack did the prigging for both of us. For him the milling of kens was not just for the gelt. He was never happier than when dubbing a jigger or starring a glaze. He loved the thrill of it, like that crank pleasure coves get from the lush or at the gaming table.

And he was diligent in his vocation: if he had been the idle apprentice in his former trade he became the master craftsman in this new one. A skilled artificer, he created a whole new set of tools he could use for his job: little saws and chisels, files and picks. His favourite implement was one he fashioned from the spike of a halberd. He called it 'Kate', that being a cant term for a picklock.

I ran the shop and it was bene to be done with whoring for a while. But I soon twigged that I should be in charge of our flash business as well as bluffer of the boozing-ken. In spite of all his talents as a ken-miller Jack yet had no idea as to what to filch and how best to dispose of what was spoken with. And when I pattered to him that we should use Wild to fence our booty, and so keep in with the prig-napper's corporation, he went into a rage. He still smarted at the wound of mockery Wild had dealt him. This is the foolish pride of coves: us morts are well used to indignity but men set such store by their vanity. I knew that I should be running this crew but I knew, too, Jack would never tout it so. I jabbered that if we were to work any lay without the thief-taker's canting we would have to brush upon the sneak.

So I was nettled when his brother turned up ebb-water at the brandy-shop. Tom Sheppard was three years older than Jack and worked as a journeyman in Spitalfields. There he had been caught filching tools from his master and was glimmed in the paw for it. I saw the brand mark, a red T, burned into that fleshy part of the palm at the base of his thumb. Jack lent him forty shillings and tipped him prog and lush. It soon seemed clear that they would be padding it out together but I felt sure that palling up with a cove marked as a thief would surely bring trouble. And when they filched from an alehouse in Southwark, and Tom kept most of what was spoken with, I was furious. But Jack insisted he was a brother in need. 'Bl-bl-blood is blood, Bess,' he said.

We had fierce widds over this and we soon found that the heat of our quarrel matched the glim passion of our lovemaking. I felt outnumbered, though, and having no family of my own could not cant the power of that bond. Now Tom and Jack bided together in the shop by lightmans, cheapening our profits by drinking our best French cognac on tick. Then they would shab off and see their mother, Mary, who had a cribb in Clare Market. Those wild rogues were bitched by no mort but the one that squeezed them out into this world, and no other woman would ever be good enough.

Then they milled a draper's shop near their mother's ken and Jack left the goods with Tom to fence, though like his brother he knew not how to dispose of the loot safely. I feared that we might all soon be snabbled if we did not tout a bit more peery and I resolved to settle this with Jack.

One darkmans he came back when I was locking up the shop, bearing a small bundle. He had cracked the jigger of a ken on Hart Street and filched from the parlour there. There was a set of oss-chives, a pair of spectacles and a large leather-bound book, all wrapped up in a linen tablecloth.

'Took a peep at the book,' he pattered. 'It's a hand-written ledger or something. Worthless, like the glasses.'

'Not if we fence them proper,' I told him.

'What do you mean?'

'You know the prig-napper puts out full advertisements of goods recovered. There could be a reward for the book and the spectacles.'

'I ain't dealing with W-W-Wild. I told you.'

'Well, what if I did? If you let me do the fencing, things would be a lot easier. You act so crank just because he bitched you that time.'

'And you just stay b-b-bitched by him.'

'Oh, stow your widds.'

'I run my own crew, Bess.'

'Well, the cloth and the oss-chives won't fetch much. You ain't much of a prig if that's all you can click.'

Jack's glaziers flared up. He made to patter something, then thought better and shook his head. Turning on his heel, he padded it out of the shop.

'Where are you going?' I called after him.

'To f-f-filch something I can f-f-fence for myself!'

I bided a minute or two then piked after him, peery that he might do something reckless. I followed him through the maze of the Hundreds down to Drury Lane. I touted him by the Black Lion, there was yet some glim coming from that boozing-ken, and saw that he dupped in there. This was bene, I thought. We could have some lush and patter calmly. But as I padded up to the jigger I spied him through the glaze. He was with Poll Maggot.

They stood close, Jack pattering something in that intent manner of his, Poll shaking her ringlets as she nodded, her painted phiz a leering mask. She spoke something and his glaziers sparked, her paw touched his cheek, then he bussed her on the gob. I thought of dupping in and fronting them but I felt so full of wrath and disgust that I turned and shabbed off into the dark-mans.

I was in a smoky rage as I padded it back. It was bad enough that my lover was working the drop on me, but Poll was supposed to be a pal. It was hardly queer for Jack to want to play the rogue in this fashion, for he had scant experience when measured with all the coves I had docked with. And I had touted enough to cant that this crank act of lovemaking could mean nothing. Or everything. Love is a bitch, I thought, as I cut through White Horse Yard, and I was surely bitched by it.

I passed a tavern that was closing up, just a dim glow of lanterns at the back of the ken. I saw a small push around a table in the corner and knew the shape of that charmed circle of coves even before I touted the gentleman they courted. It was Jonathan Wild, of course, and I recalled that sailor pal of Billy's once pattered of how little fishes swim close to a shark, as it is safest there. And I felt myself drawn in. Before I knew it I was with that crew, hawking for his attention.

'Enough!' the prig-napper called, waving the crowd away with one paw as he scratched a note with the other. 'Can't a man get some peace?'

I stepped forward as the crowd dispersed. Wild continued writing as Quilt gathered up papers and some filched items that lay on the table. A bored-looking jade sat nearby.

'Madam,' he said, not looking up but noting the gown of one standing before him. 'If you have some business, please come to my offices at the Old Bailey in the morning.'

'Jonathan,' I pattered, and he raised his phiz.

'Edgworth Bess.' His bleach-blue glaziers flashed up at me. 'Well, well, well.'

He nodded to the chair opposite him and I sat down without thinking. I had quite forgotten that calm and controlled manner of his. He knew how to be at the centre of things, the steady eye in the mad tempest of Romeville. All at once I felt queerly at ease after all the turmoil with Jack. 'Will you have a drink with me?' he asked.

'Certainly.'

'You,' he gestured to the girl by his side, 'you can go home. Pay her off, Quilt. And pike it yourself when you're finished here.' He called to the bluffer to bring us some wine and let out a long sigh. 'I spend my days taking goods from those they don't belong to and handing them back to those who don't deserve them. Well,' he shrugged, 'what have you got for me, Bess?'

'I'm running a brandy-shop.'

'I know that. With plenty of babble over the counter and much booty under it, no doubt. The prattle is you're palled up with that stuttering apprentice.'

'Jack's my husband, yes.'

'Well, I always knew you'd be unfaithful to me.'

'That's fine of you to patter.'

'Oh, I'm more faithful than anyone I know. You wouldn't cant how faithful one has to be with so many wives. I just hope you're still true in other ways.'

'Meaning business?'

'What else?'

'Jack doesn't want to fence his loot through your corporation. It's his pride, you see.'

'His insolence, more like.'

'Perhaps. But if there's a way of doing it without him knowing all could be bene.'

'Well, something might be arranged.' He smiled and touched my paw with his. 'For a small consideration.'

I thought of jabbering that I was no longer in that trade but it was such a simple thing. The crank act of lovemaking could mean nothing. Or everything. I twigged that Wild liked to mark his territory like a dog, so we padded up the dancers to a cribb upstairs. I cant that even then some instinct taught him that Jack was his opposite, some exact enemy he might battle with. Each bore a contrary mask, one of authority, the other rebellion.

My head reasoned that I was giving myself to Wild for both of us, though my heart knew that part of my own vanity was now satisfied, that I, too, could play at adultery. But I hoped that we might be quits, Jack and me. And I was keen that this dalliance might settle my account with Wild also, even if I nursed a nagging doubt that I yet owed him a body for Punk Alice.

I got back to our ken before Jack and went to bed. He staggered up the dancers some hours later, pot-valiant and contrite. He sparked a glimstick and we talked.

'We have to work together, Jack,' I told him.

'I don't want to be a prig for the prig-napper.'

'You won't have to.'

'Then what?'

'We'll patter of it in the lightmans. Douse the glim and come to bed.'

So next day we came to an agreement. Jack would do the filching while I would see to the fencing. I sent for William Field and he came to see us at the brandy-shop. He was a sly one for sure but was an old hand in the canting-crew, and had Wild's protection (though I made sure he did not jabber that in front of my lover). We pattered of Field later between ourselves.

'I'm yet p-p-peery of that cove,' Jack told me.

'Then we'll have our own lock, a cribb or warehouse, where we might stow our goods. Then we might deal with him on our own terms.'

'Bene,' Jack agreed.

And so we were set to plan our next lay but trouble dupped in once more. Jack's brother had been foolish in disposing of the goods they had filched from the draper's shop they had milled in Clare Market. Tom had tried to sell some items to a flat cove, who had squeaked to the beaks and constables. Jack was nettled. 'The l-l-lully-prig's gone and got himself snabbled!' he snapped, as he came into the brandy-shop at darkmans. 'He's been put in the Whit.'

The Whit was what all in the canting-crew called Newgate, as it was prattled that Dick Whittington, the lord mayor with the mouser, had had the trib built there. There was no time for me to patter that I had been right all along in saying we should fence our loot peerily for now the widd might be blown on us.

For biding in the Whit with a glimmed paw meant Tom might be condemned for the tree next sessions and Jack feared his brother might not sit mum-chance.

We soon heard that we had been babbled. Tom had peached us both in the hope of being admitted King's evidence, that he might be marinated rather than scragged. The hue-and-cry was out for us so we shut up shop and shabbed off from Lewkenor Lane. Jack had a pal with a cribb in Blackmoor Street who agreed to screen us there. We would stow ourselves awhile, that was the plan.

We brushed upon the sneak by lightmans and attended to any public business in the night. We melted the hours in the sky-parlour of the ken where we could tout all that came and went upon the pad. But Jack was soon nettled by this confinement – he couldn't bear to be cooped up for long. And it didn't help that at this time I started to feel queer at peep of day, a sickness that made it hard to hold any prog.

We padded it out when we could and one afternoon touted Hell-and-Fury Sykes by Seven Dials so we stopped to learn the prattle. Hell-and-Fury did not seem to know if there was a warrant out for us, which was strange. Indeed, he adopted a manner so casual that it seemed all was bene.

'Come for a game of ninepins this darkmans,' he pattered to Jack. 'There's a boozing-ken around here with a skittle-alley. We could find us a couple of chubs.'

Sykes was known to work the drop on culls with this sport by screening his expertise and pretending to be lully at it. Then when the stakes were raised he could earn good coin in showing his true prowess.

I should have stalled Jack from this crank diversion but I was still feeling ill and out of sorts. Sykes made a clever move, for it is surely easier to lure a man into a foolish business than a serious one. These fine coves who consider morts to be driven by trifles themselves find the prospect of some little sport or wager irresistible. Of course, Jack was not to know that Hell-and-Fury was on the babble and he found himself to be the chub that night. The pair of skittle-players at the alehouse in Seven Dials proved to be constables of the parish so he was snabbled and committed for the night to the lock-up at St Giles' Roundhouse where he had come to rescue me the year before.

I bided in our cribb in Blackmoor Street, not knowing what to do, but Jack dupped in in the middle of darkmans. I was shocked by his sudden appearance. His phiz was as pale as a ghost's and indeed he seemed transported by some mad spirit.

'What happened?' I asked him.

'I escaped, Bess!' he gasped, his glaziers glim and wild. 'I k-k-kicked away from there!'

And he babbled it all to me like some soul-driver in a crank state of grace. He had been confined in a cell on the top floor of the roundhouse. He had an old razor stowed, which he had used, along with the stretcher of a chair, to mill a hole in the ceiling, spreading his mattress below to muffle the sound of falling plaster. As he dug his way out onto the roof it was nine at night with a push of people on the pad below. With the sound of tiles showering from above and the hue-and-cry that a prisoner was breaking out, there was soon a large gathering for this gape-seed. Jack quickly tied a sheet and blanket together and slid down at the back of the roundhouse into St Giles' churchyard.

'Th-th-then I jumped over the wall and joined the push,

p-p-pointing up to where I had just come from, c-c-calling, "Look! There he goes, behind the chimney!"'

He acted it all out in front of me, like a person possessed, of how amid the confusion he had shabbed off into the night. And I twigged then that this was his true art: escape. He had found what poets and other hackney-scribblers call the muse, the quickening spirit that guides the music-merchant or phiz-monger. To break in was but a simple skill for him now; to break free, that could be his real genius.

'I escaped!' he jabbered once more, as if the word itself had some enchantment to it.

And he pattered that it was in the very moment of deliverance that he had felt truly alive and at liberty.

Soon, prattle of his exploits was heard throughout the Hundreds of Drury. This would be his fame, his calling. He would cut his way through the bonds of the world and carve his name upon it. He would star the glaze of the very sky if he could and mill the ken of heaven.

As I held onto him that night, I wished I could stow him somewhere safely in my heart, yet feared that he might think of me as another shackle. But I loosened my embrace as he fell into slumber for another reason, that of a presence of something nestling between us. No, something within me. And I canted what the sickness I felt could mean now.

At peep of lightmans I padded out to see Mother Midnight, a rabbit-catcher, who used to serve us jades in the academies. She touted me up and down and had a good feel of my breasts and belly. It didn't take her long to twig that I was with child. 'You'll soon feel the quickening of it.' She sighed.

As she looked up from my body to my phiz I caught her weary

frown. I knew what she was thinking: another poor whore stuck with a squeaker. My own face was a blank, though, and she must have touted the uncertainty on it.

'Do you want to keep it?' she pattered softly.

And I felt my gob make a ghost of a smile, my head give a slight nod. 'Yes,' I said, surprised by some crank thrill.

'Then keep off the lightning, nabs,' said the rabbit-catcher, showing the gap in her grinders as she grinned at me.

I didn't know what to think as I padded back to Blackmoor Street. I wanted to jabber it all to Jack, but there was a queer chance that he was not the father. It might be Jonathan Wild's squeaker I was quick with, and I couldn't cant what to do if that was true. All I knew was that I wanted the child and nothing else mattered much.

As I dupped into our cribb Jack touted me smokily and I had a crank feeling that he suspected something.

'Where have you been?' he demanded.

'What's the matter?' I pattered. 'Don't you trust me?'

'I've been peached by my own brother, Bess. Why should I trust anyone?'

So I was peery of telling him anything yet, and I decided to sit mum-chance on it for a while.

A week later we were padding out across Leicester Fields and we came across a small push around a mort and a gentry-cove. He was making a fuss, claiming that this sly jade had tried to dive for his clickman toad. The crank cull even held it out for all to see.

'Tout this, Bess,' Jack muttered to me, and I canted that he meant to nab the watch.

'No, Jack,' I whispered to him.

But he did not heed me and in a wanton impulse snatched it right out of the man's paw. He then piked it away across the square. I carried on padding it slowly, canting that there was no better way of drawing gape-seed than running away from a crime. Sure enough, Jack flew straight into a burly sergeant of the guards outside Leicester House and so was taken. I was nettled by such foolishness and wondered fleetingly at how such an impetuous creature might make a father for my child.

But for now there was real danger at hand. As he was handed over to the constables of the watch he called out to me: 'Go and fetch Kate!'

I twigged what this meant so I shabbed off back to our cribb. I canted that he would be taken to a lock-up for the night, this time St Anne's Roundhouse in Soho. So in the middle of dark-mans I padded it up there, the spike of the halberd stowed in my petticoat. But in my haste I did not hide the kate well enough and it was touted by one of the turnkeys. I was snabbled, too, as Jack's accomplice.

At lightmans we were brought before the beak who heard the evidence that Tom had babbled, as well as the filching of the watch in Leicester Fields. He committed us both to the New Prison in Clerkenwell, recorded us as man and wife, and we were put in the same cell.

'A proper honeymoon for a Westminster wedding,' Jack quipped darkly.

I smiled at this queer jest. A rogue and a whore, our union had no gospel-shop blessing or parish record and few of the gentry-coves or middling sort would see any sanctity in our marriage. But while the flat world might sneer at how we made rough wedlock by jumping the sword, here in the hold of a filthy trib, Romeville had pronounced us and I felt a crank pride in that.

My husband had a bitter dowry, though. The governor of the New Prison had heard the prattle of Jack's escape from St Giles and was determined to keep him safe. So he was put in fetters and ankle-irons with heavy double-linked chains. Our bridal chamber was the most secure cell at the very top of the prison.

I was yet uncertain of that other proof of my matronage, the little witness that would soon turn evidence on me. The doubt of whose seed it was kept me balanced in thought. And for all I cared about Jack I coldly reasoned that this could be my way out of there. That I could plead my belly when it came to trial. I would have to patter of it soon but I was peery of blowing the widd yet.

For Jack was now peached for a handful of felonies, each one a capital charge. If it went to the next sessions at the Old Bailey there seemed no doubt he'd be condemned to scrag at the fatal tree. If he was scared he screened it well. He spent a long time just watching and waiting. Touting every inch of the four walls, the ceiling, the barred glaze of our hole. Jack yet had his tools safe and they were smuggled in piece by piece by coves and morts that came to visit. Even Poll Maggot stowed a file or two and brought it to us. I was still peery of that jade but canted it was best to keep her close where I could tout her.

By now Jack was sizing up the job. One moment as easy as a journeyman tallying a bit of piecework, the next grave as some noble architect making grand measurements (though to mill rather than to build). We had been first confined on a Wednesday, and Jack decided he would make his move on the fifth day. That

Sunday had a holiday after it and he reasoned it might divert some from our trail.

I had melted the hours thinking on how I would tell Jack about being quick with child. Having so much time to ponder just made it harder. For I now had time to reflect upon myself and that did not make for pleasant gape-seed. I had been such a wicked jade all these years, how could I hope to be a good mother? The poor squeaker stood but a queer chance of it and I was yet unsure as to who was its father.

So I sat mum-chance until Sunday. At darkmans the turnkeys left us and Jack set to work, filing at his fetters. I had stripped down to my shift and was tearing at my petticoats to make the rope as he had instructed. In that state of near-nakedness I at once felt coy and unguarded. I thought I felt something stir within and I let out a sigh. Jack looked up from his labours. 'What is it, Bess?'

'Jack . . .'

'What?'

'I'm with child.'

'Oh,' he said. He stopped his work for a moment. His glaziers went blank and seemed to peer at nothing. Then that determined frown creased his phiz once again and he continued to saw at his bonds.

I waited for him to say something more but nothing came. At last I could bear it no longer. 'Do you cant what I'm saying?' I demanded.

'Yes,' he replied. 'B-b-but there's little time. We've got to hurry.'

'But, Jack . . .'

'We'll speak of it later.'

I was nettled at this. He did not want it, I twigged. He was but a child himself. I even thought of how things would stand if it was Wild's, that I might at least find some provision from that quarter.

Jack had soon unchained himself and set to work on the glaze. The way through the window was blocked by an iron bar and an oak beam. The first he filed through without too much trouble. The second was harder, for though it was wood it was nine inches thick. So with the use of a gimlet he made a row of holes that he could then saw through easily.

I had by now plaited most of the rope with the torn sheet and petticoats. Jack climbed up onto the sill of the glaze and peeped out. Then he leaped down and came close to me, bussing me on the mouth. 'I love you, Bess,' he whispered softly.

I gasped, shocked by this sudden declaration.

He put his hand to my belly and his dark eyes glimmed. 'I w-w-wanted to say before . . .'

'What?'

'Th-th-this.' He patted me once more. 'I'm so happy for this. I'll kick away on my own, now. You stay here.'

'What do you mean?'

'You can get free another way, see? You can p-p-plead your belly, now. Say that I b-bitched you into being my accomplice. P-peach me if you have to. Just,' he touched that tender part a third time and smiled, 'just keep this one safe.'

I shook my head. I knew then that it was his. I couldn't prove it, of course, but that didn't matter any more. He loved me and the child I bore: that was all that mattered.

'I'm coming with you, Jack,' I said. 'We both are.'

So he lowered me down first and I felt I was flying over Clerkenwell. He worked the cord so slowly and carefully that I was certain I could trust him and the words he pattered. And though I knew no trust bides long in Romeville, as we shabbed off back to the Hundreds it was as if nothing could stop us or get in our way. As he dupped into Drury Lane, we caught the first glim of lightmans. It was Whit Monday and we both laughed heartily at the jest of that.

Newgate Gaol, 14th February 1726

Dear Applebee,

Do you remember that Whitsun week and how the news of
Sheppard's escape from New Prison echoed down the
Hundreds of Drury? I swear I heard a ballad of it sung in a
tavern just two days after Jack and Bess kicked away.

And soon enough there was gossip of it in the coffee-
houses. Murmurings of some miraculous gaol-break and of
the law defied. A whisper of that old terror for the gentility:
a spark of liberty. There was nothing of it yet in the newspapers or journals – the flat world did not know what to
make of it. But while Grub Street kept quiet, the canting-
crew made this act their proud boast. For it was a new kind
of story and one that belonged to them. Not the repentance
of the condemned but the disobedience of the free. It took a
while for us hackney-scribblers to work out how to set it
down but this was not just news to the flash citizens of
Romeville. The street has its own press with living stories
printed on it and the rumours that passed in those weeks
before Jack's next escapade already spoke of something like a
legend.

All looked to see how the thief-taker would act against
Sheppard, who now seemed in open dissent against his corporation, but Wild was occupied in another matter. It was whispered among those of us in the know that his great
spruce-prig lay was planned for August in Windsor, where the
Court moves for a month and holds a great instalment of the
Knights of the Garter. And sure enough he soon called us
together. We had a new dancing-master.

'I'm afraid our old caper-merchant has died in his profession,' he told us, with a gleam in his eye.

'What? From dancing?' someone asked.

'Yes,' he replied. 'The Tyburn jig. Poor Mr Lin was hanged last month at Kingston for robbery on the highway.'

And the whole crew fell into laughter. We then set to work, brushing up on our steps, perfecting the correct manner of taking a partner's hand, of marking out time and rhythm. And into this choreography we worked the delicate method of nipping bungs and filching jewels.

Another of the principal spruce-prigs was Roger Johnson, a bold fellow who ran an operation to take any stolen goods that could not be fenced safely by Wild out of the country. The thief-taker now owned a small ship that sailed to Holland or Flanders and would return with contraband.

Johnson was a sly one. It was said that he had once even testified against his own mother to save his neck. As a young man he had 'preached the parson', that felony where a rogue pretends to be a minister of the Church in order to make some fool part with their money. So he was skilled in the arts of dissembling and deception but his manner of speaking was quite coarse. Wild asked me to tutor him a little and we found a quiet corner away from the main rehearsals.

'Don't worry about the patter, Billy,' Johnson assured me, after I vainly tried to civilise his tongue. 'I can work the drop without it. What we need to twig is how to deal with the prig-napper.'

'What?'

'It'll be rum loot we'll be clicking on this lay. We can bitch a bene price out of him.'

'I don't like the sound of that, Roger.'

'Then sit mum-chance and I'll go my own way. I know how to deal with Jonathan. I'm as bad as he is.'

I laughed. 'Is it true you peached your own mother?'

'You have to be bad, Billy. In Romeville man is seldom bad enough.'

With the spruce-prigs Wild had assembled an elite crew that knew how to work a lay with some finesse. He was yet to realise that one of them was ready to use that very finesse against him.

We returned to where Hell-and-Fury Sykes was instructing those that played the part of our footmen and valets. Sykes had gained favour with Wild by babbling on Jack in Seven Dials but now he dared not show his face much amid the Hundreds of Drury. The canting-crew could still prove unruly in that quarter but the thief-taker had many spies and was certain he could bitch any cove in Romeville. That bright summer saw him approach the height of his powers and none could have imagined that a prig might pose any kind of challenge to him, least of all Jack Sheppard.

I remain sir, &c.,

William Archer Esq.

V

'Bess, is it?'

Mary Sheppard touted me with scorn when Jack introduced us. After we kicked away from the New Prison that Whit Monday we went to screen ourselves at his mother's cribb in Clare Market for the darkmans. We had not met before and in truth I was peery of her and what she might think of me. Sure enough, as we dupped in I could see she canted me as a sly jade to put the bite on her precious boy.

'Well, g-get her a ch-chair, Mother,' Jack jabbered.

By the glimstick I could twig where my lover got his dimber looks. Her pale phiz was lined with age but it yet held those fine and delicate features she had passed on to him. And those deep dark glaziers that glimmed with passion.

'A chair?' she demanded.

'Y-Y-Yes, she's, she's . . .'

'I'm quick with child, Mrs Sheppard,' I told her, and the tout of her phiz changed.

'Then why didn't you say, dear?' she pattered softly, as she bade me sit and dragged a stool over to settle by me. All her peeriness was quitted and she became warm in her manner with me as Jack tipped her a glass of brandy.

'Nearly lost this one when he first came out,' she prattled. 'Got him christened the day he was born he was such a frail one. Didn't think he'd last. Well, look at him now.'

It was clear that Jack was the glim spark of her eye and she of his. That dark cherub was bound to her through love and rebellion. And though the squeak for attention he first made to her now called out to the world, he was his mother's son right to the end. I did not want to be touted as smoky of this bond but nor would I be bitched into merely being part of their family. Me and Jack had palled up for business as well as pleasure and I had no wish to become his quiet little wife.

But as we found another cribb in the Hundreds to stow ourselves I noted a new arrogance to my lover's disposition. We had to brush upon the sneak, never knowing who to trust or what queer chance might blow the widd on us but Jack padded it with a swagger. He took to carrying a loaded popp with him at all times, and though we mostly haunted the back-alleys and night-cellars, he liked to be rigged in the finest dress.

He had milled the ken of a tailor's and filched some rum loot from the strongbox there as well as some fine apparel. Among the rigging spoken with was a suit of fine paduasoy silk with gold lace and exquisitely embroidered lappets. It had been made for a fat man and might have fetched fifteen or twenty pounds but Jack spent good money on having it tailored to fit his dimber frame.

Dupping into some flash-ken he would delight in making an impression, bitching the respect out of all the rum-coves there as well as drawing the eye of every mort and jade in the place.

He spent long days screening himself and touting out that he was not being tracked, then brief nights when he took pleasure in being the gape-seed of Romeville.

Then came the news that Joe Blueskin was out of the Compter. It was prattled that Wild had stopped paying his garnish but Blueskin had found two flat culls to stand the surety of his good behaviour. He had been up before a queer old beak who was peery to grant bail and pondered aloud how long it might be before we might see the defendant at the Old Bailey. Some wit called out, 'Three sessions!' As it turned out this grim jest was an exact prediction.

But now all Romeville jabbered of the freedom of this wild rogue and at last sat mum-chance awhile of the daring escapes of Sheppard. This nettled Jack as he had grown well used to being the toast of the canting-crew. We dupped into the Black Lion on the darkmans of Blueskin's liberty and a rum push of the flash world was there to welcome him. The room hushed as all touted to see how these two now infamous prigs would greet each other. Glazier to glazier, each man measured the other. They were of roughly the same age, though Blueskin was the older offender, having performed numberless robberies well before the other had even started as a thief. None could deny Jack's prowess, though, at the one skill all villains wish for.

'W-W-Welcome back, sir,' he said, with a nod.

Blueskin's gob widened into a grin. 'If I had been you, sir,' he replied, 'I might have been out sooner.'

The room broke into laughter and Jack raised his clanker in salutation. 'To B-B-Blueskin!' he called.

A pair of fiddlers struck up a lively air, the dancing started and so began a celebration that lasted till peep of lightmans.

Nursing a clanker of ale, as I had sworn off the lightning or any strong lush, I was content to stand back and spectate upon the revelry. Indeed, I had little need for booze or company: being with child brought a deeper happiness and its own cure for loneliness.

Jack was besieged by admirers, cove and mort alike. He seemed fair suited to his new fame, though perhaps he wore it too well. Later I touted him and Blueskin pattering intently and, for a moment, the dark rogue looked over at me. In time he padded across to where I stood. 'Elizabeth,' he announced, with a curt bow.

'Joseph,' I replied, giving his true name as well to jest at this mock formality.

We both laughed.

'So, you jumped the sword with Jack,' he said.

'I did.'

'You grew tired of waiting for me, then?'

'I was never waiting,' I said, with a scowl. 'How was the trib?'

He sighed. 'With enough garnish and good books it's not so bad. I read all of Pope's Homer.'

'You'll be a wise old man yet.'

'"Who dies in youth and vigour dies the best,"' he quoted.

'I dearly hope you don't believe that.'

'So you do care for me, after all.'

'Not you, you rogue. But you plan to pal up with Jack?'

'Perhaps.'

'Then I fear for him, that you might lead him into greater danger.'

'You are so cruel, Bess, with this harsh division of your affections.'

His smile brought out the crease of a scar, the sabre wound from when he was taken in Southwark. He was still dimber, though, and full of charm. I gave him a tight frown. 'Now, as for palling up,' I pattered.

'So cold and businesslike, with no kind words for an old friend.'

'Stow your widds, Joe, and cant on the matter at hand. We're using William Field as a fence.'

'Bene. He's an old prig.' Blueskin shrugged and touted me knowingly. 'And well connected with a certain party.'

He meant Jonathan Wild, of course.

'How does your credit stand with him?' I asked.

'I don't know. It's the old game of mouse and mouser with him. But,' he sighed, 'we all have to deal with the prig-napper in the end.'

'I'm afraid Jack doesn't see it that way.'

'Well, he's not been on the pad as long as us. He'll learn in time.'

'If he lives long enough. Just tread softly with him, can you? Then we can see about approaching Wild.'

'You're a clever one, Bess.'

'You cant that?'

'For certain. Anyone might think you were running this crew,' said Blueskin.

'I am.' I smiled at him. 'Just don't let Jack know it. He's a proud one.'

He laughed and put his phiz close to mine, a glim grin on his bleach grinders. 'He's a lucky cove,' he pattered softly. 'I'm quite smoky.'

'Listen, Blueskin,' I hissed, a paw against his chest. 'Jack's more likely the smoky one if he twigs what passed between you and me.'

'Bene.' He put his hands up and drew back. 'Bene. I'll brush upon the sneak.'

'That's the widd.'

'Here's luck, then.' He took my paw and tipped it a buss. 'And don't worry, we'll all live to a ripe old age. We'll not sack a city like those Greek prigs, just take what we need. "Chiefs, who no more in bloody fights engage, but wise through time, and narrative with age . . ."' Spouting Homer once more, he made his way back into the push of carousing, calling, "In summer days, like grasshoppers rejoice, a bloodless race, that send a feeble voice."'

I laughed and shook my head as he padded away from me. Then I turned and saw Poll Maggot a little way across the room. She had been touting us all this time, and when she caught my gaze I saw a crank smile on her phiz.

So we formed our crew: small and tight-cocked was the plan. Jack, Blueskin, William Field and myself. We rented a stable by the horse-ferry in Westminster to use as a lock for all the goods we might filch. Here we might stow any booty safely away from our cribbs and without too much concern of how to dispose of it. That would give Field time to be able to fence what was spoken with discreetly.

But as we made such peery preparations, Jack was as impetuous as ever. He now entertained the crank notion of setting himself up as a high-pad. And as he spoke of it Blueskin laughed and joined in the bold patter. Neither had any experience of the rattling-lay but I supposed that each considered the gentlemen of the road to be the most valiant of prigs and felt their accumulated fame now demanded that they might be considered among the loftiest order of the canting-crew.

They held such store by their precious reputation yet they were like boys transported by those lurid tales of highwaymen. But some ever see life as a game and let others settle the score. Indeed, I had once seen existence as but a cruel wager. Now there was a chance it might be more than that. The child growing within me had given me hope but another's soul to risk as well and in truth it frightened me. It didn't help that I was palled up with a pair of natty-lads so keen on needless hazard.

I noted a dangerous rivalry in it, too. As they were seduced by such foolish sport each desired to be the boldest ruffian. I chided Blueskin when we found ourselves alone together. 'So much for taking it easy with Jack,' I said.

'He's a wild rogue, Bess. I fear he'll never let himself be bitched by the prig-napper.'

'He's smoky of you, don't you see? Yet you goad him on.'

'Perhaps he's got a reason to be,' he said, and padded up close. 'I used to blow your coals, remember?'

'I'm his wife, Joe,' I jabbered, and turned from him.

'That's a pity.' He leaned over and whispered in my lugg, 'We could make a bargain with Jonathan without him.'

From then on I found myself peery of what Blueskin might be plotting and all the more certain that we should act upon any lay with caution. I hoped the thought of a squeaker on the way might calm Jack down yet I feared it seemed but a fancy to him as we hadn't pattered of it to anyone else and didn't plan to until it began to show. So I spoke of it in bed one darkmans.

'I don't want to be a hempen-widow, Jack,' I said, and bussed him on the cheek. 'I want my child to have its father.'

He turned his phiz to face mine and bussed me back. 'They c-can't catch me, Bess.'

This was the crank confidence of his. He had started to believe in the stories that were prattled of him. And there was no benefit in arguing at this.

'I know,' I pattered. 'But one day . . .'

'Don't w-worry. W-We'll make some rum loure and pike it to Daisyville,' he reached under the blanket to pat my belly. 'We'll raise this one far from filthy Romeville.'

So we curled up together in that fanciful dream. But as we slumbered the child moved inside me. I awoke feeling this fierce struggle within, as if the little one was trying to kick away from the prison of its own parlous fate. I rubbed the bump of it softly with my paws, hushing it with whispers that all would be well. Those lully words were as much for me as for the baby, a desperate promise to myself that I might make a good mother yet.

And Jack slept on beside me, in sweet oblivion from all those worries, no doubt dreaming of more trouble he could cause. I sighed, thinking it certainly would be good to get enough money to run away somewhere together with our child. If only there was a simple way of doing it.

William Field, at least, had a steady disposition. It was bene to have one of our crew determined on cold business. With that one queer glazier that seemed to tout elsewhere, he always had an eye on the main chance, ready to game on the shortest odds. Apprenticed in Hitchen's Mathematicians, he had been part of the canting-crew longer than any of us, and I hoped that soon he might patter the right widd in the thief-taker's lugg.

We were padding it down Drury Lane one darkmans, Jack, Field and myself, and as we got to the corner of the Strand my sweetheart pointed to a fine house, a woollen-draper's premises between a gospel-shop and the Angel tavern.

'There's a ken worth milling,' he told us.

Field was not so sure as it looked secure, but Jack pattered that he was acquainted with every part of the house and that it could be cracked at leisure. He even canted where the valuables were and was certain we could speak with three hundred pounds' worth there. So it was agreed that would be our next lay.

When I asked him later how he canted so well of the ken, he was quite coy with me.

'For God's s-sake, don't let M-Mother know,' he jabbered.

'Why ever not?'

'Because I lodged there w-w-when I was a kid.'

He prattled that many years before the draper, a certain Mr Kneebone, had taken pity on the slender circumstances of the Sheppard family and had brought Jack under his care for a while until he could be settled into a trade. So Jack knew every detail of the house and, in particular, where the strongbox was stowed.

'Poor gratitude for such kindness,' I jested, in mock solemnity, but this nettled Jack.

'I b-b-begged for no charity then or now! I'll t-take what I want!'

Jack used great stealth in the milling of the ken of his benefactor. There were large oaken bars on the cellar window at the back part of the house that he would carefully weaken at darkmans by intervals for near a fortnight. I would tout upon the pad as he made a series of holes with a gimlet, as he had done in our cell in New Prison, so when the time came to crack the place it would be a simple matter. I worked stall and lookout, canting that the jades who plied their trade on that corner would tip me a warning if they touted any constables of the watch abroad.

Then, on the night of the lay, I stood guard with Blueskin as Jack cut through the beams he had prepared and slipped through the glaze. He then opened the jigger for Blueskin to dup in and they both went up the dancers into the shop. But as I bided on the pad a rake approached quite pot-valiant.

'Ah, sweetheart,' he called. 'Come walk with me.'

I ignored the cull but he persisted, wishing to procure me for himself. I could not allow him to tarry long lest he touted what was afoot. 'Would you be ready to make love, sir?' I asked him.

'Surely,' he slurred, his glaziers beaming.

'Then you'll find it ready-made on Catherine Street,' I snapped.

'But, sweetheart—'

'Pike it!' I pattered harshly. 'Before I call my twang.'

That sent him on his way, which was bene: Jack and Blueskin were quitting the ken just at that moment. I helped them carry the booty down to the Savoy Stairs where we had a waterman biding. I noted that the bag with the silver in it seemed a little light. Then we were rowed down to the horse-ferry where we conveyed our loot to our lock there.

But this lay did not stand to bring in as much loot as they had expected. We made off with some good cloth and plate but not worth much more than fifty pounds and all canted that it would fetch less. William Field set about fencing the goods and found a cove in Bishopsgate Street, who pattered that he could dispose of some of the material. But on the darkmans he was to meet the man word got to us that Field had been snabbled, though none knew which trib he was being held at.

We became suspicious of each other. When Blueskin went to tout on the lock in Westminster two days later, Jack pattered that he would pad it with him: he was peery as to what his accomplice might be up to. But they found it milled and all filched but for a wrapper or two of no value. Some cove was playing rob-thief with us.

Then, a day or two after that, an advertisement appeared in the *Daily Post* offering twenty pounds and a pardon for anyone who would give themselves up and *discover his accomplices in the robbery of one piece of scarlet drab cloth with several pieces and remnants of colour'd broad cloth, two silver spoons, a light tye wig and other things from Mr Wm Kneebone woollen-draper at the Angel at the corner of Drury Lane and the Strand*. This was common practice of the thief-taker in directing any prig to fence the stolen goods through him for a snack of the reward mentioned. But we no longer had the loot to bargain with. It seemed a trap was being laid.

So Jack and Blueskin twigged it would be best to quit Romeville and operate beyond its confines for a spell. They resolved to act as high-pads as they had pattered and set out upon the rattling-lay. Furnished with prancers, popps and a bold disposition they rode out on the Hampstead Road.

They stalled a rattler with a ladies' maid of a gentry-mort on it and filched half-a-crown from her. The next night they came across a pot-valiant cove by a halfway house on the turnpike. Blueskin dinged him with the butt of his popp but they found only three shillings in his bung. The following darkmans they held up a stage-coach for twenty-two shillings, then retired to Blueskin's mother's brandy-shop in Wapping to avoid any hue-and-cry in the Hundreds of Drury.

I got word that they planned to tarry in the east awhile but the very next evening I received a message from Jack to meet him in a brandy-shop by Temple Bar. It was the end of lightmans when I dupped into the ken and the bluffer directed me up the dancers to a cribb above. In the gloom I could make out a figure sitting near a table by the glaze. As I entered someone sparked the glim. Then I heard the jigger close behind me and a key turning in its lock. The light now filled the room and as I spun round I caught sight of Quilt standing at the door.

'Where's Jack?' I demanded.

Quilt just nodded, glaring beyond me. I turned back and saw Jonathan Wild sitting there.

'That's what we want to know, Bess,' said Wild, pushing a stool towards me with his boot. 'Sit down.' He tapped the floor with his silver-hilted sword and patted his huge ledger book, which lay on the table beside him. His pale eyes scanned me as I sat down before him. 'I'm investigating the robbery of the house of a certain Mr Kneebone,' he pattered. 'He wants his goods back.'

'We don't have them.'

'Oh dear. Well, we'll need to peach someone, then.'

'We could make a deal.'

'What with? You've just said you don't have his goods. I want Jack for the felony.'

'What?'

'You heard me. You owe me for Punk Alice.' He prodded his ledger book. 'Remember?'

'He's my husband, Jonathan.'

'That's the pity of it, Bess. But I need a body and you owe me one. Give her a drink, Quilt.'

Wild's assistant poured out a glass and handed it to me. I drank it down quickly without thinking, then nearly choked. It was gin. Neat, but not pure. Something bitter in it. Perhaps they were trying to poison my senses, but I thought of something quickly. 'Then you can have me,' I pattered.

'What?'

'I confess.'

Wild grinned, baring that blackened grinder in his gob. But his glaziers dulled and I touted that he could not cant the drop I was working. Like a gamester I had a card in my paw he couldn't scan and it nettled him.

'Take me to the beak and I'll peach myself,' I went on. 'I know every detail of the robbery and can swear that I did it. Then you'll have your body. We'll be quits at last.'

Wild frowned. 'You'd hang in Jack's stead?'

'Yes.'

He shook his head slowly, and I twigged that he knew I was stowing something from him. His eyes touted me closely, trying to read my blank phiz. I felt a little sick – indeed, there was something queer in the lush. But I found that I could stay calm as I went through the plan in my head.

I would patter that I was guilty at the next sessions at the Old Bailey and swear that I had acted alone, without accomplices. But when the sentence was passed I would plead the belly and a jury of matrons would be called to tout that I was quick with child. This would grant me a reprieve from a scragging and maybe even a pardon. I could not forbear smiling at the prig-napper as I canted the cleverness of this scheme. He could not work the drop of it and I twigged that I had gulled him.

'No!' He stood up and went to the glaze. 'No. I won't have it. You'll hang when I want you to and not before. Bring our little friend in, Quilt.' He nodded at his henchman and followed him to the jigger so to lock it behind him. My head lolled and I felt a slight fever. Then came a yawning swoon through my whole being, my guts heaved and I retched onto the floor.

'What did you put in the lush?' I asked.

'Laudanum.' Wild sighed and padded over to me. 'It's supposed to loosen the tongue. It just made you crank.'

He handed me a wiper and I dabbed my gob with it. There was a knock on the door and Wild went to open it. A short cove dupped in after Quilt. It was William Field. The prig-napper addressed him. 'Bess here has just confessed to robbing Mr Kneebone's house,' he said, waving the sword in its scabbard in my direction. 'What do you think to that?'

Field let out a queer laugh, his squint eye touting right through me. Then, in one swift and clean movement, Wild drew his sword and held the point of it at Field's throat. There was a fearful yelp. I could tout the terror on his phiz.

'We can't have that, can we?' Wild continued. 'We must discover the true culprit.'

'Uhn?' Field croaked, his neck dry with fear.

'It's you, isn't it, William?'

'What?'

'Come on, confess it, man. Don't let an innocent party suffer on your behalf.'

'But I don't—'

'I'll tip you a fine coffin, William, and I promise you'll not be anatomised.'

The thief-taker pressed the blade so the tip now dug into the flesh.

'Please,' Field begged.

'Confess,' Wild insisted coldly. 'Or I'll gut you right now. No one will miss you.'

And so William Field admitted to the felony and even made his mark on a sheet of paper that Quilt put before him. Now I could not cant what was being played and I felt the drug rush through my blood, part sickness, part exquisite warmth.

Wild turned to me. 'So that's settled,' he said, and sheathed his sword. 'Now your part of the deal, Bess.'

'Deal?'

'Yes. You wanted a deal for Jack, didn't you? We just need to know where he is. You can let him know we've a body for the Kneebone lay.'

I spat out some more bile and felt my will slip from me. Some dread ease was taking hold of my senses. There was a cramp in my stomach but the pain of it seemed distant, like the memory of something. The lightning and foul poppy juice was poisoning my mind. I lost all care of myself or even sense of who I was. But that other self, the little soul who shared my body, called out to me and I felt for it.

'Where?' Wild repeated. 'Tell me where, then we can go and patter with him.'

I knew I had to get out of there. I had to find a safe place.

'Blueskin.' I groaned. 'Blueskin's mother.'

'The blackie's mother runs a boozing ken in Wapping,' Quilt explained. 'Rosemary Lane.'

'Then get a posse,' said Wild. 'And get Justice Blackerby to sign the warrant. I want Sheppard safe by morning.'

'What?' I pattered.

Wild laughed. 'Oh, you thought you could play me, Bess. But now you've paid the debt. Field's confessed, so he might give evidence against his accomplices. Your sweetheart's one of them. If he peaches Jack he'll get an acquittal.'

'He wasn't even there.'

'Well, that'll hardly be held against him in court.'

163

I lifted my head and looked around. My thoughts were clearer. I seemed sobered by my confession, brought round by the cold truth of what I had uttered. That I had betrayed Jack.

Quilt unlocked the door and quit the room. Wild's deputy was off to the brandy-shop in Wapping: I would have to get word there somehow. Field stood at the jigger and gave me a cock-eyed stare. I twigged that he had been a sneak and rob-thief all along.

'You can pike off, too,' Wild jabbered at him and, with a fretful giggle, Field was gone. 'Better stay with me awhile, Bess. Until Jack is nicely tucked up.'

'So, I lost the game,' I pattered, though I touted the key was still in the door.

'I didn't cant what you meant by confessing, Bess.' Wild clapped his sword on the table and sat down. 'Sheppard isn't worth it. All he ever brought you was trouble.'

I couldn't help but admire the prig-napper's guile in tricking me into peaching Jack. I had but one chance left. To shab off out of there.

'Will you keep me out of the evidence?' I edged backwards to the door.

'Of course. As for Blueskin . . .' He shrugged.

I reached out behind me, took the key from the open door and hid it behind my back.

Wild frowned. 'Where are you wandering off to? Come here.'

As he stood I piked through the jigger. He was up and after me but I slammed the door shut and held it there while I got the key in the lock. Wild hammered on the panelling with loud curses. I turned and stepped out onto the landing. I reached the top of the dancers at speed, my head still giddy from the gin and laudanum, thinking only of flight from that place. Then I lost my footing and came tumbling down the staircase.

It was but a short fall and I managed to brush myself down and totter through the brandy-shop. The drug that yet coursed through my body allowed me no pain but there was a sharp queasiness in my stomach. As I made it to the street I felt a wetness on my leg. I was bleeding from my belly.

I staggered to Mary Sheppard's cribb, which was close by. She ran to fetch Mother Midnight but it was too late. I had lost my child. They tried to take it away without my touting it but I had to look. It was a boy.

And when I saw him curled up in the member-mug I wanted to weep and weep but no more would come from me. He was a perfect little thing, like some fairy creature, with a smooth round head and heavy-lidded eyes. He looked so peaceful, a tiny hand clutching at the cord of life, with some spirit yet in him.

That was all I deserved, I thought, to have this cherub taken from me. It was what many a whore would pay for, to be rid of it. I hated myself then and wished my gross and wicked life forfeit, not this small and innocent one. I wrapped him up in a cloth and went out into the darkmans, though Mary and Mother Midnight begged me not to go abroad, fearing what I might do in the madness of grief.

Sneaking into St Giles' churchyard I dug a shallow grave with my bare hands next to the headstone of a gentry-mort and put the baby there. I remembered what Jack's mother had said about how he had been christened on the very day he was born as he had been so frail. Now our own child did not even have that chance, unblessed and peached by the old sin of that fatal Tree of Knowledge.

Then I came back to Mary's cribb in Clare Market, as I'd promised I would. Mother Midnight checked to make sure there was no more bleeding and I fell into a deep slumber, happy to be embraced by an insensible darkness. The following day Jack's Mother tried to tip me prog but all I wanted was lightning and strong lush. Anything to take away the pain of the body and the care of the mind, though there was nothing to take away the agony of my soul.

And that night I learned how Jack had been taken. At peep of day Quilt and a crew of constables broke into Blueskin's mother's brandy-shop. Jack aimed a loaded pistol at Quilt's breast and attempted to shoot him. But the popp misfired, flashing in the pan and, being thus unarmed, he was overpowered and snabbled.

He was brought back to New Prison and the next day carried before the beak who had signed his warrant and committed him to Newgate to appear at the next sessions at the Old Bailey on three indictments of house-breaking. His trial was due in three weeks.

For all of that time I was overcome with melancholia and remained ginned up and befuddled with the lush. A half-life somewhere betwixt sleep and wake, where time turns upside-down. I had dark dreams by day, lucid visions in the night. And I found that grave consolation of despair where nothing mattered so I might stand careless of my own existence.

Like some moonstruck creature of Bedlam I was taken by a queer fancy. I started to ponder on what happens to unbaptised squeakers, and of that place the Romish soul-drivers call Limbo, some bleak trib on the edge of Hell. Here my lost boy would dwell until the end of time. My Jack was in the Whit awaiting trial but our dead child was already in some condemned hold till the final judgment.

And I wondered, Why do people struggle so hard to make more life when it only brings suffering? The morts are worse than the coves since they bring us into this vile world. They commit the worst offence of all: that of hope, a felony that never goes unpunished. Such was my sadness at all of creation.

It was from then that I started to hear the voices in my head. Queer widds that peached me for being bad. Sometimes it was as if my dead baby was pattering to me saying, *Can't plead the belly, now, can you? You old trull.* And so on.

☙

Then one lightmans I awoke and my humour had lifted. I rigged myself and went out, padding it up through the Hundreds as if willed by some new purpose. At peep of day I crossed into the piazza as the market was coming to life. Sun-ruddied country girls bringing their goods from Daisyville in barrows. Carts of apples, cherries and plums, flowers and herbs arranged on stalls. It was one of those bright blue mornings when all seems well in Romeville. Life would go on, I thought, whatever happened to me.

I dupped into Moll King's for a dish of coffee. All at once my head was clear, sharpened by some edge of urgency I could not yet fathom. I had to do something, but what? I turned to Tawny Betty and asked her what day it was. It was a Thursday, she told me, though she did not know the date. Some cull looked up from his newspaper and pattered that it was the 13th of August and it was then I twigged that the sessions had started. Jack might already be on trial.

I piked it all the way through Holborn to the Old Bailey and made my way through the push that was gathered in the sessions-house front yard. Here prosecutors, witnesses and quod-culls mingled with the idle crew of spectators that come to tout the gape-seed that passes for justice. And there were hackney-scribblers, ballad-mongers and those wretched affidavit men that wear wisps of straw in their shoe-buckles to advertise that they will swear false evidence for the right price. Beyond was the spiked wall of the bail-dock, where the prisoners are kept chained and waiting for their trial. I tried to tout for Jack there amid the noise and confusion.

Above us all, the upper court was lined with grand columns, the judges' bench, the jurors' partitions, the balconies for court officials, like a huge puppet-booth, with its pulcinellos dressed in fine wigs and fur-trimmed gowns. As I arrived a case was being heard against a cove from Stepney who pleaded guilty to filching a quantity of scrap iron. He was sentenced to be glimmed in the paw.

Then Jack was called up to appear. As he climbed to the dock in the middle of the vast Justice Hall he looked small and meek, much like the boy apprentice I had first touted in the Black Lion.

'It's the prison-breaker!' someone called in the yard.

His glaziers brightened a little at this recognition but he was still like a child lost in that vast hall of justice. I felt such pity for him and a deep love that touched my own loss. Poor Jack did not even know that our child was gone. All we had now was each other. I knew that I would try anything to save him.

The clerk read out the indictments. The first, of breaking the house of William Philips and stealing diverse goods, was quickly dismissed, there not being sufficient evidence against the prisoner. The second, of breaking the house of Mary Cook of St Clement

Danes, likewise had insufficient evidence and he was acquitted of that also. For a while my spirits rose as I conceived that Jack might yet go free through some simple mistake or absence, that the old blind woman of justice, so often weak-minded and forgetful, might favour us this one time in her muddled insensibility. Then the third indictment was spoken and a witness stood to give testimony.

It was the William Kneebone of whom Jack had pattered to me, the former benefactor he had filched from. He gave detailed evidence in the prosecution of this case, of how he had found his house broken, his goods removed and that he suspected the prisoner. Then his disposition changed somewhat as he recounted how he had visited Jack in the New Prison and asked how he could have been so ungrateful to rob him after being shown such kindness. There was a sad but fond tone to his voice as he told of how the young man had confessed of being unthankful for his charity but said that he had been drawn into crime by bad company. The whole court seemed moved by this feeling of regret rather than anger – even Jack bowed his head in a penitent gesture – and it seemed that some repentance was possible with due reparations or return of the loot. Then everything changed as the next witness stepped up.

The entire sessions house quietened as Jonathan Wild's name was called by the clerk. He bowed to the judge, then scanned the courtroom slowly, as if taking possession of it, knowing it to be as much his domain as that of any begowned official before him.

'It's the prig-napper!' came the same voice from the push that had rudely announced Jack.

Already the mob had marked these men as rivals, but where

Jack seemed cowed, Wild was haughty and arrogant. I noted the sneer on his gob and knew then that I truly hated him. I cursed the thought I had once had that he might have been the father of my child. Now I could only peach him for the murder of it and brood upon my revenge. I touted my enemy closely as he turned to address the recorder.

'The prosecutor Mr Kneebone came to me desiring that I enquire after the goods that had been stolen,' he pattered. 'I told him I suspected the prisoner to have been concerned with the theft as he had committed some robberies in the neighbourhood. I have heard of Jack Sheppard before, you see, and had information that he was an acquaintance of Joseph Blake, alias Blueskin, and William Field, who is here to testify.'

The thief-taker general was making a great play of his art of detection and he now laid his best card, his affidavit man.

'Did you approach this Field?' asked the recorder.

'Yes. I sent for him and told him if he would make an ingenuous confession I might prevail with the court to make him evidence.'

Field then took the stand himself and, having acted as sneak and rob-thief, he was now ready to play the part of straw man. 'The prisoner told me and Blueskin that he knew a ken worth milling,' he babbled to the court.

The recorder then interrupted as he did not cant what he pattered and Field then explained that the prisoner had meant a house worth breaking. It was true that Jack had said this but the verbal cleverness in this testimony was putting some of the flash tongue in my lover's mouth, thus fixing him clearly as one of the canting-crew in the minds of judge and jury, as well as peaching him as the instigator of the felony. The straw man then went on to recount how he had been taken to tout the ken and was persuaded to stand lookout as Jack milled the bars of the cellar, dupped into the shop and carried off the parcels of cloth and the other goods.

I touted Jack's phiz darken with anger as Field pattered his twisted tale, and as he was called upon to make his defence he was crank and utterly lacking in composure.

'He w-w-wasn't even th-there!' he jabbered, pointing at the wretched straw man. But as Wild had pointed out at that brandy-shop in Temple Bar, giving evidence that Field was innocent couldn't stand as much of a defence. Indeed, he had now foolishly made himself the strongest advocate for his own prosecution. Poor Jack, he was so nettled by the deceitfulness of the previous testimony that he quite forgot himself. Making no patter of denial, or plea of mitigation for his guilt, he instead railed against Wild's witness, declaring him to be a seasoned prig and one who lured others into evil practices. But the more he peached Field the more he peached himself, as one was judged by the other. And being thus nettled Jack's stutter became so extreme that his whole speech seemed a crank rant of anger and resentment.

After an absence of barely ten minutes the jury returned a verdict of guilty. Sentence was to be pronounced the following day and Jack was taken back to Newgate by the quod-culls.

The next morning he was brought back into the Justice Hall to hear his sentence. When asked if he had anything to say before it was passed Jack was duly contrite and humble, pleading youth and ignorance as an excuse for his crimes.

'I b-b-beg that I m-m-might be transported to the m-m-most extreme b-boundary of His M-M-Majesty's dominions,' he jabbered earnestly.

But it was too late and there was no mercy as judgment was pronounced.

Death.

Jack called out at the fatal word and a gasp ran through the session's house yard. Death, his breath against the neck of each of the idle crew gathered for the gape-seed there, a whisper of terror to warn us. My lover's glaziers were glim with dread as they took him down but I felt no fear of that gallows scarecrow. Death. He had taken part of me already so I would not flinch if he came for the rest. For at that moment I knew the meaning of the urgent sense I had felt the day before at Moll King's. I knew what I had to do.

I found a hackney-scribbler to write a short note that I could garnish a turnkey to smuggle in to Jack. *Those that condemn you will be proved false prophets, your Bess.* I wanted to cheer him, to make him cant that he was not forsaken. But then I had to conceive the manner of his salvation. There were many plans that would have to be well laid. But we had some respite for the court had now moved to Windsor so the death warrants would not come down to Newgate until the end of the month. Wild had already left for there with his retinue. I would try to find Poll Maggot in that time for I had already devised the most cunning part of my stratagem and that sly bitch could be part of it.

Dear Applebee,

I was in Windsor that August with Jonathan Wild. The
Royal Court was held there for the month with an instalment
of the Knights of the Garter at the Castle. With so much
pomp and ceremony in one place, and now exultant at having
dealt with the troublesome Sheppard, the thief-taker general
was determined to make a grand appearance.

For he had been courting fortune fiercely, establishing his
reputation on both sides of the law. Having already petitioned
the Court of Aldermen for freedom of the City, his aspirations
grew far beyond Romeville. He advised the Privy Council on
criminal policy and now intended that his presumed title of
'Thief-taker General of Great Britain and Ireland' be made
official.

He could discourse well enough with the quality, recounting
his many adventures with a wry humour, displaying a martial
valour and a nobility of arms. But it was a dark charm that
beguiled them. He offered not only protection but also some
mystique. With all his much-vaunted methods of investigation,
his networks of intelligence, his genius of detection, he seemed
to offer an answer to that great riddle of crime. Though we in
the flash world know it as but a craft, for the flat world it is
ever a mystery. They secure their fine houses so that they may
read criminal narratives or scan prints of bold highwaymen.
They wish to be safe in their beds, but in their imaginations
also. So, the conceit that all the wickedness of the world can
be found in those who steal from their fortune comforts them,
persuading them of the pure goodness of its lawful acquisition.

They then can sleep soundly with no implications, with no evidence against them. What dread it would be to wake from that dream and find themselves impeached of being in possession of stolen goods for all this time.

So for all the whispered doubts about Wild, the rumours of his dubious methods, the world above held on dearly to this hope of security. That crime could be solved so simply. It blinded them to the bare fact that their protector was also attending each occasion as leader of a corporation of thieves. For the elegant coterie that I was part of was nothing more than a crew of well-rigged spruce-prigs. This, then, would be his boldest lay and its audacity was staggering. That at such a great occasion of state he might filch from the very nobility he courted.

'The jest of it is, Billy,' Roger Johnson remarked to me, as we lined up to dance, 'that the very presence of the prig-napper tips such a sense of security among the gentry-coves that they lose all peeriness of their possessions.'

I watched Johnson weave through the assembly, following the delicate footwork of each minuet to employ his wicked handiwork on some passing partner. Our new dancing-master had drilled us in all the most modish steps of the ballroom. And in a crowd on the walks, in the push of the long rooms or dance floors, we would steal jewellery, watches and snuff-boxes, then pass the goods quickly to a sham footman so that he might convey them quickly to some place of safety. Such was our sport that season.

But Johnson was behaving in a very strange manner. He had arrived at Windsor separately from us and was already among the court with access to the best pickings. Yet he talked in a queer gibberish in the company of the men and women of quality and had the man playing his valet interpret for him. He explained it all to me out of the earshot of the *beau monde*.

'I twigged I would never get the patter, Billy, so I bribed one of the knight-marshal's men five quid to take me to St James's Palace and have me announced there as a foreign ambassador. Then I tracked the court to Windsor. I jabber backslang to my servant and he can speak my meaning.'

He told me that he also had another accomplice with him that even the thief-taker did not know of, a young spy who could inveigle himself among the true aristocrats and learn what valuables were on offer.

'He's not much of a prig, nor a sharper,' said Johnson, 'but he can personate a gentry-cove well enough and he knows all the prattle.'

Roger was by far the boldest of our crew with a presumptuous demeanour most useful for a spruce-prig. He could be brash, though, and quite reckless. He contrived to pick the Prince of Wales's pocket by tripping him up as he passed through the crowds one evening. Another night he stole a gold watch from a lady as she danced with the King. He seemed ever undaunted in his enterprises, not least in the manner in which he dealt with Wild.

'I'm only tipping the prig-napper my loot one piece at a time,' he confided to me one night. 'I want some bene loure and I'll bide for it if I have to. I can always pike it to Holland and fence it there.'

I was not so accomplished in this lay, though unlike Johnson I could patter well. I found that a foppish and effeminate manner could be used to great effect both in enchanting the ladies, who generally delight in such harmless sport, and with the men, who would hardly wonder at any danger from one with such an unmanly demeanour. In this way I harvested a fine haul of glitter that month.

But I was dazzled by more than mere gold and gemstones while at Windsor. It was that summer that I first spied my soul's desire. A precious jewel of flesh and blood.

I watched as he made his entrance to a ball one evening, dressed exquisitely in light blue paduasoy, gliding in with such genteel deportment. When he was announced as the Honourable Adam Stonyforth he paused and held a pose of sublime decorum. He had the easy grace that only the truly noble seem wholly to possess. He casually scanned the room and I could not help but observe the delicately sculpted face, the eyes that sparkled sapphire, the budding lips of ruby.

This Adam was but a youth yet carried himself with a marvellous self-possession. I was enthralled at once by the handsome boy, and as I eased my way through the crowd towards him, I summoned all the tricks and guiles I had learned as a beau-trap. I was perhaps five or six yards from him when he looked up and held my gaze with a radiance that seemed to read my intent. A smile played on that beauteous mouth and in that very moment I was stung by the fatal dart.

Then a portly fellow blocked my path. I endeavoured to sidestep him but he held my sleeve. 'Unhand me, sir,' I hissed.

'Bootblack!' came the reply. 'Would you cut an old friend?' And there was John Gay, fat and scant of breath, dabbing at his brow with a silk handkerchief. He perused my lavish dress with sad and heavy-hooded eyes. 'Good Lord but you're looking well, Billy.'

'And yourself, sir.' I nodded, looking beyond to try to keep an eye on my young man.

'Nonsense,' Gay went on. 'I've been very ill with the colic. But what brings you here?'

I shrugged. Adam Stonyforth had turned away and was bowing to the Duchess of Queensberry.

'Opportunity?' I ventured.

Gay laughed but I was losing my quarry.

'Yes, very good,' he said. 'We're all looking for that.'

Now the duchess had taken his arm and they were wandering off. I turned to Gay with a sigh. 'Your latest play did well, I hear.'

'Yes, yes,' he said, oblivious to where my true attention was drawn. He went on to recount an improbable story of how he had read it to the Princess of Wales at Leicester House and in a fit of nerves tripped on a footstool and brought down a large screen. He was as ever playing the buffoon, even with me. 'Of course I have a position now,' he told me.

'Indeed?'

'Yes. Commissioner for the State Lottery.'

It was my turn to laugh.

'All the world's a jest, Billy,' he declared. 'And Fortune's fool oversees the luck of the draw. It brings one hundred and fifty a year and rooms in Whitehall. I yet hope for something better and with more certain provision.' He looked around wistfully. 'Something at Court, perhaps,' he murmured.

I took another chance to scan the ballroom but there was no sign of my beautiful boy. I promised myself that I would find him at the earliest opportunity.

'You have much favour,' I told Gay.

'Oh, yes, I know something of the art of pleasing great men. And I receive their civilities but few real benefits. They wonder at each other for not providing for me and I wonder at them all.'

He told me that he had just come from Chiswick where he had been staying with Burlington, and that in September he was to be at Bath with Lord Scarborough. Ever keen to insist upon his status as a poor and honest poet, he was nonetheless happy enough to live off the hospitality of the rich. It struck me that Gay was something of a spruce-prig himself, slyly picking the pockets of his patrons as he took luxury at their expense. He was surely no beggar, but for his livelihood and his art it often suited him to present the attitude of one.

He looked me up and down once more. 'Well, Bootblack,' he said. 'What's this? It appears you have some prospects. I've not seen your ticket come up in the Lottery. You've gained some patronage of your own, perhaps?'

'In a manner of speaking.' I nodded to where Wild was conversing with Sir William Thompson, the solicitor general.

'Why, Billy,' Gay beamed at me, 'you naughty boy.'

Of course he remembered the robbery of Burlington and how I had known more than I should have of that affair. I endeavoured to change the subject and to talk of my own writing, though I had little to offer. But for much hack-work in Grub Street, I had composed a few ballads and scenarios for another harlequinade, mostly dialogue for the Zannis, the white-clad fools who play the lowly parts. But now I felt sure that a great muse lay in wait for me, and as my companion talked, I wondered idly what my feelings for this handsome young Adam might inspire.

But Gay was keen to learn more about Wild and even to make his acquaintance, which was not hard to arrange since he was staying at a tavern near to the thief-taker's lodgings and for once the poet played the host. A private room was procured and a fine dinner laid out with much wine and liquor: a haunch of venison stuffed with oysters in a claret sauce, a fig pudding with cinnamon custard.

'Billy tells me that you're a famous playwright,' said Wild, once I had introduced them to each other.

'Well . . .' The poet grinned and made a little bow.

'Don't have much time for the playhouse, I'm afraid. I saw *Cato* at the Drury Lane Theatre a few years back.'

Gay coughed and took a sip of burgundy. I knew how low his opinion was of Addison's tragedy. 'And what did you make of it, sir?' he enquired curtly.

'In truth I shed few tears for that philosopher,' the thief-taker replied. 'I was happy enough to see Caesar take charge.'

Gay laughed.

'In matters of state,' Wild went on, 'there's something to be said for the law of arms, the right of conquest.'

'Indeed.'

'In my business, too. Not that there's not something to be said for virtue. But without its opposite I'd have no employment. Nor others too. You've heard of this pamphlet, this fabling of the bees?'

'De Mandeville?' The poet smiled.

'Well, some Dutchman. Says that private vice brings public benefit. He has a point, wouldn't you say?'

There was a knock on the door and someone calling for Wild. One of the spruce-prigs had a silver snuff-box and a

ladies' gold repeating watch for him. The thief-taker dealt with
him swiftly, dismissing the man with a wave of his hand.

'I must apologise, sir. But you see the industry of it? An
instalment, a very busy time, sir. Nothing like it for this trade,
except maybe a coronation. And the expenses? Well,' he shook
his head, 'I had a marchioness apply to me lately after the
recovery of a diamond buckle. I asked her how much she
would give and she answered twenty guineas. I told her:
"Madam you offer nothing! It cost the gentleman who took it
forty for his coach, equipage and other matters to make it to
Windsor!"'

I was astonished at how open Wild was in Gay's presence,
both in his dealings and the cold explanation of them. This
was his hubris. The thief-taker had reached such heights that
summer that he imagined no harm could reach him. And from
this lofty pride he assumed he might yet control the depths.

'There seems a similitude in dealings between the high and
the low life,' Gay suggested.

'Yes, sir. And I have to tutor them both. The rough manners
of polite society and the fine etiquette of the underworld.'

'Really? An etiquette?'

'Why, yes, sir. And a protocol much more delicate than that
of the *beau monde*. Those born rich might misbehave but these
prigs must learn all the correct modes of custom and propriety:
their very lives depend on it. After all, it is a matter of taste
that determines if we prosecute hard or soften the evidence.
And it is only through their decorum that I will know whether
to acquit or whether to peach 'em!'

'To peach 'em!' Gay echoed with delight.

'Yes, then you'll see the rogues better-mannered than the

gentry, all acting according to convention. Quick to heed threats, as they know how to utter them, and ready to hand over booty as easily as they filch it. And if they act without such courtesy, well, they face being scragged, of course. The gallows is an extreme measure, sir, but it certainly promotes moderation.'

Wild continued to discourse on his profession well into the night. Gay sat agog at all the details of his knavish practices and intrigues. Being lavished with much food and wine made his guest most liberal in his commentary, and having a writer of such renown present did as much to loosen the villain's tongue. To get a confession from a proud malefactor, it is always better to call for a poet than a priest. For all the worldly gain and honour Wild sought, I think the prospect of the immortal fame of a dramatist's pen seemed irresistible.

But little did he know then how soon his story would be told, or how his account would be framed. The only matter that seemed to worry him that evening was Roger Johnson, who had departed early from Windsor taking most of his loot with him.

'That cove should mind his manners,' he told me later. 'If you tout him first, let him know I want to see him.'

Though each spare moment I vainly sought another, for it seemed my young beau had disappeared also. I asked after Adam Stonyforth and in every discourse I had among that genteel assembly I found occasion to mention his name. No one knew much about him and at times it seemed he had appeared to me in a dream. A dream that I had no desire to wake from.

So, as the month ended Wild and his entourage returned to

London laden with booty. It had been a summer of enchantment and I nursed the fancy of a treasure yet to be discovered. But we arrived in Romeville to find it in an uproar.

Your humble author,

William Archer Esq.

VI

I⸆ was on the last day of August, with St Bartholomew's Fair in full riot, that Poll Maggot and I padded it through the push on Smithfield. The market place was alive with entertainments: we passed rope-dancing and puppet-shows, booths of curiosity and quack-selling. But we were preparing our own conjuring act as we made our way up by Pie Corner to Newgate Gaol.

I knew of an old Jacobite that dupped into the Black Lion who had spent five years in that grim trib, a scrub of a fellow the natty-lads used to mock as Captain Queer Nabs. Once a gentry-cove that refused to swear allegiance to the new King, he had ended up a beggar from all the privations to be found in the stinking dungeons of the Whit. Yet he was always heard to say that it cheered him to tout the tower of Newgate. Well, I took this for the crank patter of the moonstruck until he explained it to me. And this was it: 'Because it reminds me, my dear, I am *outside* that foul place.'

From outside it looks bene enough, like a gatehouse of some rum palace with columns and statues of dimber morts bearing carved names like *Mercy* and *Truth* and suchlike. The one called *Liberty* has a cat curled up at her feet, which is prattled to be the very mouser of Dick Whittington, the man who had the place built. These handsome decorations span the old city gate like some triumphal arch, but in truth it is a mouth of hell. And once inside, the filth and noise of the place hits you right in the phiz, as does its ghastly stink.

We padded in through the main entrance by the south side of the gate and up to the keeper's lodge. Here the quod-culls asked us who we wanted to see and what they were to us.

'Jack Sheppard,' I pattered. 'He's my husband.'

'And this one?' another demanded, pointing at Poll Maggot.

'Didn't you know,' I gave him a sly smile, 'that the famous Jack has two wives?'

Though I had told her to keep her bonnet down, I could not resist peeping at Poll's phiz to scan how she took this jest. I wanted to twig if there was any truth in it. I had been smoky of her since I'd spied her with Jack at the Black Lion. But I couldn't tout her glaziers or tell much from the grin on her gob. Like any jade she was well used to screening her feelings. And this was a good thing in truth as I needed to stall the quod-culls of being peery of Poll and not to gaze too long on her looks.

As it was they were happy to take three shillings' garnish from both of us for the visit, and another eighteen pence to bring Jack down from the condemned hold to the grille. This was a hatch above the jigger barred by a row of iron spikes that one could peep through and patter with the prisoner. Once the quod-cull had touted that my lover's darbies were secure and the door firmly locked he went back to where his pals were drinking in the lodge. This was around the corner of a small porch that led to a passage to another part of the prison, so though they were very close to the gaolers we were out of their sight.

Jack had been in the Whit for over a fortnight and had prattled slyly with a couple of his fellow condemned on the chances of kicking away together. These other two coves had delayed in the enterprise, jabbering of some hope of a reprieve. But they dallied too long for their warrants came and they were taken for the tree, though they were able to pass on to Jack what files, saws and watch-springs they had gathered.

I had counselled him by messages that he was better off acting alone. He was ready to try his hand but I assured him there would be every benefit in waiting until the very last moment. I had a bene plan and though he had clearly mastered many an art in milling a trib, he was to follow my instructions on this escapade knowing that only I could make certain his deliverance.

And so he bided until the very hour his death warrant arrived. The keepers of the Whit entreated him to make good use of what time he had left and in mock-penitence he thanked them and said he would prepare. Then all it needed was the arrival of his two mistresses, ready to wail loudly by the grille, each grieving at the prospect of being his hempen-widow. So the quod-culls, in twigging that all hope had now been surrendered, let us be. And it being a holiday they tipped themselves some lush at the lodge.

Previously Jack had filed through part of his manacles and cut away at one of the spikes of the hatch in preparation. Now he began to saw at both with great industry as we screened any noise of his labours with our lamentations. Soon he had the fetters from his wrists and so could work more vehemently at the grille. I touted out at the lodge every so often but the gaolers paid us little heed, being in a deep discourse themselves. From what I could cant of their patter some of it concerned Jack's escape from New Prison and the measures concerted for his further security. I had to take care not to laugh out loud at this.

At last the spike was milled and Jack broke it off from the top of the door. This gave him a tiny opening to force himself through. He moved like an eel or some breed of serpent and I touted then this part of the magic of his craft. Like an acrobat who bends his form into a crank shape, or the posture-moll at the Rose tavern, who could pull her leg right over her head, Jack was able to twist his body in a most unnatural fashion. And in this manner he might snake through the narrowest of passages: the gap in the grille was less than a foot square.

Once he was on the other side Poll took off her dress and slipped it over Jack. Her rigging fitted his dandyprat frame neatly and that was why I needed her for this scheme: he would have looked quite lost in one of my gowns. The leg-irons could then be drawn up and hidden by the skirt, and with a bonnet pushed down low to hide his phiz this was a good enough disguise. Poll stood there stripped to her shift, I pulled out a handkerchief and bade her turn around.

'What?' She frowned at me.

'We've got to tie and gag you.'

I hadn't told her this part of the plan, reasoning that she might be nettled at the notion of being left behind in the Whit as me and Jack kicked away. I nodded to him as she began to protest and he grabbed her. I stuffed the wiper in her gob to stow her prattle and with some cord we bound her paws.

'It's the best way,' I told her. 'Then it'll look like we bitched you into it. Just sit mum-chance if they ask you anything.'

We sat her down by the hatch and padded our way slowly to the lodge. Resisting the temptation just to pike it we held onto each other like grieving sisters. Putting my arm around Jack he sobbed away, lowering his head so that it could not be touted, I then turned to make our farewells to the keepers and quod-culls and we shabbed off out of there.

On the street outside, the carnival of St Bartholomew's had spilled out onto Newgate Street as if to celebrate our own little masquerade. The push of the fair screened us well enough but we brushed upon the sneak anyhow, parting company lest the hue-and-cry be called at any moment. Jack made for the corner of the Old Bailey where a friend was waiting with a hackney coach, while I piked it down to the Blackfriars Stairs and touted for a waterman.

Jack soon arrived with his companion, a certain William Page, a butcher's apprentice he had known since childhood. No one had seen Blueskin since before the night Jack was taken, though it was prattled he was hiding out somewhere in the Hundreds. Now my husband had a new partner. This Page escorted him onto the boat quite gallantly and my lover himself played his part well, looking quite dimber as a mort. In high spirits I jested that he might attend a festival night at a molly-house and in an equally jocose mood Jack aimed a playful kick at me. And with this larking his leg-darbies slid down his shanks and the waterman saw the shackles. His glaziers grew wide with amazement and Page then let him also tout the popp he had stowed in his jacket so that he might not make any fuss. He rowed us down to the horse-ferry where we tipped him sixpence fare and an extra penny for his trouble.

Then we dupped into the White Hart, a flash-ken we knew

of. We would bide our time there until nightfall, and make our way back to the Hundreds screened by the darkmans. I had also thought that the keepers of Newgate might expect to track us westwards to St Giles but not think that we would be padding to it in the opposite direction. We made many toasts and took more lush in celebration but in time Jack and me found a quiet corner together.

As he tipped me a buss I felt so bright and happy. Then he reached out a paw and put it on my belly. 'Bess,' he pattered, but I flinched at his touch. 'W-W-What is it?'

I turned and touted him closely. I yet felt so bene at how we'd kicked away from the Whit that I fancied that by speaking the bad news then I might patter it away. 'I lost the baby, Jack,' I told him.

His phiz went blank, like that time I told him I was quick with child in the New Prison. Except this time I could cant a cold sadness in his face, the glim doused in his glaziers. I wished that I had stowed the widd a while on this.

And I felt the loss of it all over again. Something died between us that darkmans. That crank voice in my head came once more. *Stupid trull, stifled her squeaker.* But Jack said nothing. Nix my doll.

'I'm sorry,' I whispered.

I reached out to take his paw in mine but he brushed it away, standing up to jabber that it was time to go. I knew Jack to be full of sentiment that mostly came out as wrath. And I touted the anger in him, that he had been filched of something so precious. Hobbled by the fetters on his shanks and still wearing Poll Maggot's dress he stomped towards the jigger in grotesque gape-seed that mocked any grief we might have shared.

We left for another safe boozing-ken in Holborn. Romeville

was a blindman's holiday, just the glim of a link-boy here and there on the pad. As we rattled along the Strand I nestled up to Jack and he held me in an embrace. There would be time to patter later, I reasoned.

In a cribb above the tavern, a pal had brought all the tools necessary to quit Jack from his leg darbies. Then he changed his rigging and we sat down at a table laid out with prog and more lush. The mood rose once more and our spirits sang with all the excitation of the adventure. We had cheated death, after all, and had bilked Jack Ketch of a day's work. We were at liberty and, for one night at least, unfettered by fear and vexation. I was soon pot-valiant, happy and forgetful of all the plotting and suspicion. Then Poll Maggot dupped in.

A cheer went up in the room. Jack stood and made a toast. I smiled and raised a glass to her, then touted her peerily. If she had been taken by the keepers and quod-culls they should have kept her longer. It was prattled that Wild was back from Windsor and he would surely want to question her. Maybe he had already. And yet she had found time to rig herself in her best mantua gown, paint her phiz and pad it over from Vinegar Yard. What might she have squeaked so swiftly?

She strode over to where Jack stood, tossing her curls and pouting her stupid gob. 'A kiss for the girl who set you free?' she said, with a sly smile.

And Jack held her by the waist and bussed her on the lips.

'It was my lay, Poll,' I told her. 'Remember that. You were just the stall.'

'I took the risk, though. Stripping myself bare for him,' she purred, and pressed her hands on his that still gripped her green silk bodice. 'I could take off this dress for you too.'

I got up from the table and pulled her away from him. 'Get your paws off!' I told her.

'It's only a j-j-jest,' said Jack.

'Is it, Jack?' She tipped him a lewd wink. 'Is it?'

Poll then turned and we faced each other in the middle of the cribb.

'You made it here in good time, Poll.'

'No thanks to you and your crank scheme.'

'So you worked the drop with your story?'

'Oh! Help!' She quailed, playing her part once more. 'They put me in fear of my life! See how they used me?'

Everyone laughed heartily at this and I let it run awhile.

'And what did the prig-napper say?' I snapped at her.

'What?'

'Wild. He's back in Romeville. He would have wanted to see you.'

'I – I –' she stammered '– I never saw him.'

'And he would have kept you longer. Unless you babbled.'

There was a hush at this. The whole cribb caught its breath.

'She's babbled, Jack,' I said. 'We'd better pike it.'

'Like you babbled, Bess.' She turned to look at him. 'It was she that peached you out to Wild, you know.'

'That's not true!'

'So how did Quilt know where to take you, Jack?' she asked him. 'They got her in a brandy-shop by the Temple Bar and she squeaked it all for a handful of coin.'

'Liar!'

'Wild told me himself.'

'Wild?' I countered. 'But you said you didn't see Wild!'

'I mean—'

'See, Jack? Come on, or we'll be snabbled.'

Jack just stood there with a frown on his phiz. Poll stepped beside him and put her hand to his chest. 'He wants to bide with me, don't you, Jack? Like you did that time before.'

'Is that true?' I asked him. 'Have you docked this dirty trull?'

But he could only make a soundless stutter, his bleach phiz now all red with shame, and I thought what useless culls men can be. And morts so full of deceit. There they stood, side by side, choice examples of either sex, equal in size and error. And as I towered over them I was heartily sick of both breeds. It was only my height that gave me any perspective on this lay. And being a long-meg has its advantages. It gives you a long reach and a good swing, which can come in handy on the pad or with those flogging-culls that used to dup into Mother Breedlove's. Or to ding a sly little jade like Poll Maggot.

With one good punch I laid her out cold. And that settled the matter for now, though all there had heard her prattle of me peaching Jack. I turned to him and I swear he flinched as I raised my hand once more. In truth I thought about clouting him one, too, but instead I held out an empty palm to him.

'Well?' I said.

He looked down at Poll, stretched out on the floor, then up again at me. He nodded and reached out to take my paw in his. We called for Page to fetch a hackney-coach for us and to tout that all was clear on the pad. He had a cribb above a boozing-ken in Spitalfields that we could use and no one else knew of. We were both smoky of each other and had plenty to patter but we rattled eastwards without a word, sitting mum-chance on the verdict.

We arrived at a tavern called the Paul's Head and Page called to the bluffer to let us in. He showed us up the dancers to a small room, sparked a glimstick and spoke that he would be back at peep of day. He then bade us bene darkmans and left the two of us in that chamber to stand judgment on each other.

'Maggot's a lying jade,' I told him. 'I never took a penny from Wild.'

'Th-Then you p-peached me for free?'

'They tricked me, Jack, forced it out of me. But Poll must have babbled easy. That whore will sell you, you know, even if she does let you dock her for free.'

'Like you did with Blueskin?'

'What?'

'I heard it prattled you let him burn the ken after a night with you.'

'That was before I even met you!'

'He bl-blew your coals back then! Maybe he still does.'

'Don't be so crank.'

'Then you babbled to Wild.'

'Can't you cant my widds? I didn't mean to jabber where you were. He bitched it out of me.'

'Well, you w-were ever his b-bitch.'

'I saved you today, remember? Got you out of the Whit.'

'C-C-Could have done it on m-my own.'

'Stow your widds, you know that's not true!'

'I c-c-could. I could k-k-kick-away on my own. I don't n-need anybody. They p-peach you in the end.'

'I told you, Jack. They forced me. Made me drink.'

'Well, y-you always l-l-liked your l-lush, Bess.'

'They poisoned me!' I was getting really nettled by then. 'They poisoned our child!'

'What?'

A dark frown on Jack's phiz, that mark of anger I'd touted earlier. I felt the wrath rise inside me, too.

'That's when I lost it!' I shouted, padding towards him. 'I tried to patter my way out of there! Get to you in time! Warn you!'

'B-B-Bess!' Jack's glaziers were wide and glim. I was lashing out with my paws, swiping at his phiz.

'Dandyprat! Lully-prig! Chittiface!' I cursed him as I tried to land a blow.

But he grabbed my wrist and I felt that fierce strength of his. I held onto him and we found ourselves in a clinch, like two tusslers in the ring at Moorfields. We were well matched, for though I was the taller and longer-limbed his dapper body had that lithe and agile spirit that was so hard to catch hold of. And whatever differences in form we possessed, we were surely equal in sheer rage and fury that darkmans. I grabbed at his throat and tried to squeeze the life from that gutter-pipe. But he slipped through my grasp and, twisting round, swept my shanks from under me and I toppled onto the floor. Then he was on me, pulling at my hair to strike my head against the boards. I scratched at his face and tried to kick out at him. Something heavy came loose from the inside of his jacket and tumbled out with a heavy thud by my right lugg. I turned my head and touted that it was his popp. Jack noted it, too, but as he let go of me to reach for it I was able to plant my knee in his groin. With a squeal he doubled up. Rolling from him I was on my knees and the pistol in my hand.

I crouched low and, with Jack panting on the floor beside me, I held the popp against his head. His glaziers glimmed in the candlelight, wild shadows dancing around us.

'G-Go on, then,' he gasped. 'I've l-l-loaded it proper this time. It w-w-won't flash in the p-p-pan.'

There was a grin on his gob like the snarl of a wild beast. I cocked the hammer and slipped a finger through the trigger guard.

'Go on,' he goaded me.

But I pulled the barrel of the gun away from his head and pointed it against my own. *Go on*, came the voice, *it won't flash in the pan*. Yes, I thought, this could be it. All could be settled this simply.

'No!' he called, and knocked the popp from my hands.

A clap of lightning filled the cribb, then a shriek of wild laughter from me.

'Crank bitch!' Jack shouted, and I slapped his phiz.

Then we were at each other again but now our wrath turned to lust. I have said before that I never knew a man with so much passion as Jack Sheppard but that night we docked with a murderous ferocity. Perhaps this was the torment of grief, the outrage of the misbegotten, that we had conceived a glim of hope then lost it. The spark of life was gone and so we loved in death, knowing that we were both born to hang, after all.

The dawn came and it was bright and clear, though a chill blast whispered an end to summer. I woke to see Jack standing at the glaze, touting for William Page.

'I grew up around the corner from here,' he said, gazing out upon the streets of Spitalfields.

I thought then of my own lost childhood, of how I was banished from the sweet air of Daisyville. London had always meant ruin and sinfulness to me but I twigged then how Jack truly belonged to Romeville, as a squeaker as well as a wild rogue. I got up and went to him, still sensible of the marks and bruises of the night before.

'Jack,' I said, and he turned to me.

'W-W-What?'

'I didn't mean to peach you.'

'M-M-Maybe you should have.'

'No.'

'Y-Y-Yes.' He held my arms. 'L-Listen, Bess. There m-might come a time when you need to.'

'I never will. Not again.'

'You d-d-don't know. N-N-Nobody knows what they might deny when f-f-faced with the gallows. I might b-babble you.'

'I don't believe you would.'

'B-But what if . . .' Jack's phiz was a thoughtful scowl '. . . w-what if by peaching someone you c-could set them free?'

'I don't cant what you patter.'

'N-Never mind.' He smiled and bussed me on the gob.

There was a cry from below. Page had arrived and he came up the dancers with a brace of blue butcher's smocks. Jack was to disguise himself as one of that trade as they journeyed northwards out of London to some town called Chipping Warden where Page had family. There they hoped for some hospitality until the storm over the escape had blown over.

'We'll make some rum loure and pike it to Daisyville,' I pattered sadly, remembering that dream of raising a squeaker together in the countryside.

He promised to send word as soon as he was settled. In the meantime I would gather what loure I could and prepare to join him. Before they set off he bade me promise one thing. 'Look after my mother,' he said, and kissed me once more.

So I padded it back to my cribb in St Giles, puzzling over the curious words he had pattered to me that morning. *What if by peaching someone you could set them free?*

Turning into Blackmoor Street I at once became peery, certain I was being tracked by some cove. I quickened my pace and thought of piking it but I knew that would draw a hue-and-cry. And so I ducked into an alleyway that led to a back yard and entered the labyrinth that is the Hundreds of Drury.

I wove my way through, turning and retracing to throw off the scent and make certain none might follow me through that maze. At last I found myself in the passage of Orange Court where I could wait and tout for anyone who might still be on my trail. But as I caught my breath I heard my voice hissed from the shadows. As I broke cover I was grabbed by both arms. Someone pulled me to them, holding me close so I could regard his dark and fervid countenance.

'Blueskin!' I gasped.

'Bess,' he whispered once more.

He told me he had just missed being snabbled at his mother's brandy-shop when they had taken Jack. To my relief he did not seem to twig that I had squeaked. He had stowed himself in St Giles since then.

'There was a great celebration in the Hundreds when Jack kicked away from the Whit,' he said. 'Is he with you?'

'He's lying low in the countryside. I'm off to join him soon.'

'Well, good luck. I'd surely like to shab off to Daisyville myself.' He laughed. 'But I hardly think I'd pass as yeoman stock with my complexion. No, I'll stay a St Giles' Blackbird and take my chances here.'

'What will you do?'

'What else? Bide my time and try to make a deal with the prig-napper. It's prattled that Jonathan is back from Windsor.' He dupped out of the shadows and touted upon the pad. When he was sure that all was clear he patted me on the shoulder. 'Bene lightmans, Bess,' he said, with a buss. 'Be lucky.'

And then he padded off up Drury Lane.

I brushed upon the sneak all the way back to my cribb and resolved to bide indoors until the darkmans. But I was in need of prog so I tipped some coin to a dell who lodged in my ken to fetch something from the pie-seller on the corner. I loosened my rigging and stretched myself out on the bed. I was just about to shut my glaziers when a tap came on the jigger. The dell must have forgotten something, I thought.

'Come in, nabs,' I called, and the door swung open.

'Ah, a civil reception,' came a gruff voice. 'That's what we like, isn't it, Quilt?'

I sat up with a start. Jonathan Wild stood before me with his deputy at his shoulder.

'It was very rude of you shabbing off like that.' He grinned. 'Well, I have you safe, now. You're for the Poultry Compter.' He gestured a rolled-up paper at me. 'A warrant signed by Sir Frances Forbes,' he said. 'For aiding and abetting Jack Sheppard, for giving comfort and harbouring the felon.'

And so I was snabbled. The dell had not gone long enough to have sold me out. I did wonder at Blueskin and what he had pattered about dealing with the thief-taker. But it was soon clear who had squeaked as Wild was happy enough to tell me.

'Poll, yes. You know she didn't want to give me Jack but you? She gave you to me,' he clicked his fingers, 'like that.'

Newgate Gaol, 18th February 1726

Dear Applebee,

Now all of London was on the trail of Jack Sheppard. As Wild set off to apprehend Edgworth Bess, he bade me write an advertisement offering a twenty-guinea reward for the discovery of the prison-breaker and take it to the *Daily Courant*. The thief-taker general was possessed by a furious determination to settle the matter – indeed, it was seen by many as a test of his new powers, that he might truly prove who ruled the streets of Romeville.

For there was panic in the city as apprehensions of terror descended on the flat citizens of London. Fears that no property was now secure and terrible visions of a canting-crew rising in revolt behind Sheppard haunted the imaginations of the gentility. It was said that he had sworn bloody revenge on Kneebone and others he had robbed who had refused to sign a petition on his behalf. Shopkeepers boarded up their premises and hired bailiffs to stand guard at night.

My mind yet dwelled on another wanted man, the sweet fugitive of my affections. I had learned that this Honourable Adam bore a courtesy title as the youngest son of the Earl of Stonyforth, yet to come into his majority. I reasoned that it was likely he would now be at his country seat, or taking the waters at Bath or Cheltenham, and not be seen in town until late October or November. As you know, the London season generally begins at this time, when Parliament sits and the quality descends upon the city once more to quarter itself there for the winter.

So for the while I turned my attentions from the *beau*

monde to the flash world of Romeville. The Hundreds of Drury had rejoiced at Jack's liberty and in the taverns new songs were sung of his exploits. He embodied a threat not only to Wild's authority but also to his fame, so there was much work now for balladeers, pamphleteers, print-makers and journalists. All of Grub Street was pressed into the service of rendering this new spectacle, and a hackney-scribbler such as myself stood to subsist most comfortably on the famous prison-breaker's story.

I knew him through my acquaintance with Bess and Blueskin and so found employment with you, Applebee, as you now cleverly set out to secure the rights to Jack's memoirs and confession. Do you remember that you commissioned me to pen a letter from Sheppard to appear in your *Daily Journal*? Addressed 'to Jack Ketch', the hangman, this faked missive was for the most part merely a whimsical jest, a satire on how the young apprentice had cheated the gallows. But you carefully instructed me to add a postscript sending regards to the chaplain of Newgate and yourself, thus giving notice that you intended to be the sole executor of his last dying speech. Then was I dispatched in an attempt to broker this deal in person.

The tales of Sheppard, Wild and, indeed, Elizabeth Lyon were all fast assuming the nature of some modish fable. In his fictional correspondence I had joked that Jack was writing from *Terra Australies incognito*, but no one knew where he was, not even Edgworth Bess. And now she was in no position to come to his aid.

It was given out that Wild had committed her to the Poultry Compter, the little gaol found to the east of Cheapside, and was trying to force her to give evidence against

VII

'You'll not get me to babble on Jack this time,' I pattered to Wild. I had been put in a single lock-up on the Master's Side of the trib so that the prig-napper could quiz me in a private chamber.

'What makes you so certain, Bess?'

'The plain fact that I don't know where he is.'

'Then you'll bide here awhile. I'll tip you a week's garnish to keep you in the Common Ward. After that . . .' He shrugged.

'I told you, I don't know anything.'

'Well, maybe you'll hear some prattle of him in the Compter. Then make sure you bring it to me. Unless you want to end up in the Hole.'

Blueskin once pattered of a Romish scribbler who set down Hell as to be made of a set of rings, one inside the other right down to the very centre of damnation, each with a particular torment to match the sin of every lost soul. And, like all tribs, the Poultry Compter has its ranks of punishment, though they are not ordered to suit the crime but rather the station of the malefactor and how much garnish they can melt. On the Master's

Side there are individual cells with bed, chair, table and any other possessions you care to bring; the Common Ward is a crowded and clamorous dormitory; the Hole a filthy and dank pit of perdition.

'Don't sit mum-chance too long, Bess,' warned Wild, as he went to the jigger. 'After all, Jack'll peach you in the end.'

And though I canted these widds were meant to nettle me I just couldn't let them go. 'Why do you say that?' I pattered after him.

'Because I know, Bess. I've been prig-napper for over ten years now and that's the one thing I've twigged. Everybody peaches or gets peached in the end.'

Then he called for a quod-cull to take me to the Common Ward. Wild tipped me three shillings and sixpence garnish for the week, the same rate he had paid Blueskin. It was the old mouse and mouser game he was playing, never letting go of anybody until he had scragged them.

The Common Ward of the Poultry Compter was its own universe of suffering and infamy. It acted as a spunging-house for debtors, with coves done up by gaming or bubbled by the stock-jobbers. And it held every species at the scrub end of the canting-crew: vagrants, drunks, mollies and whores, picked up on the pad by constables of the watch, and dissenters who had sold crank pamphlets of heresy and sedition. There was a handful of Negroes, runaway slaves who had claimed the liberty of England's soil but had been retaken by their masters and were now safe in the Compter until the law could decide whether they were free or not. And there were even some prisoners of the Hebrew faith with a ward set aside for them, as nearby dwelled that little Israel in the City called Old Jewry. All the races of a fallen world abided here and it was up to Edgworth Bess to see how she could thrive among them.

I was touted with some respect by the other felons for being the gaol-breaker's wife, and indeed soon there was some babble of Jack. It was prattled that he was once more in Romeville and had milled a watchmaker's on Fleet Street. I nursed that glim of hope that he had come back from Daisyville to spring me from the Compter.

And soft he would come to me by darkmans, brushing upon the sneak as he dupped into my dreams. All was bene in that happy fancy where we kicked away together once more. But at peep of day he would be gone, shabbing off as I woke to the clamour of that wretched place.

Then I would yearn for him all the more by lightmans, though I would screen such tender feelings, knowing I would have to harden my heart in order to survive in the trib. I canted that I should find some lay to make coin on the inside: the loure from the prig-napper would soon be melted and, without payment to the quod-culls, I might end up in the Hole.

I twigged how it was not only the keepers who took garnish but certain prisoners. There was a crew led by a one-eyed cove named Butler Fox who worked the drop. It was a simple enough lay: Fox and his bullies would take anyone who would not pay, then 'make the black dog walk', which could mean any number of vile punishments.

So I put the bite on this Butler Fox, using the lewd charm a jade turns on a bleeding-cull, leading him on. But as he came close I stalled him.

'Jack's back in the Hundreds,' I said. 'He was touted in a boozing-ken in St Giles.'

Fox drew back, peery at what I'd pattered. My lover now inspired a crank kind of fear in many a rum cove.

'He's coming to spring me from here,' I whispered. 'But maybe we could pal up until I kick away with him.'

That sparked him up all the more, with the hint of danger that blows the coals in a cull. I allowed him the hopes of my favour but kept him at a paw's length all the time. He was a bully sure enough but an easy one to play.

I learned that Butler Fox was a debtor who owed forty pounds and, even with all the loure from the garnish, didn't expect to pay it off and be free for another two years. He hoped he might make it to the Master's Side before then, maybe get liberty of the gate. But even these meagre ambitions had become a distant fancy to him. Like many who bide too long in some sink of despair, he had grown over-familiar with a rank of degradation. The place had confined his mind as well as his person, and the Common Ward now seemed to him a tiny kingdom for him to lord it over. So I appealed to his petty vanity.

'Wild first learned his trade as prig-napper in the Compter on Wood Street,' I told him one day.

'So I hear.' His one eye popped and he made a lully grin.

'Then we might have our own corporation here in the Poultry.'

I promised to babble all the secrets of the underworld to his luggs for a rum snack of the garnish. He was bilked by this patter and my flash reputation. With my cleverness and his brutality we would work the drop together, I assured him. And we soon found an opportunity.

A troop of jades dupped into the Common Ward one lightmans, after the Society for the Reformation of Manners had raided a vaulting-school in Hart Street. Though they were a motherless crew, I touted Sukey Hawkins among them, whom I had known from Mother Breedlove's academy, playing the abbess. I nodded at her, canting that I would have to break this mort first then deal with the rest. Her phiz brightened as she saw me and she gave a gap-grindered smile. The poor trull didn't twig what she was in for.

'Sukey!' I called her over, then gave a cock of the head to a pair of Fox's crew.

'Bess.' She padded close and began to jabber of how she had been snabbled. I nodded as she spoke but my thoughts were elsewhere.

With a gang of whores in a gaol, any garnish they tip is likely to come back to them, as all the coves, prisoner and quod-cull alike, will melt their loure on the commodity that can be sold many times over. That trade needed regulation and in truth it was best done by one of our own sex. But there could be only one top mort on the Poultry so I had to bitch this jade.

She stalled, noting that my glaziers looked right through her and how a pair of coves now stood each side of her. 'Bess?' She frowned. 'What is it?'

'Make the black dog walk,' I told the two bullies.

For Sukey this meant being stripped of her fine silk and lace down to her shift and taken to the Hole. As the cellar door was unlocked it breathed out its sickly scent and groaning chorus. Sukey touted back at me as she was dragged to the slimy stairs.

'Bess!' she called, as if I still might help her.

'Have a good look, nabs,' I told her. 'See how you like it there. We'll patter later.'

So they shoved her in the Hole and the rest of the jades touted who their new mistress was. Sukey was pulled out at darkmans, whimpering and covered with filth.

'So,' I asked her, 'want any more?'

'What did I do to you, Bess?' she whined, her glaziers red and glib with tears.

'You just happened to be there, Sukey, that's the shame of it. But if you put your trust in me all can be mended.'

'You turned out a cruel one, Edgworth Bess. I heard you dinged Poll Maggot the night Jack kicked away.'

'And I'll do the same to any other sneak,' I said, rubbing my paws together. 'That jade is the reason I'm here. So stow the widd on any lay I patter to you.'

I told her then of how it would be. Once the garnish was paid, all the whores could ply their trade however they wanted but only if they handed over part of the loure to me. And they'd better not hold back any of their coin as all transactions would be carefully touted, by me, Fox's crew and the quod-culls, who would take their snack too. In that way I became Mother of the Compter and could afford a clean and dry cribb of my own.

And I gained a servant. I noted that one of the jades followed me around, bringing me prog and lush and even washing my rigging for me. She was the runt of the litter, an odd-looking dell of about sixteen with curly brown locks and little black buttons for glaziers. Lizzy, she was called, with an intent look on her phiz, always touting after me. I thought that Sukey must have put her on to me, to keep me sweet and to have a spy in my camp. When she came to my room one lightmans I challenged her on this but she denied it.

'What's your game, then?' I demanded, grabbing her by the hair.

She squealed and I threw her onto the bed.

'Come on,' I went on. 'Out with it.'

Her face flushed as she peered up at me. 'I just want . . .' she shrugged '. . . to be like you.'

'What?' I frowned at her and her button eyes grew wide and imploring.

'You're Edgworth Bess,' she gasped, as if in wonder. '*The* Edgworth Bess. I want to learn from you. Learn how you did it.'

'Did what?'

'Became so famous.'

I laughed out loud at this. I was not merely an abbess with a novice sister in my service but a bad saint to be worshipped. It seemed a crank jest indeed but I did not deny myself the benefit of it. I had her run errands and keep my cribb and rigging spotless. And she became my squeak, a little bird that could flutter about the Compter, then let me know all the prattle. I even let her share my bed to get some warmth on a cold darkmans. She gave me comfort, as a spaniel might to a gentry-mort, and I treated her as a pet to be toyed with. I used her most cruelly at times but those who willingly become slaves can only expect to be treated accordingly.

As Lizzy became my punk so I thought of my nights with Punk Alice. In prison as in a vaulting-school, morts will often go with other morts as true coves are scarce or not to be trusted in those circumstances. So I let that obedient girl pal up with me to soften the life a bit, and to have someone to tout my back.

I fancied that other prisoners in the trib shared Lizzy's devotion. I mistook fear for admiration and did not ponder much on how monstrous I had become. Having promised Butler Fox that he might learn Wild's trade in the Compter, it was me who now acted like the prig-napper, bitching all the inmates of that dire prison. I was a victim of my own insensible pride, which imagined honour in notoriety. And fame. Well, I was soon to learn the foolishness of it all.

For I yet dreamed of Jack by night, of piking off to Daisyville with him. And though I canted that we stood but a queer chance of it, this was my own secret folly that none could filch from me.

Then the widd was blown that Jack had been snabbled by a posse of quod-culls on Finchley Common. So the glim of my hopes was doused once more. Yet there was such a noise in town over him, the creature who had now become a commodity as much as a man of flesh and blood. It was pattered that it was hard to find a porter, chairman or any other who might give service on the pad since all were engaged in discourse about the prison-breaker. Masters complained of idleness in their mechanics and apprentices; wagers were made on him as each new controversy arose. There were loud jabberings that the justices planned to scrag him swiftly and incognito, though it was also prattled that the old warrant might not suffice and a new trial should be held. The Poultry itself was loud with this endless babble, and prisoner and quod-cull alike directed their questions at me.

So, I became a creature of curiosity and speculation, gulled of any private sentiment, a mere part of the gape-seed that was Jack Sheppard. I felt the push tout me with a smoky gaze and feared I might not come out of the story quite so bene. It made me yet more cruel and determined to collect as much loure as I could from the inmates of the Compter. For I had plans now that would need extra coin.

None said a widd of it to my phiz but I touted the disdain in their eyes and heard the whispers of complaint at my back. Biding in my cribb, I wondered at how I had become such a mean and vicious soul. I might even shed a tear in remembrance of some happier time. But by the cold glim of lightmans I assumed my stern manner, padding out from the confines of my cell to bitch the jades in the Compter. I now ruled most of the Common Ward, but I had not a single friend there. Or so I thought.

I soon heard that Blueskin had been trapped by Wild's posse at a flash-ken in St Giles. It was pattered that they milled the jigger of his cribb and Quilt was sent in first. Blueskin pulled out a knife and the prig-napper's deputy drew a sword in reply so the rogue was bitched, no doubt reminded of the sabre-cut he earned the last time he was taken that he yet bears the scar of. He was committed to the Whit to appear at the next sessions. That was the end, it seemed, with all of our little crew now snabbled. But I twigged through the desperation that I must not give in, for there was yet a chance to cog the dice of Fate once more. Though I had to be strong and that was never easy.

I found Lizzy in my cribb one lightmans, dutifully tidying up after me. As she looked up I touted something in those black-button glaziers. Not just terror but a dogged devotion, a queer sense of loyalty that abided no matter how badly I treated her. And that really nettled me. I felt a blaze of wrath take hold of me and I was ready to give her a sound beating. But as she flinched a dreadful sadness stayed my hand and I saw something in the phiz of the little punk that bitched me into kindness. I took her by the paw and pulled her to me. 'You've got to promise me,' I told her.

'Anything,' she whispered.

'Once you're out of the Compter, find an honest trade. Don't be like Edgworth Bess.'

Newgate Gaol, 20th February 1726

Dear Applebee,

It was an errand of mercy that took me to the bail-dock of the Old Bailey on the morning of Blueskin's trial, though I was officially there to report on it for your *Journal*. On a chill dawn at the start of the October sessions I joined the crowd of prosecutors, lawyers and court officials that had gathered, waiting for the prisoners to be brought up from Newgate. There was a pair of surgeons present, which I presumed to be witnesses, though perhaps they were measuring up some future specimens, like butchers at a flesh market. A cruel spectacle for any facing trial as the canting-crew dread dissection after death above any punishment they might be sensible of.

For that bitter dawn many of us had a flask of brandy to put some life in our own anatomies. And I spied Wild with a pint of claret in one hand as he spoke with some turnkeys. I caught his eye and he beckoned me over, prompting the thought of my charitable reason for being at the Old Bailey that morning.

I had seen Blueskin in the Whit the week before when I had gone there to take down some of Sheppard's comments. I had a book for him, knowing that to be what he most desired when in gaol. He stretched his frame as he took the air of the press-yard, blinking up at the narrow passage of light between the walls.

'I hear your boss has got Daniel Defoe working on Jack's story,' he said.

I had no idea how Blueskin had learned of your employment of this famous author in the writing of Sheppard's biography since it was supposed to be a secret.

'Well,' I shrugged, 'he's got all of his garreteers noting down what they can. Then Defoe might piece it all together.'

'Like some great work.' He smiled.

'It is the talk of London. And you're a part of it.'

Blueskin sighed. 'Not sure I like that,' he said. 'I always thought I'd make a story of my own. An epic poem – that would suit me.' Then he laughed but just a little too loudly. The tone was hollow, desperate. All at once his face froze and his eyes glared at nothing. '"Who dies in youth and vigour dies the best,"' he mused, with a fearful groan. Then he called: 'Christ, Billy, I don't want to die! Talk to Wild, can you? I'll be marinated, I don't mind that. But I don't want to die. Not yet.'

All his brave composure was cut down in an instant. He let out an awful sob, shivered, then pulled his shoulders back once more. He swiped at a tear with the back of one hand, then patted the volume I had given him. 'So, will Jack make a book?' he asked, blinking.

'Not so much a book,' I replied, all at once conscious of his jealousy at this. 'A long narrative more like.'

And though I sought to diminish Sheppard's glory for Blueskin's benefit there had already been rumours of a play or harlequinade of his life. As you know, on your behalf I had negotiated the exclusive rights of all his personal memoranda for the duration of his life for certain considerations and a retainer of eightpence a day. In a note he dictated confirming this, Sheppard had requested this fee to be transferred to his mother should he be unavailable for any period to collect it in person. As it turned out that was not a mere jest – though Sheppard's quips were now becoming as legendary as his actions. On his way to the chapel at Newgate a small file was discovered concealed in a Bible that had been passed to him by some well-wisher. I was on hand to set down his remark when the chaplain chided him and pressed him to reveal those who might have furnished this implement in such an impious manner. With great passion and with a motion of striking Sheppard declared: 'Ask me n-n-no such questions. One file's worth all the B-B-Bibles in the world!'

And so each wild rogue looks to how his song might be sung and they compete with each other for their wicked reputation as much as for loot.

'I'm worth a ballad at least,' Blueskin called to me, as he was taken back to his cell. Bidding him farewell, I promised I would talk to Wild on his behalf, but I did not manage to see the thief-taker, let alone speak with him, until the day of Blueskin's trial.

As I approached him in the bail-dock that morning he had other matters on his mind.

'Have you seen Roger Johnson?' Wild asked.

'I hear he is in Flanders.'

Johnson had taken the loot he'd filched at Windsor across the sea with him and it was rumoured that some of the *beau-monde* who had applied for the recovery of their stolen jewellery were becoming most impatient with the thief-taker's delay in finding it for them.

'Damn him,' the thief-taker muttered to himself, then turned to me. 'So, here to report for Applebee?'

'Yes.'

'Well, you'll see plenty of sport this sessions.'

'And another matter.'

'What?'

'Joe. He asked me to put in a word for him.'

'Damn these prigs, if they won't be bitched by me!'

'But—' I started to say, but at that moment they began to bring the prisoners into the bail-dock.

'Here they come,' Wild muttered darkly. 'The dead on holiday.'

The turnkeys were leading in the accused and I recognised the first. It was Simon Jacobs, the last of Valentine Carrick's old crew, indicted for feloniously stealing two guineas, three shillings and sixpence. When he spied the thief-taker he bowed his head a little and looked imploringly at him, his eyes bright with fear.

'See how these bold fellows now beg for mercy,' Wild told me. 'I've seen them piss themselves in the bail-dock before me.'

'Blueskin,' I whispered to him. 'Surely you'll find a way to spare him the rope.'

Wild took a sip of claret and slowly shook his head.

'But your acquaintance with him goes back so many years,' I urged him. 'Does that count for nothing?'

The thief-taker swallowed a mouthful of wine and let out a wistful sigh. 'Ah, the past,' he declared. 'Yes, it means so much. But what can it count for when measured with the future? Me and Joe go back, yes, but I go forward without him. No, I'm afraid I'm going to have to let him go. With that rogue scragged, this whole Sheppard business is nicely tucked up. It's a shame, but there you have it.'

He beckoned Jacobs, who came forward, still hunched over in supplication. I saw that Blueskin was close behind him.

Wild looked the first man up and down, as if measuring him for a coffin. 'I believe you'll not bring forty pounds this time,' he told him.

Jacobs let out a gasp of weary delight. The amount referred to was the reward given for a capital sentence. It meant that the man might be saved and only face transportation. I watched as the thief-taker weighed the lives in his power, as carelessly balanced as the clanker of wine he held in his right hand. He revelled in the cruel caprice of his own judgment. Spying his old accomplice at Jacob's shoulder, he could not forbear to make a pompous speech of it.

'I wish Joe was in your case, but I'm afraid he's a dead man.' He spoke loudly with a gesture to Blueskin, then turned back to Jacobs. 'But you, I'll endeavour to bring you off as a single felon. Then you'll be marinated.'

Blueskin pushed his way through and stood before Wild. 'Surely you'll put in a word for me as well as him?' he said, cocking a thumb at Jacobs.

The two men looked at each other a while. Teacher and pupil in that dread school of crime. The younger man had played the apprentice act of idleness and industry, of obedience and rebellion, just as the older indulged in a grim sport of cat and mouse, letting him run, then catching him again and again. Now the game was up. I noted how Blueskin thrust one hand into the pocket of his coat and stroked his chin with the other, expectantly.

Then Wild spoke: 'I believe you must die,' he said briskly. 'I'll send you a good book or two, and you'll not be anatomised, I promise you. I'll provide the coffin myself.'

Blueskin began to laugh, baring his teeth in a ghastly rictus that soon curled into a vicious snarl. He pulled his hand from his pocket and with a bestial howl leaped at his master's neck. The low morning sun caught the glint of a blade.

Wild squealed as Blueskin forced the knife against the loose flesh of his throat. Then his cries were muffled as the steel cut close to the windpipe, his eyes flashing in terror as his assailant tried to push it home. Two turnkeys pulled Blueskin off and the wine tipped down the thief-taker's front. Wild fumbled about the bail-dock, dropping the tankard and grasping desperately at his own neck. He made a dreadful gurgle and blood seeped through his fingers to mingle with the claret that bespattered his shirt.

I was close enough to feel a splash of wine on my cheek and flinched, for a moment thinking it might be a drop of that more precious fluid. As Wild turned and reached out to me I froze, transfixed in horror and fascination at the gruesome scene. Then the two surgeons came forward, one staunching the wound with a muslin scarf, the other calling for a servant to fetch his bag of instruments.

Blueskin looked exultant as he was dragged away, his eyes shining with a mad triumph. 'I'll be scragged with pleasure if that bastard dies first!' he called. 'I wish I could have cut off his head and thrown it to the rabble in the sessions-house yard!'

As Wild was carried away to be attended to, and the turnkeys struggled to restore order to the bail-dock, I went to find a tavern so I might compose an article that could be prepared for the press for the next day's *Journal*.

I ordered brandy as I needed a strong drink to steady my own nerves, though the shock of what I had witnessed soon turned into excitement at its dramatic possibilities. Such a macabre spectacle, like some Greek tragedy for the fallen state of Romeville. Bold Blueskin had tried to assassinate the thief-taker general and I was the nearest eye-witness. All the other journalists had been at the other side of the bail-dock.

With a trembling hand I wrote it up succinctly and tipped a ticket-porter a shilling to convey it swiftly to your desk in Blackfriars. Then I allowed myself that small celebration of a garreteer: of having the best story on Grub Street that evening. I drank to Blueskin's health, knowing there was precious little of that vitality left for him. As I raised a glass to Wild I hesitated, wondering what life on the streets would be like without him, though none of us knew yet whether Blueskin had delivered the mortal blow or not. If he had, then a whole empire might come tumbling down.

There were loud huzzahs from all parts of Newgate as Blueskin was taken to the condemned hold. With his fellow rebel Sheppard secure in the castle cell of the tower above, the whole of the Whit seemed on the edge of open revolt at their wicked example. And, indeed, there were fears for the security of that grim gaol as many of the turnkeys were yet occupied in taking prisoners to and from the Old Bailey as the October sessions proceeded.

The following morning I walked out to Moll King's coffee-house, confident that all the talk would be of Blueskin's attempt on the thief-taker's life and, indeed, all would be reading my account of it. This is the great consolation for the humble hackney-scribbler, of being the first with some great news. I even entertained the pleasant fancy of how this might advance my reputation as a writer. For though Daniel Defoe had taken command in the composition of the Sheppard narrative, now I had a story to match it, which might bring me to the attention of that great man.

But though all the talk of the town that day concerned itself with events at Newgate it was not the bloody attack on Wild that made the greatest noise. To the astonishment of London, and indeed the entire nation, Jack Sheppard had done it again. The keeper had unlocked and unbolted the double doors of his cell that morning and had found it empty but for the piles of rubble strewn about the hold. Sheppard had escaped from Newgate once more and all incredulously asked the same question: how on earth had he managed it? Edgworth Bess remains the last witness to his secrets left alive and she now abides here in the Whit. As well as all her private mysteries concerning him, she might illumine this public one. At the time there was only one answer we could give. That the devil had come in person to help him.

Your faithful author,

William Archer Esq.

VIII

'THIS, Bess,' he pattered once more. 'This. It's ours. All ours.'

Yes, the devil or Merry Old Roger took Jack Sheppard to the roof of Newgate Gaol and the prig-napper of all creation showed him the high place from which he could be peached or acquitted, just as he had with some other apprentice carpenter born to hang. And I was with him on the ledge, just the night above and all of Romeville at our feet.

Westwards lay the Hundreds, the Square of Venus, the maze of Seven Dials. South sat the great dome of St Paul's gospel-shop and Blackfriars, where the black Fleet flows into the silver Thames. By the east, the Tower, the Minories and the wasteland of Moorfields. From the north rose the dark hill of High-gate and Daisyville beyond.

Above the starlight glimmered. A sky full of gelt, the loot of Heaven. A vast and milky pad tracked across the universe, the lanterns of a million link-boys to lead us through eternal dark-mans.

Below was bedlam, the Whit in uproar. Shouts and huzzahs and chanting song. Calling out the rhythm of a double name:

Blue-skin! Blue-skin! For he was the hero of the hour. And from every cribb of that dark trib came the clatter of a clanker on the bars of a cell or any other thing that might sound out the rough music of defiance.

'Hear th-that, Bess? They're cheering Joe. And m-making a fine stall for my escape. A l-loud celebration is ever a good screen. Remember how we k-k-kicked away from the New P-Prison on Whit Monday?'

'Yes. Or how we came for you at Newgate on the day of St Bartholomew's Fair!' I called, and reached out to him, but he was yet too far from me along the ledge.

'A h-holiday for the flat culls provides a f-f-fine noise for flash labour,' he pattered on. 'And tonight is a f-feast of f-fools for the *Newgate Calendar*. For Blueskin was the rogue k-king crowned Lord of Misrule, having delivered us all from the thief-taker general. The Whit was close to m-mutiny and that was when I m-made my m-move, Bess. The quod-culls were b-b-busy enough quelling the riot.'

And so he blew the widd to me on his escape. I canted all his tricks and the heart of his talent, for to kick away like he did required an act of will so strong that he could bend others to it, just as he might twist a wire to make a picklock. That was the devil that came to help him in Newgate.

Like card-sharpers that play the passing-lay the best way to work that drop on a cull is to gull him into thinking he cants things better than you do. And that was how Jack Sheppard bitched the minds of the quod-culls at the Whit. When the keeper came to inspect his darbies that darkmans, Jack begged him to come again later in the night, imploring this so desperately that it firmly planted the very opposite thought in the hearer. So the quod-cull was abrupt in insisting that he would not visit the cell until peep of day and Jack canted that, with so many uninterrupted hours ahead, it was now his best chance to make his bid for liberty.

'I tr-tricked them, Bess,' he jabbered proudly. 'I f-fooled them all.'

As for the particular magic of his art, I knew his methods to quit himself from a pair of handcuffs. The first required him to stall the quod-cull fastening them then push his paws through the manacles so that they shackled a little further up on his forearms. That made them loose enough about his wrists for him to slip out of them with ease. If he had not the chance to divert the gaoler in such a manner he used a tiny picklock that he could hold between his grinders.

So, with his paws free he attacked the chimney-breast of the Castle hold, picking the mortar from between the bricks with the broken link from the chain of his leg-irons. An iron bar was embedded above the flue to prevent an escape through this passage but once it was removed it proved a most useful implement. He slithered upward, being as thin and lithe as a chimney-sweep, then broke through into the room above. He milled or dubbed his way through six strong doors, passing through the chapel and onto a ledge of the outside wall.

And there I touted him, high above Romeville. But he did not see me. I reached out to him.

'Jack!'

Using his cell blanket as a rope, he lowered himself onto the roof of a ken next to the gaol.

'Wait!' I jabbered. 'Wait for me!'

He found the glaze of a sky-parlour open and, lifting the sash, he dupped in. Biding a while for the glim of that ken to be doused, he then brushed upon the sneak, creeping down the dancers onto the pad. And there he was on Newgate Street.

Wait. I called out and tried to signal to him to pike it up towards Cheapside and beyond to Poultry, to come for me there. *Wait*, I then recall. *That is where I yet bide. And this is but some idle fancy.*

Wait!

❦

But the dream was doused as first glim roused me from slumber. *Wait.* I kept my glaziers shut for a moment to take one last look at him padding it up Newgate Street, bidding the watch at St Sepulchre's bene darkmans as he shabbed off down Snow Hill and away from me. *Wait.* Then I dubbed my eyes open, back in my cribb at peep of lightmans. With another wretched day in that trib staring me in the phiz.

For this whim of slumber was no escape, merely liberty of the gate for the darkmans. And my private fancy turned public romance as now all of the Common Ward stood eager for any prattle of Jack's latest flight, greedy for their snack of the gapeseed. Though I was well cheered by the news of it at first, I yet fenced a dread of something foretold in my crank vision. Of being left behind and forsaken. As days passed I was touted more peerily by all in the Compter. I noted a mocking pity in their glaziers and heard laughter at my back.

My little punk Lizzy tried to hide a newspaper from me. The *Daily Journal,* a month old, dated *Friday, 11th September.* It ran an account of how Jack had been snabbled on Finchley Common. It pattered of the ordinary chaplain's visit to his cell, of Jack confessing: '*He has hinted in dark terms, that he hath committed robberies since his escape,'* it read, *'and he denies that he was ever married to the woman who assisted him therein, and who is now in the Compter for the same, declaring that he found her a common strumpet in Drury Lane, and that she hath been the cause of all his misfortunes and misery.'*

I felt the sting of it and thought of the strange humour Jack had been in on that morning in Spitalfields and what he had pattered, but I still could not cant it. Perhaps some hackney-scribbler had put the widds in his gob. I reasoned it was just Grub Street prattle. So I paid no heed to the slander of it, though biding in my cribb I heard that crank voice in my head reading it out to me again: *common strumpet . . . cause of all his misfortunes.*

But as the babble of his fugitive adventures reached my luggs I feared greater disappointment. It was rumoured that he now kept two mistresses in a cribb in Soho. Now he tricked me too, just as he had worked the drop on the quod-culls, and his liberty knew no bounds. Perhaps he had made a pact with the devil and put his own soul in pawn or become a creature of the mob in acting out his notoriety. I glimmed with a smoky rage, but as that burned out I was left with a melancholy gloom that he had forgotten me so. I screened my feelings yet felt a terrible loneliness at the thought that all of my life now would be judged by Jack's ill fame.

Then Mary Sheppard came to tout me in the Compter, a fortnight after he had kicked away. She had padded it from St James's Palace where she had petitioned mercy for her son, begging that he might be spared death and be marinated instead.

'I didn't get to see the King, Bess,' she pattered. 'But I tipped them the petition. One of the servants there said that His Majesty had shown a great deal of interest in the case.'

I smiled at the poor old mort for I did not want to douse the glim of hope in her. I had heard the crank prattle that Jack might be pardoned and some great gentry-cove was ready to intercede on his behalf. I knew there was but a queer chance of that. Though all the flat world wondered at his exploits I canted they would never spare him.

'You've seen him?' I asked Mary.

She nodded. 'I begged him to leave the country. But though he promised to do so, I don't believe he is sincere.'

'Jack can scarce live outside Romeville,' I pattered bitterly, 'let alone in some foreign land.'

I recalled that fancy we once shared of piking it to Daisyville together and twigged for a moment that there was yet some hope. Jack was lost without me and all had gone best for him when we were palled up. He might dally with a couple of loose jades in Soho but they meant nothing and I was determined to face them down.

'Who is he with?' I demanded.

'Bess . . .' She shrugged.

'Tell me.'

'Well, you know how coves are.'

'I do.'

'He's changed, Bess. He's become quite callous towards women. Sarah, the maid who washed his linen in the Whit, got caught in an affray and had an eye blackened. Well, she told me Jack saw that and asked her how long she'd been married. And when she chided him for such a question, him knowing the contrary, he replied, "Sarah, don't deny it for I see you've got the certificate on your face."'

I laughed at this but not for long. 'Mary,' I took her by the arm, 'is it true?'

'What?'

'That he has two women now.'

'Yes.' She sighed. 'And they're both called Kate, that's the jest of it. I don't believe he cares much for either of them. It's all a big show, Bess. He's become so grand now he merely dotes upon his own name.'

'He still loves you, Mary.'

'Well, I am his mother. But I think that in his heart somewhere he still loves you, too.'

I shrugged, wishing it were true yet sitting mum-chance on the matter.

'He's not himself any more,' Mary pattered on. 'He was always a wild boy but now he seems to have so little sentiment left. He yet grows more reckless with his life. And with Tom now transported, he's all I have.'

Her other son had been marinated only days before his brother had kicked away. Poor Mary Sheppard left the Poultry Compter eyes glib with grief.

But my glaziers stayed dry. I would not give in. None would filch Edgworth Bess of her love or bitch her from a chance to prove it. Jack might indelicately break free from his promises with the vulgar use of two Kates, each a picklock for him to unfetter himself from our precious bond, but he had not escaped me yet. For we were meant to be and could be saved only by each other. So if he would not come for me, I would come for him. I would find a way.

Newgate Gaol, 23rd February 1726

Dear Applebee,

I finally caught up with Jack Sheppard at Sheer's alehouse in Maypole Alley near Clare Market on the evening of that astonishing day when he was seen about town in a reckless parade of defiance.

'I was p-padding it down past Piccadilly and I touted a p-push gathered around a pair of ballad singers in the Haymarket. The subject of their song was Sh-Sheppard,' he told me proudly, talking of himself in the third person, like some bold Caesar dictating his own history. 'And the company was very merry about the matter.'

As he recalled that little street opera, of joining the audience to his own drama, his face beamed with delight. Fame, the dream he would never wake from, fatal fame, which now laid a trap for him.

Since Wild's wounding and Sheppard's escape, the Hundreds of Drury had descended into lawless bacchanalia. With the thief-taker dispatched and the prison-breaker at large, all the flat coves feared that Romeville might soon be prey to chaos.

And it was on the last day of October that Sheppard made his rebellious appearance. The hue-and-cry was raised and I followed his trail on your behalf, to secure the story we had retained him for. It was Hallowe'en, when the world might be turned upside-down for the night.

He was spied that afternoon making merry with his two new mistresses in a tavern on Newgate Street, within the very sight of the Whit. He then hired a hackney-coach and drove along, with the windows drawn up, through the very arch of that dread prison. By evening he arrived alone at Clare Market and sent for his mother.

A crowd soon gathered, all ranks of London coming to watch his defiant promenade. I got there about ten to see him quite befuddled in drink with two pistols poking out of his fine suit jacket. Many of his flash associates urgently counselled him to withdraw while others simply drank his health and goaded him on.

I sat with him and sought to commit what he said to memory. I had gained his confidence but in truth he was ready to tell all. Just as with Wild revealing his tricks to Gay, Jack Sheppard wanted to be remembered so his tongue loosened. Speaking calmly, his stammer tempered with the drink he had taken, he told me that after his last escape he had wandered abroad in the guise of a beggar. Everywhere he heard his name mentioned as he had become once more the common discourse of the town. There was no escape from the spectacle, the carnival with but one mask: his own.

He broke into a pawnbroker's on Drury Lane one night and, hearing the occupants discourse in frightened whispers from the chamber upstairs, spoke loudly to an imaginary companion that he should shoot the first man who entered, thus putting them in fear of their lives. Along with the loot, he equipped himself with fine rigging and ornaments to furnish his next disguise. He took a black suit of clothes, a tie-wig and a silver-hilted sword, along with a gold watch, some diamond rings and a bejewelled snuff-box.

'Jack f-filched what he needed and stowed himself in a cribb in Newport Market.' Once more he adopted this detached narration. 'His m-mother came and jabbered that he should flee the kingdom, b-but he's tired of piking it, Billy.'

He smiled as he recounted the refuge he took with his two mistresses. He now contrived a sensual escape, becoming quite fugitive with his affections, exhausting every carnal posture with his pliant concubines.

'And what of Bess?' I beseeched him, knowing that, though many had condemned her, others had seen Jack's attitude to his wife as base and ungenerous.

'Poor Bess.' He let out a sad and wistful sigh. 'She's b-better off without me. Well, she has her freedom now.'

'Yet she resides in the Poultry Compter on your account.'

'I mean her fr-freedom from me. She'll have that for certain. You hackney-scribblers can m-make sure of it. My curse will yet be her b-blessing.'

'I don't understand.'

'You don't cant nothing, Billy. All those b-books. Wait till you're ready to swing, then you'll know something.'

Drunk and arrogant as he was, there was yet some eloquence to this.

'Life pikes it fast when you're b-born to hang,' he went on. 'So Jack starred the glaze of decency.'

I took this to mean that he considered morality to be transparent, that he saw through the rules before breaking them.

'F-f-fame is a draw for the wenches.'

'Indeed.' I smiled.

Jack spied me coldly for a moment, and I mused that though the lack of company can make a man fond, the excess of it can inspire a morbid humour.

'I just drank to the dregs of p-pleasure,' he declared. 'While that d-dirty old ge-gentleman looked on.'

'Who?' I asked him, and Jack burst into laughter.

'Why, Death, of course! My d-death.' He sighed. 'Death is a lusty watching-cull.'

He shook his head, took a sip of brandy, then roused himself, saying, 'Th-then this, Sheppard's last extraordinary performance, in this fine rigging.'

He cast his arms wide to display himself, to show his apparel: a black suit of paduasoy silk and all the jewellery he'd filched from the pawnbrokers to furnish his final disguise.

'He wore the clothes of an apprentice as a youth, m-masqueraded as a butcher and a beggar while on the pad, and n-now is transformed into a p-perfect gentleman!'

He picked up his glass for a toast. This was yet another flight, to become an exquisite parody of all those fine people who wished him hanged.

'Jack d-don't just take the jewels from the gentry-coves,' he boasted. 'He filches their v-very character.'

It was nearly midnight when his mother arrived. He dismissed the company and I joined the crowd that looked on as the night's drama drew to a close. Mary Sheppard sat by him and they shared three quarterns of brandy, but while he spoke intently to the one woman to whom his loyalty was never divided, the constables of the watch came for him. He was too drunk to offer much resistance. As he was taken he called, 'Help, for God's s-sake! I am in the hands of blood-hounds, help, for Christ's sake!'

He protested that his captors meant to murder him, which

indeed they did and most judicially. But none came to his rescue. In all his strange pomp and grandeur, Sheppard had quite forgot that the mob was but an idle spectator to his causeless rebellion rather than any stalwart confederate in it.

He was brought back to Newgate and weighed down with heavier fetters, double-ironed on both legs and with chains running through each side of his handcuffs. A watch was now kept on him day and night.

Another narrative was commissioned to be sold on his hanging day and Defoe took command of this work as its single author. It was thought wise, however, to keep one of us on hand to record Sheppard's remarks as he seemed ever ready to offer up quotable jests and banter. On Sunday at the prison chapel a visiting gentleman asked a turnkey which of the congregation was the famous prison-breaker. When he was pointed out, Jack declared, 'Yes, sir, I am the Sheppard, and all the g-g-gaolers in the town are my flock. I cannot stir into the country b-b-but they are all at my heels b-b-baa-ing at me.'

The condemned hold soon became vacant when it let forth Joe Blueskin to be hanged and visitors now flocked to see Sheppard there. For all the trouble he had caused the keepers and turnkeys, they were handsomely compensated with what they collected in fees. Charging four shillings to see the famous inmate, they had taken two hundred guineas by the end of that week.

So the living drama of Wild, Sheppard and Blueskin was yet being played out before our eyes. Sheppard had become the curiosity of the age as a great concourse of people came to view him on show in the theatre of Newgate. Only one poor creature was denied this privilege, which indeed should have been her right: Elizabeth Lyon, who still languished in a gaol nearby.

Your obedient author,

William Archer Esq.

IX

Lizzy touted at me with dread when she came to my cribb that lightmans.

'Jack's been taken,' she pattered all peerily. 'He's in the Whit.'

I canted that she feared I would take the news badly so I could not forbear from making a jest of it, if only to douse the mournful gawp on her phiz. 'Well, at least I know where he is now,' I quipped sharply.

But that just put the spark of shock in her black-button glaziers. 'Bess!' she gasped.

I smiled at her. 'A joke, Lizzy.' I sighed. 'You're still a flat one at heart.' For it is ever the sport of the canting-crew to laugh at bad tidings or any kind of danger. And I was not to be bitched into despair by this prospect. Yet there was some truth in my crank prattle. All the days of Jack's gallivanting were over as he now bided in the Whit and I dwelled a moment on the justice of that. The lully pride and foolishness he had displayed had led him to be taken so easily. But I canted that it was not yet the time to peach him but rather go to his aid. This might be the last cogging of the dice, after all.

Sukey Hawkins's crew of jades were due to be discharged from the Compter, and with Lizzy going, I would have a loyal mort on the outside. On the inside I worked the drop on the quod-culls with garnish and an easy charm. I twigged that one of their number, called Martin, was friendly enough. I could play that one, put the bite on him as I had done with Butler Fox. And he worked some hours at Newgate, there being a call for extra turnkeys to herd the crowds that now flocked to see the infamous Jack Sheppard. The Poultry Compter was close to the Whit, just the other end of Cheapside, so it would be simple enough to get messages to him. I was soon to conceive a lay that my lover and I might use to kick away together.

A week after Jack's snabbling came Blueskin's hanging day. He was to be scragged with a cove convicted of forging a lottery ticket and a poor black boy charged with robbery and arson. This Martin was there when the sheriff's men came to convey them to Tyburn. As their fetters were removed, the noose was placed around each neck with its cord wrapped around the body and the elbows pinioned. In the cart the forger fell into some crank argument with his escort, and Blueskin used this stall to try to unleash himself from his halter. The push that looked on stood quite mum-chance as he used his grinders on the knotted rope so that he might free his paws and jump out onto the pad; indeed, it seemed the mob clearly countenanced his attempt at piking it away. But the row was soon quelled and the officers' attention returned to him so he was secured once more.

Poor Joe. He held his composure for as long as he could, his final wish to perish bravely, like a proud rogue. But it was prat-tled that he was quite pot-valiant by the time he reached the three-legged mare. Reeling about insensibly, weeping and spouting lines of Pope's Homer, he made a sad end to his reckless life. But his journey to the tree tipped me an idea.

The next lightmans Lizzy came to bid me farewell. 'I wish I could bide here till they set you at liberty,' she pattered.

'Well, they don't intend to do that until Jack is scragged. And I need you on the outside . . .' I took hold of her paw and whispered '. . . to make sure that don't happen.'

Her little buttons brightened and she took a quick breath.

'Brush upon the sneak mind,' I told her. 'And stow the widd on what I'll now tell you.'

As I jabbered out the lay to her, I touted all my own lost youth on her eager phiz. There might yet be hope, I twigged. For Lizzy at least. Blowing the widd on my plan, I watched her peerily that she might cant every detail. We did not have much time after all.

'And let this be your last wickedness,' I pattered, tipping her a buss. 'Step lightly, nabs. Stay free.'

Thus I recalled the last words of Punk Alice to me and felt the tears well in my own glaziers. But I stifled a sob and sent her on her way.

In the meantime I had Martin smuggle a note to Jack, wrapped around a very sharp clasp knife.

Two days later, Lizzy came to visit and all was in place for Jack's kicking away. On his hanging day his leg darbies and handcuffs would be taken off in the press-yard and the sheriff's men would then bind him with the cord about the arms, but Jack would have the clasp knife stowed in the lining of his waistcoat, blade upwards. Once in the cart he would begin peerily to mill his hempen bonds, using the slight motion of his body to allow the chive to cut into the rope. With his paws free he might then jump out onto the pad at the appointed moment.

I had gathered all the garnish I could muster to secure myself liberty of the gate on the day, pattering to the quod-culls that it was my dearest wish to bid a last farewell to my husband as he went to the tree. I would give my escort the slip and meet with Lizzy at High Holborn.

Here a crew of girls would be assembled with flowers to pelt the cart, which would be Jack's signal to leap out and make his getaway. We would all make such a noise and clamour to stall the sheriff's men that he would have a clear path to kick away. For there is a hidden alleyway off that street, known as Little Turnstile, that leads to Lincoln's Inn Fields, so narrow that pursuit is nigh impossible.

And it seemed certain that the mob would not make a hue-and-cry but rather revel in the gape-seed of yet another of Sheppard's escapes. So the insensible push might act as a screen and the fame that once snared him might now set him free.

I would pike it with him through the passageway to a carriage waiting on the other side of Lincoln's Inn. Then we would quit Romeville for good and find some place where we might stow ourselves properly.

'We have but a slim chance of it, Lizzy,' I confided to her. 'But let us work this lay as best we can.'

As I touted her closely she would not meet my eyes but rather looked around peerily as if we were being spied upon. 'What?' I demanded, and grabbed hold of her.

'You know not of the other plan?'

'What other plan? I don't cant what you prattle.'

Then my little punk babbled of how Jack had pattered with

some other crew of a lay that he might use if this one failed. A design so crank and mysterious that would cheat death itself, not just the gallows.

'Oh, it is ungodly!' Her phiz darkened and she would speak no more of it.

I grew nettled at her and insisted that she blow the widd on all she knew. Lizzy's glaziers glimmed in holy terror as she pattered out its details, as if Jack had indeed made a pact with Merry Old Roger.

Newgate Gaol, 23rd February 1726

Dear Applebee,

I was soon to learn of this morbid scheme of Jack
Sheppard's last escape for I became part of the planning of it
when you sent me, in those last days before the hanging, to
confirm the final conditions of the publishing agreement with
Sheppard. You will recall that all the monies to be paid to him
and his mother had been agreed upon and the biography was
now close to completion. Defoe was putting the final touches
to *A Narrative of all the Robberies, Escapes, &c. of John Sheppard*
with the expectation that it would be a great success. There
was but one requirement left on the part of our subject: that
he would publicly sanction the work as his official account so
that we might surpass all the other tracts now being printed
for his hanging day. An advertisement had already appeared
announcing this edition and Sheppard was to carry a copy of
our pamphlet with him on the cart to Tyburn, thus
announcing it to the crowd as his authorised confession. He
agreed to do this so we moved on to his last requests.

As with Blueskin and many a wild rogue, Sheppard's greatest
dread beyond death was that his body might fall into the hands
of those grim butchers from the Surgeons Hall and be taken
there for dissection. The fear of being anatomised, of hidden
secrets revealed posthumously and of others having some
intimate knowledge denied us, is something of a terror to the
canting-crew. I pondered on what pitiful truths might be
rendered in being so torn asunder, but as we made the arrangements for his corpse to be taken from the fatal tree, Jack
Sheppard pattered something yet more strange and curious.

'I w-want a m-mourning hearse,' he told me, 'b-by the triple tree. And for you to m-make contact with some gentlemen.'

Then, to my bemused astonishment, he related the particulars of this most fantastical project. He gave out precise orders as to what was needed and of the certain parties that were to take custody of his remains after his execution. He made me swear that I would keep this secret until the very hour of his hanging.

Sheppard now assumed a kind of serenity that transcended the dismal circumstances of the condemned hold. Undaunted by the heaviest weight of the law that bore down upon him, he seemed ready to fly once more. For despite his mortal sentence his name had been granted a reprieve from oblivion, the image and idea of him spared in perpetuity. I was with him when Sir James Thornhill came to call.

'What k-k-kind of b-b-beak is he?' Sheppard asked me, as he was announced by the quod-culls.

'He's serjeant-painter to the King,' I told him.

'A phiz-monger?'

'Yes, Jack. The best in the land. He's here to work on your portrait. You're to be memorialised by a great master. It will be quite an honour.'

'An honour for him certainly,' he declared proudly, holding up his chains. 'M-M-Many have f-failed to hold Jack Sheppard long. This man might at least c-c-capture his likeness.'

But he spied the wry smile on my face and let his guard drop. 'Well,' he sighed, 'it might be bene to have my f-f-figure mounted in g-g-gilt one day. I'll be hanging in the sh-sh-sheriff's picture frame soon enough.'

Thornhill entered with a pupil from his drawing academy, an engraver by trade and an illustrator of satirical prints. The cell was cleared of visitors, though I was permitted to remain, along with the gaoler on watch. The artist set up his drawing pad and began to make a draft of Sheppard in chalk and pencil. Thornhill bade him sit at a table by the barred window of the cell. The light caught his face and in that moment he looked angelic. The deep, soulful eyes, the delicate chin, the generous mouth, all illuminated as a beatific icon. Thornhill commanded him to hold the pose and sketched quickly. Sheppard's eyes widened slightly, gazing beyond, and he glowed with the obscure charm that only the truly famous possess. Thus transfigured he lifted his manacled wrists and muscular hands, and gestured with long, elegant fingers. One hand gently clasped the edge of the table, the other pointed away, as if giving some sign of benediction.

He marvelled at his own image when it was shown to him. I noted a wistful self-love that one could hardly condemn.

'This will make a g-g-good print, sir,' he said.

'Well, I have to paint the portrait first,' Thornhill rejoined, with a frown.

'Y-Yes. That will be one p-p-picture. But th-th-then many may be m-m-made out of it.' He seemed more eager for the mechanical reproduction of his immortality than the fine art of it.

Thornhill's pupil laughed. 'It will make an excellent mezzotint,' the younger man declared. 'And run to many copies.'

Jack was due to hang in three days' time.

So all of my duties for you in this respect were now done, but for the arrangements that would need my presence on the occasion itself. In the meantime I had another commission.

John Thurmond, dancing-master at the Drury Lane Theatre, was putting together a pantomime based on Sheppard's adventures and they were in need of an extra ballad. A writer already engaged by Thurmond had requested my assistance. As I left Newgate I passed two sheriff's men by the gate talking of Jonathan Wild. A chaplain had been spied visiting his house: the latest rumour was that he was receiving last rites.

At the theatre Thurmond was looking through plans for theatrical machinery, scenery transformations, descriptions of lighting effects and set construction. There were vivid costume designs based on the *commedia dell'arte*. The production was to be called *Harlequin Sheppard*.

'Of course, his life lends itself to a great spectacle,' the caper-merchant insisted. 'We shall astonish the audience, just as he has dumbfounded the whole nation. We go on in ten days. Unless he escapes again and spoils the ending.'

'A reprieve!' a rotund figure called, as he entered. 'Surely young Jack should be spared at the end, at the very last minute! That a grim tragedy might turn into something bright and comic, like an absurd opera that ends happily. That would comply with the taste of the town. All of London is for Sheppard, is it not?'

It was John Gay. He approached the table where we stood. 'Bootblack!' He embraced me. 'I asked for you. Are you still up to mischief? I hope so. We're in need of your experience.'

'How was Bath?' I enquired.

He had spent the autumn there taking the waters. He sighed. 'Good for the colic, bad for the purse.'

'I thought you were a guest of Lord Scarborough.'

'I was. Dear Billy, you have no idea how expensive is the

generosity of nobility. One has constantly to tip the servants, you see. Well, I prosper in my own way.'

'You do?'

'Indeed. Each day I wake to find myself content with less than I had aimed at the day before. And so I grow richer. Come.' He took my arm. 'Let's to work.'

Thurmond wanted a stirring measure for the first act. There was much stage business of mime and dance in presenting Sheppard's escape, full of artifice and illusion. What was needed was something shockingly dramatic as a contrast. I suddenly thought of what I had witnessed in the bail-dock and suggested that we use the incident of Blueskin cutting the thief-taker's throat.

'Excellent!' Gay rubbed his hands together in glee. 'The ballad of a rogue with a knife. We'll have a murder, too.'

'But no one seems certain whether Wild is dead or not,' I cautioned him.

There had been much speculation as to his fate and all of London seemed cautious to act in anything until this matter was settled. John Gay, however, showed uncharacteristic alacrity. 'Let's finish him off,' he declared, making a cutting gesture with his hand against his own neck. 'With a Newgate garland!'

And that became the title of our song, recounting how brave Blueskin might have dispatched the thief-taker to the grave. I was glad that we might give Blueskin a ballad, and Gay was full of energy and a kind of bloodthirsty playfulness. I confess that I did not contribute too much to the eventual lyrics. The first two lines, with a bit of flash in them, are certainly mine:

> *Ye gallants of Newgate, whose fingers are nice*
> *In diving in pockets or cogging of dice.*

But the rest of it really does belong to my friend, and it was Gay who decided that we should set it to the air of the old song 'Packington's Pound'. He hummed it to me.

'Ben Jonson used it in *Bartholomew Fair*. You know, the song about the cutpurse? Some in the audience might get that. It's a nine-line verse,' he tapped out the rhythm, 'like a Spenserian stanza, except it doesn't end with an alexandrine but rather an eleven-syllable couplet.'

Gay had a fine and melodious ear. Having once written the libretto for a pastoral opera by a great German composer, he had an equal sensibility for the catch of a tavern or a street serenade. And he was able to work some sharp satire to our cheap ditty, comparing the honest crimes of the poor with those of the rich:

> *Some by publick revenues, which pass'd through their hands,*
> *Have purchas'd clean houses, and bought dirty lands:*
> *Some to steal from a charity think it no sin,*
> *Which, at home (says the proverb) does always begin.*

He ever had a poetic instinct for the exchange of values. From exquisite aria to rough ballad, his muse ran high or low but was never of the middling sort.

It was the last of twilight as I walked home from the theatre to my lodgings in Henrietta Street. A purpled sky stretched over the piazza, lights were coming on in the windows, and link-boys were sparking up their torches. I noted a crowd of gentlemen gathered by Moll King's as I passed by. The London season had begun and a fresh battalion of young bloods had descended from the shires for the delights of the wicked city. New apparel and charmingly coltish manners marked many of them as mere squires of fashion and in town for the first time.

As I wistfully scanned what might be my prey as a beau-trap I spied one of that number who stood apart from the rest, his back to me. There was something in his poise and deportment, a detached air that drew me to him. I had no conscious intention that night but some curious impulse must have inspired me to approach the young man. To think that in that fortuitous moment I might simply have walked on by.

I came close and he appeared to be looking at some distant prospect or opportunity. Then he turned to face me. And there he was, with those sculpted cheeks, sky-blue eyes and ripe mouth that opened with a bright smile. This was the very youth I had sought all these months and I could not hold back the joyful announcement of my discovery.

'The Honourable Adam Stonyforth,' I declared clumsily.

He gracefully bestowed on me a charming frown. I felt utterly foolish.

'I fear you have me at a disadvantage, sir,' he retorted softly, with a playful hint of reproach.

'Forgive me.' I hastily composed myself. 'I saw you at Windsor. William Archer Esquire.'

A gentle smile played on Adam's lips and, with a firm handshake, we held each other's gaze.

'I am new to London,' he told me.

'Indeed.'

'Is it really so obvious?'

'Allow me to show you around. I know all of its charms. And its dangers.'

The young aristocrat sighed. 'But I'm afraid I'm quite lacking in funds. I await my father's allowance. Until then I have quite meagre means.'

'Then you shall be my guest, sir.' I raised a hand as I spied his hesitance. 'I insist.'

I would like to think that this offer was born of purest charity but even as I was enchanted by his beauty I was yet driven by all the instincts learned from my years on the street. For there is no better way for a beau-trap to cultivate a cull than to have them in their debt. This art of polite deception had become my second nature, and just as the guinea-dropper works his lay by offering some coin as a lure to a greater theft, so I could not help but think of my generosity as an investment.

So I stood him a dish of coffee, entreating Tawny Betty to lace it well with arrack, and proceeded with a delicate interrogation of his circumstances. He intimated that it would not be long before he came into his majority. Fleetingly I mused how I might win his affections and reap a small fortune also.

We strolled across Covent Garden where all the bloods and belles congregated, dressed up in their finery, keen to see and be seen, to make assignations.

'This is the great Square of Venus,' I told him with an idle gesture at the cobbles, 'where all of London comes to seek love.'

We supped at the Shakespeare's Head on turtle soup, roast

veal and some fine burgundy. Having hinted at some independent means, I announced my vocation as that of a poet, and to my satisfaction this impressed him greatly. Casually exaggerating my acquaintance with Swift and Pope, I boasted that I was collaborating on major works with both Daniel Defoe and John Gay. I dreamed of patronage even as I gazed at that beautiful creature.

I quoted some of the more *outré* lines of Rochester's verse and closely observed his reaction. He laughed with a knowing amusement that suggested he might share my cursed nature, but it was yet early and I was determined to relish this evening as merely a divine fancy. It was quite the relief I needed from all the hours spent in the foul air of Newgate. And so we walked through the town together, my arm in his.

Reaching White's coffee-house we entered in search of wits, and though I was only able to summon up a couple of gin-raddled Grub Street philosophers, I nevertheless passed them off to Adam as 'two of the greatest thinkers of our age'.

We then proceeded to the Rose tavern, in full riot as we arrived. A posture-girl stripped off and climbed upon the table. With a huge pewter dish for a stage and a lighted candle as a prop she executed a series of quite astonishing poses for the assembly.

After that I took my new friend to a gaming house in Brydges Street, cautioning him to observe carefully before placing any bet. I discreetly signified to him how dice were cogged and cards sharped. In this way I sought both to gain yet more of his trust, and to persuade against any habit in this perilous sport that might endanger a future legacy I already saw as partly my own.

Leaving there, we visited several alehouses and gin-shops, though I was careful to steer our course from any flash tavern where one of the canting-crew might blow the widd on me. It was nearly midnight when we staggered out onto Drury Lane, very merry and quite drunk. I knew that it was now the time to ask Adam if he wished to end the night with a visit to some academy or vaulting-school. Mother Griffith's in King Street would stand me commission for any culls I brought there. But the young man looked at me coyly and gave a little shrug.

'I fear I'm not much one for the ladies, Billy,' he confessed.

So I suggested he come to my rooms for one last drink. I lit a fire and opened a bottle of cognac. I stood close to Adam as I made a toast and, detecting something plaintive in those pale blue eyes, leaned in closer still. I ventured a tentative kiss, a gentle buss against his full red lips. I was wary of making him fearful of me so I acted softly.

But all at once I felt his mouth press hungrily on mine. One of his hands clawed at my breast, the other slyly unbuttoned my breeches. I was surprised and indeed enchanted to find the modesty he had displayed in other matters utterly absent here. He later confessed that as a youth on his country estate there had been many opportunities for sportive capers with manservants and stable-boys, though he swore none had taken full possession of him.

That was to be my pleasure. I still remember the intoxicating lust that overcame me as I held his smoothly curved haunches and of how he gasped in pained ecstasy. My mind choked with joyful oblivion and for an instant this sublime creature was mine and I his. Afterwards in an embrace of possession we were lulled into slumber.

I awoke in the depths of night, my head befuddled. Adam had rolled from me, and as I reached out to him, I felt a pang in my heart. At first I took it as guilt, for all of the lustful and avaricious designs I had on this noble youth and the careless manner in which I had corrupted him. But there was something more, an unfamiliar dread that held me. And so I felt for the first time the fear that is love.

Later, when he thought me sleeping I opened my eyes to watch Adam by my dressing-table. He stood and spied himself in the looking-glass with a gaze of wonder on his face. Like Narcissus peering into the pool, I thought, so rudely conscious of his own beauty.

It was then I conceived of some great work and all my dreams of becoming a poet assembled in that moment. For this would be verse that came straight from the heart, love and art exquisitely combined. And however I might profit from this sublime creature, I would then have a gift to make me worthy of his affection. An ode I would write for him that would preserve his youth and radiance for ever. I would transform him as Narcissus, the subject of a great pastoral epic.

I lost the next day in a delicious haze of sentiment and sensuality, idly scribbling notes and finishing off the cognac. I rose at peep of day, and vaguely noting the crowds filing beneath my window, I dimly fancied them as some audience to this great new drama in my life. Then my mind stirred and my soul came down to earth: I had grim duties to attend upon. The mob was already making their way up to St Giles for the procession. It was Jack Sheppard's hanging day.

Your obedient author,

William Archer Esq.

X

THE press-yard was crowded when they brought Jack down from the chapel that lightmans, not just with the push of quod-culls and soul-drivers but also those curious coves who tip money to the keepers to tout the condemned take their last holy sacra-ment. I struggled to get close enough that he might spy me but there were too many around him.

I had melted bene garnish in return for liberty of the gate and to be taken down to the Whit to bid him farewell. With two escorts eyeing me peerily, Martin and one other who was not so friendly, I tried to twig how I might give them the slip and shab off to where Lizzy and her crew were biding.

Jack touted around calmly as the under sheriff made a formal demand for his body and a blacksmith knocked off the leg darbies from his shanks with a block and hammer. But when the sheriff's men came forward to put the noose over his neck and bind him with the cord he grew nettled. 'Wait!' he jabbered, holding up his paws with the handcuffs still fastened. 'What about these?'

'Why, you imp of mischief,' pattered the under sheriff with a smile on his gob. 'Do you think we'd try to deliver you without irons about your wrists?'

If he remained handcuffed he would not be able to free himself with the knife as planned. Jack raised his fambles as if to strike the man, there was a struggle and those who guarded me stepped forward to assist in bitching the prisoner. The quod-culls soon held him fast and, peery of Jack's protests, the under sheriff made a thorough search of his person. All at once he staggered back, squealing like a stuck gruntling. He had found the chive stowed in the waistcoat with its sharp blade outwards. Holding up a bleeding paw he ordered the weapon to be taken. Now we were done up and the whole lay milled.

I did not know what to do but I took this opportunity to shab off quietly. None touted me leave and brushing upon the sneak I made it to the lodge. Then I heard loud voices at my back so I piked it out onto Newgate Street. I canted that I had to get off the pad and screen myself so I made for the push gathered outside St Sepulchre's.

The street was lined with coves and morts all drawn to the gape-seed, as if every soul of Romeville was abroad that day to tout it. And the dancers in front of the gospel-shop were pushed with dells, heart-struck girls that made Jack their fondest sweet-heart. They sported bene rigging, white gowns and silken scarves, like bridesmaids to a grim wedding, with bunches of flowers and baskets of nosegays. I stowed myself there among them.

All these kitlings were jabbering excitedly. I touted one young fledgling sobbing openly as if it was her own true love going to the tree that lightmans. *Crank bitch*, I thought, and doused the urge to slap her, for what could Jack really mean to her or to any of these lully jades? I yet felt nothing but emptiness. But I twigged in that moment that it is ever easier to make a public spectacle of sham mourning than to feel the fearful candour of it in your own heart.

But though I was not ready to grieve I knew then all was lost. What could I do now? The great bell of the church tolled as the procession approached and the mob stood mum-chance awhile as the drab soul-driver prayed: 'All good people, pray heartily unto God for this poor sinner who is now going to his death and for whom the bell doth toll. You who are condemned to die, repent with lamentable tears.'

I felt helpless. Now that the widd was blown on our lay there was nothing left. Just one last thing, I thought desperately. One last tout at my lover. To bid him farewell, for him to tip me a buss to mend the wound of all the queer things pattered. It was my right to be with him at the end: that was how the story should be told. This was how it must finish, I canted.

I spied Martin and the other quod-cull on the pad in front of the procession, seeking me out in the crowd. The city marshal slowly led the parade on horseback. A posse of constables and mounted javelin men tracked after him. I touted Charles Hitchen riding proudly, but not Jonathan Wild, whose glory was now filched by Blueskin's blade. Then the cart came into view.

'Ask mercy of the Lord for the salvation of your soul through the merits of the death and passion of Jesus Christ, who now sits on the right hand of God to make intercession for you, if you penitently return to Him,' the soul-driver droned on.

I never saw Jack look so dimber as he did that day. He held himself proudly, trim and dapper in his fine suit of black silk. As the cart halted before the gospel-shop and his pale phiz turned to scan the push I swear his glaziers caught mine. He lifted his manacled paws and gave a shrug as if to patter that the game was up. Then that rascal smile spread across his gob and I wondered if he was thinking of that other crank scheme of his. But I could not believe that was yet another chance for him.

'The Lord have mercy on you.'

I just wanted Jack to utter my name. Though it might babble me to the quod-culls I needed some acknowledgment. Now you might tip me some credit, I beseeched him silently. I felt gulled of my part in his life, in his death. Mocked by all the morts around me who laid claim to him as their idol.

'Christ have mercy on you.'

'Jack!' I shouted, and piked it towards the cart.

I touted his glaziers glim a little as he spied me coming to him. That fine mouth quivered as if ready to stutter his love.

'Jack!' I called out to him once more.

But then I was mobbed as all the dells around me joined in the rush. *Jack!* They jabbered together in a chorus. *Jack!* They blew kisses and a shower of blooms was thrown up at him. *Jack!* His smile widened into a grin and he waved a shackled paw. But he did not see me now: he saw only the crowd.

Then the carriage pulled away, down the slope of Snow Hill, crossing the narrow bridge over the Fleet to the cheers and huzzahs of the multitude. The streets were filled from Holborn through St Giles and all the way to Tyburn. All of London had turned out for his sacrifice. I had lost him to the great push of Romeville.

I made to track after the black parade but a paw grabbed me. I turned to see Martin.

'Bess,' he pattered sternly, as I struggled from him.

Then the other quod-cull came and they snabbled me together.

And so we padded it back to the Compter. On our way I spied a pamphlet seller with the latest account of Jack's widds and actions. *A Narrative of all the Robberies, Escapes, &c. of John Sheppard* it named itself. Here was babbled his genuine last words, the cove assured me, so I tipped him the sixpence and carried it with me to the trib.

In my own cribb there, I scanned the thing slowly. In truth, I canted not what I was touting for, only that life works the drop on us with false hope. For though I dearly wished for some small benefit of his affections, here he peached me once more with his bitter widds. *A more wicked, deceitful, and lascivious wretch there is not living in England*, he prattled of me in ink upon a page. *She has proved my bane.*

There are those who say words cannot hurt and that only injuries to the body itself can leave a wound. But coves who patter such a lie are fools or lullies. For I might bear any pain upon the flesh or bone but this damning injury set out in black and white. Widds marked out for ever that might cast a spell and damn me. This was the imprint of his dying breath, a curse that might call out beyond the grave. All Romeville yet waited upon his execution but here was the true end for me. The story printed and my shameful part set down for all to read. All might know now that he did not love me. And so I was left alone and forsaken with such cruel thoughts.

She has proved my bane. A cruel babble that fed the crank voice inside my skull. Like my lost child that called out from Limbo. It now began to patter once more and would not stop.

My heart was truly milled and every hope doused, for this queer jabber was the worst horror of all.

Dear Applebee,

You revealed a certain foreknowledge of your own of Jack Sheppard's final escape attempt. I had fully expected you to laugh out loud when I spoke of his grotesque and fanciful scheme to cheat the gallows and the assistance he required from us in its operation. But you nodded quite soberly, contradicting me as I protested at its absurdity.

'You're too young to remember Half-hanged Smith,' you said.

'Half-hanged Smith?'

'Some twenty years ago. When I was but a garreteer like you. What a story that was.'

You then related the most astonishing tale to be chronicled in the *Newgate Calendar* as you agreed to Jack's terms. For he had confided to me a method for the resurrection of a hanged man and that he knew of a crew ready to perform it. Forgive me for quoting your words back at you but it would be good for the record to recount that actual precedent for this Tyburn miracle.

'In 1705 a certain John Smith was sentenced to hang for stealing a padlock from a warehouse door,' you told me. 'He went to the gallows on Christmas Eve and perhaps some charity of the season allowed him to be cut down early. He was taken to a house nearby, resuscitated by a surgeon and reprieved, since this is the law in such rare cases. From then on he was always known as Half-hanged Smith.

'He recalled that as he swung his spirits rose in a strange commotion, forcing their way to his head. He saw a great blaze of light and lost all sense of pain.

'Smith was in such agony when he was revived,' you laughed, 'that he cursed those who had brought him back and wished them hanged!'

'Do you really think it can be done?' I asked you.

'It's worth the gamble, Billy. With the rights to the account of it, think how many pamphlets we could sell.'

So I was there to help carry out such a phenomenon and on your behalf to see that Sheppard played his part of the bargain. A great crowd greeted him at the triple tree, a vast assembly that went on all the way across Hyde Park. As the hangman made ready with the hempen cord, Sheppard held up the printed copy of his narrative, announcing it as his authentic memoir and last dying confession, thus fulfilling his final obligation to us, his publishers. I then took it from him and signalled to the gazetteers we had in the crowd who all carried bundles of the biography, ready to be sold to an eager audience.

All that was left for me to do now was fulfil his last wish. I turned to him and noticed that he shivered.

'J-j-just the cold,' he said, shrugging the silk lapels of the fine black suit he had worn when he was taken. 'Didn't want to wear some drab topcoat over this fine p-p-paduasoy. I h-have to look my best now that I am to k-k-kick away at last.'

The rope was secured to the cross-bar of the fatal tree and the cart was made ready to pull away. Now I had to set in motion the strange request he had made in the condemned cell. This was to be his last bid to cheat the noose.

He was to be plucked from the tree as soon as the sheriff's men and constables might allow and a hearse would then convey him to a house nearby. There his body was to be wrapped in warm blankets and conveyed to a bed where blood-letting and vigorous friction applied to the limbs might bring back the circulation.

The carriage was ready as were the men who would follow this procedure. A premises near to Tyburn had been bespoken for the resuscitation and a physician employed to oversee this feat of Lazarus. All of this had been paid for by you.

'Is the h-hearse ready?' asked Sheppard.

I nodded.

'Th-Th-Then I'm happy.'

I'm not sure what faith he had in this, his last bid for freedom, or if he simply knew this instant as his best to die. I'd wager he would have been uncertain as to his own humour in that moment of truth. His spirit made a semblance of happiness. Perhaps that was enough.

But whatever the state of his mind or soul, his body surely put up a terrible struggle. That nimble frame, so slight and lithe, that had leaped o'er walls and rooftops, was now too light to bear him down in swift mercy. As the cart pulled away and he took flight upon air, he lacked the weight that might snap his neck or strangle him quickly out of suffering. His person began to spasm, his eyes bulged and a bloody froth bubbled from his mouth. He twisted and thrashed in silent agony as he danced the Tyburn jig.

The crowd seemed to hold its breath as the last of Sheppard's was choked out of him. A few could not forbear to laugh or even make jests at this obscene comedy, but they were soon silenced by the rest. For though some feign to laugh in the face of Death, here that gentleman out-stared us all, playing poor Jack Sheppard like a puppet.

It was eleven minutes by my watch before he shuddered into stillness. I wondered if he had yet seen the light that Half-hanged Smith had spoken of. And I mused on any chance that he might be restored to the continued suffering of existence. Then a soldier broke through the cordon surrounding the gallows and cut the body down. I signalled for the hearse to draw up closer and went to the foot of the fatal tree with a pair of pamphlet sellers. As we lifted him the flesh was still warm, though I could not tell if there was life in it yet.

As we took him to the prepared coach the throng began to move in closer, hundreds of eyes gazing in wonder on his mortal remains. Some came forward to reach out to touch the dead man. A woman held up her sick child so that Sheppard's numb hand might brush against its forehead.

The constables and sheriff's men could no longer hold back the crowd and we soon risked being mobbed. Then one of the men arranging the attempted resuscitation made his way through the multitude in an urgent manner. 'Be quick about it!' he gasped. 'The surgeon's waiting.'

He meant, of course, the doctor in a nearby house making ready to perform the unlikely miracle. But as soon as the fool uttered that dread word there came accusations among the assembly that we were those fiends who intended to steal Sheppard's body and take it off to be anatomised. *Surgeon!* The hated name echoed all around us and we were swarmed by a furious crew as we made for the hearse. *Surgeon!*

Sheppard's slack form was pulled from us and lifted high, like a trophy. As I opened my mouth to say something I was struck from behind and for a few seconds my mind closed into darkness.

When I opened my eyes I was on my hands and knees, a wounded animal with a head that roared in pain. I crawled towards the carriage and saw that the mob was making a fierce attack upon it. The driver had jumped down and now retreated under a hail of stones and mud. The horses were loosed from the shafts and whipped away as the coach was broken and pulled apart.

I got to my feet and turned to see the corpse tossed about on a seething mass of humanity, his fine suit now in tatters, his battered body lolling among them, like a broken doll. Any hope of reviving him was now utterly lost. Instead the hungry mob took possession of him, all struggling for some part of the vagabond sacrifice. They sought to claim him, as if that limp idol might finally speak from the depths and give voice to the outcast and the lawless. But it was too late. He was dead and now but a dumb prophet for their jabbering rage.

Your humble author & faithful garreteer of old,

William Archer Esq.

XI

S_{HE} *has proved my bane*, the voice jabbered, *she has proved my bane*, the widds in my luggs a hateful song. As I padded it by lightmans, the whole of Romeville seemed to peach me and I had to kick away from there. The voice would not leave me alone. Calling me wicked names: *dirtywhorebitchtrull, dirtywhorebitchtrull*. I had to make my own escape.

I heard how they had fought over Jack's corpse, touting for the royal touch of his dead bones or even a scrap of his rigging for a keepsake, grasping at his remains as a holy relic of the canting-crew. The mob had marched back to St Giles with the body. There was a wake in a boozing-ken where Jack was laid out and a riot in the Hundreds, with grim rumours among the flat-coves that Sheppard's ghost was abroad, leading a wraithlike crew that would burn down the Whit and mill every trib in Romeville. The beaks and the constables called for a company of Foot Guards to quell the revolt. By midnight the soldiers doused the unrest and formed an escort as the mortal remains were taken to St Martin-in-the-Fields' churchyard. The masses stood quietly as the dead rogue was afforded such queer military honours and order was restored to London as my dear Jack was lowered to his grave.

And then they anatomised his spirit as surely as the surgeons might have dissected his body. All took their snack of his fame and memory. All except me, of course. Many a time after I would meet a cove who had touted Jack but once upon the pad in his lifetime, yet swore him as his dearest pal. Everybody pattered that they had known him in some way. Only poor Bess, who had been closest to him yet denied even a scrap of his legacy, could honestly admit to ignorance of him. For in despair I no longer canted who he truly was. And all now canted me as the fatal woman who had led him to the fatal tree. So was I disinherited as every memorial peached me and whispered in my mind, *Wicked. Deceitful. Lascivious.*

I was discharged from the Poultry Compter barely a fortnight later without bail and I shabbed off back to St Giles. I was glad to be out of the trib but on the outside none would let me grieve. This was my bitter freedom. All the Hundreds of Drury touted me peerily. *Wicked.* Few dared patter anything to my phiz but instead pointed the finger and I would catch a queer look or the breath of a whisper. *Deceitful.* I was bad luck to others so I padded alone. *Lascivious.* And I never was so lonely with only ghosts for company. Jack dead, Blueskin dead, Mother Breedlove dead, Punk Alice dead – they tracked my steps through Romeville.

I thought of calling upon Mary Sheppard. But I could not bear the thought of any accusation in the grieving glaziers of that poor woman. So I steered clear of her too.

I even pondered on seeking out my little punk Lizzy but twigged what a crank notion that would be. For if she had found an honest trade it would be far from bene my turning up and the flat-coves she worked for knowing that she once ran with the canting-crew. What I dreaded more was that she might be in some vaulting-school or working upon the pad, all her youth and innocence filched, every spark doused from those bright black glaziers. Another soul damned by Edgworth Bess. *Wicked, deceitful, lascivious.*

I had but one friend now, my old pal the lush. I spent my days in boozing-kens and gin-shops, my nights working the buttock-and-file once more. Then one peep of day I woke and twigged I had to take flight, to kick away from it all.

So I found myself shabbing off eastwards that lightmans; with Jack's curses on my back, I was cast out of the Hundreds. A cruel wind blew down Cheapside as I passed a scrub of a beggar singing a ballad.

> *Away, sweet ducks with greedy eyes,*
> *From London walk up Holborn,*
> *Him that stole your clothes he flies*
> *With hempen wings to Tyburn.*

I dropped a penny in his dish but as I walked along my own song came once more. *She has proved my bane. She has proved my bane.* The catch of it kept rattling through my head.

I wrapped my shawl tight against the cold air and turned south towards the river. The sky was as grey as the lead on a church roof with scarce a glim of the day left in it. And all I felt of love was pain, yet I still tracked it as it piked from me. I touted for grief and a sorrow that might find its own end.

I was at London Bridge without canting what had brought me there. But as I walked along the narrow pad between the high kens built upon it I wondered if it was death itself that I was looking for. *Go on, jump*, the voice pattered. At the middle arch I looked down at the black and filthy water rushing below, a strong deep tide that would carry me out beyond Wapping and away from sadness for ever. *Go on, no one will miss you*. A chill ran through me. I needed a drink so I carried on over to the other side of the river.

I made it to the Turkish Shore, as us in Romeville proper call the south side of the Thames. I was in the Borough, with that big gospel-shop to my left, and I dupped into a boozing-ken on the pad there. I took some lightning, then some wine, and I found a place by the fire. Some cull offered to tip me supper but I had no stomach for prog. I thought the lush might calm me. Then I felt restless and staggered out into the night once more.

I wandered through gloomy streets with gloomy names: Dirty Lane, Melancholy Walk, Dead Man's Place. This was the Liberty of the Clink, I remembered. Punk Alice and I had padded back from Southwark Fair one year and she had pointed out these streets and pattered that it was here that in ages past the jades of Bankside had licence to ply their trade. But as the theatres and playhouses moved north this region's business had declined until it became a site for the very lowest forms of whoredom. I remember how Alice had jested cruelly that the poor old trulls gathered in this place were 'fit only for Gropecunt Lane'. Now as darkmans fell with a dull glim coming from some of the glazes of the flash-kens, I twigged what crank fancy might have brought me here.

I came to a wasteland, and as I started to pad across it, I felt as though somebody was tracking me. I thought of piking it, then touted some lights ahead, the lanterns of link-boys perhaps, and made my way towards them. It was then I noted the wooden crosses stuck into the earth. I was in a pauper's burial ground.

As I approached the flickering glim I could make out a crew of figures gathered round a grave. An ancient mort came out to greet me as I padded closer. *Dirtywhorebitchtrull*, the voice pattered.

Hush, I told it.

'Have you come for Sarah?' the woman asked me.

'Sarah?'

'Clatty Sarah – you know? Pox got her in the end.'

'No, I . . .' I didn't know what to say.

'Lost, are you?' The woman laughed, opening her gob wide to show one single grinder poking up like a tombstone. 'Ah, a good place to be lost, nabs. You're in fine company. All are lost here.'

'What is this place?'

'Why, it's Cross Bones, nabs. Given by the Bishop of Winchester for those single women forbidden the rites of the Church as they continue their sinful life. We share it with the poor of the parish now. We bury at night as they do by day. The night belongs to us, after all.'

'A whore's graveyard?'

'Yes, nabs. A place of rest for all the poor jades. And for their squeakers lost or stifled.'

I felt my eyes prick with tears as I thought of that little creature in Limbo I had buried in St Giles' churchyard with my own paws. The old woman touted the sadness in my glaziers. She reached out and took me by the hand. 'Perhaps you'd like to pay your last respects,' she said.

'Yes.' There was a sob in my voice. 'I'd like that.'

She led me to where the others stood by the freshly dug earth.

All were morts but for one: an old and wizened soul-driver, whose phiz showed such an affection for this small congregation that he might once have been their keeping-cull. As he droned the last prayers for the dead, the women took turns to drop a handful of earth into the grave.

'They call me Mother Mort,' said my companion, 'in the way of a jest as our word for woman is the Frenchified word for death. Well, we morts are here for it as surely as we are for birth. I have been rabbit-catcher as well as grave-digger in my time. And a whore, of course. Now I am mother of the dead, Cross Bones is my academy. My jades still lie on their backs in the cold ground but they can keep their shanks closed now and rest until eternity. Poor Sarah. Well, the pox got her in the end.'

I took a pawful of dirt and tossed it into the hole. As I mourned a jade I had never known, I felt calm and the voice stowed its widds awhile. And I canted then where this darkmans had led me, the meaning of this crank pilgrimage to Cross Bones. Cursed by love I had found sanctuary in a wasteland, the fatal woman among the outcast dead. I belonged here with none any better than me. And I found grief among my own kind, an old crone and a crew of pox-ridden trulls: a sisterhood. I wept with them, with myself. We can only truly grieve for ourselves, after all.

THREE

—

The

FATAL
TREE

Newgate Gaol, 28th February 1726

Dear Applebee,

We come now to the final act, to recount what became of the forsaken widow of infamous Jack Sheppard. And to learn of the strange fate of Jonathan Wild, of how the fall of that wicked statesman framed her progress. In this we will turn to my part in this story and, indeed, the very circumstances that eventually brought me to Newgate to tell it. As the day of judgment approaches, the noose of this tale tightens, and our subject yet stands in a most perilous position.

For it is but three days until the March sessions begin and I have now heard final notice of the actual bill to be preferred to the Grand Jury and here is a record of her indictment:
Elizabeth Lyon, alias Sheppard, alias Edgworth Bess, is indicted for breaking and entering the house of Edward Bury, and stealing six silver spoons, a pair of silver tongs, a silver strainer, a gown, and a handkerchief, on the 31st January, in the night.

I do not believe she has any witnesses to speak on her behalf and her only defence as to how she came to be in possession of the spoons is that: 'They were left to me by my dear Jack Sheppard and I had just fetched them out of pawn.' An absurd claim but frankly I fear for the poor woman's reason. Recounting these parts of her narrative has not been easy for her. Confession might be good for the soul but it certainly takes its toll on the mind. And though she seems destined for the fatal tree, I do wish the court might bestow some mercy upon her. For all of London was once possessed by an obsession with the events she was caught up in and had transformed its story into its own capricious fantasies.

'Come, Billy,' said John Gay, as he hustled us from our seats as the curtain came down on the first night of *Harlequin Sheppard*. 'Now to escape the serpent's tongue.'

My friend was a master in the art of detecting theatrical failure, mostly from bitter experience, and his judgment certainly did not fail him now. And, indeed, along with the boos and the slow hand-claps that greeted the finale of the wretched pantomime, there came the snakelike sibilance that, in the verdict of the *Weekly Journal's* review, saw it 'dismiss'd with a universal hiss'.

And so we beat a retreat from the Drury Lane theatre to a nearby tavern to nurse a minor wound. We had furnished but one ballad for Thurmond's dismal farce after all, and that had been the high point of the evening. Though even then there had been catcalls among the applause, members of Wild's corporation among the audience, I supposed. Sent by a thief-taker sorely vexed to learn that he had been so brutally assassi-nated in song. For news had come to us just before the performance began that he wasn't dead after all.

'We were wrong to try to kill Jonathan off in our ballad,' said Gay, as we shared a pint of wine. 'That was bad luck. He is yet a most intriguing character.'

'Well, he is said to be in rude health,' I replied. 'And seeks to rule Romeville once more.'

'The thief and the thief-taker,' he went on. 'That could be the heart of the drama. And there must be love, too. A woman, yes, perhaps two, like those two jades Jack paraded himself with on the day he was taken.'

I mused at how poor Bess had been so ill-used even in the telling of Sheppard's story, but swiftly picked up on Gay's theme. 'Perhaps we should try our hand at this Newgate pastoral,' I suggested rather too quickly, and at once regretted my utterance.

Gay shook his head thoughtfully, and I feared he had judged me presumptuous. 'No, Billy,' he said. 'It is time to let this story settle awhile.'

'Perhaps.' I sighed.

Presented barely a fortnight after Sheppard's hanging, it was generally felt that *Harlequin Sheppard* had been staged with indecent haste to capitalise on Jack's death with a gaudy pantomime, a spectacle far too crude to compete with the vivid drama of his actual life.

'Besides,' Gay went on. 'I am planning a book of fables that I might inscribe to the Prince of Wales's child, William.'

So the hapless jester was still bidding for preferment at Court. I managed to stow my impatience at the tedious trait of servility that threatened to shackle his true genius, and to screen my disappointment at a lost opportunity to properly collaborate with a true poet. But the latter sentiment was not so hard to suppress for in the last two weeks my whole life had changed.

For I had fallen in love and found my own excellent muse at last. I merely confided my plans for a poetic epic to Gay but he swiftly guessed the rest of it.

'Naughty Billy,' he said, with a delighted clap. 'Inspired by some gorgeous boy, no doubt. Well, it is an excellent subject. Narcissus, I mean. For this is the beginnings of art, of artfulness.'

'What do you mean?'

'When man realised that his image could be reproduced by nature it led him to try the same with artifice. That exquisite vanity of mock-creation. Though a lack of beauty rarely impedes the excess of *amour propre* suffered by Narcissus.' Gay sniffed. 'Well, I am more like poor Echo. For what is the writer than one cursed to copy words that others have uttered? Like the nymph sighing on the wind and, as you know, like Echo I repeat myself endlessly!'

We laughed and I poured us both another glass.

Later I walked him back to his rooms in Whitehall. When we reached the end of the Strand he put his arm through mine and drew me close. 'You know,' he spoke softly as if in conspiracy, 'in one version a *male* suitor kills himself for Narcissus's sake. It's not in Ovid so you won't find it in Dryden's translation. The Greek Conon tells it thus: the youth Aminias was spurned in the form of a gift.'

'A gift?'

'Yes. Narcissus sends the poor fool a sword to kill himself with. And as Aminias commits that act of self-slaughter he calls out for the gods to bestow upon Narcissus the curse of self-love.'

'How wondrous,' I murmured, thinking of little but the amorous possibilities in this tragedy.

'Yes, indeed,' said Gay, patting my hand. 'But be careful, Billy.'

Harlequin Sheppard closed after scarcely a week's run. Some thought it would have been better received at John Rich's theatre in Lincoln's Inn Fields, where an audience was more used to such modish novelties, but I could not think other than that it deserved to fail.

In December I moved into new lodgings with Adam. We

took four rooms in a house in Cavendish Square, ready furnished, and hired a manservant. It was all on my credit at first, as we had to wait until the spring for all the fruits of my companion's inheritance.

I remember a languid winter of short days and long nights. My friend had such a genial indolence, sleeping sometimes until the early evening in voluptuous repose. Oft-times I would spy him in slumber through the day, strangely jealous of the dreams that held him. Then I would sit by the fire to read or jot down some lines of my pastoral. By night we would go abroad in London, to the opera or a playhouse. Such a fine pair of young bloods, so well-dressed and handsome. I made sure we were noticed at all of the important gatherings, for this was to be my way into the *beau monde* at last. I saw every introduction to a person of quality as a future subscription for my great work of poetry.

At a ball at Lord Burlington's I spied Roger Johnson, no doubt working some spruce-prig lay. It was rumoured that he had come back to London having heard of Wild's wounding and had some plans to set himself up as the new thief-taker. With the recovery of Wild's health this move now seemed doubtful.

Roger had given me a knowing look when he saw me with my young nobleman and I felt the reproach of familiarity. It was so plain to a fellow sharper that I was playing the beau-trap, I felt a stab of remorse that my purest sentiments were tarnished in this manner. So I sought to steer Adam away from his implicating gaze, but as I turned to him, I found he had already made himself scarce.

I did all I could to assuage my guilt. I spoke my devotion to him on many occasions, often with some gift or token to accompany the words. I would take him to Mother Clap's or some other molly-house so that we might be with our own kind to speak and act freely. Of course I relished the looks from the other madges there when they saw my handsome young lover. But I also took the chance to unscreen my tender feelings for all to see. For though I could not think all my intentions entirely unselfish, I knew that the bright spark of love I felt was sincere.

And with that I began to set down my verse epic in heroic couplets. I was calling it *The Vision of Narcissus* and I had the opening lines:

> *Born of comely nymph and lusty water-sprite*
> *Beauteous boy of ev'ry maid or swain's delight*
> *Disdaining all the vainly proffered kisses*
> *Proud and haughty was the fair Narcissus*

This would be my great work, I was certain of it. But I had wasted so much time and money that winter that I was at ebb-water once again. By the end of January most of my capital was used up. In pursuit of art and love I had let my Grub Street trade slip. What I really needed was to make some quick coin.

It was with trepidation that I called upon Wild at his offices in the Old Bailey but, given my circumstances, I could not forgo the opportunity for any lay he might be planning. And I wagered that he might be willing to pay for information on Roger Johnson, who still held some of the loot from the Windsor instalment.

'Here's the murderer, Quilt,' Wild rebuked me, as I entered. 'He who tried to kill me with a song.'

'Sir, I am truly sorry,' I declared, noting the red seam at his neck that marked Blueskin's wounding.

'What – because I am not dead?' Wild let out a harsh cackle. 'What do you want, Billy?'

'Well, I was wondering if there was any work.'

'Work? The impudence of the man. There's nothing, Billy. I've told all my prigs. The current trade is so slack that I had to inform the Prince of Wales's household the theft of a gold watch from that gentry-ken is past all hopes of recovery.'

'I saw Roger Johnson the other evening.'

'Johnson?' He frowned. 'What do you know of him?'

'Only that he was at the Earl of Burlington's.'

'Well, I'm waiting for some babble on him presently. The fool has got into some dispute with a fence. You know Tom Edwards, the bluffer of the Goat tavern? He's got a warrant out for Johnson over some missing goods and has threatened to have him arrested. What's the matter, Billy? You made some good loure last season. Have you been living beyond your means?'

'Very much so.'

'Then sit down, man. Quilt, make some prattle-broth,' he called to his deputy, then turned back to me. 'We might see if there's anything for you.'

We took tea together and talked awhile, and I realised that Wild was himself keen for any information as he had lost a good deal of control of his corporation since his wounding and seemed desperate to restore his power at all costs. Jack Sheppard's hanging had made him deeply unpopular with the canting-crew. And he dreaded that the gentility might lose their faith in him also, that any decline in his authority might prompt questions to be raised about his nefarious practices.

There was a knock at the door and one of his men rushed in.

'What is it?' Wild demanded.

'It's Johnson, sir. Edwards touted him upon the pad at Stratford and snabbled him.'

'Where's he being held?'

'At a boozing-ken in the village.'

'Right, Quilt,' he snapped, as he got to his feet. 'Get a posse together. We'll ride out there and take him back. Then we can have the rest of the Windsor haul once he's safe.'

'We're a bit short of men, sir.'

'Well, Billy will join us. Won't you, Billy?'

I shrugged. 'I'd hardly be much use,' I reasoned. 'I'm not much of a high-pad.'

'Nonsense. It'll be good to have you on the strength.'

'I don't think so.'

'I insist,' Wild declared, with a mirthless grin, drawing out a pistol and holding it to my face. 'Here.'

Shocked, I sat up in my chair. 'There's really no need for that,' I protested.

'No, no. The popp's for you,' he said, and handed it to me. 'We're going armed. Ride with us, Billy. It'll be a chance for you to make amends for your slanderous ditty. And twenty guineas if we take him.'

'And a share of the loot?' I bargained.

Wild sighed. 'Very well,' he agreed.

While the horses were brought for us, Quilt complained

that we didn't yet have a warrant. Wild held up his gun. 'This will do,' he pattered darkly, and stowed it in his jacket.

And so we set out eastwards at a gallop. I feared that in his impetuous haste to reassert his dominance Wild was ready to act far too rashly so I resolved to hang back in the posse at any sign of danger.

We made quite a noise of it as we rode into Stratford. As we approached the tavern where Johnson was being held, two men came out to witness the commotion. They appeared to be armed.

'They've got muskets, sir!' one of the crew shouted.

Instantly Wild pulled out his pistol and discharged it in their direction. Then all bedlam broke loose.

The two men ran back into the boozing-ken. The posse dismounted and made an attack on the premises. Under a hail of bullets and broken glass the occupants quickly parleyed a surrender without returning a shot. For there were no muskets in their possession, only those long staves sported by constables of the watch.

'We are officers of the peace, sir!' their leader protested.

'And I am the thief-taker general!' Wild thundered. 'Where is Roger Johnson?'

'We have a warrant, signed by the justices, to hold him here.'

Johnson had been officially arrested and Wild had now broken the King's peace; he risked being taken himself. A loud argument continued, with Wild's crew making further threats. Only one of their number stood back from the fray, with a pistol yet undischarged. Myself. And it was with a calm detachment that I noticed a certain party creeping out by a side door of the tavern. I quietly followed him round, gun in hand.

'Roger,' I called to him, as he padded to where a horse was tethered.

He turned and smiled. 'Billy. Well, who'd have thought the old prig-napper would come back to life? Time for me to shab off, I'd say.'

I raised my pistol and pointed it at him. 'I think not.'

'Come on, nabs. That popp doesn't suit you. You're not going to shoot me, are you?'

I cocked the hammer. 'Sorry, Roger, I really need the reward money. And Wild's even promised a snack of what you spoke with at Windsor.'

Johnson sighed. 'Look, I don't even know where all of it is any more, Billy. You could ask that young cove you've palled up with for some of it.'

'What?'

'That natty-lad I touted you with at the gentry-ken the other darkmans.'

I grinned at such foolishness. 'He's no natty-lad, Roger.'

'No? Remember I pattered of a secret accomplice I had at Windsor. The one dab at personating the quality.'

'He's the Honourable Adam Stonyforth,' I insisted, but the smile fell from my face.

'Yes, yes. Still working that drop of being the youngest son of an earl, is he? Waiting to come into his majority and all that. Well, he's dab at the rob-thief, Billy. Still owes me two diamond brooches and a silver snuff-box.'

'Wait . . .'

My head throbbed in dreadful panic as all the delicate

workings of my finely jewelled dream began to fall apart. Roger mounted the horse and looked down at me with a frown on his phiz. 'He's not put the bite on you, has he? Oh dear, Billy.' He began to laugh. 'Oh dear.'

As he took hold of the reins I raised the pistol. 'Wait!' I called out once more in desperation, as if to hold back all of reality.

He spurred the steed and rode off. I fired my gun into the air above me in a kind of mournful fury, with all my dearest hopes blown skywards.

The shot brought Wild and the posse from out of the tavern to watch Roger Johnson gallop off towards the coast, no doubt to cross over to Flanders once more.

So we headed back to London, the thief-taker in a murderous humour, myself in an incredulous daze. I cursed myself that I could have been so stupid, to be taken in so easily. I watched Adam carefully now, biding my time for the right moment to confront him with my knowledge of the truth. But the days passed and the worst of it was that I loved him yet.

In the meantime a rumour started that a warrant had been issued for Wild's arrest for firing upon officers of the watch. It was prattled that there were many justices suspicious of his practices who had long wished to prosecute him. Now they could make their move.

On the 15th February the high constable of Holborn and two others of that division detained Wild on Wood Street. He was escorted to a spunging-house nearby to be held until a magistrate could examine him. So the thief-taker was taken.

And it was when the dark history of this great regulator of

crime approached its climax that you called upon me, Applebee, to serve as garreteer once more. I certainly needed the money and some distraction from my predicament. You had again proved yourself the cleverest publisher in all of London, earning yet more capital by printing its sordid chronicle. For you had now secured the rights to Jonathan Wild's memoirs just as you had with Jack Sheppard's.

Your sincere and faithful correspondent,

William Archer Esq.

XII

I was in the Black Lion with a crew of shoplifters when a bung-nipper dupped in with the prattle.

'Wild's been snabbled!' he jabbered.

Once we had recovered our astonished senses a toast was called for and much lush taken. Indeed, when the widd was blown throughout the Hundreds a general revelry commenced that would last until peep of lightmans, such was the delight of the canting-crew at the fate of the prig-napper. I was touched by that jocose spirit myself, a commodity I had lacked for a long time. I had nursed such a burning hatred for Wild and now felt an urge of curiosity also. This news was like the fall of a great tyrant in history. And his iniquitous career had been so much a part of my own story that I was keen to be a witness to the end of it. I canted that it might tip some meaning to my wretched life.

So I shabbed off early from the boozing-ken and piked it down to where Wild was being held. There was already a push outside the ken, eager to tout this gape-seed. I soon twigged that most of the coves and morts there were flat types, full of bene anger now that disgrace had descended on their esteemed protector. Those of us in the flash world already knew him for what he was, but for the honest and God-fearing this now sparked them with a glim of wrath. For they had been gulled of their very senses by his wicked deception and thus nettled came to jabber their indignation.

Wild sat waiting for the beak, unable to stand as his shanks had suffered a sudden attack of the gout. As we dupped in to confront him, he made a speech from a chair, as ever seeking to kick away from his crimes with some clever patter. 'I wonder, good people, what it is you would see?' he said.

An insult was shouted from the back of the crowd but Wild held up a paw and waited for the mob to settle.

'I am a poor, honest man who has done all I could to serve people when they have had the misfortune to lose their goods by the villainy of thieves!'

'Liar!' another called.

'This is the malice of my enemies, see?' He stabbed at the air with one finger, then sighed and spoke more softly. 'I am now in custody, about to go before a magistrate who, I hope, will do me justice. Why should you insult me? Please, as you see me here before you, lame in body, afflicted in mind, please do not make me more uneasy than I can bear!'

There were yet more cries from the assembled crew but many hushed as they touted how haggard and lamentable this once dreaded man now appeared, the stern eyes now milky-blue and imploring. I twigged something quite shocking on his phiz now: weakness. And fear.

'If I have offended against the law, it will punish me.' He groaned. 'But it gives you no right to use me ill, unheard and unconvicted!'

Somebody laughed and I canted then that his spell was broken. The charm he once possessed was lost, that power to bitch us all to his will gone. He spied me in the push and called, 'Bess! Help me! Fetch Quilt. Do something, please!'

I could not forbear to smile at how he begged. Yet if he had ordered me, even then, I might have followed his command, so used was I to do his bidding. I touted the lully-child in his glaziers but felt no pity, only disdain. Now that he was so feeble and helpless, it was safe to truly despise him.

So I padded up to where he sat. I caught the grin on his gob as he spied my approach.

'Bess,' he pattered, with a sudden glim in his eye. 'My dear Bess. I knew you would not forsake me. You'll do something for me, won't you?'

I leaned over him, my phiz above his and pattered, 'Nix my doll.'

Then I turned my back on him and shabbed off onto the pad.

Wild was committed to Newgate that darkmans and from then on I found that I could peach him for all my woes in life. It was bene to have one place to stow all my wrath and hatred for it quelled the crank patter in my head awhile.

And the rest of Romeville was now free to make a jest of the prig-napper's misfortune. In the week that followed I touted a newspaper and read that Jonathan Wild was to be charged: *with buying jewels, knowing them to be stolen at the late Instalment at Windsor.* It went on to prattle of that reckless spruce-prig Roger Johnson who had been helped to kick away and concluded of Wild that: *in the interim, he is pretty secure, and very much afflicted with the gout, which may in time, by a receipt from Jack Ketch Esq., be ('tis thought) effectually cur'd.* The press did not sit mum-chance on the verdict now but rather seemed certain he was headed for the fatal tree. And I was happy for that.

The Old Bailey was soon presented a bene paper called a Warrant of Detainer, with hard evidence of sworn witnesses, that listed the many crimes of his corporation and proved him done up for good, though now so many charges were being brought against him across the kingdom that it might take until Doomsday to answer them all.

So we were free of the prig-napper but with his decline came the rise of another power to try to bitch Romeville, as I was soon to discover.

I had been padding it with this crew of shoplifters when one of that number was caught filching. He babbled me, squeaking that I had seduced him into going thieving.

This was but a crank tale and there was no evidence or case for me to answer. Yet I was the wicked Edgworth Bess, the fatal woman, my name and notoriety a public matter and that was enough of an indictment.

I was snabbled by two constables of the Society for the Reformation of Manners. They laughed when I asked them for a warrant signed by a beak.

'This is summary justice, Bess,' one of them pattered. 'We've got new powers. No more thief-takers for the likes of you to do deals with.'

'No more corrupt practices,' the other added, 'of acquitting the devil if he peaches a lesser demon. We do not mean to regulate crime but to root out its cause. You know the cause of crime?'

I thought of answering, 'Poverty,' but twigged it was better to sit mum-chance.

'Vice!' he hissed, with the relish of sanctimony. 'Profanity, debauchery, temptations of the flesh that lead the weak to commit monstrous acts.'

'Fornication, sodomy,' his fellow rejoined. 'We intend to clean the streets of this filth. Let every whore and scoundrel know it.'

And thus I was peached to be of loose, idle and disorderly conduct and committed to Tothill Fields Bridewell for six weeks to be cured of my wickedness. That place was a different kind of trib from the Whit or the Compter: it was a house of correction where the poor, vagrant and sinful might be reformed through hard labour. A bene number of jades touted working upon the pad were sent there. We were set to beating hemp, breaking the fibre with heavy mallets on a stump, making it ready to be woven into rope. This was surely to remind us of the cord we might swing from one day and a cruel jest to a hempen-widow like myself.

The keepers there did not live from garnish but rather the gelt made from our labour so it served them to make us work and they padded about with canes at the ready. There was a pillory and a whipping post but, in truth, order was kept more by the utterance of discipline than the action of it. Here they did not punish our bodies so much as rule our minds and bitch our souls obedient. A chaplain would read scripture and make us parrot the catechism at mealtimes or on Sundays. The quod-culls touted that we toiled in silence and did not fall into any wicked discourse with each other. The only words we were meant to hear were those that might correct us from our evil ways. And so the peaching jabber in my head started up once more.

The head keeper or governor would pad his rounds every lightmans, a fat cove with a queerly jocose look on his phiz, who seemed particulary happy to have nabbed such an infamous creature as myself. 'Be happy in your work, Elizabeth Lyon,' he bade me. 'Here you might be saved, nay, improved even.' He went into some crank sermon on punishment, using my Jack as an example, pattering that when a scragging becomes gape-seed and the push cheer the condemned, it might encourage crime rather than deter it. Far better was to chasten offenders behind a closed jigger and screened from the public. And here in a well-ordered ken, he concluded, we might be bitched into goodness.

'But remember, Elizabeth Lyon,' he went on, 'though the mob might not see you, you are ever being watched here, just as the good Lord watches over us all.'

And these widds about being touted all the time nettled me, making me peery of myself. Were there peepholes in this house of correction? Might I be anatomised by unseen glaziers? I wondered. I thought of that tiny cribb in Mother Breedlove's, the dark closet with a grille from which jades and culls could be scanned unawares. Perhaps there was a great master we could never see, an all-powerful watching-cull ever gazing upon our sinfulness.

Fettered by invisible darbies made of their widds and their way of canting, I beat out the hemp in the endless measure: *one-two-three-four-five; one-two-three-four-five.* And the rhythm of work gave a grim music for that hateful refrain: *she-has-proved-my-bane; she-has-proved-my-bane.*

But at odd moments we inmates of the bridewell would patter to each other, whispering our own words and thoughts when we could. There was yet more prattle of the prig-napper. He had lately been indicted of filching and fencing some yards of lace, lifted from a shop by Holborn Bridge. A minor felony compared to all of his great crimes but enough to scrag him and a simple case to prosecute. He was due for trial at the May sessions. I hoped I might be at liberty in time for his hanging day.

So now I corrected my own thoughts as I brought down the mallet, canting how he had taken all those I held dear: Punk Alice and Blueskin, and he had seen Jack hanged and made him truant of my affections. He had caused the death of that poor little squeaker that dwelled in Limbo. Now I would hammer away thinking of Jonathan Wild. *He-has-proved-my-bane* was the song in my head now, *he-has-proved-my-bane.*

The governor dupped in and touted the smile on my phiz. Not twigging what I was truly thinking, he pattered, 'Behold how happy Elizabeth Lyon is in her work! There is hope for you yet.'

And indeed there was. Hope for vengeance. I fancied that I was beating out the very rope that would scrag the thief-taker general and that a curse might fall on every master, taking them all to the fatal tree in the end.

Dear Applebee,

It is something strange that a man's life should be made a kind of romance before his face, wrote Daniel Defoe, in the preface to his narrative of Wild's life that you commissioned that May. It is a line that haunts me yet.

So I was pressed into your service to assist in recording the fall of 'Jonathan the Great', as one Grub Street wit cruelly dubbed him. Thus the thief-taker, too, was invited to join the audience of his own tragedy, though it swiftly assumed more the character of cruel pantomime than any classical drama. I spied him on the morning of his trial, waiting in the bail-dock near the very spot where Blueskin had tried to murder him seven months before. The bleak jest of this ignominious return was not lost on Jonathan.

'I wish to God Joe's blade had been sharper,' he lamented, touching the scar on his throat quite tenderly. 'I might have been spared this misery.'

I was there to deliver copies of a pamphlet you had agreed to print for Wild as part of his publishing deal. Grandly titled: *A List of the Persons, Discovered, Apprehended and Convicted of Several Robberies on the Highway; and also for Burglaries and House-Breakings; and also the Several Persons here-under named, for Returning from Transportation, by Jonathan Wild*. It provided a catalogue of the many felons he had brought to justice in the hope that this might mitigate the meagre charges against him. And, as instructed by Wild, I was to distribute this tract to the jurors and court officials that morning in the bail-dock and sessions-house yard.

But this ploy proved a dreadful mistake. With its obvious intent to influence the jury, the very substance of his paper, listing as it did some seventy-five men and women hanged or transported by his own hand, served only to cast the thief-taker in the worst possible light for it implied that Wild had simply seen to the organisation of crime itself. And as the proceedings began, counsel for the King stood up with a copy of the pamphlet in his hand.

'This crude advertisement for the prisoner's deeds,' he declared, 'should be unwarrantable and not to be suffered in any court of law. But it should be noted that it might prove only that the prisoner has set up a corporation of thieves with a trade of felony. And that with the constant practice of procuring stolen goods, it is no surprise that he has it within his power to detect those several malefactors he was concerned with.'

So at one stroke every tick of credit now moved over to the debit side of Wild's great ledger.

He was charged with two indictments: the first for stealing and the second for receiving fifty yards of lace, valued at forty pounds. All of London now looked to his inglorious decline, that the great thief-taker general could be brought down by a low, squalid offence and hanged by such a delicate length of cloth.

Now it was his turn in that great puppet-booth of the Old Bailey. Indeed, the court seemed intent to befool him, to play and pull strings as he had done so often before, for Wild's counsel was allowed to argue for an acquittal from the first charge. But this brief reprieve served only to prolong his agony.

It became clear that the prosecution intended to press home the lesser charge, as if to humiliate him utterly by convicting him with the minor misdemeanour by which he had impeached and hanged so many others. It was a grim burlesque to watch him squirm as he realised he was trapped. His last attempt to save his own neck was to plead mitigation that the names of the thieves had been left off this second indictment and he might discover for the court who the 'persons unnamed' might be. At this the counsel for the King rose once more.

'Well, this is a most surprising plea,' he quipped, 'for a man to say, "I am guiltier than you are aware of, and therefore I ought to suffer the less."'

The jury found him guilty. And here were the beginnings of his utter dissolution. He looked dazed and haggard as he stood to make his speech before sentencing.

'My lord, I hope, even in the sad condition in which I stand, I may pretend to some little merit in respect of the service I have done my country, in delivering it from some of the greatest pests with which it was ever troubled. My lord, I have brought many bold and daring malefactors to just punishment even at the hazard of my own life, my body being covered with scars I received in these undertakings,' he declared, in a feeble voice. 'I submit myself wholly to His Majesty's mercy, and humbly beg a favourable report of my case.'

But sentence of death was duly passed upon him, and as the verdict became public knowledge he became a target for further satire and the sharp justice of comedy.

Barely a week before Wild's trial Walpole's lord chancellor,

the Earl of Macclesfield, had been tried and found guilty of
selling offices, receiving bribes and embezzling over one
hundred thousand pounds of Chancery funds. He had been
fined thirty thousand yet was set to be released from the
Tower that summer. Many jested that Wild had simply not
stolen enough to make himself safe.

And with the fall of Jonathan the Great there came the
familiar complaint that politicians, bankers, stock-jobbers and
corrupt aristocrats had also been screened from justice while
lesser thieves went to the tree. That old rake the Duke of
Wharton, who had been Hell-and-Fury's master, wrote a poem
in which, instead of being condemned to hang, the thief-taker
was employed to recover the eight-million-pound Exchequer
deficit that had never been properly explained.

As I worked on Wild's official biography, I watched as he
became a figure of cruel mirth, keenly aware of the grim irony
of his life. For my existence had also become something of a
farce. And I had been played as fool.

It is said among the canting-crew that those who work
the trap will surely be trapped themselves one day. And so I
had laid a snare for myself and scarce knew any way out of
it.

Yet I dreaded the occasion when I might have it out with
my supposed beloved. In the meantime I slyly learned all I
could about him. My 'Honourable Adam' was, of course,
nothing of the sort, lacking that distinction in morals as well
as breeding. Oh, yes, he had grown up on a country estate, but
as a servant, not as the scion of some great family. And he had
been dismissed from that household in some unspoken
disgrace that was not hard to guess at. He quickly learned all

his wicked tricks from Roger Johnson and others, and how to work the drop by masking himself as the charming but flat beau from the country.

And he continued with this façade until I could bear it no longer. I was deeply in debt, though regretfully nowhere near the great sum of Macclesfield's. I owed two hundred and fifty pounds, a dangerously middling amount that might at any moment send me to the Fleet, the Marshalsea or some other cheerless spunging-house. When Adam once again asked me for a loan and mentioned his fanciful allowance, at last I loudly spoke of all I knew of him and his circumstances.

'Well, perhaps neither of us is what we pretend to be,' he replied coldly. 'William Archer Esquire, the great poet indeed. You're just a hackney-scribbler and a spruce-prig!'

'Adam . . .'

'And to think you tried to put the bite on me with this doggerel.'

He picked up some loose pages from my desk and sailed them across the room. He surely knew where to slip the blade and I should have thrown him out then but I could not bear to.

For it was too late. I might have seen him for what he was sooner, but Punk Alice was proved right. Love is a masquerade. Love is an exquisitely painted screen.

So I let him stay.

'We're well suited, Billy,' he told me. 'A pair of counterfeits.'

We would talk of working some lay together but Adam was lazy and unreliable. I knew that he was always on the lookout for a better prospect, some rich lord to be his patron. But in truth he was not quite bad enough. It pains me to admit it but

I had proved an easy fool for him. He would have to work a lot harder to make it as a noble's favourite or any kind of courtier. I doubted he would have much to live on once his looks were in decline. But he would use me up, I was sure of that, burn the ken and leave me with no face but my own. I was his keeping-cull, his bleeding-cull and he was bleeding me dry.

That muse of the looking-glass now turned to taunt me. When I had caught Adam's visage in the mirror that morning and fancied that look of wonder in Arcadia, of the boy seeing his reflection for the first time in the deep and clear pool, I had not realised it to be a well-practised gaze: of foppish satisfaction rather than of youthful discovery. I cursed myself for having prophesied Narcissus, for the one I loved was as horribly spoiled with self-love and held little affection for anyone else.

Yet for all his low tricks and selfish manners, nothing doused the glim of desire he fired in me. I wanted him so badly that I let him ruin me. It was all I deserved, I suppose, for all the culls I had bilked in my time. I dived for any meagre scrap of his affection and could even stand his hate so long as there was some lust in it, but the thought of his indifference was the hardest to bear. Yet I knew that he would cast me off once there was nothing left to filch. I feared so much for the day that he would leave me.

He cost me dearly yet he would cheapen himself with others. Whenever we were out in public I would spy his eyes scan every man's form or countenance. And there was scant refinement to his taste: he was slave to no beauty but his own. All he seemed to care about was the sensual worship of others, no matter how wanting in grace and beauty they might be. His lack of decorum could be quite shocking.

One night at Mother Clap's he made a bargain with Dip-candle Polly right in front of me as I was buying drinks. Off they went to the chapel together as I stood there aghast. On that occasion I determined I would pad off home on my own but as I made for the door Charles Hitchen came in and hailed me. Wild was still all the talk of London so we found a table to sit down and gossip.

'Have you seen him in Newgate?' Hitchen asked me.

'I'm going there tomorrow.'

'Poor Jonathan.' He sighed.

'I thought you'd be happy to see the last of him.'

'Oh, I'm happy enough to see that baboon scragged. But it might be a bad end for all of us.'

'What do you mean? Surely you could be thief-taker once more.'

He laughed. 'Oh, no, Billy. I'm under marshal merely in name now. They'd never let me back in power. The Society, I mean.'

'The Society?'

'The Society for the Reformation of Manners, Billy. They're on the march again. Romeville is indulging in some spasm of morality with Wild's scragging. I've been *persona non grata* with the Society ever since that pamphlet.'

'It was scandalous,' I rejoined rather too quickly.

Hitchen frowned. 'You know, for all the libels the worst thing was the part of it that peached me as a sodomite. That was quite beyond the wit of Jonathan, and I often wonder who penned it for him.'

I coughed and looked away.

'So. I'll never make it as thief-taker general now. Instead, expect a crusade.' He leaned in close to me, his eyes darting to and fro. 'And be careful. There's spies in the molly-houses.'

'But you protect them.'

'I did, Billy, but only with Wild's sanction. The Society won't make any deals with thieves or bawds, like Wild did. Once he's tucked up they'll be busy again and there's not much I can do about it.'

The next morning I made my way to Newgate. It looked like rain so I took a hackney-carriage: I couldn't bear the thought of a day in the Whit in a damp jacket. It had poured down most of May and the coachman told me that haymakers had come up from the country, starving from lack of work. A low ceiling of grey cloud made all of Romeville seem a gloomy cribb.

Defoe had nearly completed Wild's story. I was there to take notes of any comments made before his final confession and to convey any last requirements he might have. The thief-taker general looked ghastly. He had eaten nothing for two days and was once more stricken with gout. The chaplain had reported that he could not walk to chapel or allow anyone to help convey him there. He did not wish to be spied by his enemies, he said, who would whisper and point at him.

He sat crouched over in the corner of the condemned hold, wigless and ragged, clutching a Bible in trembling hands. As I approached he tapped at the side of his head, where a silver plate had been fitted long ago to fix a fracture. 'I've something of a terrible disorder of the brain, Billy,' he muttered. 'I keep telling them. And all my wounds. I suffer so.'

He licked a dirty finger and opened the Bible at a page he had marked. 'See here, Billy, it says, "Cursed is every one that hangeth on a tree." What do you think it means? I asked the soul-driver but he couldn't give me a satisfactory answer.'

He passed the book to me and I looked down on the Epistle of St Paul to the Galatians as Wild prodded his finger at the verse. I read: *Christ hath redeemed us from the curse of the law, being made a curse for us; for it is written, cursed is every one that hangeth on a tree.* I had no idea what it signified but his bloodshot eyes gaped imploringly so I said, 'Perhaps it means that you are free of the curse of the law.'

'Yes.' He nodded, taking the Bible back to cradle it once more. 'Yes.'

'Mr Applebee—' I began.

'Wait!' he gasped. 'Here's another one. Now, you'll know this, with all your classical poetry, Billy. How is it that the Greeks and the Romans came to be so glorious in history, the ones that killed themselves that is, if self-murder be a crime?'

'I'm sorry.' I shrugged. 'I was never properly educated in such matters.'

Wild threw back his head and let out a dry cackle. 'Never properly educated,' he repeated. 'That's good.'

'Now, Mr Applebee,' I went on, 'he would like to know if you have any last requests.'

Wild was suddenly still. He stared at me a moment, then said, 'Yes, but not from him.'

'What?'

'I wouldn't trust him to get it for me. From you.' He pointed, then clawed a hand to pull me close.

'What do you want?' I asked him.

He whispered back, 'Get me some laudanum, Billy.'

So I procured a small bottle of that tincture of opium from an apothecary in St Giles. The drug is said to make men and women quite careless of their fate and I reasoned that he wished to be thus insensible on his hanging day. But the night before he was due for the tree, and after taking the sacrament, he swallowed all the laudanum to cheat the noose. But as he grew drowsy his two fellows in the hold perceived his sickness and endeavoured to rouse him, taking him by the arms and walking him around the cell a little. This motion awakened him, and as his countenance turned pale, he sweated and spewed out much of the bitter potion.

Wild had begged for a closed carriage to take him to Tyburn but his request was denied. He chose to wear a simple callimanco nightgown, rather than any fine clothes, to indicate humility in the face of judgment. This humble fashion for the gallows had been started by one of the many highwaymen the thief-taker had earned forty pounds from in reward for his hanging. And so, heavily drugged and already in his burial shroud, Wild was taken out to the cart as the ugly mob awaited his final journey.

So we reach Wild's final chapter, Elizabeth Lyon's too, as tomorrow is her trial. Would that she could afford a lawyer like Wild's for her defence counsel, to argue her indictment or to plead for mercy and mitigation for I do not imagine it will go well for her in the morning. What follows is the last of her story but for the final confession. We will have that from her if she is sentenced for the tree and that might complete the work. This is a wretched business, Applebee, but we must go through with it.

Your sincere but reluctant correspondent,

William Archer Esq.

XIII

I came out of the bridewell bone weary from all the hemp I had beaten, and half maddened by all the widds they had beaten into me: humility, patience, obedience, and so on. But the voice in my head had quietened a little, at least.

My paws were calloused and my manners reformed, and I should have learned the habit of honest labour. Such was the promise of my moral improvement. But if there was one thing I now canted of work it was that after a long stint you surely need a good holiday.

So I dupped into the Black Lion to tout what was left of the crew there. Lush was stood me all through the darkmans and I woke up in the cribb of some rattling-cove. I took what coin I was owed from his bung, shabbed off and started again. I stayed pot-valiant for three days and washed away all the orderliness that had been milled into me at that house of correction.

Out on the pad the following lightmans, I met with a cove hawking pamphlets, prints and broadsheets. The novelty of the day was in the form of a ticket: in jest it was an invitation to the prig-napper's scragging. An engraving of his scowling phiz was edged with the inscription *Jonathan Wild Thief-taker General of Great Britain & Ireland* and below a scroll embellished with a design of the gallows, flanked by the pillory and the stocks, manacles and leg-irons, guarded by Time with his scythe and hourglass on one side, Death with his spade and dart the other. Below was a coffin. *To all the Thieves, Whores, Pick-pockets, Family Fellowes, &c. in Great Britain & Ireland*, it read. *Gentlemen & Ladies, You are hereby desir'd to accompany ye Pious Mr J_____ W___ from his Seat at Whittington's Colledge to ye Tripple Tree, where he's to make his last Exit on _____; and his Corps to be carry'd from thence to be decently interr'd amongst his Ancestors. Please bring this Ticket with you.*

When the cove learned that I was Edgworth Bess he let me have one gratis. Before he tipped it to me he pulled out the stub of a pencil and scrawled *24th May* in the space on the ticket. Wild's hanging was next Monday, in two days' time.

So that weekend saw great celebration throughout the Hundreds of Drury. On the eve of his scragging, the boozing-kens and gin-shops were pushed with all those wishing to commemorate the bene retirement of the prig-napper. For the whores and rogues it was time to toast all of those in the canting-crew that had been peached for the tree by him. And I was content that I had made it out of the bridewell in time to tout him dance the Tyburn jig.

On Monday all Romeville was there to see him off. As the cart rattled from Newgate it was pelted with stones, mud, rotten fruit and dung as the mob jeered his final procession. Wild tried to cower between the two high-pads and the queer bit-maker that were his fellow passengers, but some cove high up in a glaze by Holborn managed to land a missile on his crown so that blood ran right down his phiz.

I joined the great push that waited merrily for him at Tyburn. He looked crank and insensible in his white shroud, clutching a Bible, his gob open and glaziers gaping at some infinite distance. It was prattled that he had taken of the same drug he tipped me that night at the brandy-shop when he made me babble. I thought of that grim darkmans and hated him all the more. His old pal Jack Ketch turned off the high-pads first, and while they were swinging Wild stood with the queer bit-maker as a soul-driver bade them sing some psalm together. Stupefied, the prig-napper mouthed the words of the dismal ditty like a moonstruck lully. The bastard looked already half gone.

Then the coiner was strung up. The poor cove had been fervent in his prayers and devotions and now tried to make some last dying speech, but nothing could be heard above all the foul oaths and curses directed towards Wild. As the executioner pattered to his old employer that he might take more time to prepare himself, the crowd became all the more nettled. Some started to batter at the cart and there were loud threats to Jack Ketch that he would be dinged if he did not dispatch the villain without delay.

So the hangman fixed the hempen-cord and a great shout went out from the multitude as the cart pulled away. In his nightgown and with a blank phiz, Wild looked to go easy, so weak it had not been deemed needful to bind his hands. But as he was turned off he stretched out a weary paw to catch the rigging of the queer bit-maker. With a fickle grasp he clung to the hanged man and swung with him awhile, slackening his own rope for a few seconds' reprieve. Then, with his strength gone, he let go of his grim dancing partner and as the cord went tight he began to twitch.

The mob let out an awful groan, that disdainful beast pitiless to the end. I mused that the governor of the bridewell might be right in what he pattered on this crank spectacle of punishment. Of how the audience might cheer a villain or hiss some fallen master. And all at once I wondered what on earth I had hoped to tout by coming here.

My head was all mizzy, for in truth I had taken far too much lush in the last few days and was sick to my guts with bile and melancholy. But I knew of a bitter and certain regret: that I had been gulled of my vengeance. I had expected some sentiment of deliverance in Wild's scragging yet felt nothing but a thick head and a sour stomach.

Nix my doll.

Then something strange sparked in my senses. My glaziers pricked as I blinked against the low sunlight. Christ, I sobbed, I can't weep for Wild, can I? But life plays a poor jest on a jade. I scarce could shed a tear for Jack yet here it came, my lamentation.

For a great hate can be mourned as much as a great love: it can prove more certain and glim as fiercely. It is hate that keeps you warm on a cold day, fires the belly when you're hungry. And the hate that had taken me through the bad days bore the name of Jonathan Wild.

And I canted then that I would miss the bastard prig-napper. He had tracked my every footstep upon the wicked pad, blown my flash name that first night in Moll King's. He had made me what I was and I rightly hated him for it. But I would miss him and so would all of Romeville. For in truth he was our creature, conjured from the queer fancy of the gentry-coves and canting-crew alike. And he yet haunts our blindman's holiday. We might peach him now but we dreamed him before.

So I stood staring at the fatal tree long after all had been cut from its branches and the push had dispersed. As the sun came down over Paddington and a crew of scrub beggars scavenged the garbage that littered the wasteground of Tyburn I turned to pad it back to the Hundreds. But who would be there? I canted that I was truly on my own now with no one to hate but myself once more.

And I feared the crank patter in my head turning back on me again. *She has proved my bane*, that dread refrain, sad song of my brain. But when it came now it was not the jabber of accusation but a soft whisper that babbled of another mort. It led me west instead of east, to the broad space trampled flat where the pad from Daisyville ends. This was my road, I twigged, the Edgworth Road. The long straight Roman pad that had brought me here in disgrace all those years ago. This had been my road to ruin, I canted. What if I was to track it back to its beginning?

Then I remembered the vow I had once made and I knew what I had to do.

She has proved my bane.

Three days later I took a rattler out to Edgworth. I wore a fine mantua gown of light blue silk and carried all the trappings of a gentry-mort. But I had murder in my heart and a popp in my bung.

I arrived at that gentry-ken of my childhood to find the gate unlocked and rusty. I gave it a shove, and it groaned like a sad squeaker. I padded up the gravel path that had not been raked or weeded in an age, through a park that had become a wilderness. I touted that the lawn was unmown and the once sharply trimmed hedges of the ornamental garden grown wildly into a savage labyrinth. The summerhouse had collapsed; the fish pond was a stagnant pool.

There was a wagon by the front entrance of the house, and workmen appeared to be dismantling the portico, carefully taking apart its columns and conveying them to the cart. They paid me no heed as I passed them by.

The jigger was open and there was no sign of a footman, so I dupped in and called out. I looked around the hall to tout the chandelier missing, the walls plundered of pictures and ornaments, and what furniture remaining shrouded in dust-sheets. Then I heard footsteps on the marble floor as Fenton, the old master of the household, approached. His livery was a little shabby now, his phiz sallow and careworn but he still bore the proud deportment of a soldier.

'Forgive me, madam,' he said, with a bow, 'but Lady Steevens is not at home to visitors today.'

'It's Bess, Fenton,' I told him. 'Bess Lyon.'

With a squint he leaned closer. Then his glaziers widened and the hint of a smile traced itself on his gob. 'Bess? What – that lanky girl? Well, well, you're a fine lady now.'

'I shouldn't think so, Fenton. But what happened? What happened to the house?'

'The master died two years ago leaving terrible debts. He lost everything in the Bubble, you see. Everything has been sold off, even parts of the building.'

'The servants?'

'All gone.'

'But she's still here?'

'The mistress? Yes. She has been counselled to go and live with relatives but she won't leave. I don't think she can quite face up to it yet. And so I stay on. I couldn't leave her on her own.'

'Where is she?'

'Please, Bess.' He made as if to block my path. 'She's very delicate.'

I side-stepped the master of the household and went looking for Lady Steevens. I found her huddled in a wing-chair by the great fireplace. Startled, she looked up at me, her mean face shrunken with age.

'Who?' she hooted, like a scared bird. 'Who? Who are you?'

'It's Elizabeth Lyon, Lady Steevens.'

'Oh,' she said, scanning my rigging and taking me for a gentry-mort. 'Do please sit down. I'll call for some tea.'

I twigged then that she had no idea who I was.

'There's no need,' I said, and took the seat opposite her.

'But you haven't been announced.' She looked around the room and frowned, as if noticing its queer state for the first time. 'I'm afraid the house is being renovated at present, so we are unable to receive visitors as well as we'd like.'

'I know,' I said, with a smile. 'It's hard being poor, isn't it, nabs?'

'What?' she asked, barely canting my widds.

'How's your son Richard?'

'Oh!' she gasped. 'Oh, my poor Richard. The smallpox took him last summer.'

I thought of the childhood sweetheart who had deceived me, wondering if I could now spare him some grief. *Will you be mine, Bess?* I mused that he might have croaked from another kind of pox but I sat mum-chance on that. *Forgive me, Mother, but she led me astray.* I fingered the outline of the pistol in my purse.

'You don't remember me, do you?'

You have let this little whore snare you, is that it?

'Er,' she winced, 'Elizabeth . . .'

This errand had not gone the way I had planned but I knew now that I would have to settle it quickly. *Go on*, the voice pattered.

'Lyon,' I reminded her. 'Bess Lyon.'

I reached into the bung and cocked the popp. Something loose clattered against the pistol.

'I'm afraid I don't,' she went on. 'My memory is, well . . . You weren't announced, you see. And with this building work, we're less inclined to invite people. May I ask the purpose of your visit?'

Now. I stood up and spoke without thinking. 'I've come to forgive you, Lady Steevens.'

'What?' She looked puzzled but, in truth, the words surprised me too.

'I forgive you,' I repeated, enjoying the crank sense of grace and power it gave me.

'What for?'

'For being a bitch.' I let out a laugh and all at once my mood lifted. 'Oh, yes, you have my pity for that. I forgive you and your pox-ridden son. And I pity you all.'

The look of shock on her phiz was priceless and I took a while to tout it properly. As I uncocked the popp my fingers felt a round object nestling by the butt. I pulled it out and saw it was a guinea. The exact sum I had first been bought with when Richard slipped a gold coin into my eager paw all those years ago. This was the token of my betrayal, the price of my ruin.

'Here,' I pattered, handing it to the old gentry-mort who sat agog before me. 'Take back your wages of sin. It looks like you'll need it.'

Then I padded out, bidding Fenton farewell on the way.

I came back to Romeville in bene humour. The voice was gone. For now, at least. I fenced the popp and had some prog in a tavern in Holborn. I canted then that there was another mort I had to make my peace with. And it was her forgiveness I now sought. So I went to a brandy-shop and bought a bottle of fine cognac, then made my way to Clare Market.

Mary Sheppard smiled when she touted me by the jigger of her cribb. She bade me dup in and we sat down and took lush together. 'Why didn't you come before, nabs?' she asked me.

'I was ashamed.'

'Stow your widds, Bess.'

'Truly. Those things Jack said about me.'

She shrugged. 'Jack always had a queer gob. Even as a squeaker.'

'But I did babble to Wild. I didn't mean to, but—' I took a gulp of air. It came out as a sob.

'Listen.' Mary put her paw on mine. 'I was there, Bess. I remember.'

'You remember?'

'Yes. That night you lost your child. I fetched Mother Midnight but it was too late. We thought we might lose you, too. That was Wild's doing. I don't blame you for blowing the widd on Jack to that bastard.'

I swiped a tear from my glaziers. 'Thanks, Mary,' I said, and poured us another.

'On the night he was last snabbled, me and Jack drank brandy together,' she recalled. 'You know what he told me?'

'What?'

'I asked him about these two women of his. He pattered there was only two women he loved.'

I sighed. Mary Sheppard grinned and showed her crooked grinders.

'No, not what you think, Bess. Not those two Kates.'

'No? Who, then?'

'Well, me first, nabs, being his dear old mother and all.'

'And who besides?'

'Some mort called Edgworth Bess.'

'I don't believe you.'

'I'm not lying, nabs. That's what he jabbered. You were his first and his best.'

'He was pot-valiant that darkmans.'

'Yes, and doesn't that make coves patter gospel? Listen, he told me he might deny you publicly, but that was to keep you safe, so that none might track after you to get to him, as they had done before.'

'Well, it didn't work. I ended up in the Poultry Compter on his behalf.'

'But he tried. The foolish boy knew he was born to hang but he hoped you might stay at liberty—'

'By saying all those hateful things about me? And having them printed?'

'What better way to make the flat-coves certain you were no longer an accessory to his crimes?'

I recalled the crank widds Jack had pattered that peep of day in Spitalfields: *What if by peaching someone you could set them free? Is that what those cruel widds of his canted?*

'He meant his curse as a blessing, Bess. That's what he told me. He hoped it might cause you to denounce him and earn some credit from the justices.'

'I would never do that, Mary.'

'I meant to tell you all of this before, nabs. But you never came.'

My head reeled. Jack had had so many crank notions near the end yet I could not quite cant this one. But if I could believe it, I might be free of that badness in my soul. I twigged even then that this might take some time. When I left I bussed Mary on the cheek. 'I just wanted to say I'm sorry, Mary.'

'Thank you, Bess.' She bussed me back. 'There's nothing to forgive, you know that.'

But there was. I could try to forgive Jack for what he had pattered and all the suffering he had put me through. If I could simply remember the happy times. I still felt gulled of the chance to say goodbye to him properly. It was a midsummer night with yet some glim left in the sky as I padded it back to my cribb. I touted a star and made a wish. Perhaps I could even forgive myself now.

And as I come to the last part of my story I beg forgiveness from you all. For you know me now for what I am, a poor jade of the Hundreds of Drury with little opportunity to earn a living in an honest fashion. My trial is tomorrow and I might be judged then, so I pray you might lend a sympathetic ear as I relate the circumstances that have brought me here to Newgate.

As the months passed I drifted about. I had doused the voice in my head but there was yet this doleful sadness that tracked after me and oft-times I found comfort in the lush. Each lightmans I would patter to myself that now was the time to end the mourning, to quit being Jack's hempen-widow and get on with my own life. Then I would get pot-valiant by darkmans and, in exchange for free drinks in some boozing-ken, patter those tales of him that coves delight in. I canted that I should find some liberty from my past but it wasn't easy.

Some eight months later, at the end of January, I was in a gin-shop in Smithfield at peep of day with some cove I had picked up on the pad. He had half a dozen silver spoons and a silk wiper filched from a hog-butcher he used to work for. He pattered he would give me them if I docked him.

'Let's go and get some lightning,' I told him.

In the ken we tipped the mort the wiper for a bottle and set to it. The booze loosened my gob and I was soon prattling foolishly.

'I'm Edgworth Bess,' I bragged to all in the gin-shop.

Faces turned and touted me. I took the spoons from my drinking companion and held them up.

'These,' I jabbered. 'These I got from my dear Jack Sheppard. I vamped them many years ago.'

I bussed the silverware as if it were some holy relic. There were tears in my glaziers and I was taken by the deep sentiment one finds in the soul when drinking gin at dawn. For I recalled the time Jack had given me the spoons he had spoken with from the Rummer tavern in Charing Cross. They were the first things he ever stole for me.

The cove I had dupped in with was slumped over, quite pot-valiant. So I stowed the silver in my bung and shabbed off.

The next day I cursed myself for playing the drunken gape-seed once more. Worse still, I had babbled my own name to a push as I had taken those spoons. And, sure enough, when the cove was snabbled he peached me, pattering that I had seduced him to go and mill the ken with him. So I was taken to Newgate and thus indicted for felony.

It is a capital charge and if found guilty I am likely to hang for it. I have little doubt of my peril, for I know that my infamy and former offences weigh heavily against me. But, then, I have ever found the balance of circumstance dip from my favour, and cant the evenly measured scales of justice are but a queer fancy of the flat world.

Though I'm sure that if I am shown mercy I could mend my ways. Remember that when Jesus found a woman taken in adultery He did not condemn her but rather pattered that she should go and sin no more. And I could give up my wicked life, though in truth more because I have grown too old for this ancient profession rather than any desire for an honest trade. If that does not seem contrite enough, it is at least a sincere repentance.

If I live I will always bear the notoriety of being Edgworth Bess, for the times I padded it with Jack Sheppard, but I'll not be ashamed of that. We were enamoured in danger and infamy, and to any who jabber that we made a poor example of love I say we were the very embodiment of that instinct. For love is a thief and a whore and belongs to the darkmans. In turn we saved each other, betrayed each other, we even tried to kill each other, but who can say any different of passion except in degree or measure? I pity those who never felt the glim of such desire.

I'll ever remember that peep of lightmans when we climbed through the glaze of the sky-parlour onto the roof to tout across the city, of how Jack pattered that all of Romeville belonged to us. For a while it did.

For now I can say truly that I do not fear death. As its shadow grows near so am I more careless of it. I have had enough of life, after all, and known its delights as well as its sufferings.

If I am spared, this narrative will count as my earthly confession. When Billy approached me in the Whit and pattered that we might pal up for some mutual benefit, I jested, 'Not if I want to plead my belly. A madge-cove like you'd be no use for me!'

But now is all of my life set down and I am glad of that. If I am sentenced to hang then we shall add my final penitence where I might endeavour to make my peace with God through the soul-driver.

But I am not scared and that is a great comfort to me. Death comes for us all and none can truly be condemned to die by another for that sentence has already been passed. However justice might bitch us with it, death itself is not a penalty within its power. They can give only the time of it, and I count it a blessing that I might cant the hour of my final moment. Few of those who come to tout me swing will have so easy a passage out of life. So I make myself ready.

I only beg that I might not be anatomised. Let death provide the modesty that life denied me. I would like a fine dress to be hanged in, a good coffin, and a decent burial ground. Tip some coin to the waterman so that he may convey me across the river for I will abide on the Turkish Shore, at that pauper's cemetery where I should belong in the end. In a little grave at Cross Bones, to rest in peace with my sisterhood.

Newgate Gaol, 5th March 1726

Dear Applebee,

What follows is a brief account of the trial of Edgworth Bess.

'Elizabeth Lyon,' called the clerk of the court, 'alias Sheppard, alias Edgworth Bess.'

I spied her as she stood in the dock with a sullen look I first took for resignation. But as the bare matters of the case were laid out in the courtroom I watched her expression resolve into something else. Something far more dangerous.

The hog-butcher's wife deposed of how they had come back from market to find a window of their house broken and their goods missing. She testified that she suspected a man who had worked for her husband and found a handkerchief belonging to her in the possession of a certain Elizabeth Seymour.

And Bess gazed ahead, holding the sessions house with a fatal stare. It was a look of defiance and I prayed that she might soon soften her demeanour so that the court might soften theirs towards her. For she could not hope for justice at this hearing but only bargain for some small mercy. The man who gave her the spoons was called.

'I was drinking with the prisoner in Whitecross Street and she persuaded me to rob my master's house, and said she'd go with me and put me in the way. So I was drunk and we went together. 'Twas between four and five in the morning.'

Bess smiled and shook her head at this but it rather made her look more wanton than outraged. Elizabeth Seymour was called and when questioned admitted that she had received the handkerchief from the prisoner.

'I sell a dram of gin now and then,' she explained, 'in Peter's Lane, behind Hick's Hall. About five o'clock that morning the prisoner and Smith knocked me up. She called for a dram, and pulling out half a dozen silver teaspoons, she kissed them and said, "These were left to me by my dear Jack Sheppard, and I have just fetched them out of pawn."'

The accused nodded slowly at this, knowing that this foolish boast had snared her. She was then called to take the stand and was quizzed by the court.

'Do you truly claim that these spoons belonged to your late husband?' the judge asked her.

'No,' she replied.

'Then how did they come to be in your possession?'

I willed her to say something at this point that might counter the damning testimony of the one that impeached her. This was her only opportunity to make any kind of a defence. But she merely shrugged and pointed at the man who had so cruelly turned evidence on her, declaring, 'He picked me up in the street and gave me these spoons to lie with me, and truly I thought I might as well earn them that way myself as let another do it.'

A clerk let out a half-stifled laugh at the frankness of this admission. The recorder called for silence. Bess grinned. The jury quickly determined its verdict.

Guilty.

She nodded at this. Now was the time for her to make some sort of plea or statement of contrition. I prayed again that she might beg mercy from the court or give even a gesture of penitence. But instead she looked quite insolent, staring back at the bench as if nothing could harm her. There was even a slight smile on her lips as she waited for the judge to pass sentence upon her.

But when it came she frowned and touched her mouth with her hand as if she could not quite comprehend what was being uttered. She was puzzled, disconcerted even.

For it was a reprieve from death that so greatly surprised her.

Transportation was the sentence of the court. She wore a dazed look as they took her down, as if she had not yet recovered from the shock of her deliverance, a curious expression, something almost like disappointment. I tried to catch her eye as she was led away but she stared straight ahead as if searching for something.

I felt so happy for Bess in that moment, that she might be shown this small mercy. But my relief was short-lived, tempered as it was by my own predicament. For it was time now for me to face my own judgment.

This final letter brings bad news and not only that the prospects for the publication of the memoirs of Edgworth Bess will now suffer as she is spared the gallows. In one of your earliest missives concerning this work you cruelly quipped that for the account of her life to be a success she must surely hang for it. For, of course, the hanging day provides the best opportunity to hawk such a work, and the news of it furnishes a convenient advertisement. We know that what the public craves above all are the last dying words.

Well, now I might provide them. From the very first I promised you an authentic narrative: this would be the genuine voice of lament calling out from the condemned hold. I never knew how much you suspected of all my letters sent from

Newgate: my initial desire for anonymity; of that time when you suggested that we meet in person and I declined claiming I was 'indisposed'. Perhaps the general reader has by now surmised my predicament, but if you have already conceived it you have been polite enough to make no mention of it, and for that discretion I am heartily grateful. As now I might freely admit that I myself have been a resident of Newgate Gaol for all this time and I witnessed her trial from the bail-dock as a fellow prisoner.

Elizabeth Lyon and I were both committed to the Whit at about the same time. I suggested that I might write her history and sell it to you to provide some garnish to make both our lives more bearable here. I soon found that there was my own tale to tell and so entwined my confession with hers, taking the bold opportunity to include all the unnameable acts of my life.

For I dwell in the condemned hold, not Edgworth Bess, and must now make my peace. These are my last words.

❧

'Sodomites!' came the cries from the street outside, then a heavy hammering on the door. 'Filthy sodomites!'

It was on the last Sunday of January that Mother Clap's was raided by constables from the Society for the Reformation of Manners. A busy festival night as they broke down the door and a general panic spread throughout the assembly. Some swiftly made for the side exit, others attempted a sly retreat through the back of the house.

As the first of the officers stormed in, staves at the ready, I saw a spirited defence led by Princess Seraphina and a few of the other mollies in female attire. It has ever been my observation that the fiercest members of our tribe are those who dress as women. Indeed, such was the wrathful fury of the princess that she managed to push her way through the general assault and escape into the night.

The rest of us were increasingly trapped. It soon became clear that constables had been posted by the side doors as those who tried to make their flight that way were caught and held. I had regressed to the rear of the premises and there seemed to be some chance of slipping out by there. But not for long. I could hear voices and footfalls coming from the back-alley in ever increasing number. The molly-house was being surrounded.

But just as I was ready to make a dash for it I remembered Adam. He had been in the chapel and could surely be discovered *in flagrante delicto*. For a moment I pondered on how apt this might be since he had so often blazed offences within my sight. Then my head cursed my heart as it compelled me to go back for him.

He was buttoning his breeches as I got to him and I pulled him out of there. I ducked sharply as a constable swung his staff at my head. I kicked the man and he toppled over, blocking the path of our pursuers for just enough time to make it to the back door. But there a new battalion of the Society for the Reformation of Manners made their sortie. Outflanked and outnumbered we were thus taken.

We were rudely herded onto the street outside. I spied the righteous hatred burning in the eyes of those who now guarded us. One constable even spat in my face.

'Dirty brutes!' another called. 'Evil buggers!'

Some forty or so of us were arrested that night. I felt an awful guilt: this had been partly my fault because I had penned the wretched chapter for Wild that peached the protector of the molly-houses. Adam looked terrified as we were conveyed to Newgate at peep of day.

'Just sit mum-chance,' I whispered to him, when we were separated. 'They have little evidence but what we might tell them.'

I had to restrain the urge to touch him or show some fleeting gesture of affection as he was called away to be interrogated. For I was ever devoted to Adam in a manner that defied all reason. He yet lived with me, more out of idleness than affection. We had moved into smaller and cheaper lodgings in St Giles, which he would never cease complaining of.

I feared for him, that he might make some rash confession. This was soon justified, though I should have saved that fear for myself. For my dear Adam gave the justices long and detailed evidence of how I had defiled and corrupted him. Thus he saved his own neck and stood to gain the forty pounds' reward for information on a capital charge. I had expected him to work every low and mean drop on me but I never dreamed that he would inform on me so.

Impeached by my lover, I was charged with committing the unnatural sin of sodomy by feloniously, wickedly, devilishly and against the order of nature assaulting and carnally knowing his person. Examined by the magistrate, I might have given evidence against Adam in return for his betrayal. But what would have been the purpose of it? They would simply have indicted us both. Besides, I still loved him so I said nothing of his own transgressions. Even as he damned me I sought his salvation. And so this fool was committed to the Whit to await trial at the next sessions.

Thus I began the writing of this double narrative. I hope yet that I have done some justice to the story as little has been afforded me.

At my trial Adam played his part to devastating effect, his eyes bright with tears, his pale face flushed with sorrow as he deposed his perfidious evidence. I had evilly seduced him, he insisted, and not only viciously made use of his body but pimped him out to others for my own gain.

'But why did you conceal such filthy practices for so long?' the judge asked him.

'Fear, your honour,' Adam replied. 'And that I am an ignorant country lad and did not know the greatness of this crime. He paid me an allowance and bought me fine clothes. He corrupted me. I was only saved by the good officers that came to the molly-house. Now I might be easy with my conscience.'

I said nothing that might impeach him but admitted my guilt to the sessions house. I caught Adam's eye as he walked from the courtroom: he looked right through me with a steely gaze. And so Narcissus gave a sword to spurned Aminias that he might stab himself with it. I was found guilty and sentenced to death.

So, despite that superstition of being briefly hanged at birth, I'll not be spared the rope, after all. I'll soon join my poor mother who nearly hanged me. From the cord of life to the cord of death is but a short span.

It is all so unjust. For all my crimes I am condemned to die for the felony of love. I might have sincere remorse for my other sins, beg forgiveness from all those I have cheated or robbed, but I seek no redemption for what I am sentenced to. I recall the words of scripture that puzzled Wild, *Cursed is every one that hangeth on a tree*, and I find my own meaning. For though I might have betrayed my own kind in the past, I am determined now to bear my curse proudly to the end.

The chaplain came to take my confession and insisted upon the villainy and uncleanness of unnatural sins, which ought not to be named among people who have any remainders of civility, much less among Christians who profess the true religion.

'We are taught to deny all ungodliness and worldly lusts,' he told me. 'Especially the lusts of the flesh. God showed the evil of this sin in his visible judgments inflicted on Sodom and Gomorrah, and the neighbouring cities, in raining down fire and brimstone from Heaven and consuming them all.'

I thought of that secret gospel of Johnny Hookman's and that favourite verse of his from St John. 'He that loveth not knoweth not God,' I whisper in the darkness. 'For God is love.'

But what can we believe in God or love? For all the countless acts in both names give but little proof of either.

I am cast out from God's grace in any case. And why try to pray to Him for mercy when He forsook His own Son upon the gallows? For if Christ Himself was born to hang I have my suspicions that He pleaded evidence for that third day reprieve. If Golgotha was the triple tree, with three hanged together just as at Tyburn, two thieves either side, what then was Jesus but a thief-taker as He peached one and acquitted the other?

And as for love, well, I loved in vain yet felt its cruel blessing. A love that proved false and condemned me in the end. But perhaps it was the conceit of love I yearned for. Love is but an idea, after all. Perhaps it is an idea yet worth dying for.

But I am so scared. My death waits patiently and every minute of each hour I might feel the terror of its appointment. In vain I seek the resolution that Bess found. I dearly hope I might go calmly at the end, though I know I cannot expect a friendly reception from the mob on my hanging day. I have seen the hatred they bear for the molly and sodomite.

So in the time I have left I try to dwell on gentler sentiments. I think of the mother I never knew and dream of her final loving embrace. And in the face of mortality I ponder on childhood. These are my last words so they bring to mind my first. The vowels and consonants I mouthed as a boy, greedily suckling on each syllable. The heroic couplets of the chapbook: *A is an Archer that shot at a frog, B was a Butcher, who had a great dog.* This was ever my epic verse for it ends: *Y was a Youth, who didn't like school, Z was a Zanni, who played the fool.*

Ah, I have ever loved words and, with more time, I might have made a poet not just a hackney-scribbler. But this narrative will surely prove my final testament. I hear that John Gay is with Swift and Pope in Twickenham, working on that thieves' opera he so long talked of. Well, here is my Newgate pastoral and I entrust it to you, Applebee.

This account is now spent and we owe each other nothing. Please convey any outstanding monies to Elizabeth Lyon with my compliments. There remains but one debt to be settled. Fate presents the bill in the end and none can burn the ken or walk away free. For it is midnight and I already hear the chimes of St Sepulchre-without-Newgate tolling for my hanging day. And the bells of Old Bailey call *When will you pay me?*

Your sincere & faithful author,

William Archer Esq.

XIV

'TRANSPORTATION is not just God's mercy on miserable sinners, it is part of His divine purpose, also,' drones the chaplain.

There is a last service in the chapel at Newgate for those of us sentenced to be marinated. So we all sit in the gospel-shop and listen to the prattle of these widds.

'It fulfils the prophecy of Noah!'

'So, are we going on the Ark, then?' some wit of a low-pad calls from the back.

The whole gospel-shop breaks into laughter at this jest. The soul-driver touts us with cold glaziers and jabbers on.

'Now Noah begat three sons: Japheth, Shem and Ham. And by these were the nations of the earth divided. Those born of Japheth are the white gentiles of Europe; of Shem, those Indian races that inhabit both east and west; Ham's kin are those benighted blacks of Africa. After the flood God decreed the earth be replenished and for each nation to go forth according to their destiny.'

'Go forth and multiply, is it, Reverend?' the low-pad speaks out again. 'Well, we're all ready for that.'

This causes a little more mirth amid the flash congregation, though a pious mort at the front turns and bids the cove hush. The chaplain yet continues with his sermon, holding the ken with his mellifluous patter.

'It was said that God should enlarge Japheth, and that he shall dwell in the tents of Shem. And so this New World is given to his people as their dominion. But the sons of Ham are cursed and it is written that "a servant of servants shall he be unto his brethren".

'So, as you have been spared death for your iniquitous crimes, be thankful for your seven years' servitude, that God has made you more fortunate than those black wretches who are slaves for life. And there is yet hope for you all. Many of those transported settle and become planters, enriching themselves as they enrich that new and bountiful land. So through toil and honest labour the journey to America might be a blessed migration, a pilgrimage from your fallen state to join God's chosen people. Go with God and let God's mercy be upon you all.'

We patter amen to all that and are led out to be marched down to the Blackfriars Stairs. We are chained up two together by hand and neck.

'Two by two,' the low-pad wit jabbers. 'We really are going to the Ark. Two of every sort, two of everything that creepeth upon the earth or brusheth upon the sneak!'

Indeed there is every species of felon among us ready to embark for America, but none laughs now as we are all weary of this cove's jesting. Out upon the pad the whole crew grows sombre. A bright cold lightmans it is and, though thankful for air sweeter than the foul stink of the trib from which we have shabbed off, we are awakened to the grim journey ahead. Each of us is now quiet in our own thoughts, trying to cant the meaning of what is to come. A prig sings an old farewell ballad that soldiers are much fond of and I hear the widds at the end of one verse.

I seek no more the fine nor gay,
For each doth but remind me,
How swift the hours I passed away
With the girl I left behind me.

Many a glazier grows glib with tears at the song, yet we are happy for the plain sadness of it for it is time to say goodbye and each needs a fair snack of the grief. I think of what might lie beyond, twigging that picking tobacco cannot be so bad as beating hemp, but seven years of it? I have heard some prattle of coves with loure enough to buy their freedom. I have some coin stowed: five guineas sewn into the lining of my rigging. The last payment from Billy Archer, bless him. It might make my passage more bearable at least.

We reach Ludgate Hill and there is a small push lining the pad. Our procession is not as grand as that to Tyburn, yet there is oft-times notice of it in newspapers, and here some public to tout those condemned to marination. I pray that I am not spied upon for I have no wish to be gape-seed any more.

I decide that my new life will start from today – wherever I am headed, be it Virginia or Maryland – that this New World will be a new story and a tale I will tell myself. I am thankful to Billy for penning my past but now I must write my own future. The sad catch of the ballad is a lugg-worm in my brain: *How swift the hours I passed away, With the girl I left behind me.*

Poor Billy. I think of him and all the others I have lost. As we reach the Blackfriars Stairs to be loaded onto a barge, some coves and morts come forward to say goodbye to the convicts they know. The pity of it is that there is no one left to bid me farewell. My little punk Lizzy, perhaps, but I do not tout her in the push. A bene part of me cants it for the best if she has forgotten me. And as we climb aboard the barge I have a crank thought: what if I was to forget myself?

For if Jack was true when he pattered that he meant to set me free with his cruel widds, is it not time for me to take that liberty for myself? My youth is now spent and, in truth, I grew too fast and saw too much. I have been judged an old offender yet I am but four-and-twenty. Now I might come of age and forsake the foolish dell I once was.

So I am crossing the water not to the Turkish Shore for a pauper's grave in a whore's cemetery but to a whole new continent. My flesh trembles at the cold and something else yet. As we sail under the bridge, past the Tower down to where the convict ship is moored in Wapping, I cant that my fear has returned. Not the fear of death but of life. The dread that comes with any glim of hope.

Embarking, we come before a cove of the ship's company, a manifest of the cargo in his paws. His glaziers spark a little as he checks me on the list.

'Edgworth Bess, is it?' he asks, a grin on his gob.

'No,' I patter. 'That jade yet bides in the Hundreds. My name is Elizabeth Lyon.'

We wait for the turn of the tide then cast off on the ebb-current, all praying for a safe crossing. I look back to tout the last of Romeville. And the girl I left behind me.

POSTSCRIPT

Elizabeth Lyon was transported to America aboard the *Loyal Margaret* in June 1726 and disembarked at Annapolis, Maryland, on 1st October of that year.

Billy Archer is a fictional character but three men were hanged for sodomy on 9th May 1726, following the raid on Mother Clap's molly-house. Their names were Gabriel Lawrence, William Griffin and Thomas Wright.

In April 1727, Charles Hitchen was convicted of attempted sodomy and sentenced to six months' imprisonment and to stand in the pillory for a day. He was pilloried brutally by a vicious mob and died soon after his release from gaol, never having fully recovered from this ordeal.

John Gay's 'Newgate pastoral', *The Beggar's Opera*, premièred at the Lincoln's Inn Fields Theatre on 29th January 1728, produced by John Rich. An immediate success that became the most popular play of the eighteenth century, it was said that it 'made Gay rich and Rich gay'.

GLOSSARY

abbess a brothel-keeper

academy a brothel

autem-diver a pickpocket who preys on a church congregation

babble to inform on

beak a magistrate

bene good

bilk to cheat

bit coin

bite a con; **put the bite on** to work a con

bitch to force or dominate

bleach blond or pale

bleeding-cull a prostitute's client who is easy to manipulate

blindman's holiday darkness

blow the coals to arouse

blow the widd to give the game away

bluffer an innkeeper

boozing-ken a tavern or alehouse

born under a threepenny planet born unlucky

brush upon the sneak to step lightly

bung a purse or pocket

bung-nipper a cutpurse or pickpocket

burn the ken to leave without paying

buss kiss

buttock a female prostitute

buttock-broker a madam or brothel-keeper

buttock-and-file a female prostitute who picks pockets

buttock-and-twang a female prostitute teamed with a man who beats up and robs her clients; also the name of this racket

cant to understand (usually to know the flash language)

canting-crew those who inhabit the flash world and speak its language

caper-merchant a dancing-master

chittiface a little puny child

chub an inexperienced player or gambler

clanker a tankard

click to rob

clickman toad a pocket watch

cog to cheat at dice

commodity vagina

cove a man

Covent Garden gout syphilis

crack to break open

cracksman a house-breaker

crank foolish, eccentric, capricious

cribb a room or lodgings

cull a man who might be prey to those in the flash world

dab good, expert

Daisyville the countryside

dancers stairs

dandyprat a puny little fellow

darbies shackles or fetters

darkmans night

dell a young female prostitute

dimber good-looking

ding to knock down

dive to pickpocket

dock to fuck

done up to be ruined (usually by gambling)

douse the glim to put out the light

drop a con or scam; **work the drop** work a con

dub to pick or open

dub the jigger to pick the lock of a door

dup to enter

ebb-water reduced circumstances

fam a ring

famble a hand

festival night a drag night in a molly-house

file to pick a pocket

flash the language of the underworld; *adj*. underworld, criminal

flash-ken a den of thieves

flat a respectable member of

society; *adj.* respectable, lawful

flogging-cull a cull who likes to be whipped

gaol fever typhus spread by lice in prison

game of flats a game of cards or sexual activity between women

game pullet a young female who is preyed upon

garnish fees charged by prison staff for any comfort

gelt money

gob a mouth

gape-seed a spectacle

gentry-cove a gentleman

gentry-mort a gentlewoman

gentry-ken a gentleman's house, a mansion

glaze a window

glaziers eyes

glib smooth

glim a light, flame or fire, to shine

glimmed in the paw burned in the hand, branded as a punishment

glimstick a candle

gospel-shop a church

grinders teeth

guinea-dropper a cheat who pretends to find money on the street as a lure to a cull

gull to cheat

hempen-widow a woman whose husband has been hanged

high-pad one who robs on horseback, a highwayman

Hundreds of Drury the region around Drury Lane known for vice and prostitution

house of civil reception a brothel

jade a working girl, prostitute

jabber to talk

jigger a door

kate a picklock

keeping-cull a man who keeps a mistress

ken a house

ken-miller a house-breaker

kick away to escape

kid-lay a con whereby an errand boy is relieved of his goods

kitling a young woman preyed upon

lay any kind of criminal scheme

lightmans day

lightning gin

link-boy one who lights the way by lantern in the streets at night

lock premises for storing stolen goods

long-meg a tall, long-limbed woman

long-shanks a tall, long-limbed man

loure money

low-pad one who robs on foot, a foot-pad

luggs ears

lully a child or simpleton, childish or simple-minded

lully-prig the lowest kind of thief

lush alcoholic drink

machine penis

make to steal

madge a male homosexual

marinated transported

melt to spend; to melt loure to spend money

member-mug a chamber-pot

Merry Old Roger the devil

mill to break

mother a brothel-keeper

molly a male homosexual or transvestite

moon-curser a link-boy who robs his clients

mort a woman

mouser a cat

mum to remain silent; to sit mum-chance to remain silent in the hope of being acquitted

music-merchant a composer

nab to steal, to take

nabs a friend of either sex

natty-lads young thieves

nettle to annoy

nim-gimmer a doctor

nix my doll nothing

no face except one's own without coin, broke

nunnery a brothel

oss-chives bone-handled knives

pad a road or street

pad, pad it to walk, to go upon the street

pal up to work together

patter to talk

peach to impeach or accuse

peep of day dawn

peery wary

phiz a face

phiz-monger a portrait artist

pike to run, to run away

plead the belly declare oneself pregnant to secure an acquittal

popp a pistol

posture-moll a stripper

pot-valiant drunk

prattle to gossip

prattle-broth tea

prig a thief

prig-napper a thief-taker

prog food

punk a little whore

push a crowd

queer bad, wrong

queer bit-maker a maker of counterfeit coin

queer bluffer a devious inn-keeper

quod-cull a gaoler

rabbit-catcher a midwife

rattling-cove a coachman

rattling-lay stealing from coaches

ride dragon on St George sexual intercourse where a woman is on top of a man

rigging clothing

Romeville London

rum good

St Giles' Blackbird a black or mixed-race person living in this quarter of London

St Giles' Greek another term for the flash language

school a brothel

scrag to hang; scragged hanged

screen to cover, to cover up, to hide

scrub a ragamuffin

shab off to sneak away

shanks legs

sharper a cheat or conman

sky-parlour garret or room at the top of a house

smoke to suspect

smoky jealous, suspicious

snabbled taken or arrested by the authorities

snack a share

soul-driver a priest or parson

spark to set light to

speak with to steal

spruce-prig a thief who dresses in fine clothes and operates at balls and society occasions

spunging-house a debtors' prison

squeak to inform

squeaker a child

stifle a squeaker to murder a child

stallion a pimp or whoremaster

stall to distract

star the glaze to cut the glass of a window

stow to hide

stow the widd to keep quiet, not give the game away

stow your widds to shut up

tip to give

tout to see, spy, look out

track to follow

trib prison (from tribulation)

trull an old female prostitute

Turkish shore the Lambeth, Southwark and Rotherhithe side of the Thames

twang a man who works the buttock-and-twang

twig to deduce

vamp to pawn

vaulting-school a brothel

watching-cull a prostitute's client who likes to watch, a voyeur

Westminster wedding a whore and a rogue's marriage ceremony

whipped at the cart's arse tied to the back of a moving cart and whipped along the street – the punishment for women convicted of brothel-keeping

Whit, the Newgate gaol

widd a word

wiper a handkerchief

ACKNOWLEDGEMENTS

A most invaluable resource has been the Proceedings of the Old Bailey, 1674-1913, (www.oldbailey.org), not least in providing the court reports of Jack Sheppard, Jonathan Wild, Joseph 'Blueskin' Blake and, of course, Elizabeth Lyon. My thanks to all involved in this comprehensive and very accessible archive.

I have been well served by contemporary accounts of the period, but I'm also grateful to many secondary sources that provided much insight and context for this novel. In particular Rictor Norton's groundbreaking work on gay culture in eighteenth-century London, *Mother Clap's Molly House* (Gay Men's Press, 1992), and David Nokes' magnificent biography *John Gay: A Profession of Friendship* (Oxford University Press, 1995). I cannot hope to acknowledge all my debts to the facts, only admit to my own fanciful mistakes in fiction. What follows is a selected bibliography.

CONTEMPORARY SOURCES

Anon, *A New Canting Dictionary*, London, 1725

Anon, *A Narrative of All the Robberies, Escapes, &c of John Sheppard*, London, 1724

Defoe, Daniel, *Moll Flanders*, London, 1722

The History of the Remarkable Life of John Sheppard, London, 1724

The True and Genuine Account of the Life and Actions of Jonathan Wild, London, 1726

Gay, John, *Trivia: or The Art of Walking the Streets of London*, London, 1726

The Beggar's Opera, London, 1727

Hitchen, Charles, *The Regulator: or A Discovery of the Conduct of Thieves and Thief-Takers*, London, 1718

Hogarth, William, *A Harlot's Progress*, London, 1731

A Rake's Progress, London, 1735

Industry and Idleness, London, 1747

Richard Hutton's Complaints Book: The Notebook of the Steward of the Quaker Workhouse at Clerkenwell 1711-1737 (ed. Tim Hitchcock, London, London Record Society, 1987)

Johnson, Capt. Charles, *A General and True History of the Lives and Actions of the Most Famous Highwaymen etc.*, London, 1734

Thurmond, John, *Harlequin Sheppard*, London, 1724

Wild, Jonathan, *An Answer to a Late Insolent Libel*, London, 1718

Modern Accounts

Arnold, Catherine, *City of Sin: London and its Vices*, London, Simon & Schuster, 2010

Bleackley, Horace, *Jack Sheppard*, Edinburgh, William Hodge & Company, 1933

Burford, EJ, *Wits, Wenches and Wantons*, London, Robert Hale, 1986

Gatrell, Vic, *The First Bohemians*, London, Allen Lane, 2013

Hilton, Lisa, *Mistress Peachum's Pleasure*, London, Weidenfeld & Nicolson, 2005

Holmes, Richard, (introduction) *Defoe on Sheppard and Wild*, London, HarperCollins, 2004

Howson, Gerald, *Thief-Taker General*, London, Hutchinson, 1970

Lineburgh, Peter, *The London Hanged*, Cambridge University Press, 1991

Moore, Lucy, *The Thieves' Opera*, London, Viking, 1997

Lyons, FJ, *Jonathan Wild, Prince of Robbers*, London, Michael Joseph, 1936

Nokes, David, *John Gay: A Profession of Friendship*, Oxford University Press, 1995

Norton, Rictor, *Mother Clap's Molly House*, London, Gay Men's Press, 1992

Novak, Maximillian E, *Daniel Defoe: Master of Fictions*, Oxford University Press, 2001

Uglow, Jenny, *Hogarth: A Life and a World*, London, Faber & Faber, 1997

Winton, Calhoun, *John Gay and the London Theatre*, The University Press of Kentucky, 1993

OTHER SOURCES & INSPIRATIONS

I'd like to thank Nicola Freeman and the British Library, whose invitation to me to participate in the 2013-14 exhibition *Georgians Revealed* provided the first spark for this novel; St Bride's Foundation Library and Workshop for providing the practical historical background to the printing trade and Grub Street; Marc Almond and John Harle for the performance of their song-cycle *The Tyburn Tree* at the Barbican on 2nd March 2014 (where Marc channelled the demonic persona of a Newgate prison chaplain); the Friends of Cross Bones who have lovingly preserved the site of the pauper women's grave-yard depicted in this book; and Stephen Webster for his Hogarthian tales of life as a London apprentice. And I was inspired, as ever, by the memory of my dear friend Bruce

Reynolds (1931-2013), latter-day highwayman and master of the criminal narrative.

Thanks and praise also to: Jonny Geller for all of his support and encouragement, Carole Welch for her meticulous care with the text, Francine Toon, Hazel Orme, all at Hodder & Stoughton, friends, family, fellow hackney-scribblers and early readers of the work – Chris Cope, Mandy Colleran, Andrew Heckert, Stephanie Theobald and Peter Ross at the Guildhall Library, who was kind enough to pass on the details of Elizabeth Lyon's landing certificate for her arrival in America. If anyone out there has any knowledge of what might have happened to her after that, please let me know.

JAKE ARNOTT

The Long Firm

*'I'll tell you what happens now,' Harry says, reading my mind.
'You can go now. We're quits. You don't talk to anybody about
anything. You've had a taste of what will happen if you do.'*

Meet Harry Starks: club owner, racketeer, porn king,
sociology graduate and Judy Garland fan. To be in his orbit
is to be caught up in the music, the parties, the people and
the sex of the Swinging Sixties. But behind the rough charm
and cheap glamour is a man prepared to do what it takes to
get what he wants.

'Compulsive reading, powerful writing'
Dominic Bradbury, *The Times*

'One of the smartest, funniest and most original novels you
will read all year . . . every bit as cool, stylish and venomous
as the London in which it's set'
John Tague, *Independent on Sunday*

'Terrific . . . its effect is both shocking and exhilarating'
John Preston, *Sunday Telegraph*

'Outstanding . . . Arnott's recreation of the decadent,
dangerous atmosphere of the times is immaculate'
Eldon King, *Observer*

SCEPTRE

JAKE ARNOTT

He Kills Coppers

During the long hot summer of 1966, a senseless murder
shocks the nation and brings the World Cup euphoria to an
abrupt end. Yet it marks a beginning for three men, who are
inextricably linked to the crime and its consequences: an
ambitious detective struggling with his conscience; a tabloid
journalist with a nose for a nasty story; and a disaffected
thief, haunted by his violent past.

Spanning three decades of profound social change, this
gripping novel explores corruption on both sides of the law
and at the very heart of the state.

'Brilliant . . . You won't be able to put it down'
Mark Sanderson, *Sunday Telegraph* Summer Reading

'The story and its characters ride perfectly within the
setting . . . It propels Arnott even further into a league
of his own'
Christopher Fowler, *Independent on Sunday*

'Arnott's tough and streetwise novel packs
a powerful punch'
Simon Shaw, *Mail on Sunday*

'A wonderful mix of period detail and atmosphere,
this is a fine, evocative novel'
Stuart Price, *Independent*

SCEPTRE

JAKE ARNOTT

truecrime

It's 1995, and crime is the new cool. Actress Julie wants none of it as she comes to terms with her hidden criminal roots. But her public-school boyfriend is going all mockney and writing the script of his 'classic British gangster movie'. Meanwhile, 'Geezer' Gaz, wannabe villain, is losing control as he preys on the Essex rave scene. And sixties gang boss Harry Starks is back to haunt them all . . .

New lads meet old lags, celebrity villains mix with media types and Cool Britannia is stripped bare in wickedly sardonic fashion. Welcome to Cruel Britannia.

'Sparklingly witty, immensely profound . . . His fictional (or, more accurately, factional) characters bristle with authenticity . . . It should be read as a matter of urgency'
Erwin James, *Guardian*

'*truecrime* brings the trilogy into the 1990s, and it blows the gaff sky high . . . the most expansive, ironical and funny novel of the series'
David Isaacson, *Daily Telegraph*

'A beacon-bright satire . . . a literary triumph'
Metro

SCEPTRE

JAKE ARNOTT

Johnny Come Home

As the dreams of the 1960s give way to anger and political unrest in the '70s, the charismatic anarchist Declan O'Connell commits suicide, leaving his boyfriend Pearson and fellow squatter Nina to try to make sense of what has happened.

Enter Sweet Thing, a streetwise rent boy, who has an uncanny hold over glam rock star Johnny Chrome; and in the wings lurks Detective Sergeant Walker of the newly formed Bomb Squad, who knows more about O'Connell than anyone ever suspected. The course of all their lives is about to change forever.

'Hypnotic, feverish and altogether wonderful . . . As Arnott argues with urgent, spellbinding power, it was a decade aflame rather than just flaming'
Patrick Ness, *Guardian*

'Beautifully observed and brilliantly paced . . . a fascinating portrait of impotence and amorality'
Michael Arditti, *Independent*

'Funny, sexy, touching, too, but it is the undertow of dread beneath the antics that makes it a serious achievement'
Mark Sanderson, *Evening Standard*

SCEPTRE